BILE AND BLOOD

BILE AND BLOOD

THE GALAXY HANGS ON THE BRINK
OF CHAOS. SOMEONE IS ABOUT
TO GIVE IT A SHOVE.

KATHERINE FRANKLIN

ISBN 978-1-915007-04-9 (E-book edition)
ISBN 978-1-915007-05-6 (Paperback edition)
ISBN 978-1-915007-06-3 (Hardcover edition)

This is a work of fiction. Any similarities to real persons, living or dead, are coincidental and not intended by the author. Characters are the products of the author's imagination.

No content in this book or its cover was generated, to the author's knowledge, using machine-learning algorithms or artificial intelligence.

Cover design and formatting by Design for Writers.

First edition: 2023

Published in the United Kingdom.

Contact: katherine@FranklyWrites.com
Visit www.FranklyWrites.com

To my husband, for asking 'Will it blend?'

Now please stop hogging the dedications
so someone else can have a turn.

PREVIOUSLY, IN *THE EMPYREAN*...

EMPYREAN FIRE BURNED THE planet Everatus IV, taking the life of Palia's young son. Palia herself escaped in an emergency shuttle, shocked unconscious by the flames of a force that underpins everything in this galaxy. The Empyrean is a sixth sense accessible to a few fading bloodlines in the Hegemony Palia lives in, more widespread in the Protectorate, where emotions are suppressed across the population. Empyrrics can sense emotions using the Empyrean, strip them, convert them into energy and hurl them back against their owners.

Palia was rescued by two Protectorate spies, Ferrash and Bek, who spotted her shuttle amidst the planetary debris. They brought her to the Protectorate, where she discovered the shock of the planet's death had made her empyrric. They fled the capital together and began their search for answers in earnest.

They discovered that it was Palia's second cousin, the Magister of the Hegemony, who destroyed Everatus IV using a weapon that could remove an empyrric's connection to the Empyrean. Disillusion and betrayal saw the spies defect from the Protectorate, and Palia recruited her old flame Fabien to lead a coup against the Magister.

After a fight aboard the flagship, Palia and Ferrash defeated the Magister together. But Palia's inexperience with the Empyrean led to her destroying all her memories of Ferrash and stripping Ferrash of all his emotions. Ferrash slipped into the shadows, leaving Palia alone.

Now, Palia is determined to find Ferrash and repair the damage she caused, but Ferrash has his own agenda. With a fragile ceasefire holding between Hegemony and Protectorate, can Palia find him before it's too late?

Have you forgotten what happened in *The Empyrean* or want to find out more about the *Galaxy of Exiles*? Check out the wiki at www.worldanvil. com/w/galaxy-of-exiles-franklywrites

CHAPTER ONE

PALIA HAD NEVER BEEN to a funeral. All her grandparents had died before she was born and the tour of duty she had undertaken as part of her mandatory service, in peacetime as it was, had been remarkably uneventful. She had never been to the Origin system either, yet here she was, on the curated world of Viken's Garden, burying her son.

There was nothing to bury. When the Magister had burned Everatus IV in Empyrean fire, he had torn Derren away with it. If you were a stickler for common belief, then it was the tides of empyrric energy known as Varna – only visible to the naked eye when travelling between nexuses or witnessing the Empyrean's use – where souls went when people died. If you believed that, you believed in the transfer of energy from one source to another. A practical, physical perspective. If the belief held true, it meant Derren's soul was trapped somewhere in the nexite batteries of the Hegemony's flagship, along with everything else that had died on the planet.

Palia didn't know what she believed.

Blinking awake from where she had retreated to the depths of her mind, she realised everyone was waiting for her. She couldn't see her mother, but she felt the cold heat of her gaze. Fabien stood to one side with tears in his eyes, framed by the trunks of two whisper-trees that became entwined amongst their upper branches. A steady breeze brushed against her skin. It carried upon it the scent of fresh life, of bare earth, of water running to meet the sea. Life, on a world of death. Or perhaps it was the other way round?

Palia drew a breath past the tightness in her chest and stepped forwards, then knelt to pick up the sapling the curator had placed there for her. Its leaves rustled when she lifted it, bright and glimmering. Green, of course. How did nobody get the irony of that? Green was the colour of the flames, and everything that had gone wrong since. A wave of nausea rose to her throat at the memory of the inferno siphoning him away. She hadn't been fast enough. She hadn't been close. He hadn't deserved to die, and he had deserved better than her.

'Do you have any words for him?' the curator asked. Her words were gentle, but Palia resented them nonetheless.

Palia lowered the sapling into its pre-dug hole and pushed her fingers into the loose soil. 'If I did, I should have said them while he was alive.' After a few pats to firm up the soil around its trunk, she pushed herself upright. 'There's no point now.' *Nothing that makes up for it.*

For the thousandth time, she felt the guilt of not being able to save him and not being able to mourn him for so long afterwards. She was past that stage now, she hoped. Half-welcome grief sat curdling in her gut, aching in her bones, clutching at her throat. Palia clenched her fists tight, grinding soil into her palms, but it wasn't the grief that made her do it. It was the emotions she saw in the landscape of the Empyrean – in others, not herself. They judged her. Maybe they didn't mean to, but they judged her, the mother of the dead and the only one with a face unmarked by tears.

She was sick of it. Sick of reuniting with people she had known since childhood and having their deepest feelings laid bare to her. The sooner she could get out of here and back to finding Ferrash, the better. It was the only one of her mistakes she still had the power to fix – she hoped.

'I... could say something, if you aren't able,' Fabien offered.

Palia nodded, flashed him a half-grateful smile, then turned on a heel and walked away. The pressure of everyone's gazes weighed upon her back.

Overhead, the light of Origin's star glimmered through the emerald canopy. Palia was happy she had come here, at least – happy to put Derren's memory to rest, even if she couldn't speak for his soul, or his remains. If he *was* in Varna, perhaps some part of what once was him would become life on this planet, at peace, in time.

Leaves crunched behind her. Palia tensed her shoulders, not wanting to turn and see who it was in case it was someone she didn't want to speak to.

'Are you okay?' a woman asked.

Palia relaxed. It was just Emesi, a friend from her time in the Hegemony military.

'I...' Palia's words caught in her throat. Grief bubbled up from where she had left it. *'Fires*, why do those three words always do that?'

'Oh *ancestors*, Palia, I'm sorry. I just...' Emesi stepped in front of her and bundled her into a tight hug, her mohawk tickling the side of her face. 'I never know what to say.'

'I know.' When Emesi drew back to regard her with a raised eyebrow, Palia stammered, 'I mean, I don't know... I mean, I do, but...' She hissed air out between her teeth. 'Ah, forget it.'

'It's that confusing?'

'It was at first. Now, it's just confusing to explain.'

'But you're coping with it?'

Palia hesitated. Bright sympathy pulsed from Emesi's core – along with a tangle of curiosity, and excitement, and fear. The realisation brought with it a wash of sadness. More than ever, Palia wanted to be away from here. All her old friends, alien enough after her long absence, were made more alien now the Empyrean made her see them so completely.

But Palia sighed and said, 'I'm coping.'

Emesi kept her stare fixed on her a few moments longer, trying to read in Palia what Palia could tell at a glance. Then she nodded and glanced over Palia's shoulder. Her mouth opened and closed while she pondered her next words. 'I... I'm sorry about Derren. When I heard, I...'

When Emesi had heard, she had probably been surprised that Derren existed at all. A misunderstanding, plus some heavy assumptions and legally questionable actions on the part of Palia's mother, meant that her son had been grown in a vat without her knowledge. Like most people, Palia had placed her genetic material in storage the moment she was old enough. Better safe than sorry, or so she thought. Palia found out Derren existed a month before his birth and chose to keep him despite the anger that had lodged in her heart. The moment they had taken Derren from the vats, Palia had cut herself off from her friends and family to live on the fringe of Hegemony space, far from everyone else. She certainly hadn't stopped to tell her friends about him.

And there it was, nestled at the centre of Emesi's being: resentment for that fact. It was a leap to assume the cause – the Empyrean didn't reveal such details – but a logical one.

'What's done is done,' said Palia. The words were familiar by now.

Emesi nodded and stared at the stream rushing past to her left. 'Where are you headed next?'

'I can't say,' Palia said, and the tone of her voice caught Emesi's attention. When Emesi looked up, she almost seemed impressed.

'War gives us all interesting jobs. I wish you luck with yours. Are you leaving straight away?' Palia nodded. 'You might want to speak with your mother, first.'

'I don't.'

'I didn't get the impression she would leave you with a choice.'

Palia sighed and cast an eye in the direction of the landing pad. 'Thanks for the warning. I'd better head off.'

They said their goodbyes and parted ways – probably for the last time, Palia thought. Whatever commonality had been between them was gone.

On the walk back to the shuttles, Palia distracted herself with the wildlife she passed. Colourful birds darted from branch to branch within the canopy, singing as they went and chasing loud insects through the leaves. One passed by inches from her face, unafraid of human presence. From time to time she spotted barklizards resting between tree roots. A whole family of them watched her pass from the safety of their trunk-bored nest, their eyelids flickering. She categorised them all, matched them to archive records, made notes of her own. Anything to keep her mind occupied. Anything to keep it away from the void.

Days were short on Viken's Garden. The sun shone directly overhead by the time Palia reached the vine-covered shuttle post that served as the planet's only landing zone. She squinted at the sky, hoping to catch sight of the flagship in orbit but coming away disappointed.

She started up the entrance ramp and sent a message to Bek via her implants. <I'll be joining you in a few minutes.> She wondered what he had been up to while she was gone.

<Done already?> he sent back.

<Doesn't take long to plant a tree.>

<There wasn't a celebration or anything?>

<That was it.>

Palia passed by the reception kiosk and nodded to the automated assistant, then booked a shuttle launch via her implants and made her way to its hangar.

Bek had never seen a child. He hadn't grown up in a society that structured its culture around them. He hadn't, in many respects, grown up at all. Was she setting his expectations for every funeral?

<There's usually a party,> she sent. <There will be one. I'm just not going to be there.>

<Oh.>

Only one word, but Palia couldn't help projecting disgust onto it. Something new and precious to Bek's mind was gone, and she didn't have anything to say.

Decontaminant spray washed over her as she stepped through the hangar boundary, cementing the weariness in her face. She frowned at the ground beneath her feet as she walked. Seamless floor panels gave way to the shuttle ramp, then to anti-static carpet.

'Palia,' her mother called.

Startled, Palia fell the rest of the way to her seat and landed with a thump. Her mother stood beyond the shuttle door. Before Palia could protest, she entered the cabin, the door resealing behind her. The engines hummed to life.

Palia spammed the command to cancel the launch order.

'Were you going to leave without speaking to me at all?' From the tone of her mother's voice, she could have been speaking about something as harmless as forgetting to clean her teeth. But there was pain buried behind her eyes, clawing at her heart.

Palia hated that she could see it. She hated that her new sense could humanise in seconds people she had spent years demonising. She hated that she couldn't cast aside what she saw just as much as she hated herself for being bitter enough to try. She pressed her lips together, tried to keep her words in check.

'I hadn't intended to speak to you ever again, if I could help it,' Palia said. 'Apparently, I couldn't.'

Flickering needles of hurt pricked her mother's skin in the landscape of the Empyrean, and she lowered herself onto a seat opposite Palia. Her gaze flicked over Palia's hair, which Palia hadn't seen the point in dyeing since the death of Everatus IV had shocked it white. Her mother's hair was still hazel, the colour they used to share, but grey streaked it here and there.

'I'm sorry about Derren,' her mother said.

Sorry that he died, or sorry that he existed? It's a bit late to apologise for the latter.

After a few more moments' silence, her mother added, 'I'd like to know what happened afterwards. If you want to tell me.'

'I don't.'

'Palia, you were gone for years, you nearly died and then... I don't even know what happened after that. Fabien won't tell me anything. That woman from the arsaeria just shrugged. Your ship has no designation, so I couldn't send a message. All I know, I got from the news feeds. The *news feeds*, Palia! They say you became empyrric, *killed the Magister* and stopped the Protectorate homeworld getting... burned? Blown up? I don't know.'

Palia shrugged. 'That's pretty much it.'

Her mother scoffed, and Palia noted the frustration rising in her with weary resignation. 'But how did you escape Everatus Four? Where did you go afterwards? I just... I want to understand, Palia.'

'You've never wanted to understand before.' This was a woman so prone to misunderstanding that she had interpreted 'my daughter is in a relationship' as 'my daughter certainly wants to stay with this man forever and a surprise child will be a perfect gift' – not that Palia pretended to understand what had been going through her mother's head back then.

What could Palia say, anyway? That she was picked up by spies and they took her into the Protectorate? That they hatched a plan against the Magister together? That she killed people to do it? Good people? Allies? That she fell in love with someone and couldn't even remember his face?

'I know I did wrong by you and Derren.' Her mother leaned towards her, hands palm upwards on each knee, begging. 'I didn't understand until it was too late but I tried, I *tried* afterwards. And you didn't give me a chance, you just—'

'Left. *Zashen* right I left,' Palia cursed, then dropped to a whisper, as if saying it here, on this funeral world, was a crime. 'You gave me a son I never asked for, a son I never signed for—'

'I offered to sign for him.'

'He was my blood!' As she said it, her control slipped, and sheets of green light flickered around her arms. Her mother pressed herself against the side of the shuttle. 'If you wanted someone else to carry on the family for you, you should have used your own. Not mine. Not Fabien's. You forged our signatures on the contract, so don't tell me you didn't know it was wrong, that it wasn't against the law.'

'I—'

'Get out.'

'At least speak to your—'

'Out!'

With a strangled cry – of frustration or fear, Palia couldn't tell – her mother bolted from her seat and exited the shuttle. As soon as she had, Palia threw a command to the shuttle's computer and launched herself far, far away from the planet, her family, and whatever parts of her old life she might still have been able to recover.

There had been no going back after the flames, and there never would be. All she could do now was keep running forwards, after Ferrash.

CHAPTER TWO

FERRASH TRIED TO IGNORE the way his hands shook as he clipped the ends of his belt together, but his mind fixated on it. The shaking was a sign of weakness. A sign he'd taken too many emotional inhibitors. A sign of how messed up things had become in the depths of his subconscious. And, as sights went, it was the safest one in the room.

Rustling sounded from the bed behind him. The woman's breathing – heavy, but fast being wrested to normality – cut a sawblade through the silence.

Ferrash gritted his teeth and reached over to a small side table for his pistol and coat. The contents of his stomach made a foray into his throat, and he did all he could not to throw up the little he'd eaten that day. It was just the drugs. Too many inhibitors, combined with whatever they'd given him to get through this. That was all. He shrugged into his coat, gripped his pistol tight enough to ground himself in reality.

His obligation here was done. His years of dodging the breeding programme were over, but maybe now he'd participated, the Protectorate would wait a few years before asking again. With any luck, the programme wouldn't exist by then anyway. The sooner he left and put it behind him, the better.

'Are you unwell?' the woman behind him asked.

Ferrash curled his fingers in the air halfway to the door membrane, then dropped his hand and glanced over his shoulder.

The attendant stood bathed in the murky amber of the room's lighting panels, her eyes flat, reflecting most of it back at him. Her expression held no curiosity, as there had been none in her voice. She stepped back into her underwear with an almost robotic precision.

'I'm well, Attendant,' Ferrash said. A part of him barely recognised his own voice, an intentionally dull monotone.

The attendant – one of the more junior ranks of keeper, though a keeper nonetheless – paused with one trouser leg on, one off. 'There is a troubled note to you. If you are not in your right mind, the process may have been inefficient. You should recentre yourself so there may be a second attempt.'

'That won't be necessary.' He caught himself before he thought on her words too much. 'Any trouble on my part won't have affected the results.' Besides, he had other duties to attend to.

'You took longer than expected.'

On detecting a slight hesitation in her words, Ferrash regarded her more closely. Her white-flecked eyebrows had dipped a fraction lower, and her posture struck him as... not vulnerable, but uncertain. For a second, he saw Palia's face in hers, but the image vanished in the time it took to drum across the surface of his heart.

It was the attendant's first time in the programme. Any descendant of an empyrric bloodline had to participate – her as a full-blooded empyrric, Ferrash with an empyrric mother. The Keepers needed to keep their numbers strong, and empyrrics could only be born naturally, not created in the vats. Hence the breeding programme. The act they had just done was illegal for any other purpose in the Protectorate.

So of course she didn't know how it was supposed to work. The preparatory material boiled down to a minute-long projection with scientific annotations and blunt instructions. She'd probably had the *splitting* thing playing in her implants through it all. Biology didn't like sticking to scripts.

Ferrash cleared his throat, pushing the thought to the back of his mind. 'Time taken doesn't impact anything as long as the criteria were satisfied.'

She said nothing, but if Ferrash were a keeper like her, he'd surely have seen doubt radiating from her.

'It just doesn't work like that.' He almost said *trust me*, but experience wasn't the best admission, given the circumstances.

The attendant pulled her robe from its hook on the wall, so he made for the door, but he didn't miss her final words.

'Given your previous success, I shall take your judgement as sound.'

The door membrane resolidified over her last word, swallowing it. Ferrash held its memory at arm's length until he had navigated the three staircases and long corridor that led to the comparative freedom of the outside world.

Snow slashed across his cheeks. He drew in a stinging breath and let it out slowly, trying to loosen the tension he'd worked up, balling his hands into fists to stop the tremors. He strode into the storm, kicking drifts of snow from the floor. The roads here didn't attract many visitors. Too many keepers nearby.

That's why he only let his attention fall on the attendant's words when he was clear of the Keepers' buildings.

Previous success? Ferrash had been dodging the breeding programme for over a decade. This was his first tasking as well as hers – no 'previous' example existed, success or no. So what did she mean? It couldn't just be strange ideas about what free agents got up to in their free time; the wording was too specific. She referred to one incident in particular. Problem was, the only child he had fathered was dead. Unless…

Something sick curled in the pit of his stomach and he hissed a slow breath into the night air. Things like this were dangerous to think about. He had to focus on the mission.

It was a mild night, for Hesperex. But for the occasional flurry, snow fell uninterrupted by the wind. Its usual icy knives had been sheathed. Now he had put more distance between himself and The Hotel – or the Residence of the Empyrric Procreation Programme – plenty of people walked the streets. The lights on the buildings around him did little to cut through the gloom, and twilight shaded the vatborn's usually garish clothes a muted grayscale.

Ferrash followed the accumulating crowd, keeping an eye out for any signs of unrest. Ever since the purge, when the Protectorate leadership and the Keepers had killed large swathes of the population suspected to be harbouring rebellious intent, people had been worryingly quiet. Their rebellious intent hadn't disappeared; it had just been pressed down into a volcano long overdue eruption. The line that the Keepers protected the Protectorate had never quite rung so untrue.

The crowd led him down a ramp to the next level, which shielded itself from the snow thanks to the floor of the surface level. Snow swirled in from air grates in the ceiling and caught in the dim night lights, but they were spared the worst of the weather down here.

A message appeared in his implants. <Exchange Triff 5-70-42. Don't be late.> The sender had redacted their details. It was clumsy enough that Ferrash could have figured it out, but he didn't need to. Vannis Proglimen may have thought this meeting was his idea, but Ferrash had arranged it.

Don't be late. Ferrash rolled his eyes. He wasn't about to be late. Too much rode on this. He rested his hand on his pistol and split off from the crowd to wait at a nearby lift. Triff 5-70-42 was a coordinate two levels down, in a textiles warehouse that hadn't been touched for the past few months. Fewer bodies to clothe, since the purge.

He shoved aside a brief tick of anger as he stood staring down the shaft, waiting for the lift to arrive. The purge was partly Proglimen's fault. As the Proctor, he held power of veto over some of the Primary Committee's decisions. If he thought the committee and its chair weren't holding true to the Protectorate's values, it was his job to let them know about it. But he hadn't vetoed the purge. Ferrash had seen the results: bodies lining the streets; blood in the gutters; informants choking down gas; soldiers beaten and broken; a whole city block reclaimed by freezing ocean, faces gasping for air even as they froze;

the planet Munab invaded and bombed. It had been the reason he and Bek had defected.

Not that *that* had lasted.

In the wake of that cleanup – the evidence of which had been tidied away with a rapidity only the Protectorate could muster – what was left of the popular conscience latched onto old stories and breathed new life into them. With casualties so indiscriminate, the simple, long-rumoured answer suggested itself: a secret police. The Reiart. Whispers ran between the vats of every planet. Even members of the Primary Committee spent their days looking over their shoulders, waiting for a knife between their shoulder blades. The Proctor, Proglimen, thought he controlled the Reiart. He was safe. He didn't need to worry. But clearly he had noticed a few orders of his gone awry, a few actions carried out he hadn't authorised. A little was expected. A lot was a worry. So he had demanded to meet an operative for answers.

With a hydraulic groan, the lift rose from the ground and its doors opened to accept Ferrash. Two vatborn joined him in silence. They hugged the wall on the right-hand side, keeping as much distance between them and him as possible, and they shrank away from his eyes when he glanced at them. The next level down, they left him alone.

Ferrash gripped his pistol tighter. Muscle memory filled in for the anxiety he should have felt. Its absence disturbed him almost as much as if he had been using no inhibitors at all. With doses like this, there was always a risk the emotions would never return... but did he have anything left worth keeping?

By the time he reached the warehouse, the cold had made his nose numb. He cupped his hands to his face and blew to warm it, scanning the racks of clothes to either side as he walked.

'Stop there' a man called. 'Hands where I can see them.'

Ferrash obliged and glanced to his left. 'Proctor.'

Surprised, the man jerked forwards into the light. The hood he wore stopped any light reaching his face, but it gleamed from the furniture of the pistol he had aimed at Ferrash. *'Keepers... How...?'*

He ran his free hand over his jaw and tried to regain his composure, with a little success. 'You come here in the open, with your face out for anyone to see, and you call me *by title*? Do you even know how the game works?'

'It's not a game,' Ferrash said. 'It's a job. I'd figure you'd know that, if you're the one in charge.'

Proglimen shook his head, his lips pressed into a hard line. 'I know my orders used to make it to your commander. Either they don't anymore, or they're not listening. I need to speak with them.'

'No, you don't.'

'What?'

'You really think you had control, don't you?'

Proglimen took another step, and the pistol became a blurred shape a foot from his skull. 'I called you here.'

'True enough. As you said, you wanted to talk. You sent an order out. Someone answered.' Ferrash shrugged, hands still in the air by his head. 'I'd forgive you for thinking you called the shots, but you never did.'

As he spoke, Ferrash monitored the emotional undercurrents in Proglimen's face: doubt, anger, concern, impulse. When his finger tightened on the trigger, Ferrash took hold of his wrist, pivoted, and swept the man's legs out from under him with a kick. Proglimen yelped and dropped the pistol before crashing down onto his hip.

Still holding onto his wrist, Ferrash drew his own pistol and aimed it between the man's wide eyes. 'You should have vetoed the purge, Proctor.'

'You're making a mistake.' Proglimen's lips curled into a snarl. 'The Reiart will flay you alive if you kill me. And why would I have vetoed it? They were splitters. Rebels. It was in the Protectorate's interest to...'

'Spare me the threats.' *And spare me your excuses.* There was no point carrying on with this. Ferrash had come here to kill the man; he didn't need to draw it out. Proglimen was a weak link in the chain, more worried about pandering to the needs of the Protectorate's committees and their stifling grip on power than to the people. He was a weak link who had cost billions of lives by doing nothing.

Weak link he may be, but everything in the Protectorate was chained to his actions, and that's why Ferrash had to take his place.

Ferrash toggled the safety on his pistol. Proglimen's eyes widened, a hint of indignation stealing across their mirrored surfaces. 'You can't. The Reiart—'

He put a shot through Proglimen's skull. 'I am the Reiart.'

CHAPTER THREE

By the time the shuttle reached the flagship, Palia was struggling to keep her breathing under control, let alone the Empyrean. The energy roiled inside her – clutching, grabbing, oscillating within the bounds of its existence as her doubt and anger fuelled it. It was right to forgive, but she couldn't.

Why did she really not want to tell her mother what had happened? Palia forced herself to slow down and think about it. She gripped tight to the fabric of her trousers and glared at the approaching hangar, breathing in, breathing out, trying to slow everything down. Green light flickered in the corner of her eye. She ignored it. The truth was, this was what she didn't want people to see. She didn't want them to see how being empyrric had changed her. She didn't want to see the fear in them, all day every day, wherever she went. She wondered how the Keepers coped. Then she tried to stop wondering, to stop thinking at all and just let everything wash past her.

Bit by bit, the thoughts submerged themselves. Bit by bit, she relaxed. When Palia opened her eyes again, the shuttle had landed inside one of the flagship's main hangars, surrounded by the reassuring blur of everyday existence.

She knew the other funeral guests would be making their way back here soon, after the celebration, so she started to walk. She could have gone straight back to her ship, since it was refuelling nearby, but she didn't think she could face Bek so soon after facing everyone else's judgement. Instead, she let him know she was making a detour and headed for Fabien's chambers. He wouldn't be there yet, of course, but she could wait for him alone.

The corridors were quiet. The ship's time marked it near evening, and most would be sharing a meal with friends and family, or on their way to do so. The few people she did pass nodded respectfully to her.

'Mater Tennic!' a merchant called to her as he solidified the membrane to his storefront. He rushed to halt the process now that he had seen her.

Palia winced. Ever since she had stopped the previous Magister's attempt to attack Hesperex, the people who lived on the flagship had seen her as their personal saviour. In reality, the only danger they had been in was from the Protectorate fleets, and Palia had done little to stop *them*. Quite the opposite, in fact. But the public had fixated on the story of a mother's revenge and so always gave her a mother's prefix, no matter how much she hated its association.

'Please, Mater Tennic, I would like you to have this.' As the membrane dissolved again, the man reached through and pulled out a large bottle. He presented it to her, and she tried to decline with a polite gesture, but he pressed it into her hands. 'Spored Spicewine, straight from the flats of Seylenon. Please, take it. For your troubles.'

'I...' Palia tried not to sigh. 'Thank you.'

The merchant, apparently pleased by a gift given, grinned at her and set off down the corridor whistling. Palia carried on, clasping the bottle to her breast.

In Fabien's chambers, she slumped onto the nearest couch, still hugging the wine, and shut her eyes.

<Fabien? Are you on your way back?> she sent.

<No, but I can be.>

<Don't rush on my account. Can we talk when you get here? I'm in your quarters.>

<Of course. Help yourself if you need anything to eat or drink.>

Palia raised an eyebrow at the bottle of wine. <I'm good.>

Two hours later, the two glasses of spicewine Palia had poured had bloomed, filling the room with its subtle aroma. She stood on the balcony, which had a prime view over the local community gardens. The far boundary hazed in the distance, only becoming clearer where it curved inwards to form a man-made bowl of greenery. Thousands of people milled about, gathered in raucous laughter or animated debate. Couples – and triples, and more besides – kissed in the shade of orchards while children splashed and screamed in the central lake.

Palia watched them, her eyes glassy. She only paid attention to the Empyrean, its ebb and flow marked by the discrete points that made up the crowd. Somewhere out there, she sensed other empyrrics – their psyches etched curious black holes into the fabric of the Empyrean. She counted two, at the moment, and one of those was the woman assigned as her new patron. Pins prickled at Palia's insides at the thought of whatever she might teach her. 'After the funeral', the woman had said. Tomorrow? Next week? Any time was too soon.

'Sorry I kept you waiting.'

Palia turned from the window to see Fabien folding his cloak over the back of the couch.

'It's okay,' she said. 'It's not like I have anything better to do.' *Except track down Ferrash.*

Fabien eyed the bottle and glasses. 'A sitting-down kind of talk, I see?'

She sighed, letting her shoulders slump, and went to sit on the couch. 'Yeah, I guess it is.' She picked up the glass nearest her and swirled its contents. Fine gold bands wound through the dark liquid, thread-thin and glowing with their own luminosity, marking the presence of the spores introduced during the fermentation process. Weird thing to add to a drink, really. She took a sip, and tiny bursts of flavour fizzed along her tongue.

Fabien lowered himself to the seat beside her and examined the other glass. 'Is this one of mine?'

'A gift from an admirer.' She raised an eyebrow. 'Again.'

He grimaced. 'At least they'll be out of your orbit soon, unlike your mother. I've had calls from her daily. Five years she goes without needing to check on you and as soon as you reappear, she wants to know everything. I will admit I can sympathise, but I understand why you cut her out. Was that what you needed to talk about?'

'No.' With a grimace of her own, Palia cupped the glass in both hands and rested her wrists on her thighs so it dangled between her legs, refracting light across them. 'I guess I just want to know if I'm doing the right thing.'

'In going after Ferrash?'

'Yes. No. In... everything.' She chewed at her lower lip, trying to tug words out of her emotions rather than flames for a change. 'Everyone hates me for what happened with Derren. They hate me for leaving. They hate me for staying away. And as for Ash... I made him leave. I forgot about him, I put him in that position. What if he hates me for it? What if he doesn't even need saving, or finding? What if he's happy enough where he is?'

'He's in the Protectorate.'

'And?'

'By law, I'm not sure he's allowed to be happy.' Fabien's lips curled up a fraction, almost in apology for what was half joke, half terrifying truth.

Palia sighed and attempted to gather her thoughts. As usual, there were no words behind the 'why's she asked herself – just an awful, gut-wrenching churn that stabbed through her chest and wrapped a tight band around her shoulders. She just *had* to go after him. She *had* to make things right. And she couldn't explain it. With a shudder, she brought the lid down on that emotion and pushed it aside. While she may have forgotten Ferrash, she hadn't forgotten the tug of that emotion and what it could make her do. She recalled the blistering light of an inferno in the Empyrean, the unstoppable hunger of it as it reached out to devour everything around her. She remembered love building upon new and uncertain love until the air was thick with feedback potential, boiling, tearing, cascading... and then nothing. Waking up empty, with gaps her mind couldn't comprehend.

Fabien squeezed her knee, and she threw him a strained smile. 'I just... I'm not sure I'm equipped for this. I'm not sure I'm a good person.'

'Does it matter if you're not?' He kept a straight face, but she caught the flash of sympathy her words had sparked in him.

'It does to me.'

He nodded, and they remained in companionable silence for the next few minutes, sipping at their wine and listening to the sounds of life beyond the balcony.

At length, Fabien said, 'Whatever you do next, whether you go after him or not, that's for you to decide.' That was true enough. The Consulate had made Palia a pestor following the Magister's death – the previous Magister's, of course. Fabien was Magister now. The Consulate had voted him in shortly after the events around Hesperex. He ruled the Hegemony, and Palia's new position as pestor made her an independent investigator who answered to no one, as long as she acted in pursuit of her objectives. That, officially, was to continue investigating the prototype technology the Magister had been planning to unleash on Hesperex. It just so happened that that objective would take her to the places she would be most likely to find Ferrash.

'I'll support you either way,' Fabien continued, 'but you should know that we've had word of him.'

Palia snapped her head round. 'Where?' They had lost all trace of him after the fight with the Magister. Some sign, any sign, would finally give her somewhere to start.

'Bek found the lead, since your ship's apparently still in the Protectorate's contacts. An execution order came through for Ferrash.' When Palia started at this, Fabien winced and raised a hand to calm her. 'For him to carry out, sorry, not *for* him. The target's on Munab, so we can safely assume that's where he's headed.'

'But why?' Palia shook her head. 'He and Bek defected. How can he be back working for them?'

Fabien shrugged. 'Did they ever tell anyone they defected? Or take any direct action against the Protectorate?'

'Well, no...'

'Then I suppose as far as the Protectorate are concerned, it never happened.'

She conceded the point. 'Who's the target?'

'Ellit Progaeryon, the commander of the mechanised division down there.'

Palia dug around the painful gaps in her memories, trying to recall what she could of their time on Munab. It took a while, but she remembered there had been another man down there with them, and his name might have been Ellit. And...

'I think he was Ash's father?' she said.

Fabien blinked, taken aback. 'I... wouldn't know.'

'It must be a front. He must be going to save him, not kill him. And I've seen those mechs, Fabien. They're massive! It'll be easy to find him. And if I find him, I find Ash.' Palia grinned, but her smile fell when she saw Fabien's expression.

'Palia, Munab's still in the middle of a civil war. Even if you manage to get onto the surface, which side will you fight for? If you back the populace and people find out where you're from... We still have a truce. We can't commit *anyone* to Munab unless we want our war to resume.'

'So it's a civil war that Ash is heading straight into the middle of. If anything, that's *more* reason to go after him.' She tapped a finger against the side of her glass. 'I can cloak myself with the Empyrean.'

'You can?'

'Well no, not personally, but I know other empyrrics can do it.' When Ferrash had been kidnapped on Sirat, the empyrric the old Magister had sent to do it had removed all trace of their presence from the witnesses' minds. Palia wouldn't know where to start, but she wasn't about to admit that. 'Besides, if I can break my own memories, it can't be that hard to break someone else's.'

Fabien pressed his lips into a thin line. 'You broke your own memories because you went up against a trained empyrric before you could control your own power and tried to do something no one had done before. At least spend some time learning from Archivist Lilesh before you go after him. By then, we might have found a way to sneak you onto the surface. And I... I would appreciate it, knowing you went in prepared.'

After a large sip from her glass, Palia set it back on the table, almost sloshing the remnants over the rim. 'When I fought the Magister, it was because I didn't have time to do anything else. I was there, he was there, and he needed to be stopped. This is the same! You think Ash'll hang around down there?'

'You can always pick up his trail after—'

'Can I? We couldn't pick up his trail leaving the flagship, and we knew exactly where he started that time. All we have now is a kill order and a whole planet to search. Spot the difference?' She worked the muscles in her jaw before continuing. 'If I wait, I lose him. I just need an excuse to explain why I'm going.'

For a while, Fabien said nothing. He stared at a painted metal panel on the wall opposite, tracing the abstract shapes and bold colours with an unfocused gaze. 'We never recovered all our data from Munab,' he said. 'You picked up the prototype, but that's all we got. If there's anything still down there and the Protectorate get hold of it...'

Then the Protectorate would be able to replicate the technology the Magister had incorporated into the flagship. The Protectorate landing themselves with the power to burn whole planets out of the sky wasn't something she wanted to think about. She wasn't sure they even had the resources to pull it off, but it was still a real concern. Thanks to the previous Magister's underhand dealing with an underground movement on Munab, any remnants of the prototype's research were sitting ducks for capture.

'You want me to make sure they don't fall into the wrong hands?' Palia asked. That was as good an excuse as any.

Fabien exhaled, thinking. Then he looked her in the eye and nodded. 'If there is yet anything to find, yes. If not, find him.'

CHAPTER FOUR

IT HAD BEEN A week since the funeral, and Fabien had been neck deep in conversations at all hours of day and night since then. He desperately wanted to sleep, but it was daytime here. The lights on the Carabalite forge ring synchronised to the day-night cycle of Carabal's main colony, Volta, at almost the polar opposite of Standard Chron. It was the Hegemony's greatest hub of commerce, industry... and time lag. Fabien tried not to let his fatigue show to the dozen-or-so engineers standing in front of him. Still, one of them must have noticed, because they nudged a mug of coffee across the standing desk towards him. Fabien accepted it with an audible groan of relief and some mouthed words of thanks.

He took a sip and closed his eyes. Several seconds later, he asked, 'Is everyone present?'

The project lead spoke up. 'System architect's down on Volta sorting out a problem at the freight docks, but we can catch her up.' She stood with her arms folded across from him, the grey hair on one side of her head shaved away to reveal bold tattoos over her dark scalp. If Fabien remembered right, she used to fly with the arsaeria. Or maybe she still did – the Hegemony's most impressive architects came from among their artistic troupes, but they did most of their work as contractors.

Fabien nodded. 'I would be grateful for that. You have all been made aware of the need for secrecy?'

They all nodded. Good. His consul shifted audibly on her feet beside him. *His* consul. Not long ago, that rank had been his. Now that he was Magister of the Hegemony, all twenty consuls reported to him. The idea took some getting used to.

Fabien drew a deep breath. 'I'm sure you have all heard about the demise of the previous Magister. The reports circulated through the news feeds should have explained that his death prevented him from committing a war crime, the pursuit of which had already come at the cost of one of our own citizens.' He waited until he saw signs of agreement before continuing. A shuttle passed by the viewscreen above them, heading for where the flagship sat moored on a kilo-metre-long docking boom further along the ring. Given the flagship's size, its misshapen flank still took up most of the screen. 'This is all true, but what they won't have explained is the nature of the weapon he planned to use.'

At this, Fabien gestured to the viewscreen. 'Over a year ago, the Magister docked the flagship at this ring for a major refit. I know some of you were involved with it. You probably noticed a lot of nexite being shipped in-system and you probably thought it was to upgrade the ship's nexite drive. It did, but that was a side effect. The Magister had a separate team of engineers working on a secret project alongside the other work, which involved laying nexite all through the ship's structure, not just the drive shaft and lance. We don't know exactly what the changes were. We haven't been able to track down anyone who worked on them.'

Eyes downcast, Fabien took another sip of coffee and winced at its bitterness. Making people disappear was underhand. If they posed a significant danger to the public, he could understand and perhaps hesitantly make that decision, but disappearing them just to keep silence? That was a Protectorate trick. Fabien had been good friends with Magister Lavennon – or he thought he had. It was hard to believe he would stoop to that level. Hard to believe he wanted the Empyrean gone that badly.

'Do you know what the weapon does?' the project lead asked.

Fabien let the steam from the mug wash over his face and sting his eyes. 'It kills planets. It strips them bare.'

'Oh, *zash*.' She leant back, grimacing. 'Everatus Four, right? Your kid?'

'Yes.'

'All that was the– was Lavennon's weapon?'

'From an admittedly limited sample size' – Fabien stole a phrase a physicist had used some weeks earlier; he liked the bitter way it twisted in his mouth – 'we think the weapon strips empyrric energy from a target and siphons it up to the flagship, where it's stored in nexite batteries. We're not sure how much the process was aided by Lavennon's own ability, as an empyrric, but it certainly requires empyrric control. That charging process alone makes it a dangerous weapon. Magister Lavennon planned to unleash it upon Hesperex, but we can't tell exactly how it would have worked. It either would have caused outright destruction or, as prior investigation indicates, removed the ability to command the Empyrean from every keeper on Hesperex.'

One of the engineers – a balding man incongruously draped in translucent silkmesh – raised an eyebrow. 'You killed a Magister just to save a bunch of mirror-eyes?'

'Yes.' Fabien held his gaze. He shouldn't have to justify it with any other explanation. War crimes were crimes for a reason, and the thought of what might have happened was abhorrent no matter who was at the receiving end. Those in the Protectorate were called mirror-eyes for their lack of emotion, but that didn't make them justifiable targets. 'Whatever the weapon was, it went untested. For all we knew, it could just as easily have backfired and killed everyone aboard. If Lavennon had intended to knock out the Keepers, then that was a nobler goal in principle, but his methodology and rank subterfuge were hardly indicators of good intentions.'

'Tech not worth scrapping though, aye?'

Fabien nodded, grim-faced. 'I don't want you to remove any of the upgrades from the ship. I just want you to take a look at it and see if you can come to an understanding on how it works. If we can repurpose it as a solution against empyrrics before anyone else does, we will.' If not, and it was a planet-killing monster of a thing, he could only ever let it be a deterrent. But the opportunity to declaw the Keepers by cutting them off from the Empyrean was too good an opportunity not to look into.

'Is there a deadline?' asked the project lead.

'No. Just go as fast as you deem possible and send me any insights as soon as you find them.' Fabien thought of Palia, on her way to Munab as they spoke. 'I might be able to send you more information for reference soon, in any case.'

'That'll be perfect. We'll draw up a plan and get started right away.'

With a smile, Fabien thanked the project lead and her team, then left them to it. The consul followed him, her bare feet almost silent on the moss-carpeted floor. Disapproval radiated from her. It burned into his back as he walked, and he caught her frowning at him in the reflection on the overhead glass. Consul Esselia was a voidfarer, her unnervingly tall frame a sign of childhood on low-gravity ships. As was fashionable amongst those who lived her life, she wore no clothes, with the exception of her cloak of office. Trace her family back far enough, and they had built the Carabalite forge ring. Old blood, but never before this high in politics. She was new to the role, reluctant to speak her mind.

'You have thoughts, Esselia?' he asked.

Her stride faltered, and her gaze flicked to meet his in the glass. 'We need every advantage against the Protectorate we can get. We can't afford to protect mirror-eyes when we know they'll just turn against us at the next opportunity. They're not—'

'Not people?'

'No! I mean, they are, but they're all programmed to obey.' Esselia sighed. 'If the Protectorate deleted one of our worlds, they'd be taking out children and civilians in the mix. If Lavennon had deleted Hesperex, it would have been different. No children, no non-combatants. And from what I hear, the planet's an iceball, so it's not like there's any wildlife to get upset about. What differentiates it from any other target?'

Fabien let out a breath of air, half laugh, half exasperation. 'You can't honestly think every soul on Hesperex is in the military.'

'Who said they had souls?'

Before he could process her words, movement caught his eye. He stopped and squinted up towards the thin scrap of sky that hid behind the looming bulk of the flagship. There: flashes in the dark. The telltale bursts of warheads.

He focused on his implants and opened a channel to the consulate chambers back aboard the flagship, linking Esselia into the conversation. <Are we under attack?> he sent.

There was a pause – slight, but noticeable – then a sub-consul replied, <An unauthorised vessel has exited the nexus. Ships from the system and guardian fleets have moved to intercept.>

<Show me.>

A moment later, a live feed of the incident streamed into his mind's eye. A small, box-shaped ship jinked through every angle as it tried to dodge incoming missiles, but it had already sustained heavy damage. Sparks stuttered and guttered into flame by one of its thrusters, and a patch along one side was blackened.

Esselia sent, <Protectorate ship.>

Her message didn't convey any sentiment, but he wondered if she was resisting the urge to say she told him so.

<Intercepting ships have jammed communications,> sent the sub-consul, <but they were transmitting the moment they left the nexus. I have instructed intelligence to decrypt its contents from the nexus logs.>

<Is it armed?> Fabien asked.

<No. One crew member, no armaments.>

'A scout ship,' he said. Whatever it had seen, it had already transmitted back to the Protectorate. <Instruct the fleets to disable it and bring the occupant in for—>

Fabien cut off the thought half formed as the Protectorate ship exploded. Metal and gas flew outwards to map their trajectories across the emptiness of space. He blinked, recalling the sillhouette of the pilot under its canopy moments before destruction. That hadn't been a missile strike. That had been self-destruction. He wondered if any emotion had crossed the pilot's face, if they had had second thoughts about ending themself just for the sake of secrecy.

Fabien sighed. <Call a meeting in the chambers. I have a feeling our truce might be over.>

'This scouting run's a symptom,' Esselia said. 'The Protectorate'll be making more movements. They'll have coordinated this. We need a coordinated response.'

'We'll have one.' He turned to face her, to impress how much he meant it with a glance, then turned again to stride down the corridor. There should be a shuttle waiting for them at the next dock. They could head straight to the consulate chambers from there.

Esselia sped up to walk beside him. 'Are we sticking with the contingency? Because I don't think—'

'That it's aggressive enough, I know.' Esselia favoured offense. 'Let's take a look at the whole situation first. If this is all we have so far, then yes, we stick with the contingency.' The contingency meant staying on the defensive, positioning fleets at Rembra and Orlax to head off the most likely candidates for Protectorate incursion. 'If there are movements, and there's a threat we need to meet, we meet it.'

She shot him a sideways glance, eyes narrowed. 'You sound like you have something else planned.'

'I think we should send a fleet to Munab. If we occupy their fleets above the planet, we draw fire away from ground targets. And if we can turn the tide in favour of the resident population, we have ourselves potential allies. The Protectorate loses a planet full of valuable resources; we gain a stepping stone into the heart of Protectorate space.'

'Nice plan, as long as it doesn't hinge on trusting new allies as far as we can vent them. I'm still not happy about the gaps it leaves in our ability to counterattack.'

'Don't worry about that.'

The moss carpet gave way to smooth metal, which reflected the lights above them. Fabien veered towards the docking hatch on the left.

Esselia waited for him to open the hatch and duck through before following. 'You have more ships hidden up your robes?'

'No, but I know a planet that does.'

As the hatch door irised shut, Esselia drew the folds of her cloak about herself and buckled her harness. Her brows drew low over her eyes, which sparkled with wary curiosity.

'You're going to petition Rythe?' she asked.

'I am.'

'They're isolationist. They don't want war. They won't want anything to do with this.'

Fabien raised his hands and shrugged. 'I can hardly call myself an ambassador for the people if I don't at least *try* diplomacy.'

She snorted. 'I suppose it's served you well so far.'

It had, but Rythe would be a tough sell. While it was true that the Hegemony had helped them against the Protectorate in the past and patrolled the Rythian Breach in the decades since, Rythe needed better reasons to go to war. His thoughts drifted to Palia again, to her mission on Munab, where the technology to strip the Empyrean from an empyrric had been developed. There had never been a better time to petition them for help.

Because if there was one thing the Stewardship of Rythe hated more than getting involved, it was empyrrics.

CHAPTER FIVE

LAYING A TRAIL TO Munab had been a good call. The kill order on Progaeryon – his father – was something Ferrash had put in the system himself. When the enforcer who handled him and Bek had received the order, he'd assigned them to it straight away. Ferrash had accepted without hesitation – anything less was a bad move when ordered to kill blood relations. 'Family' wasn't a concept the Protectorate encouraged. Nor were second thoughts.

In any case, he had no plans to go to Munab. Ferrash was pretty sure his father was dead, not that it mattered, and no one would look into his results further than he could fabricate them. He'd send a ship and say he was on it, but he wouldn't be. He would be right here on Hesperex, where he could do the most damage.

Morning made itself known through the smell of paste and brew, and through the queues that formed at regular intervals along the streets by the pastehouses. Ferrash stood in one of those queues now, periodically shuffling from side to side to dislodge any snow. The fact that the queues had spilled out onto the street even here, in the capital district of Five-Fifty-Four, indicated how scarce supplies had become. The situation worsened every year. He squinted up into the sky. Somewhere up there, orbiting a star he couldn't see, were the last remnants of a ring station – the Protectorate's failed attempt at growing crops out in space with as little human input as possible. By the time bureaucracy killed the project, Hesperex was well on its way into its current ice age. There hadn't been clear skies over Five-Fifty-Four in centuries.

'...whole lot be o'tat, si'ter,' someone said nearby.

Ferrash blinked a couple of times to unfreeze his brain. The two vatborn in the queue ahead of him stood close to each other, and they murmured in low voices. Both were wrapped in thick coats, but one wore the deep red of the star shipbound, the other the orange of the landers. An unlikely pair for conversation, and talking in lowspeak to boot.

The lander inclined her head a fraction. 'Tey pack us onto yo ship, vatter. Many us.'

The person she had called vatter – one of many the Protectorate grew sexless to avoid urges (and by extension, overpopulation) – shivered in their coat. They probably worked in a ship's engine rooms. If they worked anywhere else onboard, they would be used to biting cold.

'We told go to t'splitter world,' they said.

'Not to glasshearts?' the woman asked.

They shook their head. 'We fight we. Vatter to vatter.'

'Splitter-vatter?'

They shrugged, though the glance they gave their companion was uncertain. 'Splitter is splitter.'

Neither had noticed Ferrash listening; if he hadn't set his implants to boost audio, he wouldn't have heard them.

As they shuffled forwards in the queue, the shipbound vatter asked, 'Si'ter?'

'Aye?'

'On t'ship, when you take to splitter world... Keepers be tere. Everywhere. Dinnet look edible.'

'I take care.'

Without looking at each other, they brushed shoulders, the movement almost imperceptible. Ferrash looked away. Thanks to a Kept attack on production facilities at Vike 1 and 2, the Protectorate's supplies of emotional inhibitors had stalled. Already trying to recover their stocks from overuse during the purge, they now had too little to cover demand. If what the vatter said was accurate and the fighting was about to get more intense on Munab, demand would only increase. The deficit was starting to show. Ferrash was lucky he had his own stockpile – and his own suppliers.

When the queue finally worked its way round to the counter, Ferrash accepted his serving and took it over to a bench in the corner next to some vat tenders. The thick, chemical smell coming off them gave away their occupation.

Ferrash barely glanced at the paste as he spooned it into his mouth. He had so much to do, so many contacts checking in all the time. He had to be ready to don his disguise as the Proctor and infiltrate the Primary Committee before anyone noticed Proglimen was gone. Work like that took a lot of prep. The sides of his skull seemed to press inwards, compressing everything inside until thought was a buzzing hum of pain. Inhibitors couldn't fix that. This wasn't emotion – it was brain tiredness. Running implants too hard, too fast, for too long. Never switching off. Never leaving things to rest. Only the face-slapping smell of brew, and the inherent danger of standing out, kept him from falling face-first into his bowl. And if he slept, he dreamed of *her*, no matter how much inhibitor he had taken.

How long now? Three days? Four since he had slept? Time was invisible on Hesperex, and he couldn't spare the processing power to run it by his implants.

Just as he struggled to rise above a wave of tired vertigo, the brew in his mug began to tremble. He squinted at it, then at a spoon rattling across the table opposite him. In the distance, a dull roar grew from nothing and expanded. Louder, louder, and it encompassed the entire room.

Curiosity was frowned upon, but Ferrash had finished his meal, so he deposited the utensils on a conveyor and headed back outside. Snow cut into him, shocking after the mild indoors. Ahead, framed by the surrounding buildings, the blizzard pulsed with swatches of blue and orange. Engine flares? He checked his direction. They were coming from the spaceport alright, but to make a ruckus this big, there had to be lots of them leaving, and big ones, too. Those ships hadn't left dock since... well, probably since before he was born. They were war ships. Fighting ships. Going-all-in ships. They hadn't even launched for the attack at the prison station, let alone the invasion of Munab.

He started towards the spacers' Academy and brought up a contact in his implants. <Ida, you grounded?>

No reply. Ferrash trudged through the endless snow for another few blocks before anything came through.

<Busy overseeing launch schedule. Why?> Ida sent.

<I need updates.>

Another pause. <I can make time, if I must.>

When he confirmed that yes, she must, she sent through a time and a location in one of the Academy's conference rooms. It was one of the rooms they normally rotated through for their meetings, regularly checked for bugs, located out of the sight and usual paths of anyone else working there.

His route there brought him closer to the spaceport. Soon enough, he could make out its disjointed shadow in the midst of the snow, the shapes of ships detaching from it at regular intervals. If today had been a thunder day, he might have seen them leaving over the ocean, illuminated by lightning. But they just slipped away into the night, engines screaming.

Unbidden, he recalled his last landing here – the last he had flown himself. Bek sat in the navigator's seat, Palia wrapped in a towel in the seat behind him. Her presence came swaddled in a blanket of ambivalence. His memories gave him clear-cut lines and defined borders. But for the knowledge that emotion *had been*, nothing tethered emotion to her image. As usual, it twisted his guts despite the inhibitors. Perhaps there was something so fundamentally wrong with losing the connections that tied self and memory that his body rejected it. Perhaps his already high doses weren't enough anymore.

Ferrash closed his eyes and breathed out the thoughts until only the moment remained. Then the next, and the next, until it was time to see Ida.

Stepping out from the alcove where he had been waiting, he checked the way was clear. Then he slipped through a side door and made his way to the conference room. He usually dressed the part for meetings like this, but he'd checked surveillance – everyone who worked here was busy. No one would notice him.

'This had better be important,' were the words that greeted him when he entered the room.

Ferrash sighed and narrowed his eyes at Ida. She wore her usual red uniform, the same as any other spacer's but for the insignia on her shoulders that marked her out as a void marshal. Among those who dared express themselves in the fleets, she was Night Sky. The meaning was lost anywhere but Hesperex, as the night sky here was grey and sickly, not the uninterrupted black of quieter worlds. So that was her – grey-skinned from a gene defect, grey-haired from the stress of command and a life almost up to its built-in limit.

Her mood, though... that was always black.

'Every move I make at the moment depends on so many other factors,' Ferrash said. 'I miss any intel, I mess up.'

'Funny. Thought you had all the cards.'

'A lot of those cards are dead now. I'm having to make do with scraps.'

Ida considered him for a second, then gave a light laugh. 'You can't tell me you didn't see this coming.'

Ferrash shook his head. 'I've been doing all I can to get the truce extended to peace, but I guess it wasn't enough. What happened?'

'I'll give you the quick version. The committees were pissers. They didn't like whatever you told them about the flagship – which I'd like to know myself, by the way, in case I ever go up against it – and they decided they wanted it out of the equation. They sent scout ships out to find it. They just reported back. We've new orders, and we're going to war.'

Taken aback, Ferrash furrowed his brows. 'They made the decision that fast?'

'Unlike them, I know.' Ida shifted on her feet, expression changing to one of concern. 'I think there's new leadership in play, and it's not from the top. I had hoped it was you.'

He breathed out and didn't meet her eyes. This wasn't good. He had to take Proglimen's place as Proctor as soon as he could. The position would give him the power of veto over committee decisions, but he wouldn't be able to do anything drastic without raising questions. Everything he had planned was meant to happen in little steps, but everything else was moving too fast.

Ida folded her arms across her chest. 'Am I going to have to stand here while you wallow in bile or are we done? I need to be on that fleet when the last ship leaves.'

'I'm not wallowing.' When Ferrash met her gaze again, he noted that worry hid behind the hardness. Ida might be cold as Hesperex most of the time, but she kept a personality behind that. She had desires, emotions, an affair with a captain who flew with the void packs. Everything the Keepers would hate, if she wasn't so good at keeping it hidden. He sighed. 'I'm doing my best to keep up.'

'Do better. I don't want every planet to end like Munab.'

Nodding, he said, 'Just tell me what the plan is and I'll let you go.'

She straightened as if about to deliver a briefing. 'Our scout ships recently struck out in search of the enemy's flagship. They found it docked in the Carabal system. A portion of our fleets are headed to Munab to support the ground war. Those of the rest who aren't tasked to defence have been ordered to convene at Oproven. Our task following on from that hasn't been revealed.'

Ferrash grunted. 'They're trying to stop me finding out.' Not him, directly, but they must suspect someone of pulling strings – they always did – and that made them tight-lipped. That and the fact that, given the opportunity, most in the Protectorate would willingly defect.

'I'm not sure they trust anyone at the moment,' Ida said.

'Wise choice. Before the purge, the Reiart had a majority.'

Ida frowned. 'Majority of the committees?'

'Of everyone.'

She took a step towards him, teeth bared, her voice low. 'Keepers take you, why didn't you strike out then?'

'It wasn't enough. Not to do it bloodlessly.'

She withdrew towards the exit, shaking her head. 'I'll leave you to your dreams of bloodless revolutions, Reiart. Some of us have a real war to fight.'

Ferrash stood in the dark of the conference room after she had left, staring at the bare walls, trying to work out where he had gone wrong. He didn't try for long. The cause didn't matter; he had to keep moving forwards. He had no time for retrospect. Not now. With a sick feeling curling around his hollowed-out soul, he realised he'd have to jump ahead a phase. There was one last thing to do before he could take Proglimen's place.

There was nothing else for it. It was time to visit his mother.

CHAPTER SIX

FERRASH HAD SPENT EVERY moment since leaving his mother's grasp doing his best to avoid her. The occasional run-in was almost guaranteed – Hesperex housed headquarters for both the Keepers and the External Security Force, and they sometimes got sent after the same targets – but he'd only managed to find himself within sight of her on five occasions in over a decade. He'd shrugged off any reaction each time. Doing otherwise would have been suicide, given that as an empyrric, she would have been able to see anything he felt.

Now, though, he needed to find her. Ferrash could get a disguise good enough to pass as Proglimen in front of the committees, even faking his genetics, but his mother would recognise him under all that. He couldn't infiltrate the Primary Committee and start pulling the thickest strings only to have his mother dash it all – and him, probably. So before he could begin the rest of the plan, he had to take her out of the picture. Talk her out of it, with any luck.

Ferrash knew just how quickly his mother could kill him if he made a mistake. In public, on the streets of Hesperex, he would be gone in an instant. Even if he got her in private, things would be the same – just maybe he'd die slower. He needed help.

Help, as it turned out, lived twenty-two levels below the surface of Five-Fifty-Four – about the lowest level you could reach before you hit the furnaces. Ferrash didn't visit often. He didn't like spending that long in a lift. Forced to take the journey now after grabbing a couple of hours' sleep, he paced when alone, sat when tired, and was relieved when the doors finally opened.

The lift opened onto a long corridor, wide enough to fit Ferrash's ship through, if he could have got it there in the first place. This far down, the overhead lights struggled to pierce the gloom. Blue light pooled at intervals on either side, marking where the corridor branched off into algae chambers. He breathed in deep. Humidity hung in the air, and as he took his first step away from the lift, a droplet fell from the curve of a slipped cable above him. Ferrash watched it fall, heard its echoes fill the empty space.

He strode to the nearest patch of light and tried to relax into the silence, but couldn't. For a moment his mind hung in vertigo, grasping at a release valve that had nothing to release, rocked by the phantom absence of the tension he thought he needed to drain.

The reaction only lasted long enough for him to pause and wonder at it. In that time, he opened the airlock membranes to the algae chamber and stepped through, his eyes adjusting to the change in light level.

In the corridor, light wasn't important. In here, it was life. Algae tubes stretched a hundred metres above him and to either side, each rotating cylinder coming together to form a tunnel of vital nutrients. Or perhaps this wasn't an algae chamber – perhaps this was the stuff that fed the vats, the organic goop that birthed the workforce of the galaxy's most populous nation. Ferrash didn't know which, and he didn't care. He just walked on, cross-referenced his implants' map with the room ahead of him and then, when he reached the fourth set of tube segments, he turned right.

Here he found a narrow gap between the segments that ran all the way to the wall. Ferrash counted the first floor tile, the second, the third... When he found the fourth, he lifted it by a cracked corner and moved it to one side. Every time he visited, Hesperex's quiet rebellion used a different entrance. That was good. Smart. Sensible. As with all the others, this entrance was out of view of all security cameras. Easy enough to trick the ones he'd passed into thinking he'd never been here by having his auxiliary AI generate some fake footage.

Ferrash dropped through the gap and landed in a crouch on the floor of an access tunnel. Cold gripped him in an instant. It had been mild in the chamber. Its algae tubes were heated, and that heat bled off into the surrounding room. Access tunnels didn't need to be heated. Vatborn could freeze down here and it would just be one fewer mouth to feed.

Ten metres down the tunnel, he stopped to open a hatch that had been marked as out of order. He stepped through, closed it behind him, and squinted ahead in the faint glow the hatch light provided.

A strip of metal ran above the clear top of the tunnel, fading away on either side as the press of oceanic water obscured the floor of the level above. Beneath his feet lay the depths and, somewhere, Hesperex's ocean floor. A massive light pulsed in the distance and set the hair on the back of his neck on end. He glimpsed flickers of movement in the corners of his eyes, but they vanished when he turned to look. If life still existed in the ocean, it was either too clever or fast for the Protectorate to catch, or there was little enough to make it worth the effort. Ferrash pushed through the primal reluctance of water surrounding him and carried on, hunching his shoulders to fit. His footsteps echoed.

Soon enough, his neck ached from holding it at an odd angle. A hundred metres down the tunnel, he dropped into a crouch instead, intending to go the rest of the way on his toes and knuckles. That's when he saw her.

Directly below him, obscured by his bent legs and warped by the glass, Palia floated in the water. Ferrash's heart lurched in his chest. He jerked away, smashing his head against the top of the tunnel, but even through the new pain he could see her. She had her hands pressed against the tunnel wall, and her eyes locked onto him as he sat staring.

She wasn't breathing. She floated outside in Hesperex's ocean and she wasn't a block of ice. Her hair looked dry. Her clothes, too. Once Ferrash recovered from the initial shock, he shuffled a hesitant fraction closer. She seemed so real, more real than the memories she'd left him with could paint her, as if he could swim outside and take hold of her, bring her in from the cold. But she couldn't be real, because she looked alive and couldn't be. Because if she was anywhere, looking for him, she was on Munab.

If she's looking for me at all. A dull twinge muscled through the fug of his emotions. Palia hadn't recognised him, after the Magister's death. Why would she look for someone she didn't know anymore? In theory, he shouldn't care. But beneath it all, there still lurked some stubborn notion that things *had* to go back to the way they were. A dangerous notion.

As Ferrash stared into the fake Palia's eyes, he palmed another syringe from an inside pocket, stabbed its contents into the track-marked flesh of his arm. He waited for dullness to push through his veins, into his mind, but nothing came. Just a fuzzing at the edge of his vision, a fluctuation in his heartrate, a slight tremor through each of his muscles. Up against the limit. He should stop. Recover. Work on processing everything naturally.

How could it be so hard to shake the grief of losing an emotion you could no longer feel?

Palia's image flickered, merged into the ocean, then reformed. This time a darker face and darker eyes. Hair the shade of a cave's pitch night. A face he had left on Munab as a teenager, a memory that had never left him. He closed his eyes. With so much context stripped from recent memory, his time with his first love seemed fresher, her snuffing-out at his mother's hands like it was yesterday.

But she was a lie, as well.

Ferrash beat once against the floor with the butt of his pistol, and her image fell into darkness. A creature made of more shadow than flesh pulsated and shot away into the depths, leaving a thin trail of bubbles in its wake.

He knew what it was: the creature the Reiart had been named for, believed to be extinct, apparently just elusive. That was in its nature. Rumour had it that it took people from your memories and became them to lure you into the water after it. He wondered when might have been the last time anyone in the Protectorate cared about someone enough to do so.

He stared after it a moment longer, then continued on his way. The people he was going to see would take this sighting as an omen. Ferrash wasn't superstitious. It was just a delay.

'You took your time.'

Ferrash shot a glare towards the source of the voice. He'd barely been out of the tunnel a second and he'd already been spotted.

'You been waiting here all day?' Ferrash asked.

The man – he went by the name of Son, dark-skinned, with a narrow face and sharp eyes – gave a genuine smile and put a hand on Ferrash's elbow to steer him. They walked away from the wall together. Ferrash took quick stock of the room: people crammed to bursting, clustered beneath a low-hanging swathe of fabric studded with lights; groups in huddles, chatting; trade stalls lining the walls; a makeshift shack packed to the brim with assorted tech.

'The threads are drawing closer, tighter,' said Son. 'We must act fast to survive their closing, and you are as entwined with fate as any of us.'

Ferrash inclined his head, but his thoughts charged ahead, accelerated by his implants. He had arranged a meeting with the Technocracy, not with Son. With his religion's penchant for prophecy and foresight, had he just predicted Ferrash would make another visit soon and decided to wait for him? If that was the case, he needed to make his excuses and leave.

'Actually, I—'

Son cut him off. 'Since the purge, we've all been forced further underground. The Technocracy run their operations from down here, now. I didn't realise Ducat was another contact of yours, but when they gave your description, I realised we had both been doing business with the same man.'

The same Reiart was what Son meant, but he couldn't say that with so many people around. Not unless he meant to blow everything, and Ferrash could see that he didn't. Still, he cursed at the thought of two wires crossed, at one more weak spot where everything could spiral into blood.

Ferrash scanned the room again, but couldn't see his other contact anywhere. 'Ducat couldn't come themself?'

'They're busy again now the war has restarted. They have a lot of tasks to juggle, but they said they could carve out enough time to speak to you.'

Nice to know they still had that much respect, at least. 'Where?'

Son pointed at the shack Ferrash had seen earlier.

'Bit public. Anywhere better?'

'It goes further at the back. You will have your privacy. Ducat is inside.'

'Okay.' Ferrash sighed, then nodded thanks to Son and moved from his grasp. The two techs manning the shack paid him no attention as he passed. They were up to their elbows in machine parts, with data-screens lighting up the air around them, their eyes flicking between them and their task. Ferrash had no idea what they were working on. Could have been weapons, could have been hydroponics. Tech was much a muchness when it was stripped.

A membrane sealed off the back of the shack. Ferrash pressed a hand against it, watched the material slither back into its housing. He had to step through and open another before he made it into the shack proper. Harsher lights seared into his eyes. He blinked, taking in the clean benches, the large air filtration units, the robots and techs working together.

Ducat paced at the far end of the room, their thin arms gesticulating as they spoke. Ferrash's go-to Technocracy contact had tattooed a number across one side of their hairless scalp since last Ferrash had seen them.

"Ey, brutta.' Ducat broke off their conversation mid-speech and clapped their hands together – as much a greeting as most learned away from the vats, with touch often denied to them.

'Vatter.' Ferrash inclined his head.

A gesture from Ducat's hand saw a membrane close around the two of them, masking their conversation from the room's other occupants. 'You after more of t' inhibitors? Supply is low. Getting in hands is difficult. Or you after more wordspeak on the happenings? We hear a lot of t'ose.'

'This'll be more difficult, trust me.'

Ducat pursed their lips, head cocked to one side, then grinned and leaned back against a bench full of ocular implants stacked in sealed chambers. 'Makes it interestin'. You need?'

'Nexite grenades. A couple for me, a few more rigged throughout a section of Five-Fifty-Four to be set off at my command. A couple of your people for an ambush.'

The muscle over Ducat's eye crept up – if they had been born with eyebrows, one would have been raised. 'Huntin' keepers? Triff's wrong grid-city to do it in. Plenty quieter places.'

'I'm after one in particular. She isn't due out of Five-Fifty-Four for another few months.'

'So wait.'

Ferrash shook his head. 'No time for that.' Then, on a whim and because it lined up with some of the figures that had been taunting him since the purge, he said, 'That number on your head, are they your losses?'

Ducat's eyes crinkled in the corners. 'All vatters lost, yes. T'ere to remind me to keep as a snowrat. Quiet-as.'

'Expect to add a few more zeroes to that if my plan doesn't get off the ground.'

Eyes harder now, Ducat nodded. 'What else?'

'The difficult part. I know you've been experimenting with containment systems. Nexite null boxes that block the Empyrean inside or out. Do you have a working prototype?'

They nodded.

'How big?'

'Hand-size. Tested it wit' Sargen Saturis before t'ey killed him.'

'How long would it take you to build one big enough to fit a human?'

Ducat leaned back and folded their arms across their chest. 'Week, but I could sell all my knowhow and still be short for nexite.'

'Can't you move a few shipments around? You're still running supplies for the fleets, right?'

'Can do. Can't do unnoticed.'

'I'll handle that.' Ferrash was pretty sure Ducat *could* run those supplies unnoticed, but from the way they shifted on their feet, the slightest hint of aggression creeping into their movements, he guessed the purge had left them on edge. Wary. He couldn't blame them. If Ferrash did the legwork himself he might ease some of that, if not earn a little more trust.

Nodding, Ducat shifted their gaze around the room, at all the tech stored there. 'You send 'em here once you done, ey? Got t'ings could need testin' on a live greenling.'

'I have other things in mind for this one. But with any luck, you won't need to test whatever you've got once I'm through.'

'True?' The brow muscle rose again, then Ducat dismissed the membrane and turned to fiddle at a datascreen beside the ocular implants. 'T'is all?'

'Did you get that data I sent you?'

Ducat nodded. 'Interestin' tech. Needs scalin' up but I no clue what it does. It what I wanted testin' on a greenling for.'

'You won't be able to test it, trust me. And it doesn't necessarily need to be bigger. It just needs something to power it. Try pointing a nexite buoy at it and see what happens.'

'Oh, sure, sure. Zap mystery tech wit' ot'er tech an' see what happen. Reason you don't work for me. What else?'

'Just a reconstruction mesh.'

Ducat snorted and shook their head. 'Mesh is big expense, but not biggest you ask tonight. One in cupboard over t'ere. Better bring back when done.'

'Thank you. I will.' As long as he didn't die wearing the thing while it disguised him as Proglimen.

'All good t'en. Week, and box be ready for you. Return here?'

'Sure.' Ferrash reached over and placed a hand on Ducat's shoulder so that one finger rested on the skin of their neck. He made it look like a friendly – if culturally out-of-place – touch, but the brief contact was all it took to push his instructions through to Ducat's implants. They could read them at leisure. 'I'll let you know if there are any changes.'

'Understood. Don't go lookin' edible.'

Ferrash took his cue, retrieved a bag containing the reconstruction mesh and retreated from the techs. As he left the room and its displaced people behind him, he braced himself once more for the dark.

There were worse monsters on the surface than there were in the deep.

CHAPTER SEVEN

FABIEN WAS BUSY IN his chambers on the flagship, packing the last of his things for his trip to Rythe, when Consul Theowe charged through the open door and launched straight into an angry tirade.

'Outrageous. Simply outrageous.' The consul's braided beard bobbed against his chest. His hand, white-knuckled, gripped the sash of his robe. 'That's what the people will think of this. Scant weeks as Magister and already you go head bowed to Rythe. A display of weakness, to a single planet!'

Fabien backed away from the door and let go of his bags so he could gesture the consul to sit. He managed a polite smile, even with his mind caught in a blank state of momentary surprise. As intended, no doubt. He took a second to calm his pulse. Theowe was an old hand – a consul of some two decades' experience, wearing the robes since before Fabien had even started his career. But he was Fabien's subordinate now, and no matter how much Fabien preferred to collaborate than lead, he had to remember that.

As Theowe strode past to sit in a recliner, Fabien asked, 'Is that what the people would say, or what you say? The last I checked, you were a consul, not a plebian crow. Do you claim to be their voice regardless?'

Theowe sank back into the recliner, legs crossed, glowering. 'I do not, Magister, but that does not mean I am incapable of prediction. The ancestors themselves will be muttering about this, mark my words.'

'I'm afraid the ancestors had their say while they were alive. I understand your point, though. Most decisions make someone grumble.' Fabien clasped his hands behind his back and strode towards the balcony, facing out over the communal gardens. 'But most people live their lives, and until a decision affects them, it means nothing. So this will be.'

Theowe grunted. Not an angry sound, just an old man settling down to think. The tirade had just been a front, thought up or worked up in advance to catch Fabien off guard. Beneath it all, the man was perfectly prepared for conversation. 'All our people are military, Magister, at some stage in their lives. If they aren't in service, they'll know someone who is.'

'That doesn't change their opinion on Rythe.'

'It makes them proud. They will see you going to Rythe for help before they have had a chance to prove themselves, and it will hurt that pride.'

'Would they prefer I send them against the Protectorate without trying to better the odds?' Out in the gardens, a wheelkite floated in the breeze, buoyed about on its air bladder. It rose and fell, no control over its path. If Fabien stumbled in his new role as Magister, perhaps his path would be the same – nudged this way and that by the whims of his twenty consuls.

Consul Theowe made a scritching sound, nails on fabric. 'They would prefer you didn't go against the Protectorate at all, I think.'

Fabien thought of Consul Esselia, stubborn and doubtful. 'So I have heard.'

'I disagree with those ones.' Theowe's voice was harsher now. Strong. 'The Protectorate needs stamping out. Hit them while they're already fighting amongst themselves and we have a chance to nip any future attacks in the bud. But Rythe... we don't need their help.'

'So it's your pride you speak for now?' Fabien turned, eyebrow raised, to see Theowe leaning forwards with his fists clenched on his lap. 'Consider it this way: We have been patrolling the Rythian Breach for over two decades since the war. Going to Rythe now isn't asking for help, it's asking for repayment. Rythe has spent too long isolating itself from the rest of the galaxy. It's time for it to step into the light.'

Fabien would have gone further, but as he spoke the last few words, a reminder flashed up in his implants. *Fires.*

Theowe opened his mouth to reply. Fabien cut him off. 'I'm sorry, consul, but I need to get to a meeting, and then I need to get aboard the ship to Rythe. It can't wait. We can catch up on this later if—'

'That won't be necessary.' Theowe waved him off and rose, calm now, perfectly so, like he had never been angry at all. He left the chambers without another word, leaving Fabien to lock the door membrane behind him and set off towards the archives.

The archivist Lilesh was more than a data keeper. She was empyrric, from an old bloodline, renowned and feared in equal measure throughout the Hegemony. She shared the archives with none of the other empyrrics aboard the flagship, though that didn't mean she kept the place to herself. Some of its rooms were host to carnal acts, impressive in both regularity and scale, so bizarre that they bypassed usual indifference and raised worried eyebrows.

Approaching, Fabien caught sight of a couple of naked legs flitting around a corner, accompanied by giggling. He rolled his eyes and kept on to the archives proper. The 'meeting' rooms were just a power source, open to all. Whether Lilesh enjoyed her rowdy surroundings or whether she just tolerated them for the advantage they conveyed, he didn't know. In any case, in a pinch, the archivist had enough energy at her fingertips to last as long as anyone would stand against her. A good thing she hadn't been on the flagship when he and Palia had gone after the Magister. A good thing Fabien had told her not to be there.

'You're late,' she said.

Startled, he snapped his head to the left where Archivist Lilesh stood, hands clasped behind her back, eyes narrowed at the data-screens before her. She hadn't turned to face him. She didn't need to to know he was there.

'I got held up,' he said. 'I'm sure the ship will wait for me.'

'I'm not as convinced mine will.' With a wave of her hand, she dismissed the screens. They folded back into the wall, back into the databanks stored there, separate from the rest of the ship's networked architecture.

Fabien frowned. 'They know you're to go with them.'

'Know, certainly.' Lilesh picked her way across to another wall, another set of databanks. No one would know what they were, without being told. Lilesh could pinpoint exactly where to go without a second's thought. 'Whether they wish me to go with them is another matter. Hegemony empyrrics are much like magnets. Most often, we greet with opposing poles.'

'To my knowledge, Palia was taught the Keepers' way. Or some of it.'

'Yes. Which brings me to my main point of concern.' Lilesh paused, tapping one finger against the edge of the wall, but she didn't bring forth a screen. 'I know the one she goes in search of. Or know of. You might say our respective employment overlaps.'

Fabien had told her all of this when he briefed her, imagining she already knew. 'He's a spy, yes.'

'He's dangerous.'

'Most spies are, if they're not incompetent to the point of comedy.'

'Well,' Lilesh straightened and stared straight at him, 'This one more than most.'

'How so?'

'I can't say for certain. We have scant few insights into Protectorate networks. All I know is he gets involved in a lot of their most important work, acting alone – which directly contradicts the laws of free agency. Our agents have encountered him once or twice and never come out well from it. Until he got involved with Palia Tennic, we assumed he worked for Lariss or the Confederated Outer Reach, as he has been observed going against his own people on occasion, without reserve. Now that we know the truth, I have reason to believe he works for a branch apart from ordinary Protectorate intelligence. A rumoured branch, very much a sword held over their people's heads. A secret police.'

A section of wall pulsed by Lilesh's head, painting the sharp lines of her face emerald for a fraction of a second before fading back into the paintwork. Fabien shivered. He didn't know if it was the reminder of the power Lilesh possessed or the worry clawing at his insides that made him do so.

He licked his lips, finding them suddenly dry. 'Is there a chance he could have misrepresented himself to Palia, during their acquaintance?'

'A chance? I would say a certainty. Only the extent remains to be gathered. But you met the man. What would you say?'

'I would say I'm perhaps not the best judge of character.' Fabien grimaced, thinking of the previous magister. Then his implants registered a message that his ship was ready for departure.

Sighing, he rubbed a hand along his jaw, felt the scrape of stubble he hadn't had chance to shave off yet. 'You'll be with her, Archivist. Teach her. Keep her out of trouble.'

'And should Progmannae prove himself an enemy?' Lilesh's eyes were cold. Dark. Fabien fancied he could see himself reflected in them, so looked away.

'Kill him.'

CHAPTER EIGHT

FERRASH CONSIDERED DONNING PROGLIMEN'S disguise straight away and using his new identity as Proctor as a pretext to lure his mother to a meeting, but it wouldn't work. Contacting her would leave a trace, and if she mysteriously went missing afterwards, someone would trace it back to him.

So he went with what he'd been calling the 'poke and hope' method: Poke the wasp nest and hope you didn't get stung.

Once Ferrash moved enough nexite around, Ducat got the box Ferrash planned to trap his mother in ready in three days. Ducat gave Ferrash three people for the mission, but only one of those would be staying with him for the duration. It had to do with that number tattooed onto Ducat's scalp, Ferrash thought, and didn't blame them for the fact.

When Ducat indicated that was all, Ferrash and the others left the Technocracy's shack behind and struck out for the surface in silence. Ferrash gave the others a location in case they had to split up on the way, but no further details than that. Not that he didn't trust them. The truth was somewhere between his not wanting them to rattle if caught and not wanting to frighten them with the details. Those could come later, when they were ready to begin.

Some hours later, they arrived at a safe room near the surface – a different one to the room he had passed a night in with Bek and Palia when they had brought her to Hesperex. This floor of the building lay a level below the surface of the city, but damage to the surface had left a jagged hole in its metal floor, leaving the streets beneath it open to the storm-clad sky. Ferrash stared up at that sky through the tiniest slit of his building's window. With any luck, it would stay this dark and miserable for the duration of what he had planned. No, scratch that. No luck needed. Hesperex was always dark and miserable.

'So what's the plan?' one of Ducat's people – one of the two women in the group – asked from behind him.

Ferrash turned to face her. She had most of the group's nexite grenades stuffed inside her many patchwork pockets. She was probably a prog. Too aged to be vatborn, with hair stark grey against gnarled dark skin. She eyed him, doubtful, gaze lingering on the scars on his face.

He brushed a finger against the scars without meaning to and asked, 'What's your name?' without really knowing why.

'Aude.'

'Just Aude?'

'To you, yes.'

Grimacing, he took in the others. One was a short woman, bone-thin but fresh-faced, a lock of bright blonde hair just visible within the shadows of her coat hood. The other was a boy no more than ten years old. Ducat had assigned him over with some reluctance, and the boy had passed through the throng of Son's Observers to reverent looks and hushed whispers. Ferrash hadn't asked who was here to do which job, hadn't wanted to know which person would be staying with him after setup to help catch his mother. Now he wanted to. He wanted to make sure it wasn't this scrap of a kid with too-old eyes and a thick white streak running through his black hair.

'You two?' Ferrash asked.

'Limor,' said the short woman. Her voice grated, and its halting rhythm suggested she was unused to speaking. She jerked her chin towards the boy. 'Boy does not speak.'

Boy just looked at him, unnervingly steady, and Ferrash found he couldn't hold that gaze.

'Okay,' Ferrash said. 'What's Ducat already told you?'

Aude started pulling grenades from her pockets, one by one, and setting them down on a dust-covered table. 'We hunt keepers.' She caressed the grip of a holstered pistol with her free hand.

'We hunt keepers, yes. But we hunt one of them alive. You understand that?'

Aude's eyes flashed, but she shrugged.

Ferrash bit back a sigh. 'In eight hours, the Keepers' patrol routes will bring a group of three keepers along the street outside. One of those keepers will be a head justicar. It's her we need to capture.' When Aude's lips began to form the word 'why', he sped on. 'We need to take out her escort, then draw her far enough down through the levels that it'll take too long for help to reach her, or find her. Ducat has seen to it that her cage is in position near the furnaces. That's where we need to get her.'

Limor's nose crinkled. 'At least two-tens and four levels down. You will die before one. Keepers fast.'

Ferrash nodded. 'So I need to be faster. Got a plan for that.' He dug a metal spike from one of his pockets and held it out on his palm, to a blank-faced response.

Bek would have known what it was, but Bek wasn't here. Ferrash dismissed the pang of loneliness that brought and put the spike away with a sigh. 'Eight hours may sound a lot, but it's not. Could take a while for both parts of the set-up. Aude, I've sent you a map with locations marked out. I need you to set up the nexite grenades on a proximity trigger to either side of the street there so they take any empyrric passing through out of action. Keep them dormant – I'll activate them when I'm ready. Take Limor. Make sure you're not seen. When it's done... who's staying behind?'

Aude tapped her shoulder once.

'Okay.' Not the boy. Good. 'You come back here, you get a weapon ready and you wait to sight out that window when I signal. All clear?'

'Clear enough,' she said.

Boy tapped his own shoulder as Aude had, still holding Ferrash in his gaze. *What about me?*

'You come with me.'

Aude folded her arms across her chest. 'Prefer them when they can't ask questions, huh?'

'Funny.'

Boy was happy enough to follow him, even if both women watched him go with more than a little uncertainty. Ferrash wondered why they even listened to him. He meant nothing to them; their acceptance rested on Ducat's word alone.

Hesperex only had one mountain. Or rather, Hesperex had only one mountain that the Protectorate in all its millennia had never been able to build upon. It overshadowed a quarter of Five-Fifty-Four, the buildings nearest its slopes mostly abandoned from the cold. They walked the crowded streets towards it now, though they couldn't see it once they passed the slash in the ceiling. Boy's presence was a weight at Ferrash's side, constantly in mind even when out of sight, his footsteps barely audible. He wasn't sure why he'd brought Boy. His silent gaze was more reproach than existed in either woman's words.

'Have you ever seen a snowshriek?' Ferrash asked.

In the corner of his eye, Boy nodded. His eyes darted over and back, mirror-bright.

'Good.'

Normally, Ferrash would be content with silence – or as silent as the wind-chilled streets of Five-Fifty-Four got with hundreds of people filling most roads – but something about Boy made him want to fill it. It didn't matter what with. He just needed noise. Human noise. The lie that everything was normal. But he couldn't just open his mouth and chatter, not with so many unspeaking people around. He and Boy followed the trails of other workers, mingling with groups on the way from one shift to another, slipping away when that group went where they didn't mean to follow. A pair walking alone wasn't uncommon, but a boy drew eyes.

In that way, shuttled from one street to the next, they came to the mountain edge. Here, grey-sided city blocks had ceded to avalanche after avalanche. Ferrash had been on Hesperex when the first one came – a white mass as innocent as cloud but roaring with the violence of thunder. Two weeks, it had taken them, to dig the buildings out. They'd been hive-houses, full of vatborn, and their bodies were taken frozen stiff to feed the vats anew. Four months later, there had been another avalanche. They left it buried, after the third.

Squinting up into the clouds, Ferrash picked out snowshrieks wheeling high above, drifting down to a nearby rooftop every now and then on their two triangular wings. The creatures were hard to spot, their dappled grey-white plumage perfect camouflage against snow. Boy followed his gaze.

'That's what we're after,' Ferrash said. 'The getaway.'

No one had seen them come here. Ferrash had led them on a circuitous route for the last couple of blocks, half through the shells of abandoned buildings, until they braved the upper level. He had looped or doctored whatever cameras might have recorded them along the way via his implants.

He realised, as he started up a snowdrift into the shell of the snowshrieks' building, that he was waiting for Boy to say something. It was like having something sat in your peripheral, waiting for it to move, unable to look at it until it did.

Dim light reflected from the snow. Ferrash sank up to his knees in it, struggled to kick through. 'Did you ever talk?'

Silence, of course. But when he peered back over his shoulder, the boy gave a small nod.

'Did you serve the Keepers long?'

Another nod, and this time, a moment of connection in that gaze of his. Here was another prog, like Ferrash. Another cog ground through the Keepers' machine.

Ferrash lifted his face to the wind, let it cut, chill and sharp, across what little of it was exposed. Then they passed under the doorway, and the wind reduced to howling around the entrance. He kicked the last of the snow off his legs to join the scattering near the door, then scanned around for the nearest stairs.

When he found them, he set off up, explaining to Boy as he went. 'Those snowshrieks nest at the top of this building. Not sure how many, but at least one pair. That spike I showed you earlier? If we sneak close enough, we can use it to... tame one of them.'

Boy cocked his head. *How?*

'Spike's called a neuriger. Inserted near the brain stem, it gives you remote control over most animals. Plan is we get one and I can fly it to escape the head justicar.'

For the next two floors, Boy dropped his gaze, burning into each step they passed. Ferrash kept glancing at him, convinced of something weighty building up. Was he thinking about how you got the neuriger near the brain stem? Did he object to hurting an animal for this? Or was it the notion of being controlled, in the way no doubt his life had been controlled and painful before he left the Keepers' care?

At last, as they reached the top of the final flight of stairs, Boy opened his mouth and asked, 'Why do you want her alive?'

Ferrash pulled at an access hatch above them, then paused, holding the stowed ladder closed. He looked over to Boy. Where snow glare filtered through the hatch, it painted Boy's curly hair silver and shone from the lenses of his eyes. Powder snow drifted down, feather-light against his gloved knuckles.

For the next several seconds, Ferrash stood there, wondering in the path of that straight stare how much he could reasonably tell, and how much he should.

'I need her help,' Ferrash said at last. The words felt flat. Lifeless.

'She will kill you.'

Breaking the stare, Ferrash lowered the ladder and started up it. 'Not if I'm careful.'

'She will kill you, and she will kill Aude.'

Again, Ferrash hesitated – this time at the top of the ladder, with his head poking out into the freezing air. He breathed in deep, felt the chill slide down his throat like he was breathing in the snow that banked the hatch.

'She won't.' But his mother probably would kill Aude. Aude's job was to fire the first shot, alone in that room. It didn't matter how clear her escape path was – when she fired, she'd be noticed, and she'd probably be killed before she could get away or Ferrash could distract them. Why couldn't he feel anything? More than emotionally, more than what the inhibitors worked against, why couldn't he see Aude and the others as more than parts in an equation? More than just numbers? He'd reduced everyone to that. Ferrash let the core of people slide over the surface of his mind and pass on, unregistered. Sensible. Pragmatic. Couldn't get tied down by remorse like Ducat with their tattooed death count.

But there was Boy, standing doubtful beneath him.

'The head justicar's my mother. Won't want to kill me. Might want to hurt me, and hurt me bad, but that's all the more reason for her to chase me. I'll make good bait.'

'She will catch you.'

Across the roof, shapes moved, camouflaged against the snow. Ferrash gestured for Boy to follow him up the rungs.

'Help me catch one of these,' Ferrash said, 'and she'll have a hard time of it.'

CHAPTER NINE

FERRASH AND BOY CAUGHT themselves a snowshriek with surprising ease – in part thanks to Boy pinning one of its wings before it could fly away. Ferrash had made sure to grab hold of its short beak before it could tear a chunk out of him in retaliation, and its two stubby legs couldn't reach to claw at them. With the neuriger connected and controlling its actions, Ferrash had sent Boy along with it to the network of maintenance shafts Ferrash planned to lure his mother down. Boy's instructions were simple: stay out of the way, stay calm, release the snowshriek when signalled and get back to Ducat as fast as possible afterwards.

Ferrash had made his way back towards the safe room, and now he dropped down from the rooftop he had used as a shortcut, letting a snowbank cushion his fall. His skin itched where his hood's seams rubbed against it – he had changed into a patchwork workers' coat for the ambush.

To catch a Keeper, pretend you are Kept.

As the Keepers' head justicar on Hesperex, Ayt Mannae – Ferrash's mother – had been tasked with eliminating the Kept. Completely, and without mercy. It meant that the people she protected were less scared of her than of other keepers. Keeping the public safe from terrorists tended to paint a good image in people's minds, and the Kept were indiscriminate enough in their attacks that few questioned the label. Ferrash knew better.

Above him, a lighting panel near the broken edge of the ceiling flickered. Its guttering light strobed the surrounding buildings, slums in all but the solidity of their construction. On the outside, they looked the same snow-beaten drab as any other buildings on Hesperex, but the rooms inside held nothing more than hives for people – alcoves just big enough for a vatborn to lie in, stacked one atop the other in a comb pattern to make use of as much space as possible. Go far enough north and you'd find buildings just like these, but frozen over when their systems failed, the people inside preserved the way they'd been abandoned. Ferrash imagined none of them had dared say anything. They'd lain in their boxes, thinking their brothers and sisters and vatters would report them if they complained about the cold. They'd lain there, pretending, freezing, dying. And what had the Protectorate done? Left them there, testament to their failure.

Ferrash dusted himself off and crept to the next intersection, then peered left.

There. Three of them. Harsh lights washed most of the colour from their green robes, but he knew what they were: three keepers patrolling a problem area for anyone breaking second-shift curfew. He'd lifted the schedule from the Keepers' database, so it was no surprise to see his mother among them – that's what he'd been aiming for. Besides, he needed to avoid surprises around people who could see emotions. It was Ferrash who needed to surprise *them*. Thankfully, their desire not to advertise their patrols meant they didn't bring siggeriths with them. Three keepers, he could take. A thirty-foot-tall prime siggerith? Not so much.

Ferrash called to the others in his implants and pulled his pistol from under his coat. The keepers moved forwards, breath misting around their hoods, heads scanning from side to side as they looked for trouble. His mother stood out at the front of the group in her armoured robes.

A shard of light flashed from the window of the safe room opposite. One of the keepers at the back of the group snapped their head in its direction, but the next second the back of their skull exploded with a *crack* that echoed along the street. His mother whirled around as they crumpled to the floor. She made a grasping motion with one hand. The window shone with fierce green light and shattered, spilling shards of glass in a glittering rain to the snow below, then the flames leapt across the gap between them and his mother to coil around her arms. Aude was gone, just as Boy had predicted.

Don't underestimate Ayt Mannae.

Ferrash knew that, but still he raised his pistol and pulled the trigger. Her other escort fell. One keeper left. It shouldn't have been this easy. The next part, though – that would be hard.

Ferrash turned and sprinted from the sight of blood and Empyrean fire licking over the ice. Catching hold of the corner of the building, he swung himself around it. Blinding light shot past him. It hissed into the air in the space he had just vacated. He sent an activation command to the nexite grenades through his implants and stayed numb, waiting for the sound he hoped would come next.

Footsteps crunched closer. Walking, not running – he didn't think he had ever seen his mother run. When they passed the trigger point for the nexite grenades, there was a dull thump, and a low buzz sounded at just the right frequency to set his teeth on edge. His mother hissed in frustration.

Ferrash pushed himself off the wall and ran, boots pounding against the hard-packed snow, coat flapping in the air behind him. With Ayt's senses dazzled by the nexite, he might just avoid getting caught and killed before he had her trapped. *Keep moving. Don't stop. Just run.* Lights shining into the snowy breeze cast surreal shadows. Then he moved past the scar in the ceiling, and the snow stopped. His breath screamed through the quiet, though it would be a while until he was tired. He was counting on that.

He aimed for the stairs to the next level down. The floor tiles surrounding it crept from dull grey to emerald; the hair on the back of his neck prickled. He threw himself into the opening the second the air above became a sheet of blinding flame. Too close. Too close, and he had to keep moving.

The urge to move was base. Instinctual. The inhibitors had dulled any panic and the calculation it left in its wake was too slow to keep up with anything but big-picture objectives. Muscles flung him forwards, and his brain picked the direction.

Something tugged at his soul. An image of Palia sitting across from him flashed across his mind, white-haired and concentrating in the moments just before she killed him. Memory rearing its head out of context or his mother trying to tear them away, he couldn't tell.

Gritting his teeth, Ferrash pulled a disc grenade from his pocket and flicked it back at his mother. In the moment it took her to deal with it, he blew the bolts on a pre-prepared maintenance hatch to his right and leapt inside, knowing she would follow after.

He fell into a metal crevasse, exactly as planned. The trick was in not hitting the bottom. As long as they had set everything up right... He reached out with his implants, found nothing.

Blood. Where was the snowshriek?

Ferrash reached again and caught onto the trailing edge of a signal, weak and receding in the distance. Cursing, he tugged at it with a mental shout of command. How far did this shaft go? He'd measured it so there should be time before hitting the bottom, but any delay was a bad one. He craned his neck up, but he couldn't make out anything in the dark. For all he knew, Ayt could be right on top of him. She could move faster than he could fall. That's why he needed the snowshriek – for that and landing intact.

Wingbeats punched through the dark. Ferrash swung his body around as best he could to line up with the snowshriek's flight path. The neuriger link might give him full control of that path, but moving two bodies at the same time – one less willing than the other – wasn't easy. The creature slammed into his chest with enough force to knock the air out of him. He clung on, fingers digging into its pale feathers as he dragged himself up to lie on its back. He took care not to rip the neuriger out the back of its skull as he did so – if he did, the snowshriek would regain control of its body, and that wouldn't end well for either of them. Instead, he aimed it towards the other maintenance hatch several levels below and a block away horizontally. It struggled, its wingspan barely providing enough lift to account for his extra weight, but the landing only needed to be survivable.

Ferrash peered over his shoulder. Green flared in the dark behind and above him, a curved shield against the air, reflecting off the metal walls to either side. Ayt followed him, siphoning her own energy to adjust the direction of her fall and pursuit. The pain mesh embedded on the side of his face twinged as if in sympathy. For a moment, panic cut through the numbness, but he had adjusted the codes on it years ago. She shouldn't be able to use it against him.

He urged the snowshriek faster, just in case.

He had fallen a long way before the snowshriek caught him, and the heat of the low-level furnaces pressed closer. Level twenty-five beckoned. Ferrash could just make out the hatch's outline, orange with the glow of industrial furnaces. It showed on the overlay in his implants, too, mapped in wirelines from architectural twins older than he was. Older than anyone could be. Older even than Hesperex's ice age.

Ferrash glanced over his shoulder. The green flashes came faster now, bursting in the dark one after the other. By their size and the time between blasts, he reckoned she was going fast. Maybe faster than him.

Hissing under his breath, he pushed the snowshriek into a steep dive and let it pick up speed. Warm air slid over his skin and ripped the hood from his head to ruffle his hair. He ducked as a thick strand of cables whipped by – this section of the maintenance crevasse used to be a submarine bay back when Five-Fifty-Four had been a separate city, but the water had been pumped out and only the detritus of its old purpose remained, ready to snap his neck if he wasn't careful.

With a crack, the snowshriek flared its triangular wings and shot towards the open hatch. Ferrash pressed himself as close to its back as he could. The hatch was only about as wide as the snowshriek's body and as it tucked its wings to fit through diagonally, the lip of the hatch scraped along his shoulder blade.

The two of them swung left, but the snowshriek overshot and crashed against a tall containment vessel. Its wings slapped against the surface with a resounding *clang* but momentum kept Ferrash moving. He flew over its head and landed on the floor a few feet away, skidding along it until his lower back connected with something solid. Heat seared into him through his clothes. Ferrash cried out and twisted away. It was a section of pipe, and it must have led away from the furnaces on the floor below. Heat hazed in the air above it.

Wincing at the pain, he got to his feet and sprinted across the factory floor, wheezing as he recovered from the impact with the pipe. Not far to go. He had to make it there before she could get a clear shot in. How far behind was she?

Pale-limbed and stout, the vatborn workers hardly noticed him pass. He tumbled headlong into one of them as they carried a sheet of metal to another workstation. They fell together, faces almost touching, and Ferrash saw nothing in the other's eyes bar his own reflection. The metal sheet bounced off one corner, bending to produce a sound tunefully out of place with the surrounding monotony.

Ferrash shoved the worker aside with an apology on his lips, surging up and on to continue on his way. He couldn't stop moving. Nightmares of green fire chased him in his mind. Imagined threats hovered at his neck, no less real for the fact he couldn't see them. He vaulted over a wall of pipes, stumbled as he clipped his toe on the way down. In front of him, maybe four-hundred metres away in a straight line, stood the thick door separating this foundry from the next. Ferrash glared at it as if that would bring it closer, then glanced over his shoulder.

Ayt Mannae charged towards him like a spectre, her feet never touching the ground. Instead, like with her controlled fall through the submarine chamber, she sprang from bursts of empyrric energy. It gave the impression that she was skating on ice – body tilted forwards, arms pumping. They locked eyes across the gap between them, and a tidal wave phased into existence around her – drained, perhaps, from some of the vatborn's fear at a keeper landing in their midst. Understandable.

Ferrash triggered a command in his implants. There was an innocuous-sounding beep, then flame ripped through the base of a nearby column and tipped the whole thing sideways into Ayt's path. Metal screamed at the assault. His mother just swung her wave of energy up to shield herself, of course. But that used up the energy she was about to throw his way, which gave Ferrash a few precious seconds to make it to the exit.

The sight of the green wave splashed across his memory. *An explosion. A falling capsule. Palia melting metal and glass and spinning a shield to stop the slap of an uncaring sea...* He shook the memory out of his head. *Not now.*

Ferrash sprinted through the exit, grabbed hold of the lip on the far edge of the two-metre-thick wall and threw himself to the left, out of sight. Above the doorframe, the security camera opened up a broadcast channel straight to his implants. He watched his mother approach, trailing fire in her wake. As fast as he could, he checked all the protocols were set up. But she was gaining, and there was only one way to truly tell.

He sent the command.

With Ayt halfway through the gap, two smooth slabs of nexite fell from the outer edges and sealed her inside. She slammed against the nearest slab, but it didn't budge. Then she grew quiet, and he could picture her trying to draw upon the Empyrean. Ferrash walked up to her new prison with his pistol ready just in case she got out, somehow.

No one had tried this before. If he'd been paying for the nexite shipments... well, he wouldn't have been able to. The Protectorate didn't have money as a concept amongst its citizenry, not really. But Ferrash had diverted a little bit here, fudged a few of the numbers there and sweet-talked the Technocracy into doing the hard work for him – which wasn't difficult, considering how excited they got about any opportunity to invent something new.

Chest heaving, he took a few moments to close his eyes and get his body back under control. When he opened them, the prison was still sat there like a standing green coffin, he was still alive, and his mother's cold amber eyes were burning into him through a transparent patch of nexite.

Ferrash allowed himself a grim smile.

'You miss me?' he asked.

CHAPTER TEN

'Mata?'

Palia looked up from her datascreen to where Derren knelt, fidgeting the artificial grass beneath him with his toes. The Ado-model robot stood inactive in the distance, plugged into its repair station for a diagnostic and software upgrade. It meant she would have to devote all her time to her son for the next day or so. For a change, Palia welcomed the opportunity. She had been struggling to get to grips with a training course in spectral analysis for the past few weeks, almost non-stop, and this break came as a relief.

Derren pointed to the toy on the ground in front of him. It was a model of a kariassid, printed in flexible material from some of her observational data. It couldn't mimic the way a real kariassid could shift through shape and opacity and substance, but it was a close approximation – like a flat worm, with a membranous skin oscillating around it.

'What is it?' Palia asked.

'How does it fly if it doesn't have wings?'

Smiling, she shuffled closer to Derren across the grass and started explaining, as much as she could. She liked this room – the light levels, the grass, the ambient sounds, even the smells... she had set it all up to match the world where she had grown up. Coming to sit in it every now and then took her away from Everatus IV, just for a little while.

She watched Derren as she spoke. None of the usual guilt she felt around him surfaced. She didn't feel bound. She wasn't withdrawn. She wasn't afraid. She filled herself with the moment – with the dappled light falling on his curls, the undisguised plays of emotion upon his face.

And at the back of it, somewhere: sorrow. More profound and wrenching than anything else she felt, there was sorrow. It twisted at her gut and drained colour from the room, until everything she could see was just shades of green and flames licked at the edges of her vision. Derren turned to face her, his eye sockets hollow. White-hot sparks flickered on the edges of his lashes. Palia jerked back, but the landscape flowed with her, tugged out of shape. Derren's body contorted, limbs shapeless, mouth opening into a wordless scream. She saw the eyes behind his eyes, behind the flames – the normal ones that should have been where the sockets were – and saw that they judged her.

Palia turned, weightless. She tried to swim through a mire of her mind's devising. Everywhere she turned, another face. The Kept woman Palia had bisected in the Munabi Wilds clutched her two halves together and wailed. The guards Palia had killed on the prison station formed a sea of their screams. Empyrean fire wove through their forms, danced with the dead, trailed along the dissolving edges of Austela's wings, until everything Palia saw twisted together into flame just as the kariassid had done on Everatus IV.

Wherever Palia turned, they were there, calling her from Varna. Behind them all, the face that wasn't a face, the dream that wasn't even a memory, nothing but a mirror reflecting her own soul back at her.

She didn't like what she saw.

Palia woke shivering. Sweat beaded along her arms and her forehead felt drenched with it, but she made no move to wipe it away. She screwed her eyes shut and tried to slow her breathing, alert to any sound from the rest of the room. Someone rustled, mumbled something. Perhaps it was Bek – he had been talking in his sleep the past few nights, or perhaps he usually did so and it was another thing Palia had forgotten.

She opened her eyes a crack. Bek lay in the bunk diagonally across from her, sprawled on his front with one arm and most of his hair dangling over the side. His fingers twitched, but he was sound asleep. Propping herself up on one elbow, Palia checked the rest of the sleeping quarters, but no one was awake. She thought that might be Tessa curled up underneath her blankets, but it was hard to tell with no body parts outside the mound. Archivist Lilesh's bed was empty, the bedding folded back over the end.

Palia checked the time: o-four by standard chron. Early, but she wouldn't be able to get back to sleep with her heart still racing.

Trying to make as little noise as possible, Palia rolled out of bed, hesitated, then slipped a poncho over her head before leaving the room. Engine noise filled the otherwise silent ship, familiar among the ghosts of memories. The sound calmed her a little, as if clinging onto its memory was all the reassurance she needed that everything would turn out okay. But it wouldn't. Not if she kept having these nightmares. Not if she lost her grip on reality.

She caught sight of Derren, sometimes, in quieter waking moments. Never before the funeral, but in the days since on their way to Munab. Was it longing? Was it her mind clinging to what it could remember? Or did her connection to the Empyrean really let her see into Varna, and it worked as the stories told?

Archivist Lilesh would know. Palia stepped into the canteen to find the woman at a table beneath the viewscreen. Despite the hour, Lilesh had her thick hair tugged back into its customary bun, and she seemed as fresh and rested as every time Palia saw her. That wasn't often, for sure – Palia had been avoiding her new patron since her assignment. That ended today.

'Are you just going to stand there all day?' Lilesh asked. She sent an almost-invisible nudge through the Empyrean and the chair opposite her slid back to make room for Palia.

After a moment's pause, Palia took the offered seat and lowered herself into it, eyeing Lilesh warily across the table. 'Do you always use it for things as trivial as shunting chairs?'

'It?' Lilesh's gaze didn't leave the datascreen she held. In the time spent waiting for Palia to talk, she had continued with her day job – which rarely seemed to respect the limits of what constituted 'day'.

'The Empyrean.'

'I only usually bother with trivialities when I need to make an impression, but this?' This time, her gaze met Palia's, dark irises flashing with the strength of stone. 'All those emotions of yours have to go somewhere.'

'You've been... taking them from me?'

'Your nightmares were rather emotionally productive. If I hadn't siphoned the excess, no doubt there would be a hole in the hull over your bunk.'

Palia frowned and glanced towards the sleeping quarters. She didn't like sharing with another empyrric, didn't like knowing that everything she felt was on display. Was it so obvious?

'You're welcome,' said Lilesh.

Biting back the response that came to mind, Palia stared at the reverse of Lilesh's datascreen and said, 'Don't you dream?'

'No.'

When Lilesh didn't elaborate, Palia prodded further. 'How not?'

The archivist leaned back in her seat and placed the datascreen face-down on the table, then clasped her hands in front of her. 'Does this mean you're finally ready to take my advice?'

Palia shrugged, then nodded. 'I need all the advice I can get. I just...' She had been avoiding her. Avoiding it.

'You're scared.'

'Yes.'

'For someone untrained, you have quite the kill count. Most in your situation would have burned themselves before others.'

That would have been for the best. 'There were too many.'

'Oh, it wasn't a compliment.' Lilesh raised an eyebrow, but her posture remained unchanged. 'If it were up to me, we would take this ship back to the nearest planet and stop for as long as it took to train you properly.'

Palia began shaking her head before Lilesh finished her sentence. 'We don't have that long.'

'Then I'm sure you can imagine my displeasure at it *not* being up to me.'

She frowned and opened her mouth to ask for clarification, but Lilesh beat her to it.

'You outrank me, in case you had forgotten, Pestor.'

Palia grunted. It kept slipping her mind. To her, the newfound rank was just a cover to get close to Ferrash. To Fabien, it was a means to a goal, wrapped around a favour to a friend. To Lilesh, it was apparently a hindrance. Palia rubbed at her eye, feeling the weight of the dream settle back down on her. If she went without speaking or listening too long, she felt a nagging pressure at the back of her skull, like a thousand mouths pressed close to her ear, ready to burst into voices. She peered up at Lilesh through the fingers of that hand and wondered where the boundary lay between her rank and the archivist's responsibility.

'Do you have... doubts?' Palia asked. 'About me being able to pull this off?'

'Certainly. Even if you were trained, your mind isn't in the right place.'

'What would it take to get it there?'

Lilesh studied her, tapping one manicured nail against the knuckles of her other hand, and Palia shivered. Sitting there under the archivist's gaze, every part of her felt exposed.

At length, she said, 'Tell me what troubles you, and I will answer as best I can.'

Palia let out a breath. A part of her had hoped Lilesh would be able to voice the emotions she couldn't put words to. She shrugged, shaking her head. A bright patch of light slid past in the glimpse of Varna beyond the viewscreen.

'There's a lot of trouble to unpack,' Palia said.

'I'm here to help you. Give it a try.'

'I guess... I'm worried I'll take things too far.'

'By losing control as you did in the prison?'

'No, not like that.' Palia shot her a hard look. How many of her mistakes did she already know about? 'I mean... going too far out of choice. Maybe the wrong choice.'

'The Magister told me there was a man you loved.'

So Fabien had briefed her on that, too. 'I think so, but I don't remember him.'

Again, that piercing examination. Palia did her best not to squirm where she sat. She picked at her fingernails.

'You feel a loose thread, don't you?' Lilesh said, head cocked to one side, voice laced with curiosity. 'An emotion where there is no reason for emotion to be. Fire without fuel.'

Palia dug a nail deep into her palm, but said nothing.

'Your problems go deeper than that, though. I felt what you felt in the night. The guilt. You need to let it go.'

Easier said than done. 'I have a lot to feel guilty for.'

'So do we all. But tell me, will you feel guiltier still if you cause more death by your distraction? If you kill the last of your allies? If you kill him? Far better to stop this mission and train with me until you are ready to save him.'

Save him? Did Ferrash even need saving? He was Protectorate, on a Protectorate world, living a life that by all accounts he knew perfectly well how to lead. 'Who am I saving him from, really? Me? It's too late for that. You're...'

Palia trailed off, leaving 'right' on the tip of her tongue. Outside, beyond the viewscreen, a sleek ship swam into view, then another and another behind it. When she called up an overlay in her implants to identify them, it identified the biggest as the *Gigamet Carvan* – and as she could only see a fraction of it, she had no trouble believing it really was the largest ship in the Hegemony, outside the flagship itself. She looked over to Lilesh, but the archivist had risen to her feet at the sight, just as surprised as Palia.

'Are we meant to have an escort?' Palia asked, though the idea of an escort this massive was ludicrous.

Lilesh shook her head, her eyes focused inwards on her implants. 'This is not for us. This is for the war.' She frowned. 'The Magister is sending aid to Munab.'

Staring back through the viewscreen at the arsenal accompanying them, Palia tried to paint a new picture around the pieces. What was Fabien up to? 'This isn't a covert mission anymore.'

'Mater Tennic...'

'Don't "Mater Tennic" me, Archivist.' Palia had never been enough a mother for the title to feel it belonged to her. 'I was just about ready to agree with you, but this changes things. Fabien's just sent troops to join a war and Ferrash is on the other side. If I don't find him as soon as possible, he might not be alive to find later.'

'A few moments ago, your anxieties swelled around the notion of your guilt, not around his ability to survive. Given his former – and perhaps current – role, do you not think he can take care of himself?'

'What does it matter?' Palia gestured at the ships assembled outside and laughed. 'We have a fleet behind us. When will we ever have a better chance to find him?'

Archivist Lilesh said nothing. From the distance in her eyes, Palia wondered if she was composing a message to Fabien at the same time as taking part in their conversation.

'Besides,' Palia said, 'there's data down there that Fabien doesn't want falling into the wrong hands. Covert would have been simple. Fighting gets messy. If we leave it until the war has run its course, the damage might have been done already.'

Lilesh's eyes flicked back into focus, her gaze darting towards the ships before landing back on Palia. 'This will not end well.'

'But it will end.' That was all she asked for.

CHAPTER ELEVEN

THEY WERE STILL SEVERAL hours from the Munabi nexus, so Lilesh went to rouse the others from the sleeping quarters while Palia raised the display table from the floor in the lounge. As Palia examined the information she had on Munab, she felt the ghost of another's actions superimposed onto her own. She knew better than to fixate on them or turn to look. There would be nothing there but confusion – a void that would suck her in and perhaps spit her out again, but as something not quite herself.

She wanted so much to remember. Every bone ached to follow the shadows the void cast on the world.

'Thought we were going over this later? Bit early, Pal. Could've let me sleep.'

Palia looked over her shoulder to see Bek walk through the door naked. She offered him a hesitant smile, which was only blearily returned, and inclined her head to a mug on the other side of the table.

'Ah, maybe I'll forgive you.' Bek all but lunged for the mug and took a large gulp before she could warn him about the temperature.

He hadn't said the words with malice, but Palia cringed at them anyway. No matter how much he had supported her since she had pushed Ferrash away, there had always been resentment in him. Resentment, blame and fear. Some of that he aimed at himself, some at her, though she could tell it pained him to feel that way. It had been an accident, but it had still been her fault. In any case, she had never asked for Bek's forgiveness and he hadn't given it. Another reason to find Ferrash.

While she pretended to examine the information before her, Palia opened a tentative eye onto the Empyrean. Where Bek stood, there was calm. Around his chest, though, bright sparks rattled against the confines of his bones. Anger, perhaps. It was hard to tell.

She checked over her shoulder for the others. It sounded like they were having a conversation further down the ship. Turning back to Bek, Palia asked, 'Do you really think he'll do it?'

'Hmm?' Bek raised an eyebrow over the rim of his mug. Its steam had brought a faint flush to his face.

'Do you really think he'll kill his father? Progaeryon?'

Bek held her gaze for a few seconds, then frowned and rested his mug on the table. He tapped a light rhythm on its surface with the fingers on his free hand. 'Don't understand what'd stop him.'

Palia frowned. 'He's his—'

'Father, yeah. That's why I said I don't understand.' He shrugged and faced the viewscreen, which washed his face with light. 'Ash'd never met him before Munab. Killing him might just be the same as killing anyone else. But it's blood. They share that. I don't know if that changes things.'

It wasn't the answer Palia had been hoping for, and her shoulders fell as she considered it. What if this, too, was her fault? Was Ferrash having to prove himself thanks to his association with her? Was assassinating his father the price he had to pay to earn the Protectorate's trust again? She didn't know. She couldn't remember enough to work it out, and that was what grated at her nerves every day.

Bek stared past the viewscreen, his brows furrowed.

'What's wrong?' she asked.

Blinking, he stalled with his mouth open for a while before shaking his head. 'Nothing. Just thought there was something off about this, but... It's nothing.' His voice carried a new edge to it and he shifted on his feet to close his stance. Whatever the thought was, he had withdrawn, and was holding it close to his chest.

You can trust me, Palia wanted to say. But he couldn't, of course. She couldn't even trust herself.

As she considered what to say, footsteps echoed along the corridor. Archivist Lilesh arrived with the arsaerian technician Tessa close behind. White ribbons wound their way around the horns that followed the curve of Tessa's scalp – she hadn't removed them since the death of her sister aboard the flagship. She didn't look at Palia at all as she passed, and a fresh jab of anxiety needled Palia's guts.

'At your direction, Pestor,' Lilesh said.

Palia took a deep breath, nodded. Then she brought the display table to life and spread her hands out on the surface, where the ground of Munab lay flat, calm and unscarred by war. She wondered how much it had changed. Of all she remembered, only the invasion kept coming back to her. Before and after was void-ridden, but she recalled a swarm of ships chewing over the planet's surface, raining fire and hail down upon it. How Munab had survived at all, she couldn't imagine. But she would soon see how much a toll the war had taken. And they would be bringing a fresh one along with them.

She took a few seconds to close her eyes and focus. When she came back, she put as much strength and confidence into her voice as she could and said, 'Right, this is what we know...'

They exited the Munabi nexus five hours later unprepared for what they would see. Strapped into their seats in the cockpit, all they could do was gawp at the scene laid out ahead.

Fire blossomed in the void before them. Each burst flashed for the barest second before being consumed by the vacuum, but hundreds spawned in the sky every second. Palia recognised a flak screen when she saw one. Behind that wall of light, somewhere, lay the Protectorate fleet. Perhaps Munab hid behind it as well, though they couldn't see it. Palia squinted in response to the light. She could almost convince herself that the heat of the explosions had reached her, even across all that space. One of the cockpit displays tracked the paths of incoming missiles, but none made it past the screen.

She craned her head to look around the full extent of the canopy. When a fleet travelled through the tubes of a nexus and the subsequent Varna lanes that cut through space, they could engage formation-locking protocols with any allied ships travelling with them. Bek must have tagged them into those formations, because they sat at the rear of a diamond cloud of assault ships. Without atmosphere to haze the distance between them, each ship stood out in crisp white sillhouette against the darkness. Directly above them was a different story. There, the uppermost ship blended into the underside of the *Gigamet Carvan*, which split the view almost horizon to conceptual horizon.

'Is that our flak screen or theirs?' Palia asked.

Bek kneaded his jaw with one hand, eyes reflecting orange from the flames. 'Theirs.'

A second after his reply, the flak became less frequent, then dropped off altogether. She squinted to make out anything behind it, but the distance between them was so vast that only something as obvious as a wall of explosions could catch her eye.

What she did notice was Munab, an angry orange dot a little to their right, hiding beneath the bow of the *Carvan*. A storm raged on its surface. Flashes studded its atmosphere. Was it a storm, or had the battle upon it grown so large that it could be seen from space? Every so often, a glimmer of light reflected from a swarm of objects close to the planet. That must be the Protectorate fleet, then. Quiet. Grey. Lurking.

Nothing happened. There had been fire and flame, but now a void yawned between their fleets with only the slightest specks of interference. Palia flexed her fingers on the arms of her chair. If she leaned into the silence, she could open her senses to the Empyrean without intending to. Her awareness spread from Bek to Tessa to the nearest ships and beyond, picking up excitement, nerves, determination. She noted the threads on the surface of Lilesh's soul, but skirted around the void in her core.

When the silence became too much, Palia said, 'Can we slip through the lines and—?'

She stopped when she found a transmission from Bek in her implants. It was a video captured from a close-up of the Protectorate fleet, showing row after row of indistinguishable grey hulks. As she opened her mouth to ask why he had sent it, something flashed across the picture. It was as if an invisible needle had stabbed into them – a line of debris just *appeared* from nowhere, and if she looked hard enough she thought she could make out a hole in one of the Protectorate ships.

At once, her breath left her, and chills made her arms heavy. Her fleet had broken out the railguns. Packed so tight together for their bombardment of Munab, the Protectorate hadn't stood much chance of avoiding them. A twisted flash of anger and sorrow from Bek made her glance his way, but he kept his appearance neutral.

Railguns were the lightning strikes of space. You could spend your whole life in fear of getting struck and most of the time, for most people, you would be fine. The other times, those rare instances when fear flashed into bright significance, you were dead. Of course ships had ways to mitigate the threat. They could seal around a breach if they were big enough and if they weren't, they weren't likely to get hit in the first place. Stand in the way and you were lucky. Dead and gone in an instant. Less fortunate and you would be sucked out into the void to gasp for final breaths that would never come.

Worse, though, to watch it. Silent. Sudden. If you turned from it, you wouldn't know it had happened. Death should come with explosions and screams and tearing metal. It shouldn't just be light smeared across the dark.

Sat there, with hundreds or more ships waiting almost invisibly distant, Palia couldn't help waiting for her own lightning strike. Theirs was a small ship. If, by chance or design, a railgun strike took them now... Oblivion's teeth chattered by her ear.

Palia glanced back inside the cockpit to take her mind off the fleets only to see Tessa wriggling her fingers above her lap, her gaze unfocused. Palia frowned, trying to follow her movements.

'What are you doing?' she asked.

Tessa's attention flicked to her, then to the canopy, then back to her implants. 'Capturing this moment on record.'

'I thought... aren't you a technician?'

'A lighting technician. I craft projection sets. Mai was always better at it than I was, but...' Tessa shrugged. Mai was dead, and that was Palia's fault.

Unsure what to say, Palia looked back out of the canopy. The Protectorate wouldn't launch their own railgun slugs – unlike conventional missiles, you couldn't easily control them once launched. If the target moved out of the way in time, the slug would just keep going until it hit something. That something was the nexus – the only way in and out of the system for both ships and data. Destroying it would mean consigning everyone in the system to exile for as long as it took for someone to notice and send a replacement – or build one, since there was rarely a spare to hand.

Archivist Lilesh glowered at the *Carvan* as its manoeuvring thrusters flickered off from a brief burn. 'What does the prestain think she's doing? We should still be firing on them. We have the advantage.'

'Light's taking a while to reach us,' Bek said. 'Hold on.'

He made a couple of gestures at the control panels and rapped his fingers on his armrest as he waited for an image to appear. Lilesh was right – sat next to a nexus, the empyrric lance likely to be aboard the *Carvan* would be able to fire indefinitely. Since the Protectorate couldn't fire their railguns, their only option was conventional missiles, but they needed to make a decision first. Move in front of the planet and the Hegemony wouldn't risk railguns either, but they would still have the nexus in the background stopping the Protectorate using theirs. Close the distance and, as soon as the presiding captain aboard the *Carvan* gave orders, they would be scrap. Move to the side to get a better angle on the fleet and they would be leaving Munab open to attack.

'Communication burst between the *Carvan* and the Protectorate fleet a couple of minutes ago.' Bek had a finger to his ear, listening. 'Captain's not fired because she's warning them to stand down.'

Lilesh tutted. 'They won't.'

Nodding, Bek pointed to a console, which flickered to show a different close-up of the Protectorate fleet. The ships had changed position, and Palia caught flashes of their thrusters firing to move them away from the planet. The third option, then.

'This is drone footage?' Palia asked.

'Yeah. Five-second delay between observed and live.'

Light flared in the canopy above them and Palia winced. The *Carvan*'s main engine pulsed in a plume behind it. Thrusters set along its length fired to point it towards the Protectorate's anticipated new position. Across the rest of the fleet, engines burst into life. The fighters in their formation pirouetted to face the other way, towards Munab, and towards orbital combat. Bek swore as he worked the control column to turn with their more agile manoeuvres.

Palia's heart beat faster in her chest. They were splitting from the rest of the fleet to make landfall, with any number of orbital and planetary defences barring their way. She gripped tighter still to the armrests of what used to be Ferrash's chair and felt some small comfort in the fact it might be his again soon, that the ghost she sat within would be filled and flesh and whole.

Burns complete, their formation's engines cut off. The two halves of the fleet peeled away from each other like flocks of birds wheeling in search of different roosts, sliding silently to their destinations across the stars. She waited for weapon impacts to flash back into being, for lightning to cut its unheralded destruction into their midst... but nothing came. Just two fleets matching pace with each other, waiting for sight of a bared throat to lunge at with open jaws.

Palia tucked her chin down to cover her own throat, then waited for the war to come.

CHAPTER TWELVE

FERRASH TRUDGED THROUGH THE snow, shivering. His heart hammered in his chest, beating against ribs that felt like ice. His breath came in shuddering gasps. Each one was a shock to his system – a gulp of freezing air in, a great huff as his lungs rejected the cold. He clenched and unclenched his hands, fighting the urge to rub warmth into his face through the wrappings in case his nose broke off in the process. The cold bit into his skull, pressed against his teeth and clamped his legs as he struggled to place them one after the other.

The mountain was death. Everyone knew that. The mountain had been death as long as humans had inhabited Hesperex and the ice age had only made it deadlier.

What better place to hide?

Glancing over his shoulder, he took in the snow-shrouded sprawl of Five-Fifty-Four. It was dawn, and above the swirl of Hesperex's permanent storms, it almost looked beautiful. Weak light filtered through the atmosphere from the dying sun, subtly lifting the edges of each undulation. It seemed that the snow of the mountainside stretched on forever, and but for the Tower of Voices spearing through into the crisp air, he could have pretended that was all there was to it. That it was just him, an empty planet, and a box containing his disgruntled mother.

Ferrash glared at the box. He'd asked the Technocracy to build it well insulated, which meant his mother was warm and cosy, albeit imprisoned, while he was out here freezing off all the bits he wanted to keep on. With any luck, the pistoning spider legs hauling it after him were making it an uncomfortable ride. He wished the maintenance tram he'd brought it to the edge of the mountain on had stretched further – he could have saved them both the walk.

He turned and kept walking, just in case the machine kept going and stabbed a claw through his foot.

Overlaid on his implants, a marker indicated remaining distance to the bunker. Just two hundred metres away. A few hundred long, cold steps and he would be warm. Five more minutes on the mountain and, like most who had tried to ascend it before him, he would be dead. Though his whole body screamed at the effort, he kept walking. The world narrowed to a slit just covering the ground ahead, his movement to one foot after the other, his thoughts to nothing. At one point, the snow shifted just in front of his feet and he almost tripped as something living darted away. He stared after it, watching the blur of a creature vanish into land where no life could live, but he never stopped moving.

A hundred metres more... Ferrash felt his mind slipping. Unthought lapsed into memory, and he stumbled as he remembered walking the flat streets of Five-Fifty-Four and tried to place his feet deeper than the ground allowed. Palia intermittently walked in front of him, behind him, by his side, shivering as he had ceased to shiver. He tried to push her image away, but it just drifted back like the snow. His mind had mapped its context to this situation and latched onto it. Thinking of Bek instead brought him guilt, and any emotion was better than the silence of a memory with feelings carved away from it.

As Ferrash wondered what Bek was up to now, his foot jarred against something hidden under the snow and he fell forwards. He landed hard on his left arm and cried out, but the box stabbing towards him kicked his brain into gear. He rose to one knee, panting, then to his feet. Instructing the box to wait, he scraped a patch of snow aside with his feet. Bare metal. He'd made it, as long as he still had the wits to get inside.

Ferrash staggered back from the hatch and commanded it open. To his relief, it shot up, scattering a rain of snow into the air around him. He lurched into the opening and slammed the hatch shut again the second the box was through.

Wobbling on his feet, he resisted the urge to lean back against the wall, slide down it and fall asleep. It would be warmer closer to the hideout's generators and he had to keep moving long enough to let the air heat him. He fumbled in his pocket as he walked, gloved fingers struggling to extract the ration bar he'd brought with him. He took an end in each hand and – a little hesitant in case his fingers cracked before the bar did – snapped it in two. Warmth flooded through it. Waiting for it to heat all the way through was maddening. Waiting for the toxic gases to dissipate after he'd opened the packet was almost more than he could bear.

At last, he fell onto a worn chair in the generator room and wolfed down the bar. A heavy tiredness settled over him as he warmed and, with a last, wary glance at the box as it manoeuvred itself upright in the room next door, he slipped into a deep and dream-filled sleep.

He woke ten hours later with the echoes of dreams playing around his head. Most nights, memory played after memory in an uninterrupted sequence from the events of Everatus IV, resuming from where it had left off each time. But most nights he didn't really sleep, he just ached as his brain charged on ahead of its allotted time. Last night had been different. The memories had collided with one another, played out of order. Would they carry on from where they had been the next night, or would he have to start over?

Groaning, he drew himself upright. He swore when he saw the box. *Better not have died in there*. He doubted it. The box's legs had retracted into its framework now that it was stowed against the bare metal wall, a small puddle underneath it the only sign of its journey through the snow. Beneath the translucent nexite, he could just about make out a squat shadow the height of his waist.

He drew in a deep breath, stood up, then curled his fingers into one sleeve to get at the hidden syringe. Before he pressed it into his wrist, he paused, beset by the memory of a syringe in one hand, Palia's hand squeezing the other – then a clean movement to inflict the inhibitors on her before she could react. Those events were out of order, and he was halfway to reconstructing them before he shook his head and brought his thoughts back to reality. Depressing the plunger didn't push the memories out of his system, but they calmed the annoyance they had caused.

Ferrash walked through the arch separating the generator room from the main room and rapped his knuckles against the front of the box when he reached the far wall. 'You awake?'

'I am,' his mother replied.

Ferrash tried to respond, but his throat moved in silence, as if hearing a voice from so long ago had denied him his own. He cleared his throat, but when he tried to speak again, his mind went blank. He'd rehearsed this a thousand times in his head, planned it all down to the last letter, but this? How could it ever work?

Movement in the box. 'Were you planning to leave me like this, or did you drag me all the way up here for a reason?'

'I have a reason.'

'Care to enlighten me?'

It should have come as no surprise that her voice was so devoid of emotion, but it stung anyway, the fact that he had made so little impact on her. He folded his arms across his chest and stared at the shape in the box. Despite the inhibitors, despite his own manufactured sense of calm, he struggled to get the next words out of his mouth.

'I need your help,' he said. The request was a bet. Getting rid of her or keeping her imprisoned would have made more sense. But if she disappeared, the committees would be more alert to anything out of the ordinary, like cracks in the façade of Proglimen's borrowed face. For Ferrash's disguise to be most effective, ideally, he needed her alive. He couldn't tell her about his plan to impersonate Proglimen, not yet, but he had something better to dangle under her nose.

For a moment, his mother's shadow sat still. The generator's hum expanded to fill the silence, whining to the same tune as the overhead lights. Then the shadow slid up from its place of rest and her face came into view by the translucent slit at the front of the box. Ferrash stared into his mother's eyes, so much the reflection of his own, and as much as he wanted to tear his gaze away, he couldn't.

He had lived under the watch of Ayt Mannae for fifteen years. In those fifteen years, he had been taught by her, threatened by her, hurt by her, and never heard anything from her that marked her as human. She might as well have been a robot assigned to his care. He had never seen her smile, or heard her cry or laugh.

She laughed now.

He narrowed his eyes and hers stared back: cold, inert, uncaring. The laugh was so at odds that it prickled the hairs on the back of his neck. It was a threat that he couldn't account for.

'You kill my attendants, imprison me and carry me to a hideaway all to ask for my help? Until now I believed I had raised a son, not a simpleton.'

Ferrash snorted. 'Raised me? Almost killed me, more like. A lot. Gella did more to raise me than you ever did.'

'Gella? The vatborn free agent who requisitioned you? The same agent stupid enough to get executed for dissention?'

'How'd you know about that? Been checking up on me?'

'The woman convinced me you would be more useful to the Protectorate following her example. I kept watch to ensure that remained true.'

'So what, if I'd screwed up with the ESF, you'd have taken me back? Kept teaching me to be something I'm not?'

'I would have found a placement more suited to your abilities. Underperforming free agents tend to find their lives somewhat shortened. Better in use somewhere than a corpse.'

'I'm touched by your concern, truly.' Ferrash gave her a skewed smile. 'To answer your question, sure, I could've just found you and talked, but that raises two problems. One: The Protectorate doesn't go in for familial chit-chat, and there's no good reason for an agent – for anyone, really – to go talk to a Keeper, unless they get given the kind of mission that's meant to get them killed. No excuses, a lot of suspicion. At the risk of sounding like I care myself, which I don't, a lot of that suspicion would have landed on your lap, too. We'd both lose.

'Two, and this is the most important one: sure I could have just asked, but I've got you in that box because I'm pretty sure your first reaction to what I'm going to ask for would be to kill me.'

It was hard to tell, but she might have shrugged behind the nexite. 'No doubt you make an accurate assessment. What is it? Are you running with the Kept now? Need I point out the irony of asking a Keeper's help whilst in alliance with those who wish all empyrrics dead?'

If they were talking irony, they could look no further than the fact most Kept were themselves empyrric. He knew that. She knew that. It was irrelevant, though.

'I'm not working with the Kept,' he said. 'Don't want much to do with them if I can help it.' He wanted to keep an eye on them, and he needed them in the fight to come, but he couldn't let them come out on top. Or intact. It irked him that he had no contacts within their ranks. Empyrrics just couldn't be trusted.

'Elaborate.' One word from his mother. A command, really. A petulant voice in the back of his head told him to disobey just to spite her.

He stared at her, measuring the weight of the words to come. 'You're aware of the Reiart?'

'A myth. An excuse for unsanctioned killings, for military involvement in committee affairs, for conflict between the two security forces.'

'Hmm.' Ferrash smiled. 'Maybe you don't know so much. The Reiart is real. They killed Gella, and backtracking from her murder took me to them. Talked my way into a job. Got my hands dirty for a few years. Enough of that and I wound up in command. Funny how easy that is when things are kept so secret that no one really knows each other.'

Her voice dry, Ayt said, 'Congratulations.'

'I'm not in it for the career. I'm in it for the Protectorate. The real Protectorate, that is, not the committees and the vats and the death of emotion. The people. They're who the Protectorate is, who it's always said it is but only ever kept pushing down. The Protectorate isn't what it should be, and it needs to change. So that's what I'm doing. I have everything set up. A little longer and it'll all change in a flash, as little blood spilled as possible.'

'So why do you need my help?'

'The Keepers and the Kept. They're problems. The Empyrean is a problem. And thanks to the Hegemony, I have a way to fix it. I just need an empyrric. I need you.'

CHAPTER THIRTEEN

'LET ME OUT OF this box,' said Ferrash's mother.

Ferrash blinked. He'd been expecting a request for clarification, or something relevant to their discussion. The change of topic momentarily threw him.

'What,' he asked, 'so you can kill me?'

'No, so I can urinate.'

'...And then kill me?'

'I have been in here for hours, listening to the electrics and wondering if you had frozen to death. The air in here is already stale. Let me out, or I can assure you it will soon smell significantly worse.'

She *had* been in there for hours, breathing in the stale air that filtered into her box – stale air mixed with microscopic nexite particles during the filtration process. Ferrash made a show of entering an unlock sequence on the outside of the box while he actually checked its readouts. No official records or experiments measured how much nexite an empyrric had to inhale before it affected their ability to access the Empyrean. Unofficially, the Reiart had known its effects far before Ferrash had joined them. The Kept, too, had contributed data, albeit unwittingly. Too little nexite and the empyrric would disintegrate you a little slower than usual. So much that they were breathing more nexite than air and, believe it or not, they suffocated.

Length of exposure. That was key. It varied for each individual, but over ten hours was long enough, wasn't it?

Ferrash keyed in the real code, stepped back.

The second the door slid up, she came for him, arms raised, hands grasping for the fabric of his coat. His implants' scanning suite detected the tell-tale electronic squawk of the pain mesh that would deal her an instant burst of agony she could convert into empyrric energy. Ferrash darted back, leaned out of her reach and knocked her arms away with a forearm. Confusion registered as a flicker in his mother's eyes. Nothing emerald glinted from her. No flames, no drain, no death. In that moment, they were finally on equal terms, and on equal terms, he could beat her.

With a twist of his arm, he grabbed onto her wrist and yanked her off balance. She regained her composure and tried to drive a knee into his groin, but he stepped back and swept her other leg out from under her with a well-placed roundhouse. By the time she hit the floor, he had his pistol trained on her skull.

Half-raised off the floor already, she stared at it, then him. Her muscles relaxed. She rose to her feet with the lined skin of her face still twitching to the tune of the pain mesh whose wires snaked beneath it.

Ferrash inclined his head to the left. 'Toilet's that way.'

After a moment's stillness, Ayt nodded to him once, curt, then followed his directions. As she walked through the side door and out of sight, Ferrash let out a sigh of relief. It had worked. It had worked, and he was in control. He had anywhere between a few hours and a few days before the nexite made its way out of her system. If he hadn't convinced her to help in that time... well, he'd have to kill her. That or expect every keeper on Hesperex to come for him as soon as she made it back.

He moved to the other wall and made a little brew for himself on the hideout's heater while he waited. When he had measured out the water, he paused, then added a second measure to the jug.

'So, this plan of yours.' His mother re-emerged from the corridor, her hands tucked into the sleeves of her green robes. 'How do you intend to 'fix' the Empyrean? The Judiciary's knowledge stems largely from intelligence the ESF brought back from Hegemony reconnaissance, which stops at the fact their Magister's weapon was empyrric in nature. At a guess, the agent on that mission was you, and there are more details you haven't offered up.'

Ayt Mannae's skin had grown paler since he had last seen her, and frail. It puckered in dry folds at the major nodes of her pain mesh and thinned so much where those implants ran over the top of her scalp that he imagined he could see bone beneath. Her hair, once as thick and dark as his, dangled in a few grey strands from the uncovered patches of skull that remained. Strength still burned in her eyes. Pain had destroyed her flesh, but hardened her mind.

Ferrash sipped at his brew and indicated the other mug with a bob of his head. When she took it, he said, 'By the time I got more details, it was over. And I... decided some details were better left withheld.'

'Do you not trust your own colleagues?'

'Do you?'

She stayed silent.

'The Reiart taught me no group or system can be trusted to keep secrets. I know you Keepers have your own spies – I think I could name most of them. Word would have got back eventually, even with instructions not to let the data outside the ESF.'

'So we would object to the fix?'

'As a group, yes.' After yesterday's frozen march, Ferrash wanted to hunch his shoulders over the mug and breathe its warmth in, but he kept his back straight and gripped it close to his chest. He noticed one of the wall panels by the heater had come loose, and some of the insulation foam was poking out of it. That would need to be repaired. 'As individuals... you'd have whatever opinions you felt permitted to hold. Because the fix is about power. You'd lose all of it. Without the Empyrean, the Keepers are a separate security force at best. A bunch of lost souls at worst.'

Ayt narrowed her eyes. She hadn't touched her own brew yet, and held the mug perfectly upright in her lap. 'For someone who wants nothing to do with the Kept, this sounds a lot like something they would strive for. Is that what the Hegemony's weapon did? Target all empyrrics on a world?'

His memory showed him the room again. Palia kneeling across from him. Pain, constant and agonising. Oblivion. Funny how pain was always what you remembered, no matter how much you lost. Then waking, and facts, and theories.

'Think so,' he said. 'The prototype was capable of it on individuals, but the flagship's weapon was untested. It's not what you think, though. Didn't kill. It strips an empyrric's ability to access the Empyrean. Permanently.'

'Unless you have access to the Hegemony's flagship, this hardly helps your goal. Strip one empyrric at a time and the others will kill you.'

'Imagine it scaled up.' He crossed to the other side of the room and stared at the box. Shade pooled inside it, like the coiling potential of what it was meant to contain. Nexite was the beating heart of the galaxy. It channelled whatever unknowable energies lingered in the universe through each nexus, manipulated it to accelerate ships between stars a hundred lightyears distant. It acted as a battery, powered engines, generated anti-grav fields, charged weapons. And, if you paired it with nanotechnology and a decent dispersal system, it created ripples big enough to confuse empyrric awareness. The box hadn't really been tried before. As long as the Empyrean existed, there would always be a new use for it, a new way to make its destruction even more destructive. Sure, you could say that for any other law of the universe, but the Empyrean... If Ferrash had been more open to religion, he might have said it had been designed a weapon, and was destined to remain so.

Ferrash said, 'You always told me the Prime Nexus was more than just the first and biggest. More than just a control node.'

'It is.'

He turned, faced his mother across the length of the room. 'It's the centre, right? Of all of it. The whole empyrric flow?'

'There are no records of its origin, if there were any to begin with. Perhaps before the schism, we knew more. But yes, from our observations, that seems the case. The Prime Nexus is *the* nexus of the Empyrean. All energy flows from it and returns to it, at some stage.'

Ferrash nodded, satisfied to have it confirmed. 'The prototype implied the final weapon worked on a feedback loop. Fed energy into the empyrric, who couldn't let it out again. Or something like that. Eventually, the frequency of energy in and energy out became harmonic, or whatever equivalent applies, and creates null zones. Long enough and it all goes null. No Empyrean, no empyrric. They're blind.'

He took a deep breath. 'I was there when the Magister explained why he did it and... I don't exactly remember my motivations, but I ripped all the details from his implants before he died. There's a lot to go through, but there's enough. What happens if you turn the Empyrean against itself? What if the Magister wasn't aiming for Hesperex, he was aiming for the Prime Nexus?'

His mother's eyes fixed on a point somewhere above his head. If he reached far enough, dared to delve with his implants, would he see her mind laid out? Did she speed her thoughts through the pathways of her software, or did she limit herself to the safe organics of grey matter?

'You saw this done?' she asked.

'Yes. I... was the power source.'

'Voluntarily?' She raised the scant remaining hairs of one eyebrow.

He shrugged. 'Made sense at the time. Needed to find out what it did. Trusted them not to kill me.' Logic told him that trust might have been misplaced – in skill if not in intent.

'And the empyrric was stripped of ability, as you say?'

He shook his head. 'They were testing on themself. Would've been counter-productive to go all the way. And I guess once it started fluctuating, they wouldn't have been able to keep up the energy input.'

'So, you come to me' – Ayt walked over to examine the box herself – 'and say you want to eliminate the Empyrean. You expect me to help. You expect it to work. You expect to be able to pitch a revolution on the back of it. And you base this on the supposition of a half-baked experiment conducted by some empyrric you clearly must have shared juices with.' The look she gave him next pierced right into the heart of him. He resisted the urge to step back.

'Shared jui...? What? No, I...' He ground his teeth, frustrated as his memories fell over each other in an attempt to find context. 'I moved as circumstances dictated. Was short on time, so needed to take risks. It worked. That's all that matters.'

Ayt nodded. For the first time, a hint of emotion crept through her expression – a sly something, lurking in the corner of her lips and behind the mirror sheen of her eyes.

Cold set its claws into Ferrash's back, the mountain itself trying to shock sense into him. He reached for his pistol. Too slow. Ayt whipped a palm through the air between them and a green wall slammed him sideways. He hit the edge of the box, cracking his head against the nexite. His vision swam. Bile rose in his throat. Ferrash pushed his thought processes into his implants to bypass the nausea, but only just in time to see the second wave come at him. It struck him square on the left shoulder, tilting him into the box so that he was left hanging onto the edge with one hand, only one foot planted on the floor.

His mother's fingers curled, and a lifetime's memories let him anticipate what would come next before it happened. He locked eyes with Ayt over a room steadily colouring green. Dregs of emotions he had barely been holding onto – base, primal emotions, hard to shift, like the muscle response of fear – drained out of him. His limbs grew heavy. The distance from his free hand to the pistol at his belt became insurmountable, even when all its muscles relaxed and his arm fell to within an inch of the holster. Strength slipped from his fingers. He willed himself to fight on, to somehow defeat the inevitable and spite her for all the times she had done this before. But even his will was fuel to her, and it slithered from his mind as another wisp of Empyrean flame.

All faded. Sight, sound, sensation, gone. And the last he saw of his mother before he slipped into oblivion was her eyes, reflecting the fire she drew from his soul.

CHAPTER FOURTEEN

WHEN FABIEN'S TRANSPORT REACHED the Rythian nexus, he parted ways with it, jetting out of a launch tube in a sleek craft no more than five metres from nose to tail. The side of the nexus rushed at him, shining bright in the light of Rythe's sun, the end of the tube their transport had exited still glowing with the afterwash of their arrival. For a moment, he stayed there, decelerating between walls of dark and light, between the star-pricked void and the technology that ushered them through it. Peaceful. Devoid of scale. The nexus could be endless. Beyond it, in what part of the void lay in sight, the nebulae of the Rythian breach shimmered, its composition highlighted in colourful array by his viewscreen's filters. From here, it floated like ink in water, vague and fragile-seeming. Up close, Fabien knew it was an ever-changing mass of careening asteroids, Hegemony patrols and foolish smugglers.

He took hold of the controls and nudged the nose left until the nexus slid out of sight and he could see the ship again. It waited at anchor now, ready for his word to send the rest of the delegation after him. Just off its bow sat the planet Rythe, its giant ice caps shining bright with reflected light. He gave the engines a burst to send him towards it.

'Rythe Approach,' Fabien hailed across their channel, 'this is the *Irmet Lightskip*, requesting permission to land.'

Their reply was instant. '*Irmet Lightskip*, permission is granted. Please follow advised path.'

Fabien nodded, even though they couldn't see him, then settled in and waited for that bright, icy glare to fade into two strips of white squeezing a narrow band of green.

Rythe's ice caps shone so bright, he could see them even after landing at the equator, or so it seemed to Fabien. When he stepped out of the *Lightskip*, he had to squint against the horizon. It was only mid-morning, but the air still had that crisp, polar brightness to it, and a slight breeze chased cool air around his robes.

All at once, music split the air. Brass blared somewhere to his right and he caught a flash of metal. A voice cried out. A dozen feet stamped in unison. Blinking to get his eyes back in focus, Fabien stepped down the last rung of the ladder and faced his welcoming party. The dozen feet belonged to a dozen men and women standing at attention to either side of his exit, bedecked in crisp black uniforms edged in silver.

'Magister Honeras.' A tall woman stepped forwards and saluted, bringing her hand up so the tips of her fingers brushed her brow.

Fabien touched a hand to his shoulder in return, worried that the Hegemony's version of a salute looked over-casual. The words he had been given to say next felt alien. 'I have come seeking audience with the Steward.'

The woman nodded, her attention leaning towards appraising. 'This way, sir.' She turned on her heels and strode along the avenue of soldiers, her heels clicking on the hard stone of the landing circle.

Fabien followed, his cape flicking out behind him. A muffled bang came from behind him – the sound of a ship entering atmosphere. He didn't turn to look. Not because it would be rude, but because a far greater sight revealed itself in front of him.

A few metres away, the landing circle dropped sheer, with a narrow slab reaching out into what would have been empty space, if there hadn't been a creature standing underneath. His advisors had warned him about the vriarbeast, had shown him pictures. Far different seeing one in the flesh. All Fabien could see at that moment was the covered seating area on its back, positioned next to the slab, which must be a gangway.

With a rustle of feathers, two gold, engraved horns rose into view, followed by the bone spurs they capped, sprouting out to either side of the vriarbeast's jaw. The spurs might have just been decorative, but Fabien got the distinct impression those were what it used to spit acid, and was thankful he didn't have to find out. Its eye, full brown with no whites and only a speckling of darker black where the pupil should have been, wheeled amidst deep green feathers.

Fabien held its gaze, only realising a few seconds later that the woman had stepped aside at the gangway. She gestured for him to step aboard, a slight smile curving her lips.

Nodding, Fabien crossed the gap between stone gangway and wooden platform. He edged between two rows of seats to the other side of the creature's back, then skirted around to the front, behind the pilot – or rider, perhaps? In any case, it left him the seat with the clearest view of the way ahead.

He glanced right, eager to catch sight of his destination, but other landing circles – and beyond them, broad-canopied evergreens – blocked what lay ahead. He'd seen the capital, briefly, as he came in to land: a fortified city sat atop a hill, with the shining course of a river running through it. But then he'd been too focused on landing, and everything looked different from that high in the air anyway.

'You picked the best spot,' came a voice from the rider's seat.

Fabien leaned on the railing in front of him, jolted a little by the vriarbeast as it lumbered forwards. Now he could see the rider behind the wooden panel that would normally hide her from view. She stared straight back at him with a grin plastered across her face. She had drawn her frizzy red hair into a bun at the base of her neck, and her eyes were a dusky, light brown, verging on red. He found himself grinning back, then leaning a little further forwards still to get a better look at the vriarbeast.

'You scared of heights?' she asked.

Before he could ask why, the hard-packed earth beneath the vriarbeast's claws disappeared. For a moment, they pitched down, and his stomach began to lift away, but the vriarbeast kicked out with its hind legs, thrusting them into the air and Fabien back into his seat. Two great wings unfurled to either side, flapped once, then held open with their flight feathers curling at the tips. Fabien looked along them, into that snow-bright glare. A part of his mind wondered what Rythe would have to offer them. On the ground, they were a force to be reckoned with. In the air, in the void... no one really knew.

He looked around for a seatbelt or harness, but couldn't see anything. He glanced back to the rider, but could just see a loose strand of red fluttering behind the partition. 'You're not planning on any barrel rolls, are you?'

That provoked a peal of laughter. 'I'm not sure these ones like aerobatics.'

'You're not sure?'

She leaned around the partition to peer at him. Around them, the treetops fell away to become a green carpet stretching into the distance. 'I usually fly the smaller ones.' Now she had to shout to be heard over the wind. 'I'll admit I blagged my way into flying this one today.'

'Why?' On a hunch, he turned and looked over his shoulder, but every other seat was empty. The soldier hadn't come with him. The part of him that had spent a long few days in security briefings after becoming Magister registered a twinge of panic.

'Don't look so baffled, I'm not going to kidnap you or anything silly.' That wide grin returned, tugging at her ears. 'There are more waiting to escort you in the citadel. I just wanted to get a first nosey, see. There aren't that many outsiders come to Rythe.'

Fabien leaned an arm over the rail, lulled by the constant noise and motion of wingbeat after wingbeat. When he looked right this time, the citadel sat on the horizon, coming towards them in a gentle turn he hadn't noticed until then. It stood stone-walled and proud on a tall plateau of bare grey rock. Those walls blocked most of the city from view, besides the tips of towers and a great flat slab where one of the taller buildings must be. It dominated the surrounding landscape, however, with the famed twin waterfalls nothing more than shimmering ribbons set against the cliff. The rivers flowed through the city and palace, if he remembered right, from a great lake atop the plateau.

'Have you ever been off-world?' Fabien asked the rider.

'Not yet.'

'You'd like to, though?'

She glanced over her shoulder again, eyes crinkling. 'Seriously? Who wouldn't? I love Rythe, but ugh' – she pulled a face – 'we can be so serious. Besides, how can anyone live on one planet their whole life, knowing there's more out there, and never want to explore them?' A far-off look came over her then, and she nodded to herself, like she was counting off reasons in her head. 'It would be nice to see what other beasties there are out there, but I'd always come back for my vriars.'

'So what's the reason you haven't travelled already? If it's cost, there are probably...'

'Cost? Pfft. That's not an issue. Space is cheap.' Rich words, on a planet whose ships never seemed to leave the system. 'It's responsibility. Isn't it always?'

'You still haven't introduced yourself.'

'Nor have you.'

Fabien raised an eyebrow, and she laughed loud enough that the vriarbeast turned its head to regard her with one bespeckled eye.

'I'm Lady Charante, daughter of Lord Jelen Charante. I doubt your people briefed you so thoroughly as to have heard of us, of all people, but my father's been on and off his deathbed for the past few decades. When it wasn't wartime, I was needed here.'

'I'm sorry.'

She shrugged. 'No need to be. If anyone should be, it's the Protectorate. My father volunteered aboard one of your ships during the war. Got caught in a viral swarm. Slow-acting variant. Apparently the

Protectorate got their numbers wrong or something. He survived the war, but his lungs haven't been the same since, and nothing's worked to save them. Even transplants got re-infected.'

'I've heard of the strain. We've had no luck with our victims either, I'm afraid.'

'There you go, apologising again. Well look now, we're almost at the tower, so if you want to get any more in before I have to drop you off, speak fast, right?'

He laughed. Sure enough, the tallest tower loomed in the near distance. Little flashes of green marked where more vriarbeasts sat waiting in alcoves for passengers. As he watched, one of them dropped like a stone before spreading its wings across the tree-shaded streets and rocketing off on its task.

'Do you have any tips?' he asked, thinking the question was worth it.

Another shrug. 'I don't even know what you're here for.'

Ah. Maybe not. 'I take it my visit hasn't featured much in the news, then?'

'Oh, it has, sure. I wouldn't have known to want a nosey, otherwise. And I gather it must be something special, seeing as we don't have many Magisters visit. But it's always just "diplomacy this" and "state visit that". The news speculates all it likes, but it doesn't have a clue, and nor do I. So I don't know what tips would be useful, see?'

The vriarbeast flared its wings, making the air crack and roar past its feathers. Fabien had to lean forwards, clutching at the rail and almost shouting to be heard. 'Even general tips would be useful!'

Lady Charante said nothing, too focused on seeing them in to land. Fabien braced, expecting to be jolted and tilted backwards, but their touchdown, when it came, was gentle.

She turned to face him again as the vriarbeast folded its wings, wearing a sly smile. 'I can give you the tips I'm qualified to give, if that suits?'

Fabien leaned back in his seat, giving her a half grin to show he knew this would at least be half a joke. She chuckled when she saw it, then raised a finger in the air by her head.

'First,' she said, 'never stand in front of a vriarbeast. Second, never stand *behind* a vriarbeast. Third, never stand beneath a big one. Fourth, keep clear of the streets underneath flight routes in a thunderstorm.'

The first three had Fabien chuckling under his breath, but he frowned when she reached the fourth. 'Do they get hit often?' he asked.

'No,' she said, and grinned wider, 'but they do shit.'

So it was that when Fabien's nominated minder arrived to collect him, they left to the sound of Lady Charante cackling with laughter.

CHAPTER FIFTEEN

'WAIT,' THE FLEET OFFICERS had said. 'Just wait for the first wave to land, then you'll be safe to join them.' But Palia didn't like sitting in orbit and twiddling her thumbs, giving Ferrash plenty of time to slip between their fingers. She didn't appreciate Archivist Lilesh's insistence that this was the perfect time to train, even though Lilesh was right. Most of all, she hated watching – sitting in orbit as fires bloomed and flashed across the surface of the planet below, knowing that people died down there every second, every minute, every hour they waited.

Going down there wouldn't change that. They couldn't stop a war all on their own.

But Palia wasn't waiting.

She leaned over the back of Bek's chair, the door membrane behind her sealing them off from the rest of the ship. It was night-time, standard chron, and the other two were fast asleep. Palia had contemplated using some of Ferrash's inhibitors to stop any emotions giving her away to Lilesh but – besides the fact that there weren't any left – she still found the thought abhorrent. In any case, a lack of emotions would probably be a greater tell than anything else she might experience.

Bek stared straight out of the canopy, making minute adjustments on the controls. The belly of their part of the fleet slipped away above them. Being parked in high orbit would keep them out of the range of the Protectorate fleet's guns until the window opened again. Ground fire didn't trouble them this far out, but the closer they got to the surface, the more they risked getting noticed.

'How does it look?' Palia whispered.

'Like there can't be many left alive down there,' Bek said.

'No, I mean us. How's the approach?'

'Can't approach yet. I've burned us into an orbit that'll cross our– the *Protectorate* fleet's orbit faster.'

She tightened her grip on the chair. 'Why?'

'We're still identified as one of their ships. We still have ESF codes. We head to the surface from their position and if Ground questions us, that gives us a free pass.'

'So they'll just... let us in?'

Bek shrugged. 'Sure, unless Ash used the same codes to get here and hasn't left since. So if they shoot us down, at least we know where he is.'

'He'll be there.'

After a moment's silence, Bek turned to face her. He had his lips pressed tight together, and a strand of blond hair lay against the pallor of his face. His brows scrunched towards his nose. Emotions tangled as a dense mesh of filaments around his throat.

'Look,' he said, 'I know I told you we'd find him. I know I said it would be okay, but...' He shook his head. 'Why do you care? You don't even remember him. He's a stranger to you. I *need* to find him. He's my friend. My brother. He taught me everything good I know. And when I find him, I don't know if I'm going to hug him or slam him against a wall and ask why he didn't say goodbye. But you? How can you be so upset about it when...?' Bek made an all-encompassing gesture with one hand, let the question hang in the air.

A lump lodged in Palia's throat. She let it stay there, afraid that if she tried to swallow it might catch and re-emerge as a flood of raw emotion that Lilesh would wake to instantly. 'I messed everything up so badly, Bek. I don't remember him. I sort of remember the context of where he *was* and where he should have been, but I can never focus on the gap. I can't... I can't touch it. I can't try to get it back. It's gone, and there's nothing I can do about that.

'But...' She closed her eyes, shifted on her feet, tried to calm her thoughts. 'Everything I felt for him, it's all still there. I can't connect it to anything and it's so *frustrating*. I just... I *feel* like I love him. I don't know if I do. I don't know if I've just blown a little bit of joy out of all proportion because I've got nothing to compare it to. So I want to find him, if nothing but to fill this stupid gap with something I can understand. If he doesn't want to see me, that's fine. I'll go. I just need to see him, remember what he looks like, apologise for what I did to him.

'I don't know how much I took. He remembered to run and hide, clearly. But for all I know, he could have forgotten everything else. He could just be a husk running around, like—'

'Like the rest of the Protectorate?'

Palia sighed. 'I need to know how much I hurt him.'

'You can't fix him.'

'We don't know that. If there's anything I can do to make this right, if there's any way I can give back whatever I took, I have to try it.'

Bek nodded. 'Just try not to make it worse, right?' Not for the first time, she noticed the bags under his eyes, the tiredness worn on his face.

'Right.'

Silence returned. The Munabi desert crawled past beneath them. Swirling clouds of poisonous gasses obscured most of it, letting only the tips of some rocky mountains rise into view. On a distant horizon to their left, where the gasses churned so thick that they marred the veil of atmosphere with green-black cumulonimbi, a ripple of explosions flared into bright white-orange light. Flames already underlit the clouds a sickly brown, but now they renewed. The clouds billowed around the plumes of smoke as they rose.

How high did those fires lick? Who could still be fighting there? Given most of the Munab Palia had seen was underground, perhaps a battle raged beneath the surface. If so, the combatants were trapped – the heart of the planet on one side, a raging inferno above. Palia understood xenobiology, not climate science. She didn't know if the heat above would cook everything below.

She returned her attention to closer scenery and the approach of daylight. Little ticks blinked into view on the canopy viewscreen, highlighting the positions of other ships. The engine hummed. Quiet, like background electronics. It nudged her with a little acceleration before the inertial dampers compensated for the burn, then another moment of deceleration.

Bek altered their angle of attack so the nose pitched upwards. She couldn't see the planet anymore, which meant she wouldn't see if any missiles came for them.

'Strap in,' Bek said. 'We'll hit atmosphere soon.'

Palia buckled herself into the other seat, then used those moments of blindness to review the information she had. They had more intelligence on Munab than anyone else in the Hegemony. Bek had let her access Ferrash's archives – those he had access to – but refused to let anyone else get hold of them. So Bek gave her the map and Fabien gave her the latest troop movements.

Since Ferrash would be searching for his father, Progaeryon, to carry out the kill order, it made sense to go to where they had last seen the man – the habitation nearest to the planet's network of nexite mines in the southern desert. It didn't have a name, just a codified longitude and latitude, but the locals called it Cavemouth, for obvious reasons.

'What is this?' Lilesh's clipped voice came from behind them.

Palia jerked around in her harness to see Archivist Lilesh framed in the doorway. When had it opened? The woman's face was fire. With a growing chill, Palia watched the fabric of the Empyrean coil around her, accumulating within her limbs. No light, though. No visual tell. And Lilesh used her own emotions – Bek's remained untouched and Palia felt the same as she had before. She couldn't tell where the tide originated. Nothing clawed like fear or churned like anger. It all just pulsed, weaving around the limits of Lilesh's body, an endlessly coiling snake in bright, indecipherable lines.

'We were instructed to remain with the fleet, Pestor,' Lilesh said. 'Why are—?'

The ship rocked around them. Lilesh stumbled, but righted herself. A strand of hair slipped in front of her eyes, the only escapee from her still-immaculate bun.

Palia took the opportunity to speak before Lilesh could step in again. 'We might lose the chance to find the tech *and* Ash if we stick around waiting for too long. Once we're down there, it'll be fine. I got in touch with the forces on the ground, so they're expecting us. Their objective's just about where we need to be, so we can stick with them for a while.'

Lilesh sighed. Heatwash illuminated her face as they punched through the atmosphere. Palia had no idea what might be going through her head. 'Show me where you plan to land.'

With a glance out of the canopy at the sick, yellow clouds and the last tongues of plasma, Palia brought up the plans in her implants and shared them with Lilesh. The woman's eyes became unfocussed, and Palia looked away, her heart hammering. She didn't like the thought of so much energy standing right behind her. It made every sense in her tingle, her hands itch.

'This is quite a way back from the front lines,' Lilesh said at length.

'See, I was being careful. Thought you'd approve.' Palia inclined her head. No harm in conceding the point. 'And it'll give you plenty of opportunity to teach me as we make our way further in. You can start by teaching me however you do that.'

'Do what?'

'Keep everything hidden. Or... obscured, anyway. Untraceable.'

'There are steps to take before you reach that level, should you ever do so.'

Palia's hackles rose at the implied doubt, but she bit her tongue. 'Then we'll start with those steps. Is anyone targeting us or are we good?'

Bek shook his head. 'None yet, but I'm about to put us down behind your lines. The Protectorate pick up on that before we're well protected? Expect it to change.'

'Okay.' She turned to look at Lilesh again, waved her over to the side seat. 'You might want to strap in.'

Tessa joined them for the landing, after Bek sent a nudge to her implants to wake her up. A deep sleeper, the earlier turbulence hadn't phased her and she sat now in the remaining side seat, bleary eyed, readjusting her focus in and out on the base of Bek's neck. Palia could pretend she hadn't noticed the two of them spending time together – loudly, in a ship where you couldn't get far out of earshot – but she couldn't quite forget, or fail to draw conclusions from the comforting effect his presence seemed to have on her subdued emotions.

They touched down in silence. Palia only noticed they had landed when the ground stopped moving up in the canopy, so gently did Bek put them down.

By the time they donned their armour and lowered the ramp, an aide already stood there waiting for them. He touched a palm to his shoulder in salute, breath misting in his helmet. 'Pestor, welcome to Sixty-Fourth Legion mobile headquarters. I'm your liaison. We spoke on the relays.'

Palia nodded, grateful to be wearing a full helmet rather than the plain mask she had on her first visit. 'Adjutant Signus Cammel, right?'

The junior officer nodded, then gestured behind him. 'If you'll come with me, I need to brief you on today's operational objectives. The legion only made landfall point-five hours ago, so we have yet to make a move beyond fortifying our position.'

If this was what he called fortifying, Palia wouldn't have guessed it. They had landed on an impromptu airfield, with shuttles clustered around clear aprons and take-off zones. When she craned her neck back, she could just make out the flicker of a sky shield high above them. Of course, the real airfield was the slab of metal off to their right, which had its own shield. The aircraft carrier squatted on thick treads, steam rising from it into the dawn air. Considering the base temperature of the desert, it had to be heat still bleeding off from atmospheric re-entry.

'How long will the generator last, Adj-Sig?' Palia asked.

Cammel followed her gaze, then gave her a reassuring smile when he realised she referred to the shield. 'Indefinitely, if they don't fire at us. Under heavy bombardment, about forty-eight hours. Plenty of time to get out of the situation.'

The shield didn't look like it could withstand any kind of heavy bombardment, but looks were deceptive. They installed this same shield technology on ships and Palia knew from the fact she was still here that they could hold out. In a ship, though, it was a simple matter of travelling to a nexus to recharge. That wasn't so easy on a planet's surface.

Cammel led them towards the edge of the airfield. The soil there had been disturbed, a darker brown scattered across the usual orange around the entrance to a fortified bunker. As Palia wondered how far they would have to dig to find the Wilds, the horizon burst into light. Wincing, she planted her feet and threw her arms over her face. A few seconds later, the detonation rumbled through the ground beneath her. An ominous groan rumbled past, rattling components on nearby shuttles, and a wall of hot air slammed into her.

When she dropped her stinging arms, there was an orange ball of fire extinguishing to black smoke in the distance. In the quieter moments that followed, gunfire sounded from that direction alongside an anguished, creaking scream. Something metal. Something big. Something broken.

Palia drew a deep breath into her lungs, tasting dust and smoke through her helmet's filters. 'What was that?'

'The explosion?' Cammel asked.

'The scream.'

Cammel grimaced. 'That was one of the Munabi's mechs breaking. They're in the thick of it right now.' He held the bunker door open for them, one eyebrow raised. 'You're sure you want to go out there, Pestor?'

If that really was the mechanised division, Palia didn't have a choice – Progaeryon commanded that unit, so that was where she needed to be. She nodded, but she wondered how many keepers were out there. It wasn't the orange flames she had to watch out for, not the old familiar warmth and promise of a certain death, but the green ones, and the threat of being devoured silently from all existence.

'I'm sure.'

CHAPTER SIXTEEN

PALIA SAT IN THE back of the transport shuttle, feeling like a fraud. The four of them had been attached to a small band of forty combined *milites* and *auxes* – career soldiers and those in mandatory service. A squad of eight, including Adjutant Signus Cammel and the custodian leading them, sat in the transport with them, waiting to take off and establish positions on top of a nearby mesa overlooking Protectorate forces.

They knew Palia was empyrric. She felt their eyes on her, saw their hope and nervous excitement jostling past pre-fight nerves and bravado. Most of their attention, of course, they reserved for Lilesh. One of the *milites* had apparently fought alongside her before, and the weight of whatever stories he had told about her held sway with his friends. They kept a wary distance from her and Palia, despite their good will. Palia was glad for that – it made them less likely to notice how much her palms were sweating.

Lilesh had confiscated her gun. The custodian had tried to give her another, but a harsh look from Lilesh had made him think twice. She said Palia would learn more if she had nothing else to rely on. Palia had to agree, but she still felt defenceless.

Movement flashed in the shuttle's ceiling viewscreen: two jets streaking through the sky, bright against the dark clouds above. Engine roars followed in their wake, muted through the transport walls. Palia followed their path until they vanished over the lip of the mesa in front of them and waited for explosions, but all she heard was gunfire. A moment later, the jets appeared again, curving around to the right and back. Just a scouting run, then.

Cammel had shown her the map, given her the brief. That mesa was all that separated their forces from the Protectorate in the dust bowl below. It jutted out of the desert floor like a stamp had punched it out from beneath, towering over a mostly flat landscape. The rebels, the Munabi locals, were holed up around the underground base Palia had visited last time, outnumbered and surrounded on all sides but for the route into the deep desert. The Protectorate wanted to take back the nexite mines out there, but they had to take and hold the base, first. It wouldn't be long, without intervention – they had captured an artillery complex at the tip of the mesa, which let them rain as much fire as they wanted upon rebel forces. A lot of those rebels were stuck fighting in a town on the surface, which Palia understood to be not much more than rubble at this point. If they wanted to find the remnants of the mechanised division, it would be easier to spot them from a high vantage. If they wanted to get far without getting blasted to pieces, they had to take the complex.

<Pestor Tennic, you appear to be fearful,> Lilesh sent to her.

Palia glanced at the woman, who seemed the very image of calm but still played host to that snake of energy, coiling, ready to strike.

Palia breathed out to begin the process of calming down. <Sorry.>

<Don't be. And stop that. Who taught you to do that?>

Caught mid out-breath, Palia frowned. <Ash did. Stopped me blowing everyone up.>

<Arguably, it did not, though I appreciate that it could have been worse had you not made some attempt at control. No, that is the Keepers' way of doing things, and unless you turn yourself into a soulless automaton akin to them, it is a dangerous method. Too great a risk of explosive lapses, as you and several untethered souls in Varna are well aware.>

Palia gritted her teeth and tried not to get annoyed by the slew of justified insults. <So what do you do?>

Four more jets passed overhead, then another four, then another. The vibrations hummed through her bones. This time, they fired.

Flames burst into the air at the top of the mesa. Dust and smoke spurted after them. The shockwave passed through the shuttle, reverberating deep in her bones. They would be heading up there, soon enough. She picked up an undercurrent of tension from the soldiers around her. Experience and training in peace time was one thing, and maybe some of the *milites* had fought during the Rythian war, but there hadn't been a planet-side war in living memory that Palia knew of. Perhaps they had just realised that themselves.

Of the twelve that had flown over, eleven jets circled back.

Lilesh paused, ear cocked towards the radio.

'—craft down,' it said. 'Two batteries taken out on the ridge. Estimate one remaining. Turret neutralised. Lift in three.'

Bek leaned over to the man next to him. 'That three seconds, or—?'

The transport jolted, and puffs of noxious gas dodged away from the engine exhausts as they rose into the air. Palia followed the gas clouds' movement on the wall viewscreens until they disappeared beneath the opaque floor panels. Their shuttle hovered, suspended in the morning air, a hundred other transports arrayed in front and to either side of them. Every one of them waited, the air filled with the hum of their engines, until the jets had swept back overhead for another run. Then the row of lifters right in front of the mesa rose, white shapes against the sheer brown cliffside, their payloads of artillery pieces dangling from strops beneath them.

The jets passed overhead again, but a missile streaked out from the top of the mesa and struck one of them side on. It splintered in mid-air, nose splitting from its fuselage, scattering a rain of debris over the lifters below. The main bulk of it continued and exploded somewhere over the top of the mesa. A sick feeling settled in Palia's gut.

<Emotion is a weapon,> Lilesh sent, her eyes brightened by the flame. <That is the first thing the Empyrean teaches us. By denying their emotion, the Keepers deny the best weapon they have available, relying instead on their pain and anything they can take from those

around them. Abhorrent. Flawed. Embrace emotion instead of suppressing it, and it is yours to control.>

The row of shuttles in front of them rose just as the lifters reached the lip of the mesa. Around her, the soldiers in her squad readied their weapons. Despite the jet exploding above them and the underlying tension, they were remarkably calm. One of them told a joke that she missed the bulk of, and some of them fell into snorts of laughter. Bek laughed with them, but the smile didn't reach his eyes. Was he trying to fit in naturally, or out of habit as a spy?

The shuttle rose. The shuttles in the rows ahead of them stretched in a neat diagonal sheet to the top of the mesa, like someone had strung beads on wires connecting the sky to the ground. Palia fixed her gaze on the first row as the lifters edged forwards with their payloads strung beneath them, becoming exposed to the enemy at the top. They all flew clear. She watched for flashes over the edge that might indicate a strike, but the sky remained overcast. Still, with every metre they climbed, her heartrate rose. She turned her attention inwards, fixating on the nerves that danced there and letting them stay instead of trying to slide them away. It didn't work. The more she looked at it, the more she felt it, and green motes began to slide beneath her skin.

<It isn't exactly controllable,> she sent to Lilesh.

<I was unaware you were making an attempt to do so.>

Palia frowned at Lilesh across the hold, then one of the *milites* cried out in alarm. Whipping her head around, Palia found him and followed his stare up. A black shape hung over the edge of the mesa, almost straight above them now. It bounced against something and rolled fully over the edge, trailing black smoke behind it. Their transport jinked left to avoid it, but the shape separated into chunks as it fell. It was one of the lifters, and the rain of debris it shed now was the artillery it had been hauling to the ridge. A massive gun barrel tumbled towards them, end over end.

'Lilesh!' Palia snapped.

Lilesh raised an eyebrow as if questioning what *she* was meant to do about it, then rolled her eyes and raised a hand. Empyrean fire flashed along her arm, straight up through the ceiling viewscreen and into the falling barrel. Glitches splayed across the broken viewscreen, but Palia could just make out the barrel's shape sloughing away as it fell.

The viewscreen died. For a moment, all was still, then something slammed into the cockpit. The shuttle rang like a bell. Palia jerked sideways in her harness, the motion sending pain shooting through her neck. They began to spin, and air rushed in through the breach alongside the pained screams of one of the pilots. Palia could see his pain. It speared into the rest of his body from his legs, great stabbing lances of it, cooling almost like lava into a hard mass where his legs ended. Then it siphoned away, wending a trail to Lilesh to join the winding snake as she tore his dying soul from him.

Palia stared at the woman, who shrugged out of her harness as if they had just landed on firm ground, despite the spin pinning them to their seats. Air whistled through the hole she had seared in the roof. Every half second, the cliff flashed past behind her. Close. Very close.

Lilesh jerked her chin towards the hole in the roof. 'Shall we?'

It took Palia too long to realise what she meant, but a fraction of a second later she began struggling out of her own harness. 'Everyone up!'

The soldiers, who had been bracing for impact, hesitated before following her example. One kissed the rings on his left hand. Another ran a finger along the gems set into the flesh of her ear.

'You don't need your ancestors,' Palia said, dredging up more confidence than she felt entitled to. 'We're getting out of here.'

The moment they were all free of their harnesses, Lilesh raised a hand and sent another condensed bolt of empyrric fire through the roof.

Palia cried out as her feet were swept from under her. She flew along the pressure differential and out through the new gap behind Bek and Tessa. In her panic, she felt the Empyrean press against the confines of her soul. It crashed against her skin, trying to break free

– so she blinked into focus and let it. As the sheer cliff rushed towards them, she created a shield.

They slowed. She could almost touch the side of the cliff, if she stretched. But now they fell down instead of across, at a rate of inches rather than metres per second. Palia spotted a ledge below, but her shield hadn't reached it yet. As she watched, the green flow that formed it began to drain away, along with her panic. The latter redoubled when she caught sight of Lilesh floating in the air beside her, the flow tethered to her core.

All twelve of them touched down upon the ledge, and immediately pressed themselves back against the reassuring solidity of the cliff. Palia tried to work some moisture back into her mouth, but there was something invasive about having the Empyrean stolen from beneath her feet, even if it was well intentioned, even if it saved her life. It wasn't like Palia could have saved them all. She might not even have saved herself. She couldn't meet the soldiers' eyes. She was a fraud, a joke of an empyrric, here to satisfy her own goals at the cost of everyone else. The thought should have made her guilty, but she was done with guilt. She got angry instead. Angry that she couldn't do more. Angry that Ferrash might be in trouble. Angry that Lilesh had taken the pilot's soul to fuel their escape and hadn't been quicker to stop the barrel hitting them.

<Pull yourself together, Pestor,> said Lilesh.

Palia hissed and peered up the side of the cliff. The impact and fall had seemed to take forever, but they had only fallen a hundred metres down the face. Flak bloomed in the sky above – clearly the Protectorate had put up a renewed offensive, maybe after hiding some of their units from the initial bombardment, keeping them in reserve to avoid retaliation. She couldn't see a clear way to reach the top. Either they would have to climb, or someone would have to pick them up. Foiled before they could even get to the battle proper.

She turned to Lilesh. <You killed him. The pilot. He was still alive and you took his life from him.>

<He was already dying. There was no point leaving him to suffer.>

<But you took.> How did she raise the concept of denying a soul passage to Varna when she wasn't even sure she believed in it? When she stripped it back to logic, when she made it matter-of-fact, Lilesh's actions made undeniable sense.

Lilesh sent, <I took control of the situation. As we should do now. We need to reach the top, and soon.>

<How?>

<By following me.>

With that, the archivist coiled energy around herself again and rocketed upwards, taking all eight of the soldiers with her in a flurry of alarmed shouting and windmilling limbs. That left Palia on the ledge with Bek and Tessa. Palia stared at them, then at the figures darting over the lip of the mesa, then back at Bek and Tessa.

'I...' Palia opened and closed her mouth, flailing for words. Anger bubbled up inside her, clamping around her throat, boiling in her gut. 'Both of you, hold onto my arms. I don't want to drop you by mistake.'

Both of them hesitated. Bek's eyes reflected green back at her, and she looked down to see flames licking around her arms. The rage burned brighter. However much she tried to embrace it, she didn't know what that meant. She didn't know how to stop herself feeling angry at being angry. She didn't even know if that was what she was supposed to do.

'Just hug me or something, okay?'

Bek shrugged and flashed her a half-grin behind his helmet's clear faceplate that might have made her scold him if this were any other situation, then folded his arms around her. Uncomfortable at the wave of relief it brought her, for another human to hold her again, Palia cleared her throat.

'Tessa?'

The arsaeria, who wore a cap-style helmet and mask for lack of a helmet that fitted over her horns, hesitated. Palia didn't want to look. She didn't want to see what the woman felt. But she saw fear, and mistrust, and a little hate.

'Tessa,' she said, trying to keep her voice level, 'it's okay. I won't hurt you.' *Not like I hurt Austela.*

Tessa didn't believe her. Tessa didn't trust her. But stuck between stranding, a long drop and a potential escape, Tessa chose the lattermost. She stepped up behind Palia, slipped her arms around her waist and clung on.

Palia let out a deep breath. Then, without trying to overthink it, she let all her anger and nerves and fear bleed out from her fingertips. She fixed her eyes on the sliver where sky met cliff above them.

She hoped it would be enough.

CHAPTER SEVENTEEN

FERRASH WOKE WITH A start and cracked his head against the side of the box the moment he tried to move. He froze, listening for signs of movement outside, for anything that might give away how much danger he was in.

Nothing. Just darkness, the muffled hum of electronics, his own breathing.

He must be imprisoned somewhere other than this box, surely. His mother must have moved him. Maybe he was in the Green Jail, and any second now a couple of procurants would open him up and use him for practice. Maybe she had turned him over to the committees and he was in the Freezer, which he himself had kept supplied with dissidents and terrorists over his years as the Reiart. Resting crumpled at the bottom of the box with his shoulders curved awkwardly in the corner, Ferrash reached a tentative hand out to the box wall to check. When his skin came into contact with the nexite, the box systems interfaced with his implants.

Always build in failsafes – it was the rule just after not falling into your own traps.

Ferrash frowned. He double-checked the data. Triple-checked it. It couldn't be right, but his logs hadn't been tampered with. He was still in the hideout under the mountain, still in his box, and still alive. *Why?*

He swayed to his feet, groggier than sleep would usually leave him thanks to whatever Ayt had drained from him. He had dreamed of Palia again. Flashes of memory played out behind his eyes, bringing the frustration of not understanding her creeping back into his awareness. He reached for the syringe in his sleeve, remembered it was empty, found none in his pockets. *Great*. Sighing, he used his failsafe system to unlock and open the door.

Definitely still the hideout. The mugs spilled during the fight with his mother lay on the floor. The base's generators still hummed through the archway, so she hadn't left him to freeze to death. The thought of her leaving him alive by accident was only a little more outrageous than her doing so on purpose. Killing someone was the simplest thing an empyrric could do.

Ferrash took a couple more steps away from the box, scanning his surroundings. Was his mother here somewhere, watching him? The same way she had let him believe he would escape Munab when he was young, had waited until he was almost away to reveal she had known all along, had let him fall in love only to snatch it away as another lesson to him? They weren't memories he liked dwelling on, but in this moment they were almost comforting – a reminder of what Ayt Mannae was capable of, of who she really was. There had to be some cruel trick to this, and she would reveal it later.

Once Ferrash made sure she wasn't hiding in any of the other rooms – aware that she could just remove all memory of it if he found her – he made his way down the corridor and tried the hatch. Unlocked, it swung open, dislodging the latest drift of snow. Freezing air bit into his face, gave it a good gnaw. It convinced him he was awake, but the thought didn't fill him with joy.

What now?

The sliver of doubt chilled him more than the air. He drew a deep, shuddering breath. *Think, Ash. Think*. He wanted to go into damage-control mode, but he didn't have time. Proglimen was meant to be in today's committee meeting, in his position as Proctor. Proglimen was dead. If Ferrash didn't show up wearing his face to impersonate him, everything he'd planned would be over. Maybe it already was, but he had to operate on the assumption his mother hadn't reported him, or there was no way he could continue to operate at all.

So, with growing trepidation for everything that could go wrong in the next twenty-four hours, he booted up a pair of skis from beside the hatch and stepped out onto the mountain.

Ferrash made his way to a safe room first, far enough from the Tower of Voices to be comfortable but close enough that a tram could get him there in time for the meeting. The safe room had a tiny bathroom in it, and he huddled in the slim gap between toilet and sink so he would be able to see the mirror. He cut his hair short to match how Proglimen's had been. Hunks of it fell away until nothing remained to hide his scars and his neck felt cold and naked.

Reaching into a coat pocket, he pulled out the bag Ducat had given him and upended it over his palm. The reconstruction mesh slid out, landing in a heap of scraggly red-brown fabric, feeling almost wet against his skin.

He pinched out an edge coloured lighter than the rest between thumb and forefinger, then pressed it to the spot just behind his right ear. With a nudge from his implants, it connected. It felt like his skin writhed with bubbles where it touched, and Ferrash pressed his tongue to the roof of his mouth to suppress a shudder. These things were fine once you got used to them. He folded the rest of the mesh around his ear and across his face, smoothing it into place with his free hand. It burrowed into his flesh, itching so intensely around his eyes that tears tracked a haphazard trail down his covered cheek. When he had it over his other ear and all the way round his neck, he drew his hands away, leaned over the sink and let the accumulated revulsion out in a wordless noise of disgust. Then he splashed water on his face and looked into the mirror.

His skin rippled and distorted, twisting into something unfamiliar. The mesh became translucent over his eyes for a moment. When the blurring went away, Proglimen's face stared back at him, an alien strangeness lent to it by being reversed in the reflection.

Ferrash wanted to claw at it, but he kept staring until the urge subsided and the itching faded away. He was Proglimen now. The Proctor. Self-important, comfortably powerful, quietly paranoid. No different to most of those serving in the upper committees. The mesh had made his skin paler, greyer. His hair, darker nearer its roots, needed no further alterations now he had cut it.

It was time for the hardest part of the plan to begin.

It was fortunate that the Tower of Voices had lifts as well as stairs, or Ferrash would have arrived late and out of breath from climbing to the tip of the tallest building on Hesperex. He had never been this high before. He spared a glance out of the window when he reached the Primary Committee's floor only to see an unbroken expanse of churning grey clouds.

He wasn't sure what else he'd expected, really.

Taking a seat on one of the chairs by the window, he scanned the waiting area. Seven committee members sat around the edges of the room. That was good – it meant he wasn't the last to arrive. Ferrash paid no one any particular attention – the others were studiously avoiding each other's gazes – but checked off the faces as he noticed them.

The two women in uniform were easy. They represented the military, one for the landers and one for the shipbound, in orange and deep-red respectively. Ferrash imagined they had arrived well before the others. The Chair hadn't arrived yet, or they would all be in the chamber already. The representatives for food and water, vatters both, sat beside each other, staring down at their datascreens. The woman representing Hesperex's physical infrastructure sat directly opposite the window, the occasional flash of lightning reflecting from her eyes. Her digital counterpart wasn't there, and Ferrash knew they hadn't attended a committee meeting in months; they were so deeply immersed in trying to fix the mess that Hesperex's networks had become. The man representing the ISL narrowed his eyes when his counterpart from the ESF stepped out of the lift, and the woman who administered the vats – the role was historically always assigned to women, though no one remembered why – raised an eyebrow at the both of them.

The Chair pushed past behind them, shrugging out of his thick coat and shaking snow over the floor as he did so. He had a hard face and flinty eyes, his thinning grey hair trimmed into a neat goatee. By the time he flung the doors to the chamber open and stepped through, he had already begun an argument with Infrastructure over train scheduling.

Ferrash bit back a sigh and followed the others into the room, walking past the Chair's position at the end of the table nearest the door to take his own at the opposite end, his back to the window. The Chair tried to call order when everyone was seated, but by then it was too late. Arguments had erupted around the room.

Two minutes into the chaos, the door opened again and Ferrash felt his blood run cold. From the immediate silence, Ferrash wasn't the only one. A Keeper's arrival had that effect on people. His mother stepped in, her green robes coated in a thin dusting of snow. It took all his willpower to suppress a swell of panic. Her gaze flicked around the room, met his briefly, then fixed on the empty seat. When she pulled it out to sit down, the noise of it scraping across the floor echoed around the room.

The Chair cleared his throat. 'As we are all present,' he said, 'we shall begin.'

Ferrash feigned ambivalence, but his thoughts free-fell inside his head. Had his mother recognised him? Was she waiting to make a move? Was this the end?

He spent the next two hours doing his best to stay focused, but the Chair hadn't explained Ayt's presence yet – if he even knew why she was there – and that kept everyone on edge. Most of the agenda focused around the war on Munab, with the military representatives presenting their reports of how events had proceeded so far. The Chair went off on a half-hour rant about the Hegemony's intervention, then pivoted to asking Vats if there was something wrong with the gene code used in the Munabi vats, to have so many people turn splitter.

Besides a brief interjection here and there, Ferrash kept to his own thoughts. He could spend this first meeting getting used to how things worked, then start pushing his own agenda once he knew the limits of his believability as Proglimen.

When he felt the tension in the room shift, he pulled away from his thoughts.

The Chair was gesturing to his mother. '—of you will recognise Ayt Mannae, here today to represent the Keepers' interests.'

Ferrash didn't miss the hint of frost in the military representatives' expressions. His mother wouldn't, either. The Keepers were meant to stay clear of the political system.

Ayt rested her hands on the table, nodded her thanks to the Chair for his introduction and swept her gaze along the faces of the attendees. The movement was inherently threatening, like a predator searching a herd for weaklings. Each representative shifted a fraction as her gaze passed over them. Ferrash remained rooted to the spot, emotions walled out more thoroughly than he had ever made them before. She lingered on him longer, he thought, her eyes cold and calculating.

Then she drew her gaze away and said, 'Prior to this meeting, the Chair invited me to report on treachery within the bounds of Hesperex.' The words sent ice down Ferrash's spine, and he could have sworn he saw a corner of her lips twitch. 'As such, I have collected the results of my recent investigations into Kept activities in the sub-levels and on the surface. I apologise for their presentation being incomplete – I was recently... *waylaid*, and unable to tie everything together neatly in time.'

Ferrash stared at his mother. That had to be a direct reference to his kidnapping her. She had to know, but she hadn't said anything. She was just carrying on, letting him maintain his disguise when she could just as easily have blasted him out of the window.

Had she really just spared his life, or did she have other plans for him?

CHAPTER EIGHTEEN

THEY ALMOST DIDN'T MAKE the last few metres. With the bulk of Palia's anger already spent, she drew on an ever-rising well of panic to boost them up the cliff to the top of the mesa, but it was an unstable energy. The Empyrean came in fits and bursts, struggling to free itself from her hands. She and Tessa and Bek bobbed like leaves caught in a column of wind. For an alarming few moments, they pitched backwards. She could picture herself peeling away from the sky and falling to the ground hundreds of metres below. That was what saved her. Flame burst in silent jets from her palms and sent them skidding across the mesa's rough surface.

Palia jarred her knee against a rock, slammed her helmeted head against something solid, blinked back stars. She wanted to move, but didn't have the strength. She lay there panting, trying to figure out if she had unintentionally disintegrated her own legs or removed her muscle memory of walking.

Someone grabbed her wrist and hauled her upright – Lilesh, standing immaculate under the weak sunlight, one eyebrow cocked beneath her faceplate. Behind her, over the lip of a rocky ridge, Palia could make out their objective. The artillery complex they needed to capture sat too far distant to discern many details. Something swivelled on the roof and a few spiked anti-vehicle defences had been erected around it.

'We are not done yet, Pestor,' Lilesh said.

Palia glared at her and shook her wrist free. 'Why do you—?'

A solid roar blotted out the rest of her words. A jet passed overhead and a missile streaked from beneath its wings towards the artillery complex. The missile flitted past the building's defences and straight into it with a detonation that rocked the ground under her feet. It must have gone into a window – she couldn't see any exterior damage.

Lilesh led her along the ridge in front of them until they reached a fissure where the rest of the soldiers had gathered, waiting. Palia tried to find the rest of the assault forces by peeking over the fissure walls. As far as she could tell, they were off to the right, most of them hidden by rocky outcrops. Sporadic fire came from some of their hiding holes, but they received just as much in return. A few unaimed shells thudded into the ground around them from the uncontested Protectorate positions down below. Every now and then there would be a great *thud-thud-thud* that pulsed through the rock, but Palia couldn't tell where that came from.

They slithered down the last section to the others, Bek and Tessa following behind. The custodian leaned against the fissure wall with his arms crossed across his chest, head tilted towards a radio carried by one of the soldiers. Cammel stood closest to them, watching the custodian intently.

At first, Palia mistook the gunfire over the radio for loose pebbles falling after them, but then a voice came through.

'...gas mostly ineffective. ...ing mirrors still fir... ...be automated. How... ...proceed?'

Palia frowned and tapped Cammel on his elbow. 'What's this about gas?'

Cammel blinked at her, face tinged green and queasy behind his visor. Lilesh had jetted them up quite fast, without warning. Palia could see how that might upset a stomach.

'They tried firing gas cannisters into the complex,' he said. 'Knock-out, I think, so we could just walk in and take it.'

'Isn't there still resistance outside the complex?'

Cammel shook his head. 'It's all gone now. The Protectorate haven't had time to counter with their own air support – a lot of it has been lost in the fighting.'

Bek, who had found a rock to sit on, pulled his head out from between his knees. 'Gas won't work.'

'Are you okay?' Palia asked.

He wavered before replying. 'I've realised there are some kinds of flying I'm not too keen on.'

She grimaced. 'Sorry. Why won't it work?'

'Complex is linked to the base with a tunnel. When the gas came in, they probably just opened the hatch and let it wash away.'

One of the female milites, a heavy gunner nicknamed Steel, snorted. 'Mirrors ain't usually so tricksy. Why didn't you tell us this before?'

The woman had no idea of Bek's origins – nor did the other soldiers – but Palia wasn't sure knowing would have changed her words. Bek didn't react to it, in any case. He just shrugged. 'Thought it would've been picked up on scans,' he said.

'And they call your lot Intelligence.'

Ignoring the insult, Bek turned to the custodian. 'Is there a new plan?'

The man shook his head. 'Nae yet, but they'll probably want us assaulting the complex on foot. S'tae good a position te destroy outright.'

Bek shrugged. 'We're headed that way anyway. Might as well get started while your commanders are deciding what to do with themselves.'

The custodian narrowed his eyes at Bek, fingers tapping the body of his carbine. An echelon of jets roared past and unleashed a salvo of missiles. The shockwaves sent more rocks skittering down into the gulley to join them. Palia found it hard to draw her eyes away from the rain of shells coming from over the mesa, more and more often now. If they moved from their current position, that fire would be meant for them.

<A perfect opportunity for you to practice,> Lilesh sent.

Before Palia could reply, the custodian spoke again.

'I'll get hold o' the rest o' the band and coordinate an approach. Ye have any other insights ye've been holding back? Wait, no, hold up...'

He raised a hand before Bek could answer and turned to the woman with the radio. 'What was tha?'

'EMP strike on the complex, custodian.'

'Aye, good. We move now, then. Dinnae want to lose an advantage like tha. Move up!' He motioned forwards, over the lip of the fissure, and Palia refocused her eyes as the plans overlaid on her implants.

Around half of the soldiers streamed up over the lip before Steel jerked her chin after them. *You next.* Palia staggered forwards, trying not to show how exhausted she was, how much it felt like the flight up the cliff had drained everything vital from her.

<If I could send you a jolt of energy to get you up there, Pestor, I would. Alas, the Empyrean is not so helpful. We help ourselves. Do try to shield these poor souls from the bombardment, won't you? I'm sure they're all relying on you. Why else would they put you in the middle? Nice of them to minimise the radius for you.>

Palia drove her feet into the side of the gulley and followed the others, repeating *shut up shut up shut up* to Lilesh's messages as her mind processed them. With some reluctance, almost too spiteful to attempt it, she tried to grab hold of that anger. What did embracing it mean, really? Did it mean taking it as her own and using it without trying to remove it completely? As missiles shrieked above them, she tried that. She raised both hands and let her anger flee from her. Clawing her fingers slightly, she brought Empyrean fire into a thin sheet above their heads.

A moment later, missiles struck two hundred metres to their right and in front, sheering off a spire of rock that tumbled towards them. When it hit the shield, Palia's flames latched onto it. It fell, burning, straight towards the line of soldiers, straight towards Palia, and it vanished into motes an arm's length from the first soldier's head.

Palia gasped as the last of her anger bled out of her, eager to join the flow, too fast and strong for her to stop. The shield pulsed briefly, then vanished.

<A passable attempt,> Lilesh sent.

While Palia gathered herself, one eye on the spread-out line of soldiers in front of her, Lilesh's influence stirred through her awareness. A moment later, another shield appeared, stronger than the first, though perhaps less stable.

Palia followed the others. Whenever the bombardment struck outside their shield, tremors raced back to rock them on their feet. The custodian picked a path across the craggy floor that kept them mostly out of view of the complex. The top of the mesa wasn't as flat as Palia had thought it would be, and it boasted plenty of rocky outcrops to serve as cover.

Reassured that they weren't in immediate danger, she turned her attention to her awareness, resisting the initial vertigo of its being a wider field of view than her ordinary vision. It wasn't panoramic, per se, just dimensionally confusing, like trying to pin higher dimensions to three-dimensional space.

Lilesh's energy swirled in constant flux, as did her emotions. In fact, the winding snake that Palia had originally assumed to be a direct manipulation of energy pulled from somewhere else *was* the flow of her emotions, untapped and yet controlled. The more she tried to look at it, the more she lost her footing. When she walked into a rock wall attempting to see the minuscule cycle from emotional conception to flow to usage and where it all fed back, she gave up. If the archivist wanted to teach her, she could do better than this.

Palia wondered how Ash had taught her, for her to have taken his lessons to heart even after forgetting his existence. She looked to Bek, moving across the rock in isolation to the others, and regretted that she hadn't dared to ask for reminders.

The last stretch had them dipping down into a low crater with the complex just out of sight. It appeared again when they reached the edge of the crater, squat and innocuous, almost hidden by the ridge. At last, Palia could see the source of the deafening bursts that had been sounding at intervals – three large cannon mounted on a swivelling mound on the roof. The complex itself was a wide block with slit-style windows. Besides the roof cannon, armour-fronted turrets faced out around the approaches.

The custodian crouched down behind the ridge and waited for the rest of them to catch up. Palia reached it a few seconds later and knelt next to Steel, feeling that all-too-familiar sense of déjà vu where context skittered away from her grasp. Lilesh joined them, her shield shrinking to butt up against the crater ridge like a pitched tent. It spat fire far too close to Palia's head for comfort, and her skin crawled. She couldn't remember Ash, but she remembered most of the fight with the Magister. She remembered the Kept on Munab. She remembered Everatus IV and the kariassid disintegrating into nothingness.

Palia breathed in deep. Artillery smoke drifted through the air, blown back towards the Protectorate positions by the prevailing wind. She started to think how good it was that that would limit visibility before realising the Protectorate already couldn't see what was on the cliff, from below, unless they had a live link from above. The good news was that they were possibly firing blind; the bad news was that they were definitely firing a lot. Perhaps the complex called the shots for them. How long could Lilesh maintain a shield?

'Hey Bek,' Palia said. 'If the complex has a tunnel leading back to the base and the Protectorate have the complex, won't they have sent people down there to get to the base from the inside?'

Bek shrugged. 'Depends how many are in there. If they had enough, yeah, they'd send them down. But maintaining the position's more important. Protectorate doesn't send small teams or individuals. Not unless they're free agents.'

'Ash?' She kept her voice low so the others couldn't hear.

'Has his own mission. He'd reject this one.' But he didn't sound confident. Ash was already going to kill his father, if his orders were to be believed.

The custodian examined the complex through a short monocular. 'Dinnae look like they have any folks outside the complex. Maybe in some o' the turrets, but our fire's left most o' them smoking. Pestor, Archivist, you twos can get us there safe, aye?'

Palia peered around the side of the ridge. A hundred metres of artificially flattened land stretched between them and the complex. It commanded a strategic position over most of the local landscape, being atop the only tall landmark in miles. Thanks to the way the mesa sloped down from its position, it also had an almost uninterrupted line of sight to anyone trying to assault it on the mesa's surface. That meant them, the second they decided to break cover. Palia had covered that distance and maintained a shield before, but never for so many people.

But she'd taken out the Magister, for ancestors' sakes. This was nothing compared to—

'Stay here,' said Lilesh.

'What?' Palia dragged her gaze back and frowned at the archivist.

'This is going to be a long day. You save your energy for later. I will have it sorted in a moment.'

The custodian, who looked just as perplexed as Palia felt, glanced between the two of them. 'But...'

'There are no keepers with them. Therefore, they are defenceless. No extra effort is needed on your part.'

Was she that fed up by Palia's attempts already? Palia couldn't tell. As always, that constant ouroboros masked Lilesh's identifiable emotions, if she possessed any. In all her interactions with Lilesh, the only difference from Palia's interactions with keepers was that Lilesh didn't want to kill her – though the flight up the cliff made Palia question that.

Before any of them could stop her or ask more questions, Lilesh stepped out into the open. Steel swore and brought the barrel of her portable railgun to bear on the complex, for as much good as that would do them. Handheld could rip through armour and flesh well enough, but Palia guessed the complex had thick walls, and that would only suffer against sustained and concentrated fire. The outer turrets were maybe more vulnerable.

Lilesh apparently didn't need support. She strode straight towards the complex and kept walking, even when a dozen guns opened fire on her. The instant they did, Lilesh's serpentine energy flared and lashed out, fuelled by a burst of what for one moment was unmistakably adrenaline. Tongues of viridian green swept along the floor before her and rose. The wall flashed and hissed where missiles met it. Lilesh bounded forwards, in a walk one second and a sprint the next, her arms pumping, her feet not even touching the floor. Palia squinted, dialled the optics up in her implants to get a better look. The Empyrean showed her what it was before her eyes did – each step Lilesh took struck a cushion of the Empyrean. That cushion pushed back in turn, trampolining her faster and faster with each step. Juggling so many empyrric tasks at once – the shield, the steps, the constant flow of emotional energy – boggled Palia's mind.

More turrets swung round. The air in front of Lilesh shimmered. The ground behind her shattered. She had crossed fifty metres in the span of a few heartbeats and she crossed the remainder in half that. Another flash of green, brighter, louder, smashed through the complex wall and Lilesh disappeared inside.

The others muttered. They couldn't see inside as Palia could, with the Empyrean. They could hear the gunfire, furniture smashing, bodies being hurled aside, but they couldn't do anything more. Palia could. She kept all her attention on Lilesh, trying to work out what made her tick, and she thought she finally got it.

When a Keeper fought, they were controlled. Steady. They kept a handle on their own emotions whilst leeching off those of their enemies, with pain as a fallback if circumstances demanded it. When Lilesh fought, she was in ecstasy. That was the only way Palia could describe it, or get her head around it. The pleasure seemed almost sexual, coursing through Lilesh's whole body as an undercurrent to the serpent, as its origin. Where that emotion rose, Lilesh wove it into the flow. She kept it going. Like rain falling on a planet only to evaporate and rise again, Lilesh's arousal became Empyrean, became her weapon, then gave her the joy of killing.

That's what it was. She enjoyed the kill. She ripped the life out of people and rejoiced in it, her energies spinning in the space as if Lilesh was dancing. Maybe she was. Whatever she was doing, Palia couldn't drag her eyes away, couldn't take her mind off the beautiful chaos that was death to the Empyrean.

'She need help?' asked the custodian.

Palia shook her head.

'Ah, ye looked a mite worried fer a moment.'

'I always look like that,' she said, and forced a smile.

Lilesh's attack finished before that conversation ended. One minute there had been a complex filled with... Palia hadn't counted them, but at least a dozen Protectorate soldiers. The next, there was just Lilesh, and that damned snake. Palia's ears rang with the unnatural silence of it. Yes, fire still came up to the mesa from below, but the great booming retort of the complex's guns had stopped. Palia didn't have to worry so much about keeping her feet – the worst vibrations now were distant. The Protectorate wouldn't risk shelling so close to the complex. She wondered how long that would last. Deprived of an advantage, would they rather remove it from the field?

'It is safe,' said Lilesh through the squad channel.

After a moment's pause, they picked themselves up and jogged to the edge of the complex, keeping a wary eye on the turrets as they went. The Empyrean showed her there was no one in them. Here and there the back of a manned turret had been melted open where the essence of whoever had manned it had been dragged out as flame.

While the others entered the complex through the hole Lilesh had made in its wall – so much for keeping the fortification intact – Palia traipsed to the edge of the mesa. She stood right up close to the edge, her toes gripping the top of the cliff, her hair whipped forwards by the wind. Beneath the brightening horizon, a sea of heat-hazed grey shimmered. It reminded her of a herd migration she had once seen from above, if the herd beasts had had tanks and worn armour.

She narrowed her eyes against the glare, heart racing. Lilesh's excitement was contagious. Perhaps it lingered in the taste of the Empyrean. Perhaps Palia had always had a taste for it.

Whatever the case, she hungered for the fight to come.

CHAPTER NINETEEN

'COULD YOU STAND BACK a little?' Bek asked.

Palia looked at him over her shoulder, then joined him a safe distance from the cliff. 'I was just looking,' she said.

'Really?' He laughed, but his knuckles were white where they gripped his carbine. 'Thought watching Lilesh'd given you second thoughts.'

'About life? She's not that bad.'

Darkness fell over his face in a matter of moments. 'There's nothing left. She left no one alive.'

Behind Bek, Lilesh spoke with the custodian. Further back, a train of troops from the remainder of the band jogged over the rugged terrain to join them, alongside a light personnel carrier that Palia guessed held the new garrison for the complex.

'I don't exactly have a good track record of leaving people alive, either,' Palia said.

Bek snorted. 'Yeah, but you had no idea what you were doing.'

'Fair.' She still didn't. At least, not compared to Lilesh.

Bek glowered over his shoulder at Lilesh. 'Archivist, keeper, I see no difference. Neither leaves survivors. Neither takes prisoners. And *she's* the one your new Magister sends to teach you?'

Palia resisted the urge to protest that Fabien had her best interests at heart, that he would have done the best he could with the resources he had available. But if Lilesh was the morality the Hegemony had to offer, what did that say about them? If this was the way of Hegemony empyrrics, if learning to embrace the Empyrean's inferno got her too amped up on adrenaline to hold back…

The thought made her shiver, and she pushed it aside. Instead, she pointed towards a thick column of smoke in the dry valley behind her. 'You can see the mechanised division from up here. If we want to find Ash, we have to get to them.'

Bek's face twisted, his brows turned down but his jaw set in determination. 'You don't get it, do you? Ash taught you the way he did for a reason.'

'The way the Keepers taught him.'

Bek started to speak, but a throaty hum drowned him out. Palia turned to watch a troop transport coming in to land within the complex's generated shield. The custodian kept pace with it on the ground. It touched down next to him, muted sunlight sliding along its surface. The custodian beckoned the both of them over to join him, then gestured at the transport.

It was time to go.

Anxious to get closer to their goal, Palia started towards him, but Bek caught hold of her arm.

His next words were quieter. 'I'm still not exactly sure what he saw in you above anyone else, but at a guess, a part of it was that you never wanted to hurt anyone. Didn't want to be a Keeper, didn't want to be like her.' He nodded to Lilesh entering the transport. 'If I'm being honest, that's a lot of what I liked about you, too. So you think hard about who you'll be by the time you reach him, and imagine if that's someone he'll want anything to do with.'

Palia hesitated, but only for a moment. The hole in her mind gnawed at the bounds of her identity, more terrifying the closer she skirted to it. She wanted to scream, to get the gap out of her head, to tear it out if she had to, but she couldn't. All she could do was keep moving forwards. Stop, and the hole would scream back. She boarded the transport and strapped herself in and, though she avoided Lilesh's gaze, she could feel it against her skin.

<I think I see how you do it,> Palia sent to her.

<We will shortly have ample opportunity to see if you are correct.>

* * *

135

Moving the Protectorate lines was as simple as walking artillery to the edge of the mesa and aiming down. An hour's sustained bombardment forced their armies – minus their dead – back to join the main contingent and left a foothold just large enough for Hegemony troops to disembark. When Palia stepped out of the transport in this new territory, it was to the sight of corpses, and parts of them, littering the ground. Poisonous fog twisted through the fingers of an outstretched and severed hand, over the legs of a woman leant back against a rock as if she was only asleep, along the myriad positions of the still and silent dead.

Steel trudged along beside her, her portable railgun hefted over one shoulder, as they followed in the steps of the rest of the band. A voice called softly from somewhere nearby and Steel stopped, drawing a pistol from her belt. Palia caught sight of a Protectorate soldier groaning in the dirt just as Steel's pistol tracked to his face.

'What are you doing?' Palia grabbed Steel's wrist and tugged it aside.

Steel frowned at her. 'It's just a clone. Protectorate ain't goin' to fix it up, they'll just pump out a new one. 'Sides, he's dying.'

Palia bit back her first answer in light of the fact that two of Steel's statements, including the most important one, were at least correct. Most of the flesh between the man's hips and ankles was a blood-and-bone-strewn mess. His life dimmed even in the Empyrean.

Palia sighed and said, 'Fine, I'll do it.' Then she raised a hand and drew what remained of his life from him until the Empyrean shone from beneath his skin and his entire body writhed away into the air – perhaps into Varna, too. New energy thrummed through her bones, drummed against her skin. Now for the choice: to let it free as she would have done before, or to take it into herself and let it shape her? She chose the latter. She chose to become angry – angry at what she had just done, angry at what she was about to do, angry that she had to do it in the first place. And just as Lilesh's thrill of battle kept her energies in constant motion, Palia used the anger to nurse hers into life. They stuttered at first, but she soon had them chased into a rough circuit, nowhere near as clean or as vibrant as Lilesh's.

Steel stayed silent as they moved on from the spot where the man had been. Fear tangled with admiration within her, and the sight only made Palia angrier.

It took half an hour for them to cross the field of corpses and reach the edge of the shield that had just been set up at the base of the mesa. There they stood under its protection, staring out at the battlefield.

Jets thundered across the sky, teasing anti-aircraft fire from the Protectorate swarm. Now and then Palia caught the bright flash of Empyrean flames, though for the most part these were concentrated along the strip of land running straight away from Palia's band, where the Protectorate met the Munabi rebels. Green lashed against green, Keeper fighting against Kept.

The custodian brought his rifle up to sight through it at the enemy positions. 'Word from the prefect,' he said. 'We're straight-lining it. Got affirmation tha we should go in, get the rebel mechs out o' trouble. They've made contact, so rebels know if we cut 'cross the back of 'em to leave us be.'

He transmitted the view through his sight to the rest of their implants and highlighted the route. It drove a course not far from the entrenched front lines and ended in the smoke-shadowed town in the distance. Great bipedal mechs stood tall above the low buildings surrounding them, stark against the horizon. Palia tried to remember how many had been here on her last visit. More than six, for sure.

The feed snapped closed and the custodian lowered his rifle. 'Let's get off. Already had one o' them stompers fall today. No use losing another.'

They moved out. Bek seemed relieved to be away from the dead, but he kept glancing back over his shoulder as he walked and his hands had balled into fists. The rest of the time, he watched Tessa, whose hands moved in much the same way as she had moved them on the ship – capturing the moment on record.

As the fighting grew louder and closer, they ducked down into a dry riverbed that lent some cover. Every now and then a shell landed in the dust nearby, kicking clouds of it up and over their heads. Once, one landed on the riverbank and threw a mountain of dirt on top of the lead soldier. It filled the gulley and they had to clamber around it, tempting fate with a brief stint in open view. Lilesh still had the shield up and Palia had put some of her own energy into its creation, but she still tensed every muscle when she was up there. Smoke and fog and gunfire wavered in the heat at the front line. Palia kept fidgeting in her segmented armour as the sweat found new ways to chafe.

Her world became the pace of her feet against the rocks, the mist of her breath hitting the visor in front of her face, the rolling thunder of warfare, the concentrated effort of keeping her emotions in a steady enough cycle to help keep them shielded. Every now and then she scanned her mind to make sure it was all still there, but of course she wouldn't know if it wasn't. The existing hole would just grow wider, her encounters with its edges more frequent. If she messed up enough, maybe she would just fall in and no one would be able to retrieve her. The anxiety of that fate simmered under the boredom of their march as minutes dragged into hours.

Something moved, fast. Biting tongues of panic flared in the fabric of the Empyrean. Palia snapped back into focus and withdrew from the shield, trusting Lilesh to keep it up.

Five dust-covered figures slid down the riverbank just in front of them, armed but not attacking. The first of them was a woman. She hit the ground, caught sight of them as she pressed her back up against the bank, and cut an arm through the air in front of her. 'Cover! Take cover!'

Bek moved first, hissing as he leapt aside, but the others had their weapons trained on the newcomers. Lilesh cocked her head to one side, just for a moment, then she jumped for the bank as well. Palia felt the rumble before she heard it. Stones slipped down from the top of the slope before she could think to move. But she did, and just in time.

The tank came belching smoke and dripping oil on two great dusty tracks that spun in the empty space above them, spitting dirt into their faces. It seemed to hang there for a moment before its front end dipped and its bulk fell towards them. Lilesh brought her shield down. Her energy massed, glowing bright in the daylight, but it was Steel who struck first. The woman wedged her back against the bank, brought her railgun to her shoulder and fired until the heat sink ejected itself.

Her shots scored the underside of the tank with neat holes. This close, they likely punched all the way through, armour plating and all. But bullets couldn't fight gravity, no matter how powerful. The tank was going to crush them. The riverbed was shallow, too shallow for the bank they crouched by to offer any real protection, and dirt slithered down Palia's faceplate as the treads churned into the top of the bank.

Lilesh unleashed her energy. She sent it flying into the tank as a shockwave and in a matter of moments, it went from an unending wall a metre above their heads to a tumbling box on the other side of the riverbed. It landed on its top, one of its treads hanging loose, one wheel tilted at an odd angle. Palia looked for a side door, but the tank didn't have one, not on this side. A moment later someone started banging against the hull. Black smoke began to curl out of the barrel and from what was now the bottom of the tank. Fear sparked from emotional canvasses so placid that Palia hadn't even noticed them until now.

One of the newcomers staggered upright and stared at the tank, sighting through an eyepiece attached to their shoulder-mounted rocket launcher. The next second, a missile darted out from it and struck the tank's exposed underbelly, detonating in a ball of fire that Palia had to wince away from. She shivered. The newcomers' emotions were dull, too. She had only noticed a brief pang of regret as the tank exploded.

'You're the rebels, aye?' The custodian pushed away from the bank, dusting off his rifle.

The newcomers looked confused for a moment, most of their now fearful attention caught on Lilesh, who still shimmered faintly with aftertraces of the Empyrean. One of them nodded, but they furnished no more words and instead retreated back up the slope they had come from

While the custodian and Steel went to the edge of the bank to peer over and judge how close the front had shifted, Palia watched the tank burn. All trace of life inside it had vanished. She hoped it had been quick. There were no rebels and enemies, just those who were able to follow orders other than the Protectorate's and those who were not.

'Front's getting close for comfort,' said the custodian. 'Let's get a move on.'

They picked up the pace. Palia's heart beat a background tattoo to her footsteps, and her mind ached with the constant swirl of anger she had to maintain. The untethered whip of the love she had burned away sat within it, as much a fuel as anything else she could muster.

She could hear the mechs now. Their metallic groans carried on the wind and the stamps of their footsteps travelled through the ground beneath her. In one of those mechs, perhaps, was Ferrash's father, battling for his life against the rest of the Protectorate, unaware that the true threat might well come from his own blood.

If Palia couldn't get there first.

CHAPTER TWENTY

THE RYTHIANS HAD GIVEN Fabien a suite of rooms on the upper floor of the palace, high enough up that he had a clear view across the city's rooftops. He had stared out across them when he arrived, finding the city looked a little like a mossy rock with all the wide-canopied trees spread through its streets. But he hadn't spent long in his room since then, beyond a brief sleep and changing from one outfit to the next. They sent him on a tour of the city as soon as he woke, and the fresh air was perhaps the only thing that stopped him falling straight back to sleep.

He wasn't sure what time it was now, as he stood blinking groggily at another set of lightly embellished blue robes. They were the same robes as usual, of course. A magister's robes never got more or less formal – they were a constant, made to be recognised and, at some point, probably designed to be comfortable. In the setting of Rythe – with its thick carpets and draperies, its jewelled and braided uniforms – it seemed a little like he would be turning up to meet the steward in nothing but his underwear.

Nonetheless, that's what Fabien had come to do. So he shrugged out of his current robes, folded them neatly on a chair and donned the new ones after showering. He had no idea why he had to change between each appointment – perhaps each set of robes was slightly different and he was just too tired to notice.

At last Fabien stood, examining himself in the mirror. Who was he to be Magister? He hadn't been able to call himself young for a long time, but plenty hadn't ceased seeing that fresh-faced governor.

Naive. Hot-headed. Idealistic. And now, the figurehead. How out of his depth he felt, now that he had a moment to look at himself. His chest contracted. While he stood here, somewhere lightyears away, his people were locked in battle on Munab. Palia was fighting. And he was here. The thought set his nerves dancing. He closed his eyes.

A knock sounded at the door. 'Are you ready, sir?'

Was that Lady Charante's voice? Caught halfway between a frown and a smile, Fabien walked to the door and pulled it open. True enough, there she was, still in riding gear, though her boots looked freshly polished and she had a half-cloak slung across one shoulder.

'It's "sir" this time, is it?' Fabien raised an eyebrow.

Lady Charante rolled her eyes at a short man accompanying her. 'He'd tell me off if I were any less polite. But come on, let's get you to the steward.'

The short man frowned, perhaps annoyed at not being introduced, but dutifully fell in behind Fabien as he followed Lady Charante.

'Did the steward send you,' Fabien asked, 'or did you blag your way here as well?'

She shrugged. 'A little blagging goes a long way.'

He smiled, dropped his gaze to the floor, and stifled a laugh. He was beginning to wonder if all Lady Charante's blagging was so innocently intended, or if there were some other motivations at play – on her part or the part of those she had asked for favours. To ask would be unseemly. To ask indirectly, about her family, about any relationships of hers, might give the wrong impression. If, indeed, that would be the wrong impression.

They chatted their way to the hall of the steward, just small talk. They talked about vriarbeasts and caring for them, the different breeds and their uses, the best ways to deal with their acid and their acid temperament. They talked about the outside – the worlds beyond Rythe, and all the places Fabien had been or heard of. He hadn't been to all too many, he realised, no matter how far he had travelled. Then their talk turned to the Protectorate, which got him thinking about

Munab again. She must have sensed his change of mood when he grew silent, as she asked no further questions.

So in silence they came to the hall. Vriarbeasts had been embossed and painted on the two great doors. Two guards in black-and-chrome dress uniform flanked them, staring straight ahead. Fabien gave the guards' spears a double take. They had guns of some sort, not blades, affixed to the shafts.

The doors swung open, green-lacquered feathers glinting from the hides of the embossed vriarbeasts. Iridescent opals formed their eyes, and beneath their gaze, a path that looked to be made entirely of opal stretched across the hall from the open doorway. It ran for five metres, ten, twenty, then ended at the foot of a simple throne.

Lady Charante took a single step into the room beside him, cleared her throat and announced, 'Magister of the Empyrean Hegemony, Fabien Colia Nessus Honeras, sire.' Then she gave a sharp bow, turned and left.

The throne sat empty, but a man stood to its right-hand side with his back to Fabien. He had looked over his shoulder at their entrance and now he turned fully, silhouetted against the window that made up the rear wall. He was young, with skin as dark and smooth as the stone that made up the palace. His smile flashed white against it. Contrary to Fabien's expectations, he had dressed plainly. He wore a white shirt, unadorned and unbuttoned to his breastbone, tucked into trousers the colour of ashes. A gold chain lay where a cape might be worn, but one hadn't been attached.

'It has been some time since a Magister stood in this hall,' the steward said. His voice rang clear across the hall.

'Oh.' Fabien smiled back, but let his confusion show. 'And here I was thinking I was the first.' He couldn't imagine Rythe accepting the last Magister on their planet, let alone in this hall, as an empyrric.

'The first while still in office. Magister Frierwen joined us for a while in her retirement.' With a few more paces to the right, the steward gestured to a high-backed chair set behind the throne. 'Sat in this very seat, in fact, for most of it, passing the time with the steward before my stewardship. Come. Sit with me.'

Fabien crossed the flagstones, his footsteps echoing from the high ceiling. When he reached the chair, he found a small table set up between it and another, where the steward sat waiting.

As Fabien lowered himself into the seat, he said, 'We don't keep our titles, after we retire. We only wear them during the years of our service.'

'Of course. You prefer to mark deeds of note into names, don't you?'

'Frierwen was called Tielmar, in the end.'

The steward took hold of one of two tumblers of water that rose from the surface of the table. 'What does it mean? It doesn't translate well.' He motioned for Fabien to take the other tumbler.

'Oathbreaker, in the dialect of the plebs of her home world.' Grimacing, Fabien took hold of the tumbler and looked the steward in the eyes. 'She wasn't popular, come the end. Not with a lot of people, anyway.'

The steward held his gaze, nodded a fraction. 'Unlike you. Honeras is the name they gave you, isn't it?'

A flush rose to his cheeks unbidden. 'A while ago, yes. I resolved a lengthy trade dispute and apparently they thought that was noteworthy.'

'Hmm.'

Fabien opened his mouth to speak, but thought better of it. The steward still stared at him, his eyes piercing, the tip of one finger tracing around the rim of his glass. Did he doubt he had come across the name naturally? Plenty had tried to influence the names people chose for them. The attempts backfired more often than not. Even Frierwen had had the sense not to try fixing her image once it was marred. But here was the steward, doubting his. The name embarrassed Fabien more than it caused any pride.

Eager to move away from being the subject, Fabien asked, 'And you? Do your people call you anything, besides steward?'

Another smile flashed across the steward's face and he stopped playing with his tumbler. 'Not to my face.' He took a sip.

Fabien grinned and made the most of broken eye contact to glance left, out of the windowed wall. Here the palace looked out over the plateau's lake. The edge of it shone silver beneath the clear sky. He had thought if he looked far enough, he might have been able to see the start of the ice caps, but everything appeared closer together from space. Trees marched unbroken to the horizon here.

'You know why I came here?' Fabien said at last.

'Perhaps. Or perhaps I will only know it when I hear it from you.'

Fabien snorted, half a chuckle, and leaned forwards facing the steward. 'It's the Protectorate. They've worked themselves into a mess, the worst I've ever seen that they haven't already dealt with. A civil war on Munab. Unrest, so I hear, building elsewhere.'

'They purged that unrest,' said the steward before he could continue. 'As they do every time it appears, and will do in every cycle. People stand up, and are cut down, and are silent until the next are unwise enough to stand. This is always the way with them.' But he still had that hard look in his eyes, that testing glint.

Picking his words with even more care, Fabien said, 'Never has a whole world taken a stand and survived the consequences long enough to fight. Until Munab. They are the first step in what could be the end of the Protectorate, or the future of its reimagining. Where Munab stands, others may follow, and with each planet that does so, the Protectorate becomes weaker. There has never been a better time to strike against them, not to annihilate, but to undermine and overturn. I have sent my fleet to aid the rebels—'

'And you would ask that we send ours.' The steward reclined, casual in the midst of his great fortress palace, the fingers of one hand loosely curled, supporting his cheek.

'Or provide ground forces, yes. The sooner we can see this done, the better, and the sooner we can see the Keepers gone from this galaxy.'

As Fabien looked the steward in the eye, he received a message from Consul Esselia. <Magister, there's something you should see.>

<I'm in talks with the steward, Esselia,> he sent back.

<This is important. The Protectorate have attacked Corumma.>

<And were intercepted, surely. How many did they send?>

<We didn't see them coming. They jumped into free space. Bypassed the nexus.>

The exchange had taken less than a second, but the steward couldn't miss how Fabien's face froze at Esselia's last message.

'Trouble?' the steward asked.

Fabien nodded, closed his eyes and tried to halt the chills that were climbing up his spine. His train of thought spilled over into an unreachable abyss. He took a deep breath, held it for a moment, then let it out slowly before opening his eyes.

'I'm sorry,' Fabien said. 'There has been a development in the war. I need to deal with this. Please, consider my words. Your support would mean a great deal to us. To me.'

Not at all perturbed or surprised by this interruption, the steward said, 'Go. Lady Charante will see you back to your chambers.' This last he said with a knowing smile.

CHAPTER TWENTY-ONE

FABIEN'S SKIN ITCHED AS he followed Lady Charante back to his chambers. It wasn't just from the fact that Hegemony space had just been attacked while his back was turned – he didn't like leaving the conversation with the steward open-ended. Getting Rythe's support was vital, and the steward's motivations had layers that Fabien couldn't see beneath. Too much about Rythe was unknown. They liked it that way.

Lady Charante seemed to pick up on his agitation. 'You keep your meetings short, you do. Did it go badly?'

Fabien refocused his eyes. Lady Charante dropped back to walk beside him, her red brows forming a concerned line.

'No.' Fabien shook his head. 'It didn't go badly. I was interrupted by news from the war, that's all.'

'That's all?' One of her eyebrows darted upwards. She flashed him a quick smile. 'Not much then.' Becoming serious, she asked, 'How bad?'

'I don't know yet.' Fabien let out a long sigh. He wondered how Lady Charante had arrived to escort him so fast. She had left after dropping him at the throne room. Had she just happened to stay nearby or had she, as Fabien suspected, been instructed to remain close at hand? He shook the thought out of his head. It didn't matter either way. All that mattered in this moment was finding out about Corumma.

When they reached his chambers, Lady Charante held the door open for him and Fabien strode a few steps in before stopping. Rythe's networks only allowed him standard implant communications, not projections, and he felt like he would need the latter for this meeting.

'You alright there?' Lady Charante asked, one hand still resting on the door handle.

'Is there any way I can get projections in here?'

'Oh, sure.' She walked forwards, bootheels clicking until she crossed onto the carpet, letting the door swing closed behind her. Fabien stepped back to let her pass, then trailed behind her to the full-length mirror that sat next to one of the windows overlooking the city.

Lady Charante rapped her knuckles on the edge of the mirror. 'It's 2D only, but it should interface just fine with your implants. Give it a try.'

'Thank you.'

Fabien moved in front of the mirror and touched a hand to its surface, letting his implants work out whether they could connect. When they found something, he requested a call with Esselia. His reflection disappeared from the mirror's surface and the scenery shifted, leaving only a view of the room behind the mirror.

Lady Charante inclined her head. A strand of hair fell away from her face, shining in the light from the window. 'I'll leave you to it.'

'No.' Fabien said it without even thinking, and his throat felt suddenly tight. 'It's okay, you can stay if you want.' When she raised an eyebrow, he added, 'I have nothing to hide from you – or from Rythe. And word will get out about this anyway.'

Her gaze flicked between him and the mirror, still clear as it waited for the call to be accepted. 'I doubt your council will be thrilled to see me.'

Fabien shrugged. 'If I manage to be persuasive enough, this will be Rythe's war as well. A representative wouldn't go amiss. You can stay out of view if you want. Maybe you can claim it's another thing you've blagged your way into.' In truth, he wanted someone in the room with him. Being so far from everyone he worked with, so far away from the usual loop of news and conversation, he felt isolated. Parts of his world were burning and he couldn't see the flames.

Lady Charante huffed out a laugh, shook her head and brushed past him. She took a seat on a lounge set a few metres away and hefted her booted feet up onto the short table next to it.

Smiling as he turned back to the mirror, Fabien straightened out his robes. The call connected. He looked up to see Consul Esselia staring back at him. He might have believed she stood in front of him if it wasn't for the fact the mirror cut her feet off.

'Magister,' Esselia said, relief flooding her voice. 'Thank you for calling so quickly.'

To his left, Lady Charante stifled a cough that carried a distinct undertone of laughter. Fabien was confused about it for a moment before recognising that Esselia was naked as usual, and that would be an outlandish sight for a Rythian. He suppressed a flush of embarrassment at the realisation.

'What are our losses?' he asked. He had to know that first. What had the Protectorate destroyed?

Esselia grimaced. 'We've lost the mining station.'

Fabien drew a sharp breath through his nose. His heart jolted in his chest. 'All of it?'

She nodded. 'Not without cost to the Protectorate. Mirrors were ballsy to risk a blind jump, but a blind jump's blind. Don't know if they were doing a suicide run and actually hit their target or if they just missed, but a third of their fleet jumped right into it. It's gone.'

Esselia was right to call the move ballsy. To jump blind meant accelerating from one nexus to a specific – but inaccurate – point in space instead of a destination nexus. If it didn't leave you stranded, it rarely left you where you intended to go.

'And the other two thirds of their fleet?' Fabien tried to recall how many people had been stationed on the mining station. His imagination tugged at him. How would it have been, to be going about your work, your life, one second, then blown away into fire and void the next?

'They've taken out the regional fleet and established a blockade around the planet.'

'*Ancestors*,' Fabien swore. 'And the nexus?'

'Still intact.' Esselia shook her head in disgust. 'They at least wanted to leave themselves an escape route.'

'But they're not escaping, are they? What are they waiting for? Why Corumma?' It didn't make sense. The mining station was a valuable target, but it wasn't a nexite mine, and the Hegemony had enough raw resources beyond nexite that the loss of the station wouldn't hurt it too much. The planet of Corumma itself was only host to a small outpost, not a full colony. The fact that it wasn't self-sufficient meant a blockade was effective, but not of any strategic importance, either. The ideal course of action for the Protectorate's fleet remnants would have been to turn around and leave via the nexus as soon as they were done.

Esselia shrugged, her face twisted with unspent anger. 'I couldn't begin to imagine their motives, but we've got some advisors in speaking about it right now. I think Archivist Lilesh has sent her thoughts as well.'

'Good. Can you forward that on to me?'

'Should already be in your files. It just might not have given a notification – they get glitchy on Rythe.'

'Right, thanks. I'll check.' Fabien would have a lot of reading to do tonight, but he had expected a challenge keeping up with events. He rubbed his fingers along his cheekbone. 'We need to send a relief force through to Corumma.'

Esselia clicked her tongue and shifted on her feet. 'I think we should wait until we're done on Munab.'

'Why?' Leaving the survivors alone too long would be an abandonment.

'It'll stretch our forces too thin. We need to send something decisive through the nexus, with their fleet sat alone on the other side of it. I wouldn't put it past the mirrors to bomb the planet if they feel threatened, either, so we need the fight to be quick. Once we have Munab secured, we can divert ships back to deal with it.'

Fabien grimaced. 'How long will the outpost's supply last?'

'Two months. Plenty of time.'

It was a nice amount of time, Fabien had to admit, but he wouldn't put too much confidence in any estimates of how long it would take to secure Munab. It wasn't a familiar planet for them, and the Munabi rebels were an unknown factor. The Protectorate also had far more fleets lying in reserve – it would only take them moving one to Munab to throw everything off course. Besides, what would he tell the people on Corumma? To stay put and wait? It looked like he'd have to.

'Okay.' He nodded. 'We'll wait for now. If I'm successful here, we should at least be able to take Munab and get aid to Corumma sooner.'

'Well' – Esselia didn't look too convinced by his chances – 'good luck with that.' Her image faded back into the mirror. Fabien's reflection reappeared a moment later.

With a groan, he crossed to his bed and flopped down onto the end of it. He sat kneading his forehead in his hands, momentarily forgetting Lady Charante sat opposite him.

'Can I blag myself a question?' she asked. She had taken her feet off the table and rested her elbows on her knees, leaning towards him, her expression intent.

Fabien shot her a weak smile, expecting a question about Esselia's clothing choice – or lack thereof. 'Of course.'

'Why can't you just do what they did? Jump in behind them? Bypass the nexus?'

Before he could stop himself, he barked out a laugh. Lady Charante's expression didn't change. If anything, she looked a little confused by his outburst, and he realised she was being completely serious.

'When *they* did it, they miscalculated and smashed a third of their fleet into the mining station. For all I know, if *we* tried it, we'd miscalculate, jump into the outpost and kill all the remaining survivors.'

Lady Charante frowned and leaned back in her chair, her boots squeaking against each other. 'Might they have done it on purpose? It can't be that difficult to calculate a jump.'

'No.' He shook his head emphatically. 'Not a chance. Do you know how a nexus works?'

'Can't say I do.'

'No one can. That's why blind jumps are dangerous. We know how to interface with a nexus, but all that interfacing is done with another nexus as the end point. If you remove the endpoint it's like... like trying to triangulate a position when you only have one point. You might get the general direction right and you might know the distance, but it won't be very accurate.'

'Hmmph.' Lady Charante scrunched up her face, and Fabien couldn't help smiling at how it made her look. 'Terrible way to travel.'

He laughed again, gentler this time. 'You really haven't left Rythe, have you.'

Lady Charante gave out a little cough of a laugh and flushed, but a slight frown gave the impression she was annoyed at herself. 'Something like that.' She laughed again, and the frown vanished. 'Does it show that bad?'

'No, it's just...' Fabien waved it off. 'I guess a lot of people in the Hegemony might not know it either. It's just not a question I was expecting, that's all.'

'Well,' she leaned forwards, winked, and unfolded herself from her chair, 'I do try my best to be unexpected. Now, should we get you back to the steward?'

Fabien slid off the bed, inclined his head and gestured to the door. 'Lead the way.'

CHAPTER TWENTY-TWO

THE FIRST FERRASH HEARD of the attack, he was eating lunch in one of the Tower of Voices' upper mess halls and an automated message from Ida arrived in his implants. He opened the message, stopped chewing, swallowed.

Ida was dead. The void marshal, his highest contact in the admiralty, the woman he'd been hoping would rally the void packs against the Protectorate when the time came, was gone. The automated message wasn't so much from her as it was from her genetic identifier, which had just been wiped from the Protectorate's database along with a few hundred other names in the same log. But that couldn't be right. Her fleet had gone to Oproven, and he hadn't heard about them moving from that position. Ferrash had eyes all through the fleet, Ida's included, so unless their orders had been left right until the last moment, until they were already en-route from a nexus...

Ferrash trawled his implants for anything he might have missed. Before he could get far, the viewscreen at the far end of the hall flickered away from the stream of propaganda he'd been ignoring and switched to a view of an asteroid belt. He tapped into the newsfeed a moment before the presenter started talking, a moment before explosions flared across the screen.

Scatz.

The system on the broadcast was Corumma. He knew the name. Corumma sat squarely within Hegemony space, inside the range of the more powerful Protectorate nexuses but beyond the Hegemony's shorter range. According to the feed, Ida's fleet had just attacked it.

They had flown into the nexus in the Oproven system and shot straight out in free space, bypassing the Corumman nexus to avoid Hegemony fleets stationed nearby.

The Protectorate called it a success, spinning it as a strong blow against the enemy and a sacrifice by the people, for the people. But by launching a full fleet into free space, they had taken the risk of miscalculation. A third of the fleet had collided with a mining station, with both destroyed near instantaneously. People on Corumma might not have even heard any cries for help and if they had, they would have reached them over the nexite buoys before the light of the destruction did. Ida had been on one of those ships. The fact made Ferrash wonder how much of her fleet's demise had been miscalculation and how much had been the Protectorate disposing of unreliable assets. Ferrash hoped the void-pack captain she'd been sleeping with didn't set out for revenge, or things would get messy.

Another contact down. Another web gone dark. Ferrash still had a lot of eyes and ears out there, but he had lost most of his informants during the purge. The Reiart didn't have the reach it once did.

Before he realised what he was doing, he was halfway up the stairs. The monotone of the broadcast was lost to the rush of blood in his ears, the sound of his heart pumping: uneven, chaotic. He ran a diagnostic, noted the levels of inhibitors breaking down in his bloodstream. He looked up how much was lethal, but couldn't find a definitive answer – which was odd, because if anyone knew how much of a substance it took to kill someone, it was the Protectorate.

All those levels to the top of the tower couldn't go fast enough. The lift was too slow, the distance the committee had put between them and the people of Hesperex too great. Ferrash received a report of riots breaking out amongst the dock workers, the closest to the departed spacers, the most likely to feel their loss.

Not now. There would be time for rioting later, when Ferrash had lined up all the pieces he needed. But if public order on Hesperex broke down to the extent of rioting on the streets *now*, the committee might decide on another purge. If he couldn't stop them, the toll might leave him blind. Ferrash had a live map up with the riots marked out, and every level he moved up, the riot expanded. Not much, compared to the global population, but big enough to attract attention, to raise questions in the eyes of those who wanted control at any cost.

The lift opened onto the Primary Committee's waiting room and Ferrash strode straight across, not bothering to check the view from the window this time. The committee members liked to meet early some mornings – Ferrash suspected it was so they could speak freely without the Proctor listening in, which wasn't strictly legal. In any case, they were all there now, and they stopped talking when he walked in.

Where was Ayt in all of this? Where was his mother? Why hadn't she come after him yet? Ferrash almost wished she was a permanent committee fixture just so he knew where she was. At least she came to most meetings these days – that was probably the Keepers exerting their influence. The more time passed, the further they embedded themselves into the chain of command.

Taking his seat at the end of the table, Ferrash surveyed the room. Most of the representatives eyed him warily. Only wearing Proglimen's face and without access to his memories, Ferrash had no idea if Proglimen had known about the attack on Corumma or not. From the way it had been carried out, without even Ferrash's contacts hearing of it, he suspected not even all the members of this committee had known. The representative for the spacers didn't look pleased, and that was interesting – any orders to the fleet should have gone through her first.

Ferrash took a gamble on Proglimen's ignorance. 'Would someone like to explain why we've lost a void marshal?'

Spacers leaned forwards like she wanted to second the request, but kept her mouth shut. It would embarrass her to admit no control over her own forces – or a split within the Board of the Fist that oversaw the military. Even mired in the emotionless grey of Protectorate politics, it paid to save face.

After an awkward silence, the ISL representative cleared his throat. 'We believe, in the absence of any other evidence, that the move must have been authorised by the Reiart.'

Ferrash stared at the man, at his lie made believable by centuries of shadow and myth. Then he glanced along the length of the table at the Chair, who had set his hard features into a studied look of concern.

'You would have me believe,' Ferrash said, 'that the Reiart – a fictional entity that seems only to exist to keep you and the ESF on your toes, but in any case is supposed to deal with internal treachery – gave a specific order to Void Marshal Ida's fleet to conduct a high-risk blind assault into Hegemony space, knowing that this would likely decimate the fleet in question?'

Silence reigned around the table. The Chair hadn't altered his expression.

Ferrash leaned back in his seat. Ida's death was a fact now. He couldn't do anything to change it. If he wanted to play into his long-term goals, he would pin this on the Keepers, but he had nothing credible he could pin on them, and the Chair stank of manipulation.

Thankfully, the Proctor existed to needle the Chair. 'Fictional entities aside, I would remind those present' – and here Ferrash gave the Chair a pointed glance – 'that fleet orders must be relayed through the proper channels. These committees were put in place to ward off tyranny, not to abet it or turn a blind eye.' Ferrash knew how little that meant, considering how corrupt the system was and how many people you could bribe without even having an official currency. But he was impersonating the Proctor and, well, *this was his job*.

'Your point is noted, Proctor.' The Chair gave a forced smile. Forced, because no matter how often the man might practice it, it still lacked emotion. The smile itself was an affectation of office. At some near-forgotten point in the Protectorate's history, in the time of another Chair, that position had been raised above all others. The Protectorate had been a cult, the Chair almost worshipped. Official record stated that the committees had been strengthened to make sure no one could gain that much personal power again. Ferrash suspected the Keepers had got involved, scared that a powerful and charismatic leader might lead the people against them. That level of power had gone, but the shadow of the charisma it had once embodied remained.

The Chair's smile vanished then, and he continued, 'While the void marshal's death is regrettable, we have many other experienced personnel to stand in her stead, and our fleets remain the most numerous in the galaxy.'

And the most dated, Ferrash added in his head. He asked, 'What's the full situation on Corumma? Did we achieve anything beyond the destruction of the mining station?'

'The planet's defence forces have been taken out,' the Chair said, a little *too* fast for someone who claimed to have had no involvement, and Spacers narrowed her eyes. 'The remainder of the fleet have established a blockade.'

'And the moment the Hegemony sends forces through the nexus to recapture the system?' Spacers asked.

'Then the fleet threatens to bomb their cities until they leave.'

Ferrash kept his face neutral. The galaxy didn't have a standard definition for war crimes, not that the Protectorate would subscribe to the definition if it did, but this surely would have counted.

'So,' Ferrash said, 'we lost a good portion of a fleet just to block the Hegemony from one relatively inconsequential system, from which we can't advance and can't retreat, considering they control the nexus. It doesn't surprise me that this order didn't come through the usual hierarchy – the Board of the Fist might have actually shown some competence.'

Ferrash had expected the Chair to bristle at the insult, but he brought out the smile again. If anything, that was more frustrating.

'That's correct,' said the Chair. 'The fleet is stranded, which keeps them out of our way. As I have seen reports that not all of them were strictly *loyal*, I consider it fortuitous. Now we are able to keep the splitters at arm's length while we conduct the remainder of the war without their interference.'

A chill passed through Ferrash at the mention of loyalty, but he kept any reaction off his face. Spacers wasn't so controlled. Her face flushed, she clenched her hands into fists on the table.

'My—' she began, but the Chair cut her off.

'On the subject of loyalty, and in the spirit of transparency I *always* offer this committee, the Keepers inform me that they have uncovered a pocket of rebels in the lower levels. I imagine they will make a move soon. Our work following the purge is almost done – soon it will be a pure and loyal Protectorate we govern, with all traces of leechrot removed! It is our duty to see that comes to pass.'

Ferrash's blood ran cold at the thought of Son and Ducat hidden away in the lower levels. If the Keepers really had found them, Ferrash had to let them know. He had to get them out of there. But if the Chair had sent Ida to Corumma to die on suspicion of her being a traitor, and he suspected Ferrash played a part in that treachery, then this could also be a trap. If the first thing he did after this meeting was travel to the lower levels, the Chair would have grounds to arrest him. The Proctorate committee might very well start a coup because of it, and that would be a bloody disaster.

Still, he couldn't just leave them in this kind of trouble unaware. Ferrash kept staring at the Chair, into the cold steel of his eyes, but his mind whirred away at what he was going to do once this meeting ended. Proglimen couldn't be seen to descend to the lower levels, but Ferrash could, once he reclaimed his face.

That's when the message from Son came in.

<Keepers in the lower levels. We're under attack.>

CHAPTER TWENTY-THREE

FERRASH LEFT THE COMMITTEE chambers when he finally found a lull in the conversation and an excuse that wouldn't seem suspicious, almost forty-five minutes after Son's message. It was all he could do to walk out casually and maintain that pace until he found a safe room. He made sure to fake a different journey on the nearby cameras so they wouldn't see him arrive and leave the same place with a different face.

Then he moved as fast as he could towards the lower levels, swearing all the way.

It was clear even on the surface that a lot of keepers had been through, and recently. No one dared venture onto the streets. The people clustered in doorways and alleys and darted away when he came into view, like that would protect them if a real keeper came after them. Ferrash had tried and failed to get a message through to Son, but something was blocking all communications – and people, as one of his contacts who slipped the net had told him – from the lower levels.

Was Ayt behind this? Ferrash tried to keep the question out of his head, but it kept swinging back to spite him. He kept an eye out for green robes as the lift descended, but saw nothing. More floors went by, and the only sign of the Keepers was in their absence. Then, on the eleventh floor down, the bodies started. They lay draped over their workstations or in doorways as they had tried to flee, half melted away by the tongues of the Empyrean but not devoured completely. The keepers weren't even trying. They were just wading through, on their way to the lower levels. They had a specific target in mind.

Ferrash scanned through every channel he could. He tried to find a trace of the Keepers' objectives, but came up with nothing. He'd never had contacts in the Keepers. You couldn't trust empyrrics. But that meant he'd never gained access to their systems, which were entirely separate to any other Protectorate system. He was blind.

When the lift finally reached the level above the Observers' hideaway, Ferrash bolted through the door and sprinted for that day's floor tile. A contact sent him a camera connection. Keepers prowled just one level above him, hunting for a way down. Only a matter of time before they found the Observers. They had to move, *now*. He shimmied along the maintenance tube as fast as he could, until he fancied he could hear singing at the other end.

It *was* singing. The Observers were singing, largely out of tune but loud, and in numbers.

Ferrash shot out of the end of the tunnel and rolled to his feet. Scanning the crowd, he checked every mouthing face to see if it belonged to Son, but he wasn't there, not even on the dais under the blanketing shroud of lights. Maybe if they stopped singing for a moment, they'd hear the screams. Why'd they have to sing? Two levels up, the keepers could probably hear them. They didn't even know the danger they were in.

No time to waste looking for Son. Ferrash pulled his pistol out of his belt, aimed it at the ceiling with the mode set to sonic and pulled the trigger. It punched its own space out of the noise of the song, echoing around the room to a chorus of cries and abruptly cut-off lyrics. The Observers all turned to face him, fear in their eyes but slow to any other reaction. No sounds fell down from the upper levels. Not yet.

'Where's Son?' Ferrash asked them.

'Right here.' The man came elbowing his way out of the Technocracy's shack with Ducat close on his heels. 'What are you doing shooting holes in my ceiling? Does song offend you so?'

With a shake of his head, Ferrash jumped off the little plinth that sat below the tunnel entrance and made his way over to Son and Ducat.

He spoke low so that only the nearest might hear what he had to say. 'There are keepers two levels above you. Don't know how, but they've found out where you are. You all need to move. Now.'

'How?' Son raised both arms, let them fall down to his sides. 'The tunnel is the only way out. We made sure to seal the other entrances when we came down here. Which way are the keepers coming?'

Ferrash dug into the camera feeds again, running a recognition routine on the images to see which views held keepers. When he got the results back, he hissed and gritted his teeth. 'They've split in two. One group's in hydroponics, probably waiting for you to try escaping that way. The other's right above us. My guess is they'll burn their way down. Are you *sure* there are no other exits?' He brought up the map even as he said it, trying to find another option himself.

'Brutta?' Ducat jerked their chin at Ferrash, their eyes narrowed. 'We have a work could help wit' t'is. Old Triff under-sea tech, a level down from here.'

'A submarine?' Triff was vatter-speak for Five-Fifty-Four, and Ferrash didn't remember finding anything about ocean transport in its archives.

Ducat shrugged. 'If t'at t'word you want to speak for it.'

Around them, the crowd grew restless. Son motioned for those who had been shuffling closer to back off and give them space.

'Ducat,' said Son, 'I don't mean to criticise your people's projects, but I won't trust the Observers' lives to an experiment. Have you tested this machine? How old is it? Does it even work?'

'It is old. We fix it up, run its engines, but ot'er projects took more'f our 'ttention. There been no time for test runs, and we were 'fraid t'be heard in t'water.'

'If they can hear us, there's no point—'

'Ocean's deep,' said Ferrash. 'If we go down far enough and keep going until we hit a dead city, maybe Sixty-One-Eighty-Three, they might lose our trail. Could take them ages to find us.'

'That's miles away! Are you mad?'

'Son, don't make me remind you what waiting for the keepers'll do to you.'

Something screamed in the spaces above them before Son could reply. On the camera feeds, the glare of Empyrean flames concentrated into cutting jets. The crowd tried to back away from the noise, bumping into each other, treading on toes and crushing against the walls. Son took the scene in, his eyes shining, face twisted as he tried to work out what was best.

Son turned back to Ducat. 'How many can you take?'

Ducat's eyes flicked upwards. 'One, maybe two hundred. Will have to squeeze.'

'Not all of us.' With a last look up at the ceiling, where the keepers would soon break through, Son stepped up onto the same plinth Ferrash had just vacated and held up his arms for people to listen. At once, they fell silent, and every eye in the roomed turned to face him.

'Those noises you hear,' Son said, 'are the Keepers trying to find us. Do not panic.' He raised a hand to quell any rising conversation, but the Observers hadn't breathed a word. He was authority. They were listening.

'I ask that those born from the vats over thirty years ago follow me, while the younger among us follow Ducat. Theirs is the safest way out, but only a few may follow. Go with them now, quickly.'

Ferrash watched the crowd, his eyes narrowed, expecting there to be some protest, but the crowd parted with barely a comment. Some clasped hands with fellow vatters, but they said nothing. With a last nod to the both of them, Ducat split off and led their new contingent further into the hideout, presumably to where the Technocracy kept their submarine. Ferrash hoped they hadn't bodged the repairs. He hoped they could find sanctuary in the silence of dead cities.

'Son, you should go with them,' Ferrash said. 'You're not that old yourself, and they need your leadership.'

'They have Ducat.'

'More interested in circuits than people.'

'And we don't have time to argue about it. Now tell me, where exactly are the keepers?'

Ferrash pointed straight up, then along the tunnel behind Son. 'Nowhere else?'

He shook his head. 'Not that I can see, and there are cameras on a spread of the floor a mile in either direction that I've tabs on.'

'Good.' Son waved the remaining Observers to follow him, then began to jog away from the sea of lights.

Ferrash followed him, frowning. The keepers' flames were clearly audible now, a continuous roar interspersed with groaning metal. 'Thought you said there weren't any other ways out?'

'No unsealed ones. See that ceiling panel up there?' Son pointed, and Ferrash followed it to a thick metal plate bolted to the ceiling. As they drew closer, Son slowed down and gestured for the others not to get ahead of him. 'Is that pistol of yours any good?'

'What do you want me to do?'

'The bolts. Shoot them out.' Something metal clanged onto the floor above. 'Quick!'

Ferrash braced his pistol in both hands, used his implants to target the bolts, and fired eight shots in quick succession. The panel squealed and lifted off at one corner, but held firm. Another shot at the stubborn bolt and the whole assembly came crashing down, along with a sliding ladder from the access hatch it had been hiding. He shared a look with Son – an understanding that this way out was a slow and almost certain path to death – before they both turned and ushered the crowd forwards.

Ferrash counted them, his gaze darting between the sea of bobbing heads and the ceiling above them. There were perhaps two hundred people they needed to get up that ladder, and two feet of solid metal before the keepers reached them first. Ferrash held one side of the ladder, Son the other, the two of them bodily shoving each elderly Observer onto it as fast as they could until it was thick with bodies and Ferrash's knuckles were white with the impatience of waiting for space to clear at the bottom.

Someone cried out. A fragment of metal bounced against the floor next to a prone Observer with her hand clutched to her head. She wasn't even vatborn, Ferrash realised. She was a prog just like him, or a sannot – an unsanctioned birth – and her age didn't mark her anywhere as near death as the rest. Still she had stayed, and now she was directly under the keepers.

Ferrash stepped away from the ladder, fixated on the ceiling. Empyrean flames ate through the gap, licking at the sides as it grew wider and wider. The Observers scurried away from it like ants from a falling shadow, pressing together near the ladder until Ferrash struggled to move through them. At last, he broke free from the tide and edged along the wall to get closer to the gap.

At that moment, the flames died back. Ferrash drew a disc grenade out of an inside pocket and flicked it up, watched it curve through the human-sized hole in the roof... then fly straight back down.

Ferrash swore. He yelled to the others to get down and threw himself onto the floor. Heat and noise slammed into him, throwing him against the wall. He cradled his head against the worst of the blast but his spine hit the edge of something solid, sending pain shooting into his skull. He struggled to his feet, retching, only to fall flat on his face when his leg gave out underneath him. He grabbed at it, felt something wet, brought his hand up stained crimson. Fire reflected in the blood, its near-white light dancing over the surface of his palm.

With an unintentional snarl, Ferrash brought his pistol to bear on the keepers and started firing. Two of them stood herding the crowd into as small a space as possible, not even trying to kill them yet. Son's eyes were wide as he held the ladder. People raced up it, scrambling as fast as their hands and feet could take them.

A single flash of the Empyrean put a stop to that. One of the keepers swept an arm out in front of them and an emerald scythe arced through the air. It cut one of the Observers in two and the ladder along with him. He fell screaming into the crowd below, conscious just long enough for the pain of cauterised bisection to register. The ladder fell, cutting off their one remaining means of escape. Ferrash fired until his heat sink jammed the firing mechanism, but they turned back every shot without even bothering to look.

Beyond the ringing in his ears, he could make out other sounds from the level above. Were the Keepers still dealing with resistance up there? He wanted to check the cameras, but he couldn't take his eyes off Son, taking the hands of those beside him, gathering them all as close as he could before the slaughter.

Then another keeper dropped down from the ceiling.

It took three whole seconds for Ferrash to recognise his mother – or let his eyes believe it. In that time, she speared a beam of light through the chest of the first keeper. The second turned, stunned but quick to shift to the defensive. One of the Observers sloughed into the flame of a shield. The flames his mother threw at the other keeper wavered in the air between them, like some mental tug-of-war made visible. The crowd collectively shuffled back, attention fixed on the spot where their friend had been only moments before.

Ferrash lay where he had fallen, mouth agape, one hand clenched around the wound on his leg. It hurt to watch the fight. Flames swept the room, stabbing and whirling and probing for weaknesses. They scoured along the floor and billowed against the confines of the ceiling before being ripped away to some new purpose, the energy in constant motion, in constant use.

Then metal flashed in the corner of his eye. The keeper gasped and crumpled forwards on his knees. Behind him stood Son, bloody knife in his hand. Shoulders rising and falling, Son stared at the keeper he had stabbed as the man's body was consumed by flame, and he followed the trail those flames took back to Ayt Mannae.

She blinked, once, then turned to face Ferrash.

'Get up,' she said. 'We need to get out of here.'

CHAPTER TWENTY-FOUR

AT MIDDAY, PALIA AND the others stopped beneath an overhang of rock at the side of the riverbed to rest their feet, take on water and assess the situation. Palia's nerves were so strung-out that they had begun to beat at her constructed loop of anger, warping it out of shape, cycling her energy faster and faster in a way she wasn't comfortable with. Lilesh had shrugged and said that faster was better. Then, perhaps seeing the worry on her face or noticing a genuine threat in the fabric of the Empyrean, she suggested letting a little of it go.

So Palia sat, carving a hole into the packed dirt inch by inch, as the custodian checked for new orders. Bek sat beside her, a water bottle trembling between his hands. Ripples spread across the water's surface. Behind his faceplate, Bek stared into empty space. His emotions quivered as tight outlines around his bones, clutching tight to his chest.

'Are you okay?' Palia asked.

Bek's eyes refocused, but there was still a distance in them. A dimple appeared in the skin above one of his eyebrows. 'It just seems so... wrong. All this. Fighting each other. We all came from the same vats.'

'You've fought your own people before, on this planet.'

'That was different.' He shook his head, lips pursed. 'They were with the Kept. They'd made a choice to take that side. But here? How many people here made a choice, on either side?'

'Not many, I imagine. But the Munabi haven't surrendered. That's a choice.'

'They'd be killed even if they did, and they know that.'

Bek was right, but Palia felt like she should have something to say to make him believe that everything would work out. Maybe Ferrash would have had words for him. She didn't know. She couldn't remember what he was like.

'Pestor?' the custodian called.

Palia cut off her flames, whipping her head around to find him. 'What is it?'

The man grimaced. 'Yer nae gonna like it. Command's seen the front line shiftin', an' they nae want it shiftin' further. Want us to strike out from here, shore up the rebels' defences to stop it gettin' worse.'

'What about the mechs?'

'Lower priority, longer fight. Idea is they'll still be around fer us to swing back an' help them once we're done.'

Palia looked behind him, to where the mechs and the smoke surrounding them formed silhouettes against daylit sky. They had beaten back the Protectorate for now, and for once the town stood still, entirely under Munabi control. It wouldn't last. The Protectorate had more troops it could fling at them. More vehicles, too.

'How long could that take?' she asked.

'Long as it takes to see the rebels in good shape to stand on their own a while. Anywhere 'tween half a day an' two; it's hard to say.'

Time had already been against them. Losing more now might lose them the best chance they had to get on Ferrash's trail, might lose them the only chance they had to stop him doing something stupid. As the division commander, Progaeryon was almost certainly in one of those mechs, and Ferrash was meant to be on his way to kill him. Looking at that stack of smoke on the horizon, the silent sentinels waiting to wade into battle once more, Palia's heart burned in her chest. That untethered thread wound its anchor tighter, stretched itself to breaking point. If she turned away, might she break with it?

She turned to Lilesh, and before the archivist had finished shaking her head, Palia said, 'We should split up. We'll go on alone.'

'...Are ye sure, Pestor? Ye mean jus' the four of ye?'

'Just the four of us. It's not far to go and we'll be behind Munabi lines the whole way.'

'The journey dinnae bother me so much as tha' town. When the fightin' starts up again, ye'll be in a deathtrap.'

'If it looks too hot, we won't go in.'

The custodian sighed and looked to Lilesh for confirmation, but she just shrugged.

'Fine, fine,' he said. 'It's yer mission, Pestor, jus' make sure ye dinnae make a mess of it.'

Palia nodded. 'We'll take care.'

The rest of the band packed up and left, disappearing one by one over the lip of the riverbed. Even Cammel, who was in theory meant to accompany them for the duration of the mission, left with only a backwards glance over his shoulder. Palia wondered if she was doing the right thing.

'While you have a history of dooming those you travel with to die,' said Tessa, 'I wasn't expecting my time to come so soon.'

Palia bit her lip and did her best to look Tessa in the eye. 'No one's going to die.'

'Not if we get moving now, Pestor.' Lilesh stood straight-backed, concentrating on a spot in the distance. 'There are keepers massing to the right of the town. Even I wouldn't like wading into that fight.'

'How many?'

'More than I can deal with. Need I say more?'

'Okay.' Palia nodded and looked to each of her – acquaintances? colleagues? comrades? – in turn. 'We ready? Let's go.'

She set off at a jog, hoping that she could keep up the pace as much as she hoped the others could. She fixed her sight on the figures in the distance and promised herself she wouldn't look away, not until they were there, not until they could do something.

* * *

Forty-five minutes later, they made it to the outskirts. There wasn't much left that could be called a town anymore. The passage of mechs and heavy Protectorate tanks had flattened many of the buildings, and the mechs themselves stood rearranging piles of rubble with their feet, building them up into great barricades eight times her height. Palia's group crouched low to the ground as they came up to the closest end of the barricade. There were bodies in it – hands reached out of the rubble, dust-powdered, blood-reddened. Palia almost cut herself on the sheared-off hull of a drop pod as she sidestepped to avoid a face, perfectly serene on the floor.

Try as it might, her helmet's filters couldn't keep out the smell. Acrid and thick, it was the scent of hot metal and oil, burned things and burned people.

Queasy, Palia dropped back to walk beside Bek. 'Do you know which mech is Progaeryon's?'

He squinted through the haze at each figure in turn, frowning. 'They all look the same to me. We only made this division before deciding mechs were too expensive and unstable, so I'm not familiar with them.'

'Do you have access to any records? Can you find their identifiers from here?'

He shook his head. 'Ash might've known how to do that, but...'

Ferrash might well be doing that right now, about to beat them to the punch before they could even work out where to aim.

'Can you call them?' she asked.

'Implant-to-implant comms are probably jammed, but I can try.'

Bek diverted his attention to the task, leaving Palia to take stock of the town. In a patch a little further away, some buildings remained standing, their low-walled sides scarred with smoke. She tried to remember how it had looked the first time she had been here, vaguely remembered crowds of people hidden by heat haze. She remembered the mechs well enough, standing sentinel over the base entrance with their domed heads glinting in the sun, but everything else hurt to think about. The only people she could see in the streets now were soldiers – though perhaps they had once had other occupations.

In the corner of her eye, Bek's expression grew more and more grim. He nodded at a speaker he couldn't see, then brought his attention back.

'Bad news?' she asked.

He licked his lips, then pointed to the second-furthest mech from their position, which stood a way back from the barricade with some ammunition being hauled up rickety scaffolding beside it. 'That one's Progaeryon's.'

'Okay, that's good, right?'

'Progaeryon's not in it.'

The ground fell away beneath her feet. She could feel Lilesh and Tessa's eyes on her, on Bek, on the importance of that news. 'What?'

'He's dead. He died a month into the fighting, trying to stop saboteurs destroying the mechs in their docks. Thrown off a gantry, apparently. Fell.'

Palia stared at the space between her feet, feeling like a clamp had tightened on her skull. 'So Ash...?'

'Either already knew and isn't coming here, or has found out just the same as us and'll be heading back soon. I'm sorry.' Bek's voice caught on the apology and he cleared his throat to dislodge it. Palia wondered if he was upset that they wouldn't meet Ferrash or that Ferrash had lost his father. Further into the town, rocks rumbled and metal groaned as a mech nudged debris up to the barrier.

So what do we do now? she wanted to ask. But she couldn't. Not with everyone looking at her, expecting her to know what to do next. Though maybe, she thought, just maybe, a large part of why she had ended up raising a child alone in an otherwise uninhabited system for five years was that she never knew when it wouldn't hurt her to ask for help. Or when she was just too proud to accept it.

She rubbed a knuckle along one brow. 'Does their division still need help?'

'Said they could handle it, but... sounded like a lot of bravado. My guess is none of them've been getting much sleep lately.'

Lilesh put her hands on her hips. 'You really want to get invested in the ground war? We will be here for months, if we even survive that long.'

'No, I'm not saying we invest. But we need to get into the base if we want the rest of the Magister's prototype research. If we just stick around long enough to help them survive the next attack, a Protectorate withdrawal would give us a window to get in, get out and get off planet.'

'Did you not hear my earlier assessment? Keepers massing? That is not the kind of threat we can deal with. Besides, the Munabi still control the base. There is nothing to stop us going there now.'

Palia gritted her teeth. 'Okay, so we go in now and come back up a few hours later to find the Protectorate holds the entrance. Then we're trapped. I'd rather not be able to get in than not be able to get out.'

'Regardless, the Keepers—'

'What about the Kept?'

Lilesh tensed. 'What about them?'

'The Kept were a large part of this planet getting invaded in the first place. They've been at war with the Keepers forever, so logic puts them on the same side as the rest of the Munabi.' In an effort to back up her words, Palia closed her eyes and delved into the fabric of the Empyrean, much as she had done on the flagship and... another time she couldn't remember. A little further out and they appeared to her, like predators from the depths of an ocean, black holes drawing close the energies around them. She didn't look far enough to find the keepers on the horizon, but there were definitely other empyrrics sharing the town with them.

She opened her eyes, stared straight at Lilesh. 'If we fight alongside them, will we win?'

After a longer pause than necessary, Lilesh said, 'If they refrain from turning against us, it will even the odds.'

'Then that's what we do. Bek? Ask them where they want us.' As he did that, she wondered how Lilesh knew about the Kept, and about so much else beside. Palia had the sneaking suspicion that her role as archivist was more akin to a position as spymaster, and that she had strings connecting to far more information than Palia could give her credit for.

The mechanised division came back to Bek with restrained enthusiasm and directed them to Progaeryon's old mech, so they continued their journey along the barricade of bones. Each step took them closer to the centre of the town, where fires still raged. The mechs' shadows fell across broken buildings and ruptured sewage mains. Palia was so occupied picking a path around the latter that the mech almost came as a surprise – she only noticed it when she passed into its shadow.

She looked up and was rewarded with a large drop of oil landing on her faceplate. It looked bigger than she remembered, but smoke shrouded its head, making it hard to see where it ended and the sky began.

A door creaked open at the base of one of the mech's giant feet. An oil-stained hand popped out to hold it open, follow by a similarly stained face as a Munabi woman stepped outside. She beckoned to them all to join her.

Palia hopped across a rivulet of something that could have been oil or excrement or a combination of the two, then walked to the foot. She couldn't stop staring up the mech, struggling to keep it all in proportion in her mind. Armour covered every inch, in segmented sections over the joints, though a section of plating had been blasted off the ankle joint above her head and oily pistons glinted through the gap. One arm ended in a flat-nosed rotary cannon, the other in a thick-clawed hand. The loose end of a wire dangled from a slot on its wrist – from a harpoon, perhaps? She couldn't tell.

'In here,' said the Munabi.

Palia started and ducked through the door. The woman's feet disappeared up a ladder ahead of her. Bek shrugged when Palia turned to consult him, so she followed the woman up, taking the ladder one rung at a time. It hurt to grip the rungs too long. A thin layer of oil covered them, but they had been coated with grit to stop people slipping off. The end result was painful. Looking up the shaft of the mech's leg, she couldn't tell how far it went. Most of that was because the Munabi's backside blocked the view.

By the time they reached what Palia guessed was the mech's chest cavity, they were all gasping for breath. The Munabi had long since left them, off to duties elsewhere, and they stood in the room all alone. Palia didn't know what she had expected. A crew, at least. There had to be more than this.

While she waited for the woman to come back, Palia limped to the edge of the room and peered out through a viewscreen. They stood above the level of the barricade, so she had an uninterrupted view of the Protectorate positions outside the city. She could just about make out tiny dots of people, rows of tanks, lines upon lines of them all stretching back as far as she could see. She zoomed in as far as the resolution would hold and there, staring straight back at her, was an unmistakable field of green-robed keepers.

She backed away from the magnifier, catching eyes with Lilesh.

They were in for a tough fight.

CHAPTER TWENTY-FIVE

'How do we do this?' Palia whispered to Lilesh, pleading with her eyes, hoping for once to see some trace of humanity reflected back at her. The archivist had said there were a lot of keepers, but Palia could never have pictured there being *that* many.

Lilesh was about to answer when another Munabi appeared from a hatchway. He had clearly tried to rub the oil off his face, leaving a grimy smear across his features.

'You're the ones searching after Progaeryon?' he asked.

Palia nodded.

'Right. Which of you are the empyrrics? You two? That's good. You other two, I need one on comms and one helping with the right shoulder guns. Decide amongst yourselves but get to it. They're almost ready for another push.' He massaged his jaw and gave Palia a dark look. 'You might have noticed we're a bit understaffed. We've been fielding each mech with a complement of five of those Kept *sannots*. Last of ours died in the attack this morning. Caught by shrapnel. Pretty flames couldn't do much to help him then. We've got one more on loan from another mech, but I want him in the head with me. I like to know I can put a bullet in the back of his skull if he misbehaves.'

Palia wondered if it had been their Kept allies who had attempted the sabotage that got Progaeryon killed, or whether this was just a general dislike of them. Whatever the case, Bek and Tessa had already left. Whoever this man was, he was about to leave them, too.

'Wait!' she called.

'What is it? Haven't got all day.'

'Has anyone else been in touch with you recently? About Progaeryon?'

'No. Why would they? There's nobody cares for us but ourselves.' With that, he turned and left.

Palia's heart sank. Ferrash wasn't on Munab. If he wasn't here, that meant she had no idea where he was, or where to even begin to look for him. She considered the vastness of colonised space, all the little hidey-holes and forgotten places he could crawl into that she didn't even know about. That was if she even recognised him if she saw him, which she wouldn't. Maybe she had already passed him somewhere when Bek hadn't been with her. Or maybe Bek *had* been with her, and he just hadn't pointed him out. Palia was completely reliant on other people to spot him for her. She had taken them all on a wild chase across the galaxy for a ghost she couldn't catch.

'Focus, Pestor.' Lilesh's voice snapped her out of her thoughts.

Palia gave the archivist a small, unfeeling smile by way of thanks.

'Your answer to how we do this, Pestor, is that we survive.' Her attention fixed on the viewscreen, Lilesh drew in a deep breath and let it out as a loud sigh. 'All that matters in this fight is that the machine we stand in remains standing. You may feel the need to fight the Keepers. Don't. There are too many of them. You will lose. This is a battle of attrition.'

'I understand.'

'Do you? Do you understand how many of them will come against us? How long they will continue to do so?'

Palia let her smile widen into something a little more genuine. 'I understand that in seventeen minutes, our fleet will be directly overhead.'

Lilesh shot her a sideways glance. 'So will theirs.'

So the good news was that their fleet would be able to bombard the Protectorate's position from orbit. The bad news was that the Protectorate fleet would be able to bombard theirs as well.

Somewhere deeper within the mech, a gyroscope groaned into action. A jet screamed past outside. Palia swallowed and found another viewscreen to peer out of. So imperceptible was the mech's motion that at first, Palia's brain denied what her eyes saw. The barricade was moving further away – they were taking a step back. She couldn't see over the top of the barricade anymore, but for a sliver of the dusty horizon.

<Tessa, Bek, do either of you still have eyes on the enemy?> Palia sent.

Bek replied that there weren't any viewscreens in the comms room, so he was just as blind as they were. Tessa's answer took a little longer to come through. While Palia waited, a background chatter of motors and hydraulics played through the mech's structure. They had stopped moving, and the sound seemed to originate on one side, so she guessed at a systems test. Perhaps the other side would be next.

Tessa sent, <I can see them from the shoulder. If they come into range, you'll hear.>

Of course, Bek being on the comms meant Tessa on the shoulder guns. Palia envied her, able to see the fight approach rather than sitting in the dark. From Palia's vantage, the air carried the sound of engines in motion, of explosions. She had to blink sweat out of her eyes already, it was so hot inside the mech. Whose idea had it been to station mechs on a desert planet and not give them some kind of cooling mechanism in the crew spaces? Whose idea had it been to use mechs? Two feet could trip over anything, even thin air.

A coarse growl sounded from outside. The viewscreen showed smoke rising beyond the barricade. Those must be the Protectorate tanks. Palia turned to Lilesh, and the archivist mimed putting her hands over her ears.

Confused, Palia adjusted the sound abatement in her helmet's systems until the tanks were a distant purr. If anything, it just made her feel even more isolated from the outside world. She stared at the barricade, waiting for the first flash of green or orange to mark the start of battle. Then the whole mech boomed as its guns fired. The floor bucked underneath her. She fell, scrabbling at her helmet even as she dialled up the sound abatement in her implants. The sound vibrated through the floor, straight up her back and through her spine, shaking her teeth in her skull. She crawled to her feet with her head still ringing. Lilesh snorted with silent laughter, her shoulders shaking, one hand clenched around a handrail.

<Nice to know you have a sense of humour,> Palia sent.

<I favour slapstick.>

Palia staggered to her feet. Another shockwave hit them, but she managed to keep her footing. A rain of debris pattered against the hull, followed by a few louder clangs. When she looked back at the viewscreen, there was a chunk missing from the top of the barricade and fire and smoke belched up from behind it.

<Can you sense them?> Lilesh sent.

Palia crouched and braced herself against the wall beneath the viewscreen, her eyes closed. As she let herself slip into greater aware- ness, she slogged through the sun-like flare of Lilesh's presence in her peripheral, wading until she could judge its limits, acknowledge it in her mind and minimise her sense of it. When that was gone, nothing else remained. She had to go searching.

She found the Kept first. One directly above them, four in the mech to the left, five in the one to the right, just as the Munabi man had said. She felt, but couldn't quite place the sensation, that some of them noticed her attention and looked right back at her. It was like an extra dimension giving her a courteous nod. Palia couldn't see it, but the trace of it remained. Further out, she found it harder to maintain concentration. She had to get past the tired determination of the Munabi in the mechs first, and the pain the Kept used to fuel their powers, not so different from keepers after all, then the pain of the wounded and dying, which she mostly circumvented by ignoring anything in the town behind them. Then came the tanks, and the disturbing mental stillness of the people driving them.

Then came the keepers.

<I sense them,> Palia sent.

<About time. Ready yourself to shield.>

Palia tapped into the drumbeat tattoo of her nerves and wound it into the coiling energy that was a shadow of Lilesh's. She tried to reach further, but her awareness faltered and her head began to spin. Lilesh took her wrist in an iron grip.

<Don't take from anything outside yet. The sooner the keepers know we are here, the sooner they alter their attacks to target us specifically.>

Nodding, and with her awareness mentally superimposed upon her vision, Palia rose to peer through the viewscreen again. More shocks vibrated through her feet, but she couldn't tell which guns were which anymore. Their rounds carved smoking paths through the air above them, punching somewhere just behind the barricade. But the barricade itself was falling. Explosions pocked its length, great bursts of rock and fire ballooning out, collapsing, breaking from the top of the wall like the crest of a great wave. Tanks advanced over the shifting rubble. They crawled up one side, turrets pointing straight at her viewscreen at times, then threw themselves down the slope.

The mechs began to retreat, putting space between them and the tanks as fast as they were able, but no matter how much distance they gained, Palia could still see the tanks. The mechs might have been able to move faster, but they were big enough targets that they couldn't hide.

<Shield up,> Lilesh sent.

Palia teased the thread of energy out until it joined Lilesh's, then worked at maintaining that supply. It was the fastest way. Once beyond the confines of her own body, Lilesh could do with it as she pleased, and she was much better at shielding something as big as a mech. Palia wouldn't know where to start. She hadn't tried protecting something she was standing inside. She didn't want to try it now and blast a hole in the mech's chest by accident. She had done worse already, after all.

The first missiles struck the shield. In the slit view of the viewscreen, they burned star-bright into nothingness. Their payloads vanished.

Wherever one hit, the shield weakened for a moment, only to be replenished by the surrounding storm. The explosive retort of all that metal being fired towards them was echoed by nothing but silence, and the boom of ill-aimed shots striking the ground to either side of them. Palia clenched her fists tight by the edge of the viewscreen, keeping the shield fed with all the adrenal excitement pounding through her veins. It left her empty, and calm. She breathed out to relieve the tension, searching for the keepers again. If Lilesh and the Kept were preoccupied, perhaps Palia could be their early warning system.

Lilesh noticed the shift in her attention. <Now isn't the time to be calm, Pestor.>

Startled, Palia turned to face Lilesh. The archivist had both hands pressed against the inner hull as if she was the only thing keeping it upright. Sweat streamed down her face beneath the helmet. The moment Palia collected her thoughts to reply, something shifted in the peripheral of her awareness.

One second, she was staring at Lilesh. The next, she was sprawling. Her head spun. Her legs folded underneath her when she tried to stand. Iron sang in her mouth where she had bitten her tongue. Silence abounded. She turned down the noise abatement.

Groans and creaks grumbled through the mech. The floor had tilted a fraction from its last position. Had they been hit? Palia phrased the question to Lilesh, tried to find her in a cabin filling with smoke.

'—an go smear their *zashen* dirt in those damned mirrors of theirs. Crows in a *zashen* pack, I swear...'

'Lilesh?' Palia could hear her again now their guns had fallen silent. She wasn't sure if she'd hit her head and dreamed Lilesh swearing, though. 'Are you okay? What happened?'

Lilesh raised her hand out of the smoke and latched onto the nearest structural column, dragging herself upright. She swept her gaze around the room, eyes fixed on the ground, clearly trying to find the source of the smoke.

'We were hit,' Lilesh said.

Palia flinched as the shoulder guns chattered again. Breathing a sigh of relief to hear them firing, she looked around for a breach, but their room was still secure.

<The shield?> Palia asked.

<The Kept has it maintained, but—>

Another impact knocked both of them off their feet. Palia stayed on the floor this time. In a jolt of panic, she reached for the Empyrean, spread her awareness as far as she could. All the while, her panicked energy lashed around her body. It was a flow of sorts, but violent. Her whole body shivered with it. The keepers' presence sat out there like a great knife edge waiting to slice down on the world, the acid potential of their vacant souls a warning to steer clear.

Pain spiked as a jagged net of light in ten, twenty, forty of the keepers, unsettlingly familiar. Forty was more keepers than there were empyrrics in the Hegemony, wasn't it?

<Lilesh, they're—> Palia cut the message off halfway through thinking it. Where the keepers' pain grew, the Empyrean faded into life – controlled, unlike Lilesh's unleashed serpent. It spread across the ranks of keepers, then tapered, spear-thin. Its point sped towards them, bright enough in the fabric of the Empyrean that Palia knew it would be visible to her eyes if only she had time to look.

It struck the weak remnants of their shield just as Palia's fleet timer hit zero. A massive explosion shook the ground beneath them. The spear winked out. The keepers disappeared from her vision. She tumbled along the metal floor as it pitched and rolled, the gyroscope weakened from whatever had hit them before, no longer able to keep them still. Two more strikes sounded as concussive *booms*. Palia slipped again, her gloves squealing across the surface as she scrambled for purchase, but she fell against Lilesh at the far side of the room. Green fire pulsed along the lengths of Palia's arms. They tried to latch onto Lilesh's clothes and eat at them, but Palia jerked herself away before they had the chance.

She took a moment to draw the energy back into herself, teasing it into the flow, and stood up when she was sure the bombardment was over.

The viewscreen flickered, but stayed active, a mottled wall of smoke all she could see through it from this far away. She took a hesitant step closer, then another, reluctant to jinx the condition of the outside world. Until she saw it, they were both safe and unsafe, trapped in a world of uncertainty that at least held some chance of having a good outcome. But they hadn't died, and the Empyrean was bare of the keepers' influence for now.

When Palia finally got close enough for a good view, it was to the sight of rows of tanks burning, thrown to the side like a child's discarded toys, centred around three great craters in the soil.

Tentatively, she peered out from the hatch and up, where the Hegemony fleet hung as specs in high orbit, trading fire with something in the distance. They had made it to the orbital window. Palia let herself relax.

Then there was a flash of fire and the mech fell groaning backwards.

CHAPTER TWENTY-SIX

PALIA DIDN'T REMEMBER FALLING, but she woke on her side a moment later, everything in front of her limned with a green so vivid that its light seeped into the surroundings. It was like waking in a forest, if that forest were metal and broken and burning.

Suddenly someone yanked her up by her elbow. Palia staggered into Lilesh's arms, then regained her footing on the hull. The hatch to the ladder they had climbed up was on the floor – now a wall – in front of them. She tried hard to reconfigure her sense of direction now the mech's chest cavity had been turned on its side. Tilting her head up, she found the viewscreen. Half of it was dead, and the rest looked onto nothing but sky.

With Lilesh's hand still tight around her bicep, Palia paused, listening for any sounds of movement, mind turned to the Empyrean for any hint of activity there. Guns fired in the distance.

'I was hoping the fleet would do more damage than that,' Lilesh said. A large clump of hair had come free of her bun and hung over one half of her face. The archivist had to squint past a deep scratch in her helmet's face plate to see anything, but it didn't seem to be punctured.

Palia rolled her left shoulder and winced as pain shot through it. 'What—?'

'Keepers. They protected themselves from the hit and sent a retaliatory strike at us. The Kept had let his guard down. I couldn't dispel the shock.'

'Where did they hit?' She kept trying to get her bearings, spinning around to examine what used to be the ceiling.

<Bek? Tessa?> Palia sent.

Tessa's reply was instant. <Still alive.>

As Palia waited for Bek to reply, bile began to rise up her throat. Lilesh had to repeat herself before Palia paid attention: the keepers' strike had hit just above their level. She didn't know the extent of the damage.

<Where was Bek?> Palia asked.

Scuffling noises came from far on the other side of the ceiling that separated them from the top of the mech. Something banged against metal twice, three times, like someone trying to batter a door open. Palia rushed to the ceiling and pressed herself against it.

'Bek?'

Tessa replied. <That's me. I can't get to him. The hatch is jammed.>

Palia bit her lip hard enough to taste blood, then jogged over to one of the ladders that led to the mech's head. Behind her, she sensed Lilesh stiffen.

'Pestor, we need to get out of this wreckage.'

'Not without Bek!' She reached for the ladder and pulled herself up, gasping at renewed pain in her shoulder. Despite it, she managed to swing her legs over and get on top of it. Hoping this was the right ladder, she crawled to the hatch in the ceiling and, much to her relief, pushed it open with ease. She was less relieved when she saw what lay beyond it. The hull had crumpled inwards with the keepers' strike, buckled far enough that it touched the mech's spine, obstructing her view of the room.

Ignoring Lilesh's protests, Palia clambered over the hatch and dropped to the hull on the other side, jarring her knees against the buckled section. Oil dripped on her as she wriggled onto her stomach. She laid her cheek against the hull, craning her neck to search every part of the room.

Was that a hand poking out on the other side of the damage?

Palia swallowed her rising nausea and used her elbows to pull herself forwards. She had to skirt around the worst of the damage – she just couldn't fit through the gap – but as she got closer, she could see that yes, that was definitely a hand.

'Bek! Bek?'

<Have you found him?> Tessa asked.

Palia scrabbled over to him as fast as she could. Bek had his helmet off in favour of a mask and headset, which hung at an angle around his head, a loose wire sprouting from one of the earmuffs. His skin was pale, paler even than usual. At first Palia thought it was just from the small gash streaming blood on his forehead, but then she saw his arm.

'Bek.' She gripped one of his shoulders and gave it a light squeeze, but she couldn't take her gaze off his arm and the point at which it disappeared under the buckled hull in a pool of blood. 'Bek, please don't be dead.'

<Did you say dead?> Tessa sent. <What's happened to him? Pestor Tennic?>

Palia checked Bek's pulse. Something fluttered, but it could have been the growing vibration of tank engines outside. She licked her lips. Could she lift the wreckage away? Or would that just make the bleeding start again? It looked wrong – there wasn't enough blood. The pressure of the hull must be keeping it from flowing.

'The arm has to come off,' Lilesh said.

'Zash!' Palia flinched from the sound of Lilesh's voice, cracking her right shoulder against the hull. 'Ancestors! Warn me when you're sneaking up.' She stared at the edge of Bek's arm again, balled her hands into fists against her legs to keep them from shaking. 'If we tie it and lift the hull, we—'

'The arm's coming off.' Lilesh grabbed hold of her shoulder and tried to pull her back, but Palia kicked her away.

Chest rising and falling, she recalled the smell of burned flesh when she had scythed the Kept in two in the Munabi caves. Empyrean flames could cauterise flesh, when they were devouring it. It was the only way, but she couldn't bear the thought of hurting him, of having to explain what she had done when he woke up. She screwed her eyes tight, opened them again. Before she could change her mind, she purged the anguish of the decision, sending it shooting down her right arm where she kept it tight. When the flames formed a bright blade illuminating the room like day, she cut down into the flesh of Bek's arm just above the elbow. It sliced through like nothing was there.

Palia counted herself lucky she hadn't been able to feel the catch of bone – she might have thrown up otherwise.

'Good choice,' said Lilesh. A thin veil connected her and Bek in the Empyrean, a leeching of his pain and, it seemed, his consciousness, to Lilesh's reserves. 'Now pick him up and get moving. We don't have much time.'

Palia looped an elbow under the pit of Bek's undamaged arm and shuffled back the way she had come, struggling under his weight. She thought she could hear small-arms fire beyond the hull, beneath the sound of engines and tank treads crunching over dirt. Something made that *phwee* noise that bullets make when they skip over a metal surface, right by her head on the outer hull. Lilesh had vanished. Palia had the sudden image of being trapped alone in the corpse of a mech, cradling Bek's body until the water ran out or the tanks ran over them.

Her shoulder bumped against the lip of the hatch. When she twisted to shove Bek through the opening, Lilesh reappeared, hauling him out before Palia even had chance to ask for help. Palia clambered through after them, barely able to keep up. Lilesh found a hatch on the wall and stepped out onto the dusty ground with Bek slung over one shoulder.

<Tessa, we have Bek and we're out of the mech,> Palia sent. <Can you get out?>

Tessa had no need to reply – she and Palia locked eyes the second they both jumped out of their hatches, separated by the spread of the mech's legs. Tessa's eyes widened at the sight of Bek.

Palia turned. Beyond the mech's great splayed feet rose a second impromptu barricade. This one had artillery pieces along its length, manned by soldiers so coated with dust that they almost blended into the barricade until they moved.

When she turned back, Tessa had Bek over her shoulder instead of Lilesh, her knees wobbling under his weight.

'This has gone on quite long enough, Pestor,' Lilesh said. 'We need to go.'

Palia shook her head. Bek needed medical help, and soon, but they still had a mission. 'What about the research? We can't just leave it to the Protectorate. Think what they'll do with it.'

'Did you mark their research base on the map?'

'Yes, I...' Had the research team deleted the data when they had rescued them from the Kept? Palia couldn't remember. All the memories around it were dark.

'Then I'll get in touch with the fleet before they fly out of range. They can hit it from orbit.'

'What? No!' She might not remember the facts, but she remembered the caves, teeming with life and colour. 'We can't do that. It'll destroy the whole ecosystem.'

Lilesh eyed Palia as if she had grown extra limbs. 'Would you prefer the Keepers find a way to repeat what happened with Everatus Four and make more sonless mothers, or would you let a few sorry animals on a broken planet shuffle out of existence? One is a tragedy, the other a pity. I know which I am obliged to avoid.'

As Lilesh turned to issue the command, Palia lunged after her. She hauled at her arm. 'No. No! Don't do it. Someone else can go down there. It's—'

Lilesh backhanded her across the face. With a *whumph*, the Empyrean ballooned from the impact. Palia went flying and landed hard on her hip, skidding across the floor for several metres. Fury flashed through her skull. She rocketed upright, Empyrean fire curling from her hands and bursting at her seams.

Overhead, roughly where the Hegemony fleet sat in orbit, a light winked. Gunfire and shouts and running feet grew closer behind them.

Tessa scrambled out of the line of Palia's rage under Bek's weight. Palia stood for a moment, torn between lashing out at Lilesh and turning to face the enemy behind, between stopping an order Lilesh had probably already given and keeping them all from dying.

Snarling, Palia twisted on her feet, her anger building and building to levels so high that she couldn't imagine anyone being so burnt-up with it, let alone ever remember being so. Her tongue was welded to the roof of her mouth. Her cheeks ached under the pressure of her clenched jaw. The Empyrean swirled around her, a matrix of bright fire and dark emotions. It scared its reflection into the eyes of the Munabi soldiers retreating towards them. It glinted off the fabric of the barricade as its component parts slipped and tumbled. A moment's silence, then the barricade erupted outwards, bricks and bones bouncing from the flat bow of a tank. A prime target.

Palia drew her arms back, letting the rage build along her bones and boil in her blood. Then she flung them forwards, and all that fire punched through the air. It speared into the tank's front plating, annihilating in seconds what artillery might have struggled to pierce. Its occupants disintegrated. Her flames snuffed them out, then she re-centred and dragged their life forces back along the tail of her energy. The tank rolled forwards a few more paces before stopping, plugging the gap in the section of barricade it had torn through.

She held her breath, waiting for the rest to come. The Empyrean drenched her awareness, like the atmosphere itself was alive with its energies, like it was and always had been everywhere.

Glancing over her shoulder at Lilesh, she saw it. A thick beam of light split the sky in two. It flashed lightning fast, angling away from the fleet, there one second and gone the next. Clouds exploded away from its path. But for a low *whoom* from its passage through the sky, no sound accompanied it. Easy to believe that it had never happened. Easy to believe Palia had got carried away in the moment and seen afterimages of her own flames.

'There you are, Pestor,' said Lilesh. 'A neat incision. There was no reason for you to worry.'

Palia blinked from Lilesh to the point a mile or so distant where the beam had landed. It had seemed so insubstantial that she couldn't imagine it being a threat to the caves below. Her mind denied that such a brief and innocuous thing might have – had – just seared through the dark of the caves to take out their target. Lilesh was right, to some degree. It was precise. The damage was limited. The research wasn't theirs, but it was, hopefully, gone.

'Fine,' Palia said, dragging her mind away from the damage they might have caused. 'Let's get out of here.'

CHAPTER TWENTY-SEVEN

BIRDS FLITTED AMONGST THE foliage of the gardens in front of Palia. She had counted all of them now, she was sure of it, categorised them into their species, identified individuals, stopped one step short of giving them names. It felt surreal to go straight from the fighting on Munab to this. Fleet ships often had gardens – in fact, it was unheard of for the bigger ships *not* to have any – but the peace felt artificial. It felt like an illusion. A joke put there to mock her.

It reminded her too much of her garden on the orbital platform of Everatus IV.

'Pestor Tennic?' a woman said.

Palia looked up, expecting to see Lilesh, but it was the surgeon who had operated on Bek.

'How is he?' Palia asked.

'Awake, and if his flirting with everyone who walks past is normal behaviour for him, I'd say he seems mentally sound.'

'His arm?'

'Cleaned and covered.' The surgeon made an apologetic gesture. 'As he isn't a citizen, we haven't the scope to go beyond simple prosthetics. Regardless, we need his permission before any reparatory work. Did you want to go in and see him before we broach the conversation?'

Palia nodded, though her nerves tied themselves in knots at the thought of how Bek might react when he saw her.

'Alright. Through here.'

She followed the surgeon through the door to the ship's medical bay, stark and sanitary white, bright after all the floral colours outside. Bek lay on one of the beds near the back, making eyes at a nurse who had his back turned to him as he checked up on another patient. The wide sideways grin he wore slipped a fraction when he caught sight of Palia.

'Bek, hi,' she said. 'Sorry, I-I can go if you don't want to see me right now.'

He shook his head. 'No, it's okay.' The stump of his left arm waggled as he pushed himself upright, trying to complement the movements he made with his right, and he had to shuffle awkwardly to stay upright. He inclined his head to a chair, stump bobbing up and down, phantom hand patting the seat. 'You can tell me what happened.'

Palia shot the surgeon a questioning glance, but sat down when the woman nodded to indicate she could tell him. It wasn't like he was blind to the results, after all. The surgeon sealed the membrane behind her, blocking the space around Bek's bed from the rest of the room.

'Bek, I'm so sorry,' Palia said.

He laughed, the sound hard-edged. 'Why? You didn't cut my arm off.'

Palia sucked her lips between her teeth, put a hand over her face, tried to work out the best way to say it.

'You... *did* cut my arm off?'

'Okay, okay.' She held her hands up. *Slow down.* 'I'll start from the top and... get to that bit as soon as possible.' She explained how the keepers had downed the mech, how they had found him trapped beneath the buckled hull, how the only way to save him had been for the arm to come off. After that, she sat staring at the floor, a thousand excuses and ways to carry on the conversation filling her mind, but none of them allowed to come to her lips.

Bek sighed. 'Can't say I'm happy about it, but sounds like you didn't have a choice. Besides,' he waved his other hand at her and winked, 'this one's my favourite.'

'Wait, you're not angry?'

He fixed her with a level stare. 'Not about this. Maybe it's just the drugs they've got me on, I don't know. Think you're a splitting idiot for pushing as far as you did, though. We found Progaeryon was dead, we should have headed back. Didn't even complete the fake mission your Magister gave you.'

'Not as such, but...'

'What?'

Palia shifted in her seat, trying to escape the ergonomics it had shaped around her. 'Lilesh ordered an orbital strike on it.' Bek said nothing, just recoiled a fraction. 'I told her not to, but it was too late. The fleet sent an empyrric lance through the surface. I think it was precise enough not to do too much collateral damage, but I can't know for certain.'

'You realise there's a hab layer on top of the caves, right?'

'What?'

'Habitation. People live there.'

Palia slumped back into her chair, letting a huff of breath out through her nose. '*Zash.*'

'But as you said, precise, so' – he shrugged, then continued bitterly – 'who knows? Besides, they're just clones. Protectorate'll pump out new ones.'

Confused, it took Palia a few seconds to realise Bek must have overheard Steel on the other side of the mesa. 'Bek, she didn't mean it like that. She doesn't understand—'

'None of your lot do. And you're half right, anyway. They will just pump more of us out. Doesn't put the same people back, though. They're still dead.'

'I'm sorry.'

Bek sucked in his cheeks, staring into a middle distance beyond the privacy membrane. That left it up to Palia to break the silence, to find something good to say and get them focused on the next goal. But the thought of whether Ferrash had been on Munab without her notice had been eating at her. It gnawed in the silence between moments, and the silence that now stretched between them.

'Bek,' she said, ' you'd tell me, right? If you saw Ash?'

His forehead furrowed over his brows. 'Course I would.'

Palia breathed out a sigh of relief, conscious of Bek's gaze on her.

'What, you thought he could be standing right next to you and I wouldn't say anything? Pal...'

'Do you have a picture of him? Something to remind me what he looks like? In case you're not there.'

'Putting aside the fact that I *will* be there, no matter how many limbs I've left, sure. I've got his ID stored in my implants. Comes with an image. Here.'

The file came through to her implants and Palia hesitated over it before filing it away, unopened.

'You looking at it now?' Bek asked.

She shook her head. 'With the gaps in my memory, the way it gets sometimes... I'm not sure how I'll react. I'll look when I'm in private.'

When Bek raised an eyebrow, she blushed and opened her mouth to deny any funny business, but he waved her off. In the same moment, he caught sight of his stump and his eyes danced away again. Maybe he blanched, but it was hard to tell – his skin couldn't get much paler.

'On Hesperex,' she asked, 'do they make prosthetics?'

Tentatively, Bek drew his gaze back to the stump of his arm and examined it with pursed lips. 'No. Most vatters just get retired when they're broken. But if you're a Keeper, or you've power in the committees, or you can prove you'll be more useful to them with a fix than dead, you can get them regrown. Ash probably knows a dozen people can do it in the lower levels, provided the purge didn't catch 'em.'

Palia tried not to think too deeply on what 'retired' meant in the context of the Protectorate. 'Do you think you could get one?'

Bek inclined his head to the membrane, the stale white room beyond. 'Your friends here won't do it?'

'No, though I could probably pay for treatment on your behalf, if you wanted it done here. But I was thinking we should go to Hesperex next,' she said. 'If Ash isn't on Munab, he might be there.'

'Or he might be with the Laresics, or on Rythe, or in the Outer Reach.'

'But he might be on Hesperex. We have to start somewhere.'

Bek sighed. 'No, I agree, it's just...' He chewed his lips, as if wrestling with some unwarranted sense of guilt. 'I've been going through Ash's files. He was thorough, deleted most of them, but... there's a pattern to his actions over the last few years. He has contacts everywhere. I can't salvage enough of the data to see where, but there are a lot, and they all report back to him. I knew he had some, but I never knew the scale of it. I thought half of it was just him listening in to stuff he shouldn't.

'After the purge, I started to suspect. When he went missing...' Bek ran a hand along his scalp, letting his fingers tangle with his untied hair. 'I think he's up to something. Something he's been planning for a long time and doesn't want me involved with.'

Palia could see the hurt in his features even without the Empyrean to peer beneath. It frustrated her, to see evidence that Bek and Ferrash must have been close but have no memory of how close, of how deep that bond went, of whether either of them kept anything from the other, of how much it might hurt to have that flipped on its head.

'If he is planning something,' Bek said, 'it's more than likely going to be on Hesperex. That means we'll be wading straight into whatever mess he's about to cook up. Could ruin it.'

Palia glanced at the membrane, wishing it was one-way visible so she had something else to look at. 'What do you think it might be? At a guess? What would he choose to do with all that?'

Pity twisted as a bright coil in Bek's gut, the emotion reflected only a fraction on his face. 'Ash is an idealist, for all he doesn't always seem it. He'll be doing something good. Maybe not kind, maybe not safe, maybe not all too clever even if he tries to be, but it'll be good.'

The ship's guns boomed, far enough away that it could have been joggers running down an adjacent corridor. Palia wondered what they had fired at – the Protectorate fleet or the surface of Munab. What if Ferrash was trying to stop all that? What if he had some master plan to end the war and somehow bring peace to the Protectorate? She doubted it, but she hated herself for doubting it at the same time.

She scrunched up her face as she thought. 'If he's doing something good, and us getting in the way could ruin it... maybe we should just give up. Leave him alone.'

'Say we find him on Hesperex. If we ruin his plans, then... well, that's his fault for not telling us. If we don't, maybe we could help him.'

She could pose so many more possibilities. What if he didn't want help? What if they got there and found out he was up to no good? But she looked into Bek's eyes and saw the earnestness there, the desire to find what once was and hold it close, and never let it slip its rein again. She could appreciate that. So she nodded, and she promised that travelling to Hesperex would be the next step in their mission, as long as she could get permission for it.

As she got up, Bek reached out to grab her sleeve. He grunted when he realised he'd reached with the wrong arm. 'You haven't mentioned the others. Are they okay?'

Palia couldn't imagine he cared for the archivist's welfare, so she said, 'Tessa's fine. She was worried about you. She tried to break down the door but it was stuck on her side.'

Rather than making him blush, the words cast a shadow on Bek's face.

'What's wrong?' Palia asked.

'I'd hoped she didn't think too much of me.'

'Bek, you had sex. Even if her feelings go no further than that part of the relationship' – and when he flinched at the word, she imagined them going no further was exactly what he wanted – 'she's not going to be happy about you dying. Her being upset about that doesn't necessarily mean she wants... *exclusivity*, if that's what you're scared of. Exclusive isn't really the done thing around here, anyway.' Palia didn't know how true that held for the arsaeria, but the rumours inclined her to assume the same.

'Good. Good. Thank you.' Bek sighed and leaned back into the pillow that propped him up, letting the light from an overhead panel wash over his face. Then, with a wistful air and not a hint of humour in his voice, he said. 'I wonder how the weather is on Hesperex.'

Palia left him to enjoy his painkillers.

CHAPTER TWENTY-EIGHT

FABIEN WALLOWED SOMEWHERE JUST below consciousness, pinned down by a fug of sleep, vaguely aware of the pillow he had his face shoved into. A knocking came at his door. The sound sat in his brain for several seconds before it registered, then came again.

Groaning, he rolled out of bed, pulling upright at the last second so he didn't just flop straight onto the floor.

What time was it? These forty-eight-hour days were wreaking havoc on him. His brain felt like a pool of lead trying to run out of his eyeballs.

The knocking came again, measured and polite.

'Come in,' he said, voice thick with sleep.

The door opened and Lady Charante stepped in. Her eyebrows shot up when she caught sight of him, and Fabien rubbed a palm across his eyes to try forcing them to focus. He realised he was only wearing the thin trousers he had gone to sleep in and was both glad and a little embarrassed that it was Lady Charante who had opened the door and not one of the steward's staff.

'*Stars*, you look like vriar sick,' she said.

'Thanks.' Fabien cleared his throat so his next words wouldn't be as much of a garbled mess. 'Sorry, I'm having a little trouble getting used to the time difference.'

Lady Charante laughed and gave him a once-over. 'I can see that.'

Self-conscious at the attention, Fabien dragged himself to the wardrobe and pulled a plain tunic over his head. 'Is something wrong? I don't think I've got anything on my schedule for now.'

'Yes, sorry. I should have realised you'd be catching up on some shuteye.' She folded her arms across her chest and leaned against the doorframe, tilting her head back to regard him. 'I just figured you've been running about so much these last few days, you need a decent break.'

Fabien mirrored her stance, leaning against a windowsill and raising an eyebrow. 'I thought that's what I was doing by sleeping.'

'Yes, well.' She stared at him. 'Come on, you can't tell me you're not in the slightest bit interested by what I've planned?'

'What have you planned?'

She waved a hand. 'Ah, telling you would spoil it.' Then she slapped her thigh like she was beckoning a pet over and jerked her chin towards the corridor. 'Come on!'

Fabien followed, not quite certain how much of his obedience was due to his lack of sleep. As she led him along the corridor, he asked, 'This isn't just a very thinly veiled attempt to kidnap me, is it?'

Lady Charante just laughed.

As soon as they left the walls of the palace behind, Fabien began to wake up. The sky was grey and overcast, so he couldn't tell what time of day it was meant to be, but the chill air shocked his face. He wished he had put a jacket or some robes on. If night-time approached, it would only get colder.

Soon enough, he realised that they were heading for the vriarbeast tower. He stared up at it, its tip shrouded in mizzle, until they passed under the entrance. With the damp air pressing in, the deep, earthy, sharp-tinged scent of vriarbeasts was far more noticeable.

Lady Charante glanced back at him over her shoulder – the first time she had done so since leaving his room – and gave him another appraising look. At the bottom of the staircase, she held out a hand for him to wait and darted into a side room. She came out a moment later with a bundle of brown fabric in her arms. This she thrust at him, and Fabien turned it around a few times before realising it was a long, thick coat.

'Don't want you freezing up there,' she said.

He shrugged into it, grateful for the extra warmth, and refrained from asking where she was planning to take him. Maybe by 'up', she just meant the top of the tower, and he was in for a hands-on introduction to her world of vriarbeasts. Whatever she meant, she clearly meant it as a surprise. He would let her have that.

When he had the coat buttoned up, Lady Charante nodded, satisfied. Then she started up the stairs two at a time. Fabien's time-lagged body protested at the sight. He tried to keep up with her for the first few steps before resorting to a more normal pace. He was fairly certain he caught her chuckling at him the next time she happened to look back. In any case, he was gasping for breath by the time he reached the top.

Lady Charante clapped a hand on his shoulder. 'Come on, you'll have time to rest in a minute.'

Wheezing, Fabien staggered after her.

The stable she brought him to wasn't as large as the one he had landed in upon his arrival, and nor was the vriarbeast it contained. This one was about half the size, for a start. He could tell that even though it was curled up asleep. The feathers that rustled as its breath hissed over them were black, not green, with fine lines of yellow feathers patterning its back and face.

'Up, lazybones!' Lady Charante called to it, patting it on the rump. 'You were awake when I left you. You can't have gone back to sleep already.'

The creature snorted. Its eyelids slid open to reveal bright yellow eyes. It shook its long neck before giving Lady Charante a grudging look that might have been very similar to the one Fabien had given her earlier. He wasn't the only one whose sleep she had disturbed, clearly.

In no time at all, Lady Charante coaxed the vriarbeast to its feet and jumped onto the saddle it already wore, then hauled Fabien up behind her. The saddle had room for four passengers, with harnesses to keep them in. Fabien sat in the spot behind Lady Charante with his hands tight on the handhold that separated them.

They leapt from the side of the tower, the wind whipping Lady Charante's ponytail into his face so hard it stung. He spluttered, woken up a fraction more. The vriarbeast spread its wings – far wider than those of the larger beast – and soared.

They flew for perhaps thirty minutes, passing above the clouds and skimming over the shrouded landscape below far faster than Fabien would have thought possible. Eventually, the clouds beneath them cleared and they dipped back down again, plunging towards an oval lake that sparkled in the bowl of a forested mountain valley.

They landed on the slopes where trees gave way to rugged grass, the vriarbeast's wings snapping closed the moment it touched down.

Lady Charante hopped off, took a deep breath and said, 'Here we are.' Then she turned to help Fabien with his harness straps, freeing one leg with practiced motions before leaning across his lap to undo the other. When she was done, she took hold of his hand and helped him down to the grass. Fabien had met diplomatic aides who were less helpful.

'You know,' Fabien said, looking around, 'I do have a security attaché back at the palace. He's probably running around screaming at people and wondering where I am.'

'Oh, I ran it past him.' She waved the thought away, then started rummaging in the vriarbeast's saddlebags.

Fabien stared out across the lake. On the far horizon, the edge of the ice caps shimmered so bright he had to squint. The grass around them bustled with birds and butterflies and nodding red flowers. It looked like the sort of remote wilderness he could imagine Lady Charante enjoying, but he wondered how much a hand she had had in organising this. He found he didn't entirely care.

When he turned back, she had spread a cream blanket over the grass in front of a flat rock and placed an insulated box on it. She caught his eye and held a bottle in the air, waving two glasses at him with her other hand. 'A little something to cheer you up.'

With a smile, he went to join her on the rock. They sat beside each other, knees touching from time to time as they helped themselves to the food she had brought with her, the vriarbeast shuffling its snout through the grass beside them as it tried to catch butterflies.

After a while, Lady Charante said, 'So, what is it in the Hegemony that makes everyone want to have their tits out?'

Fabien snorted, spraying out the mouthful of wine he'd been savouring. 'I've been wondering when you were going to ask that question,' he said, although he hadn't imagined she would put it quite that colourfully. From her reaction to Consul Esselia showing up naked on their call earlier, he'd thought she would ask about it sooner.

'I'm a curious soul. Can't help myself.'

He shrugged. 'Not everyone does it. It's most popular amongst voidfarers and the arsaeria. They don't really see the need for clothes, and I guess some people see it as freeing. A few of them talk about showing the truest version of themselves.'

'Warts and all?'

'Warts and all.'

Lady Charante thought about that for a while, staring out at the ice. 'I guess they must be pretty particular about wiping their arses well, then.'

Fabien was glad he hadn't had another mouthful of wine when she said that.

'So that's not how you normally go about?' she asked.

'No, no. That's... not me.'

'I figured as much. You seemed awkward enough with your shirt off earlier.'

'I...' In normal circumstances, Fabien was perfectly content with nakedness. Changing with others, bathing with others, that was common enough back home. But Lady Charante made him aware of himself in a way that he wasn't normally.

Lady Charante laughed at the look on his face. A moment later, her expression darkened. She toyed with the stem of her wineglass, red brows knitted together. 'I heard you lost a son to this war?'

Fabien straightened his back and let out a sigh. 'Not to this war. To the magister before me.'

'Oh?'

'It wasn't intentional. He was just... collateral damage.' He picked at the grass by the side of the rock, stroked his thumbnail along the blades.

'I'm sorry,' she said.

Fabien smiled at her and jostled her shoulder. 'Now who's the one apologising for things that aren't her fault?'

'Were you with him when it happened?'

He shook his head. 'No.' Palia told him it had been instant, but he couldn't deny a part of him wished he could have been there to comfort him. He wished he could have done more than that. He wished he could have healed the rift between Palia and her mother, could have stopped her hiding herself away on Everatus IV in the first place. But it had been her private battle. She had wanted to fight it alone. He had respected that. 'His mother was with him, though.'

'Is she...?'

'She's still alive.' Fabien had never really had to talk about it before. The events surrounding Magister Lavennon's misdeeds and eventual death were practically legend across the Hegemony. Everyone knew who Palia was, and her connection to him. Someone had even commissioned a drama about it – a fact he regretted knowing as soon as he had heard it.

He glanced at Lady Charante out of the corner of his eye, conscious that his not being with them both might, perhaps, be an insult to the Rythian notion of a family unit. 'The situation between us is... complicated. We were together once, but not when Derren was born. He was grown in a vat without Palia's knowledge or permission.'

She screwed her face up in disgust. 'That's horrible.'

Fabien nodded, unable to find the words to say how much he agreed. 'Maybe if we did things more like Rythe, it would be simpler. We put our emphasis on ensuring support and enabling freedom.' He weighed his next words carefully. He suspected Lady Charante's level of access to him wasn't a coincidence on Rythe's part. 'I understand your relationships – your marriages – tend to be a little more... political?'

Lady Charante stared back at him, her expression hovering halfway between seriousness and a smile. At length, she turned to look at the lake and said, 'Sometimes. But there's an art that goes into it.' She leaned towards him a little. 'You know, the steward is skilled at many things, but he is a *devil* of a matchmaker. Only last year, he sent two of his council members on a trade mission together. Everyone thought it was a terrible idea – the two of them fought like leapvipers every time they were in the same room – but would you know it? They were engaged by the time they returned. As in love with each other as they had ever seemed to hate.'

A warmth spread through Fabien's chest as Lady Charante spoke, his heart beating a little faster with each word, with each glint of her eyes. When she finished speaking, she tucked a stray strand of hair behind her ear and glanced at him sidelong. They locked eyes, both well aware that they were being pushed together, both entirely uncaring. He found her hand on the cool surface of the rock and took it in his own, then leaned forwards to kiss her. She pressed back against him, her lips warm against his, tasting faintly of the wine and food they had just shared.

When they broke apart, Fabien matched Lady Charante's grin, ran a hand over her hair and said, 'Well, I would hate to break his winning streak.'

CHAPTER TWENTY-NINE

THE VIEW OVER RYTHE'S forest canopy was not a view Fabien could easily grow bored of. After spending most of his life on board ships, or making short hops between planets for visit after visit after visit, having a few hours to relax alone and undisturbed was a marvel. Still, as he watched the trail of vriarbeast winging their way in from the capital city's outskirts and spotted the flagship sitting in orbit above them, he knew it would be short-lived.

Rythe was a big planet. It operated at 2SC-14, which meant twice the length of a Standard Chronology day and a great chunk of time difference between him and most of the galaxy. The days felt like they could stretch on forever. In reality, the universe churned at its normal pace. Out there somewhere, his forces were putting their lives on the line for something half war, half humanitarian mission. He could relax here as much as he liked, but it would always be with that itch in the back of his skull, telling him to get back out there, to pull his weight.

This mattered, though.

He took a sip from his cup of morning *chalca* and glanced down the length of his suite. At the far end, past the dining room, greeting room and hallway, were his robes – his new robes, still being pieced together and adjusted by a joint team of fashion-minded arsaeria and Rythian tailors. That's what it was all about: joining, union, collaboration. That's what they told him, anyway, when they explained their concept of marriage. Gone was the parentage contract, the legality that didn't care who you spent your time with so long as you spent enough time with your children. The Rythians valued children – one need look no further than their nobility to see the weight they placed on them – but they valued the union that created them more. Or the same amount, perhaps. The lines were blurred.

In any case, a marriage was two things: a personal tie and one of diplomacy. He and Lady Charante already got on, but the accelerated timescale of the required diplomacy meant marriage had to happen sooner than he might have anticipated. In marrying Lady Charante, he was committing himself to a lifetime with her – and the Hegemony to an alliance with the Stewardship of Rythe – for as long as he was Magister. If it let him secure their help, he had to do it.

And it was hardly disagreeable.

His implants chimed a message: Palia, requesting a call. His heart fluttered in anticipation of sharing the news. He smiled and projected her image onto the mirror in front of him.

Palia blinked when she saw him. 'You're somewhere... quaint.'

'Rythe.'

'Oh. You're asking them for help? That'll take ages. It took centuries before they even let a delegation visit, and now you're asking them to war?'

'You're right. It would have taken ages.' Fabien tried to place the background of her image, but it could have been any ship in the fleet. At least it wasn't Munab. Archivist Lilesh had sent him her report on events. He hadn't read it yet. The archivist had made it quite clear through the tone of her message that it wouldn't make pleasant reading.

'It would have,' he said, 'but I... I had a happy accident, I guess.'

Palia raised a white-haired eyebrow. He still hadn't got used to the way it shocked her face. 'You... accidentally sweet-talked them?'

'In a sense.' He laughed, felt colour rise to his cheeks and wondered if she could tell. 'I met someone. I spent a great deal of my time talking to her rather than the Stewardship's diplomats. We came to an agreement.'

'How have you managed to make that sound contractual and romantic at the same time?'

'Well, I suppose it is.' Far from his usual experiences of romance, this one had promises bundled in with it. There was a definite point of no return, a moment of commitment. It felt right this way. No room for doubt and misconceptions. 'We've agreed to marry each other.'

In the mirror, Palia moved across the room and began to pour a cup of chai. 'Marriage? Is that even legally binding in Hegemony space?'

Fabien hadn't thought of that. One of his judicians almost certainly had, so he ought to ask them. 'It will be for me, unless I want a bunch of angry Rythians on my tail.'

'They're one planet, Fabien.'

He eyed the architecture around him: the smooth-hewn stone, the carved wood furniture, the natural fabrics. Such a contrast to their military technology. 'I get the feeling they're a lot stronger than any of us imagine, Palia.' Few ever saw a Rythian ship. Fabien had only seen four on each visit, as an escort to his arrival, and at the same distance their intelligence reports could boast of. They had nothing more. The Rythian fleet was an enigma.

'So what happens when you leave Rythe? Do you leave?' Palia asked. 'Or do you take her with you?'

'No. She's a vriarbeast breeder. If she leaves, she leaves her trade behind. I'm staying until a few days after the wedding party, then it's back to the war, but we'd like to travel together when it's over. They estimate it will take that long to prepare their fleet, anyway. They're not committing ground forces, but they need to bring some of their ships back from scouting missions.'

A colourful bird chose that moment to try battering through the window membrane and Fabien jumped at the noise. Palia's hair flashed as she turned to follow his gaze, even though the projection probably wouldn't let her.

'Fabien,' she said, her voice taking on a strained note, 'we didn't find him.'

Sighing, he paid more attention to Palia's face, noting the hard lines there, the bags under her eyes. So easy to be distracted by the unnatural white of her hair and miss everything that lay beneath.

'I know,' he said.

'We think he might be on Hesperex. I—'

'I can't let you go there, Palia.' She drew breath to argue, but Fabien held up a hand. 'Munab was different. It was already in the middle of a civil war and you would have had allies there even before our involvement. Hesperex is the capital. We've never successfully infiltrated it. And you may have been once before, but that just makes it more likely that a second appearance will draw more suspicion.'

'But—'

'If you want to argue this, you can argue it in person. Come to my wedding. Take a few more days to relax from what happened on Munab. Get the archivist out of your hair for a while. Hesperex isn't going anywhere.'

He could tell Palia still wanted to argue. She had that look in her eyes, that set jaw, those lips verging on a pout. But she was also tired and walking a very thin line between sanity and madness. Lilesh had warned him about a tipping point. While the archivist herself often seemed like she acted from the other side of that line, he trusted her opinion.

Palia agreed, in the end, so he sent her the details and found her passage to Rythe, then brought the call to a close. She had still been annoyed, not least because it had taken several days to get a call through to him.

Outside on the windowsill, the bird had come to rest. It puffed its feathers, irritated by the invisible wall that wouldn't let it past. The reaching warmth of the morning sun backlit its plumage in gold.

Someone knocked at his door. Fabien groaned and rose to his feet, expecting it to be the tailors. 'Come in!'

The door opened and a middle-aged man stepped through, his hair a close-cropped steely grey, his eyes a piercing red – some genetic mutation common to Rythe.

Fabien pulled himself a little more upright and bowed his head in greeting. 'Lord High Marshal.'

'Magister.' The marshal wore his undress uniform: a high-necked black jumper with his braids of office looped around one shoulder. 'Do you have any plans this morning?'

'I don't, unless I receive news from the fleet.' The question had been part rhetorical, mostly courtesy – the marshal would have access to his itinerary. 'Do you have something in mind?'

The marshal nodded, chest puffing, seemingly impressed by whatever he was about to state. 'The house of the steward has granted approval for you to review our forces. There are things you ought to know about it, should it be fighting by your side.'

It took a few moments for his words to register. When they did, Fabien raised his brows in surprise. He had just been given an invitation to see what no one outside Rythe had seen before, to his knowledge. He considered it odd how the marshal referred to the forces as 'it', as if they were a wholly separate and self-intelligent entity. Worth asking about later, perhaps.

'I'd be honoured to,' Fabien said, meaning it.

With a smile, the marshal turned and led the way through the palace complex, passing bustling congregations of workers making preparations for the wedding celebrations, until they came to the vriarbeast tower. Fabien kept an eye out for Lady Charante as they made their way up the spiral staircase, but he couldn't spot her attending to any of the beasts.

The beast they were to take waited ready near the top of the tower, preening its vivid green plumage on the embarkation platform that looked out over the capital city. An aide directed its acid-spitting face away from them so they could board, then the marshal encouraged it into the air, leaning into the wind with the tassels of his braid flapping behind him.

Fabien took the chance to watch Rythe unfold beneath them. This vriarbeast must have been a racing breed, clear from the smaller size and the lithe cut of its muscles. From his position in the saddle he could lean to see paved streets flash past beneath him. The great silver thread of the Eiberas river raced them to the falls. Then they passed them, the spray from where it cascaded to meet the lake below misting skywards to chill his skin.

They flew to a small section of the spaceport set aside from the passenger area – though both were small, given Rythe's few visitors. From there, they boarded a silver-hulled shuttle and headed to orbit.

'Where do you keep them?' Fabien asked as they sped out of the atmosphere. 'We didn't see any signs of a fleet on approach, aside from the escort vehicles.'

The marshal glanced at him sidelong, a corner of his lips turned upwards. 'We don't keep them in-system.'

Though it struck him as remarkably inefficient, Fabien refrained from criticising the stewardship's military strategy. Rythe only had the one nexus in their system. Unless they had come to an arrangement with a nearby system to hide their ships there, which Fabien would have heard of, the only space left was free space. If Rythe came under attack, any response would be limited by the speed of their engines. Was secrecy worth that cost? Perhaps they just relied on their knowledge of transit through the nexus for fore-warning, not that it would make a great deal of difference.

They slipped out of orbit and the marshal pointed the shuttle's nose towards the nearest edge of the Rythian breach, the thick swathe of debris-strewn nebulae that shrouded Rythe from the rest of the galaxy.

'Are we not travelling through the nexus?' Fabien asked, aware that any other travel could take months and surely the marshal wasn't about to take them on a long, dull holiday for two.

The marshal, who was busying himself with a manual check of all the cockpit instruments, just grinned. When he had completed his inspection of the last few panels, he keyed a code into a datascreen, then let his hand hover over an uncovered button on the dashboard.

'Is your harness secure?' the marshal asked.

Despite himself, Fabien hesitated. His lips were slow to form the word, 'Yes...'

The moment he said it, the marshal's grin grew wider still. He pressed his hand down on the button. In the canopy's viewscreen, the space in front of them marbled and shimmered. The ship's lights dimmed. A second engine hummed to life.

Then they ripped a hole in the universe.

CHAPTER THIRTY

THE BOX STOOD AT the side of the room, door still ajar from when Ferrash had escaped from it the other day. It was the siggerith in the room, the silent focal point that neither he nor his mother quite wanted to acknowledge. His leg ached, but the wound was shallow and he'd wrapped it with a numbing bandage. Son and the others warmed themselves in a room carved further into the mountain. They hadn't all made it up. It had been Ferrash's idea to head up to the mountain base, and a part of him wondered if he maybe should have tried a little harder to find another safe spot in the lower levels.

His mother had trailed at the back of the group, and Ferrash was well aware that those who had fallen hadn't left corpses behind.

Ayt had saved them. Ayt had covered their trail. Ayt was still here, staring at him as he clattered around the small stove, trying to do anything that meant he didn't have to look at her or speak to her. As he did, he sifted data through his implants. He had a leak in his web of contacts. Several leaks. His web had too many holes in it.

'Have you realised yet?' his mother asked.

Ferrash didn't turn around. But the silence grew and grew, pressing against his back like her gaze had weight to it.

'Realised what?' he asked eventually.

'Your mistake.'

He turned to glare at her over his shoulder, one arm shoved deep in a storage cupboard to get to a heating unit.

'Your mistake,' Ayt said, 'is believing you can achieve any of this without coming out bloody. You want a revolution. You want change.

Look at the last civil war we had and see how much death that caused.'

'That was keepers.'

She shrugged. 'So we have stronger weapons than you. A weapon is a weapon. If someone intends to cause harm, they will use whatever they have, and the strength of what they have available will only affect the scale of the disaster.'

Ferrash hauled a heating unit out of the cupboard and connected it to the three others on the stove. 'Why did you escape and leave me here only to come back and help us?' He didn't ask why she hadn't outed him as Proglimen, in case he was just being exceptionally paranoid and she had no idea.

'The Judiciary would have noticed I was missing,' she said. 'No matter how clean you think you made your trail, they would have found you and followed you here. So I went back and fed them a story about the Kept. It didn't confuse them as much as I had hoped. They already had a lead on your little group of friends.'

'You admitted you got kidnapped?' That was a career-ending move, even for a Keeper.

'I told them I allowed myself to be taken so that I could report back, or take them down myself. Given I was put in charge of keeping tabs on them, I knew of a pocket I could mention to make the lie convincing.'

'And what's your plan now?'

'You asked for my help. I intend to give it. What are your next steps?'

Ferrash finally turned to face her. He leaned against the stovetop with his hands gripping the edge. If he didn't, it would be all too easy to grip his pistol instead. 'I need a way to get on board the Prime Nexus, affect the flow of the Empyrean through it, and stay alive as long as it takes to achieve what the Magister intended.'

'What about your revolution?'

'I'll set it off when the Empyrean's gone.'

His mother made a grunt in the back of her throat and wandered over to examine the box. 'Have you thought about what happens after that?'

'There are people in the committees ready to take over. They have a long-term plan for how to settle things down again, make life fairer.'

'And in the short term, should they all die in the fighting? You are being remarkably short-sighted over this, or perhaps over-long. Think about it, Ferrash. The Protectorate works on a delicately balanced system of debt and reacquisition. We have no official currency. What we acquire from nations beyond our own we either barter for or steal. If your revolution affects the balance of the committees, it is bound to send the people you apparently care for so much spiralling into a poverty they were previously protected from, if for society's benefit more than their own. How do you plan to counteract that?'

A few weeks ago, perhaps, he would have shot down her question. He had thought of everything. There were no gaps in the plan. His algorithms all predicted a high chance of stability should everything go smoothly. But it wouldn't, would it? Nothing had been, lately, and here he was gambling with the fate of billions on the basis of a flawed model. Finance would be an alien concept to most of the committees. They would need help, guidance, resources for when they inevitably got it wrong.

'Stay here,' he said. 'I'll go talk to someone.'

Ayt shrugged as if to say she had nowhere better to be anyway, then took Ferrash's place at the stove. She hadn't left any witnesses to her betrayal, so perhaps she would wait a plausible length of time before returning to the Keepers, if she wanted to stay there undercover. It was only the need to keep his contacts safe that made Ferrash leave her there unguarded. Doubt knotted itself in his chest as he walked away. Fear spiked along the flesh of his back, but she didn't send any flames after him.

Following a series of sloped corridors further up through the mountain base, Ferrash pulled his coat tighter. It was colder up here. Fuel was scarce, so he hadn't heated it far above outside temperature. Since most of his communications were with Five-Fifty-Four, or at least relayed by contacts in the city, he didn't need to come up here often.

When he reached the comms array in its sealed room, he found it coated in a thick layer of dust. He pressed an arm over his mouth and nose and swept the chair clean before taking a seat, then did his best to dust off the controls with the end of his scarf. He cast about the space near his feet, found the generator and switched it on.

It hummed to life, red light blinking then shifting to green. The built-in heat exhaust began to kick warm air against his legs. A moment later, lights on the array began to blink on as well, indicating the status of each relay.

There were a lot more severed connections than last time. It looked like he had no way of directly contacting the far side of Hesperex anymore. Depending on the coordinates, it might be because those were mostly dead cities, after the purge, and the Protectorate had taken out some of its own infrastructure by accident or intent in the process. They hadn't repopulated the cities. The Protectorate was finally admitting that Hesperex was a lost cause. No point filling dead cities on a dead world.

He flicked a few switches and cross-referenced his implants' data to make connections to whatever arrays weren't being actively monitored. It paid to be careful. His array bounced messages around the planet hidden within the noise of other communications, but sending them right under the nose of listeners would just tempt fate.

At last, he sent, <Ducat?>

He waited for a ping to come back from one of the relays. No telling if Ducat and the Observers were still in the submarine or whether they had made it to Sixty-One-Eighty-Three. If the former, and the sub was near a low-lying relay, they should still be able to make contact. No matter where they were, they would be far enough away for a noticeable time delay between replies.

Ducat's reply came a moment later. <You have instructions?>

The discrepancy between Ducat's speech style and their implant communications always threw Ferrash at first, but the identifier was definitely theirs.

<Not instructions,> Ferrash sent. <A query. I need to find someone in the Hegemony.>

<What makes you think I'd know about that?>

Ducat was toying with him. Ferrash knew full well that they smuggled resources and intelligence between pretty much every faction out there, the Hegemony included. Locating individuals in all that mess was less Ducat's line of business than reeling off the state of shipping in each system across the galaxy, but some people were easier to keep tabs on than others, some ships harder to lose sight of.

Ferrash asked, <Do you know where the Magister is at the moment? Or the flagship? Either will do.>

<Easy answer to that. Word's all over. Admiralty's in a state about it, considering the implications.>

<That answer being...?>

<Sannot's getting married. Some woman on Rythe. And after the ceremony, boom, suddenly there'll be another fleet against us. I'd be pissing myself if I were the Admiralty, too.>

Ferrash thought back to his time on Rythe, the military that had always seemed a little too secret, the intelligence that had always seemed to know more than it let on, but never acted on any of it. If he used the same cover he had used last time, they would probably notice. If he used another... they'd probably notice anyway. They'd keep an eye on him, monitor every word he said, but they'd let him in. Maybe baiting spies was a sport for them.

<If I send you an identifier, can you secure an invitation for it?> Ferrash asked.

<Sure. Can't get you transport, though. You'll have to sort that yourself.>

Ferrash nodded, even though Ducat couldn't see him. <Not a problem. When can you have it ready by?>

<If you set off now, the invitation'll be ready by the time you get there.>

<Thanks. Send me it when it's done. How far have you got with the data I sent you?> Ferrash had given Ducat all the data he had

scraped from the prototype and the Magister's implants. He might need that technology recreated and improved upon to destroy the Empyrean for good.

<Not far, but not nowhere. Concentrating on survival now, research later.>

That was fair, and sensible, but Ferrash hoped he would be able to pull off the plan before everything went crazy. He thanked Ducat and shut the relay down.

A wedding, right in the middle of wartime. Ferrash could see the reasoning for it, especially if it brought Rythe onto the board after so many centuries' isolationism, but it felt like a sidestep away from real issues. No matter. Rythe was neutral ground – easier for Ferrash to get to than the flagship, which might well have his genetics stored in its database from his last visit. The steps he'd taken to hide his in the Protectorate might not work in the Hegemony.

He turned the array off and walked the length of corridor back to his mother. That she was still there surprised him. That she offered him a cup of brew surprised him even more. He waved away the offer.

'You have a solution?' she asked.

'I have a way to talk to the person I need to talk to.' Ferrash pulled his skis from where he had left them against the wall, checking Five-Fifty-Four's grid to make sure they didn't have any cameras trained on the mountainside.

'I'll let you know if anything comes up while you're gone,' Ayt said. 'And I'll have a think about the best way to put your plan into action on the Prime Nexus, if you could leave me the details...'

A curl of steam wafted from her mug past her eyes. She sipped from it. She seemed completely at ease but – and Ferrash couldn't tell if this was just the tension of the pain mesh or a genuine expression – her brows were downturned, her eyes narrowed not in anger, but in... something he couldn't quite place. It sent a shiver down his spine. In that moment, he wasn't afraid of her, he was afraid of her being something she was historically not.

With a huff of breath, he reached inside his coat and pulled out a data chip. He took two steps across the room, holding it out for her to take, and gritted his teeth when her hand brushed his in taking it.

'That's the backup,' he said. 'Don't lose it.'

He turned to leave, the skis over one shoulder, then hesitated. *Don't open doors that hide emotions.*

Looking back over his shoulder, he saw her sat there still, the straggly mess of her hair resting limp on her shoulders.

He cleared his throat. 'Progaeryon's dead.'

His mother didn't move, just sat there, examining the data chip as she held it in front of her face, the mug resting on one knee. Then she nodded, slowly. 'I guessed as much.'

'He wasn't a prog.' His father's name suggested he should be the progeny of the Aeryon empyrric bloodline, but that had been a lie. 'He was vatborn. Read it in his ID.'

She curled her hand around the chip. 'You met him?'

'Briefly. I wasn't there when he died. That was after I'd left Munab.'

'He offered to take you, you know, but it would have looked suspicious.'

Ferrash rolled his eyes and made to leave again. 'Don't be ridiculous.'

But she called out after him, even as he left the room behind. 'Dodging the breeding programme runs in the bloodline. You chose to run from it. We chose to alter the parameters.'

What *that* meant, Ferrash thought as he slipped out through the hatch and began to slide down the slope, was that she had known. She had known he had next to no chance of being empyrric. Yet for fifteen years of his life, she had tried to force him, tried to make him be like her.

Thank the stars he had never become so.

CHAPTER THIRTY-ONE

THE STEWARDSHIP OF RYTHE could own this galaxy if they wanted to. That's what Fabien thought as he sat staring at a sky lightyears distant from where he had been moments before, at a shining cloud of fighting ships that stretched away above and beneath and to either side. He didn't know what question to start with, but with an image to maintain that didn't involve his mouth hanging open like a loose flap of skin, he had to say *something*.

'An integral nexite drive?' Fabien asked. But it couldn't be. Nexuses and nexite drives could propel you across space, but nowhere near this fast.

The marshal shook his head. He manoeuvred them between the seemingly endless ranks of ships. 'A drive of our own devising. It doesn't contain nexite.'

That made sense. Rythe didn't import any nexite and, as far as Fabien knew, didn't mine any of their own. They wouldn't have been able to outfit a fleet this large with nexite drives. Whatever they used instead, it was something different, maybe even something the rest of the galaxy hadn't clued onto being worth anything. Fabien wondered how much other technology got missed out on just by being overlooked.

'How does it work?' Fabien asked.

'That, I'm afraid I'm not allowed to tell you. The Stewardship has to have some secrets, sir.'

Fabien was sure the Stewardship had many. 'But can it go anywhere? Anywhere in free space and back, of its own volition?'

'Yes. Your flagship can do the same.'

That was true, but the flagship had to recharge at a nexus every so often, and it was the only ship in the galaxy with such a drive. Fabien didn't know if the design would be possible in a smaller ship. Each nexus was built from the same template – the only difference between the flagship and any other nexus was that they had built a ship around it.

'And all these ships have the same engines?' Fabien asked.

'They do.'

Fabien tried to imagine the attack on Corumma if the Protectorate hadn't had to jump blind. He tried to imagine the galaxy if anyone could get wherever they wanted, whenever they wanted, without any kind of warning before they got there. He couldn't. It would be chaos.

Putting the thought behind him, Fabien examined the ships they passed. Most were incredibly small, even smaller than some of the one-man fighters his fleets fielded, with perfectly smooth, spherical hulls. They had no docking hatches, no landing gear that he could see. Some bigger, elongated shapes lurked in the distance – ships that he might conceive of as big enough to hold a reasonable crew complement. A part of him doubted they did.

'They asked me to bring you here,' the marshal said, scrolling across his data screen with one finger, 'so I could impress upon you the core notion of our armed forces.'

Fabien nodded. 'It's all driven by machines.'

'An engineered intelligence, yes. Other than the fact we have had no reason to fight, it is the reason we have avoided war until now.'

'Why?' It was an odd way to put it.

'Imagine if it wasn't just us. Imagine if everyone fought their wars with unmanned ships. How much more distant would it be, to sit back and watch dots on a screen wipe each other out, knowing that no life would be harmed? How easy to extend that sensation to the first humans caught in the crossfire, the first real ship, the first planet? If there aren't people in the cockpits pulling the triggers, there's no one to wear a conscience. Maybe it would work. Maybe wars would become like games and we would never have to spill blood again. But we doubt that.'

'What changed your minds?'

The marshal turned his head, measuring him, trying to gage a response before he had given his own. 'The Protectorate. This is an opportunity to take a world out of the hands of empyrrics. The Keepers can't draw emotions out of machines. They can't use their own essence against them. By taking Munab, we would be sending a message to the galaxy that the time for empyrrics to rule is well and truly over. Your bloodlines have almost died out. The Laresic Merchant Republic and the Confederated Outer Reach didn't have any to begin with. The Protectorate is all that's left, and they don't plan on going quietly. The house of the steward requests that Munab be handed to our administration, once the battle is done.'

Smiling, Fabien pretended to inspect the ships. He wondered if the Stewardship meant this as a threat – to have the leader of the Hegemony alone and vulnerable in free space, poised over a question of territory.

'What are your plans for the planet?' Fabien asked.

'Stabilisation, followed by a gradual ceding of control to the local population, resulting in a semi-independent relationship not too dissimilar from the way your Hegemony manages its planets.'

There were far less reasonable avenues they could pursue. Munab wouldn't be an easy sell for potential colonists, either, with its hot climate and poisonous atmosphere. The only thing of worth on its surface, that he knew of, was the nexite mines.

Fabien peered behind them in the canopy, tried to make out familiar constellations in the distance, found none. 'Can I suggest an amendment?'

'I can pass on any comments and have talks established with your consuls.'

He nodded. That was something. 'How about a joint effort? You allow some of our people to settle on the planet and integrate with the local population. You let them mine and export the planet's nexite – taxed, of course. A joint venture implies joint defence. That far into Protectorate space, they might need that extra bit of dissuasion.'

'The house's plan was to remove the nexus from the system, keep them cut off from everywhere but Rythe until they've established themselves.'

'That cuts off any route for trade, and Munab doesn't strike me as self-sufficient. Unless you would prefer us to travel via Rythe and go aboard your' – Fabien waved a hand, unsure what name Rythe's alien technology went by – 'blink ships.'

The marshal inclined his head. 'We can discuss it. Are you satisfied with the fleet? We have unmanned vehicles for ground attack, as well, just significantly fewer. Until now they've only seen service as scout ships.'

'I'm more than satisfied, thank you. And thank the house for me, for letting me see this.'

'My pleasure, sir.' A light touch on the control column and the marshal had them pointing back in the direction they had come, sighted at the dual horizon formed by the fleet. Fabien readied himself, more nervous now that he knew what was coming.

'Time to get back for your wedding,' the marshal said, and hit the button.

Lady Charante ambushed him upon their return. At the bottom of the vriarbeast tower and as soon as the marshal's back was turned, she crept out from a side room, snuck a hand around Fabien's waist and drew him into a kiss. They broke apart a moment later, her with a mischievous glint in her eyes. The marshal examined the rustic architecture of a nearby building to pretend he hadn't seen.

Fabien let a smile crease his face. 'I thought we weren't meant to see each other? Something about omens.'

'Pfft. Omens.' She waved a hand, as if wafting away a bad smell. 'That starts from tonight, anyway. Consider this a gift to last you until after.'

Thinking she meant to kiss him again, he leaned forwards, but she turned with a wink and a smile and strode back into the tower, a bundle of tack over one shoulder.

Three days to go until the wedding. Three days until he had to argue with Palia about a return to Hesperex. Three days until he had to start weighing his presence at the subsequent celebrations with the shadow of the war he was meant to be fighting.

With one day to go until his wedding, Fabien borrowed the house of the steward's council chamber for a remote consulate meeting. Those consuls still aboard the flagship in orbit were the first to fade into view, followed closely by those scattered throughout the Hegemony. Esselia didn't appear, but that was to be expected, given her posting with the fleet by Munab. Either she deemed her comms too prone to interception by the enemy or she was just too busy to reply.

'May I say, Magister,' said the remaining prime consul, 'that we all wish our heartfelt congratulations upon you for your wedding tomorrow. May your ancestors smile upon your match and upon whatever children may come into your care.'

Fabien nodded through a strained smile. The prime consul remained a staunch traditionalist, but Fabien appreciated the sentiment.

Fabien cleared his throat. 'I've called you all here today because I want to initiate the second phase of the war on the Protectorate. Those of you I have spoken to recently may already know of it, but so far I have spoken only in vague terms. Consul Esselia has organised a report into its feasibility and sent me the full details. So we have a plan, and we have a good indicator of success.'

Bringing up a projection of the galaxy, Fabien walked into the centre of the room and highlighted five systems: Hesperex, Everatus, Falles,

Lig and Empyros. Together, they formed a sort of kite bisecting the starmap, or a spear point thrust into the heart of the Protectorate. It depended on perspective.

'The plan is that we use our nexus network to drag the Prime Nexus out of the Hesperex system and into our own space. The advantages to this are twofold. One: much of the Protectorate's administration will be confined to Hesperex and unable to travel elsewhere. Two: any expansion to their range will be limited and time-consuming without the Prime Nexus' manufacturing capability. Thanks to Esselia's investigation, we have confirmed that moving the Prime Nexus should be possible. Our scientists have calculated that we need four nexus to stand a chance of moving it.

'The nexus in the Everatus system is, for obvious reasons, no longer needed. Falles, Lig and Empyros are self-sufficient systems and should be able to stand a period of isolation without any issues. However, if we choose to take this approach, we run the risk of losing one or all of the nexus we commit. Before I go any further, is that a risk we are willing to take?'

Around the room, there were nods of agreement. Fabien counted each of them, made sure that no one looked like they wanted to object. He was surprised, but only a little – the Prime Nexus was the galactic prize. Everyone wanted it. Everyone except Rythe, perhaps.

'Okay,' he said. 'Then I need someone to get in touch with the system governors for those three worlds. Let them know we plan to move their nexus, but frame it as being a defensive measure if you can. Make sure they are prepared for a few months or years of isolation if needs be, and coordinate with other systems to get them any supplies they might be missing. We can redress any imbalance later.'

After another minute or so, Fabien had his volunteers, and they promised to report back to him as soon as the planets were ready. With any luck, the war wouldn't force their hand into attempting it any sooner.

He returned to stand by his seat at the edge of the room and ran his hand along the smooth stone of its backrest. He met the gaze of each of his consulate in turn. He, maybe more than any other Magister in history, stood at a turning point, a pedestal of responsibility that was far too easy to fall from. Succeed, and the Hegemony would get back what once had been theirs: the Prime Nexus. Fail, and he would have left billions of his people in the dark.

He nodded to his consulate. 'I will speak to you all again in a couple of days, with a wife by my side and Rythe at my back. When that day comes, let's see if we even need to carry this plan out.'

CHAPTER THIRTY-TWO

IT TOOK FOUR JUMPS for Ferrash to get to Rythe. First to Munab, so he could lose himself in the chaos of the warfare there, then to Yennik, a quieter system that wasn't often monitored. After that, he jumped across the border into the Laresic Merchant Republic with Seneher, followed by Lariss itself.

On one of the trade stations orbiting Lariss, Ferrash hid himself. He made contact with the fringes of his network, got some clothes fit for Rythian nobility. He worried that if Bek was also attending the party, he might recognise Proglimen's face – or worse, Ferrash's underneath it – but he didn't have time to source a new one. He had to take his chances with Proglimen's.

Now Ferrash sat in the cockpit of a borrowed racing ship, letting the passing lights of the nexus lane soothe him through his closed eyelids as he hovered a layer of consciousness above sleep.

He could have bought more inhibitors on Lariss. Though the Laresics had no need for a stockpile, they had the technology to synthesise them from trace samples. Ferrash hadn't asked for any. As he drifted, he tried to convince himself that it was for the best, that his reliance on them had gone on long enough, that his mother had given him all the tools to control his emotions without needing inhibitors, even if she hadn't been the kindest teacher. But beneath the calm, there was a background note of panic.

Keep it together.

An alarm triggered in his implants, nudging him to wakefulness. Ferrash opened his eyes just in time to see the last of the green lights slip away. They opened onto the void of the Rythe system.

Rythe's response was almost instantaneous. Two minuscule ships hove into view either side of him, keeping pace despite his fast exit from the nexus.

'*CVL Etheron*, this is Rythe approach. Please submit your travel approval and wait outside high orbital,' came a voice over the radio.

Ferrash looked around, trying to catch a glimpse of his escort, but they had slipped beneath his canopy. He sent the files over. Today, he was Juul Aranthe, a returning Rythian expatriate in truth long deceased. Aranthe was the same identity he had taken on his last visit, so at least he was being consistent. As luck would have it, he had looked a little like a younger Proglimen back then. If Rythian intelligence matched him in their database, everything would line up at least long enough for him to get in and out.

After a few minutes' deceleration and before he had reached high orbital, the voice came back and told him he had permission to land on the surface. Breathing out a heap of tension, he took hold of the control column and keyed in a path to the landing site. Two borders down, only the palace to go.

Last time, Ferrash had travelled aboard the vriarbeast transports from spaceport to city. To save mingling with too many people who could later identify him, and so he arrived late enough that the festivities would be well underway and he could pass without notice, he chose to walk this time. It had been too long since he had walked on ground without snow, seen real trees, breathed fresh air uncorrupted by the Protectorate machine. His boots pinched as he walked, but they would settle soon enough. He had opted for the full ensemble: a slit-necked shirt, black trousers belted with a sash around his waist, a maroon half-cape sweeping over one shoulder. It would have let him freeze to death on Hesperex. Here, it was comfortably warm.

Ships continued to filter into the landing zone. Ferrash counted five – three of those shuttles from bigger ships – in the time it took him to climb the well-worn steps to the city gate.

He stood watching the last of those touch down, sunlight brushing over the hull markings that identified it as a Hegemony ship. Quite a few late arrivals, by the looks of it, but most were only there for the celebrations. They'd go on for days yet. Ferrash only intended to stay for one of those. Any longer and he risked bumping into people he shouldn't, or missing out on something back on Hesperex.

'Are you coming in, sir?'

Glancing back at the gate, Ferrash found a speaker mounted near head height. He nodded to where he thought the camera must be. 'Yes, sorry. Just admiring the view.'

The gate swung open. He marched into the streets, his cape billowing out behind him. The shadow of a vriarbeast rushed across the flagstones in front of him. In its path lay the city, the palace complex, the Magister and a difficult conversation.

When Ferrash was close enough to the palace to hear strings carried on the breeze, he noticed his mouth was bone dry. Steps faltering, he licked his lips, tempted by the streetside wine merchants. But some buried part of his mind kept pushing him forwards. Something about the palace, the way it loomed over everything... it felt portentous. Stupid way of looking at it. He was as safe here as he had ever been. Nothing special about a fancy castle on a big hill. Nothing but the associations Ferrash's memories made with the person he was there to see.

The guards at the palace entrance didn't seem to notice his strained expression. They registered his fake identifier and let him pass with courteous respect, and he strode past them. He dug a thumb beneath the fabric of his belt in lieu of gripping a pistol.

Where would Fabien be?

Ferrash forced himself to relax into the flow of the music – physically, at least, though he remained on edge. A look around the entrance hall told him this wasn't where he needed to be. Some arsaeria lounged in one corner, catching each other up on gossip. Two groups meeting each other by chance and having a conversation on the spot, he guessed, since some were well and truly drunk and the rest were just excited. Besides them, the doormen did their best to appear as furniture and an older Rythian noble snored on a lounger. Ferrash smiled at an arsaeria who happened to catch his eye, then moved deeper into the palace before they could take it as an invitation.

How did weddings work? Ferrash hadn't had time to do research. He knew there was a formal part and a celebration, and the formal part was done, but he had no idea if the celebration was meant to be structured. It didn't have an itinerary, but that didn't guarantee scheduling freedom. It just all seemed so empty. The strings drifted through unfamiliar corridors, accompanied by a conversational hum and scattered laughter, but there seemed to be no source. The next room he passed into was empty. The next hosted a line of chatting celebrants only because they were waiting by the toilets.

At a junction, he followed where he thought the strings led and suddenly found himself in an open courtyard. Thin silks separated it from the sun's rays and hundreds of people milled around an ornamental garden. Musicians sat on a flute-columned balcony directly opposite, their notes joining with the quiet burbling of an ornamental river.

Ferrash paused to take the scene in, accepted a thin cylindrical glass when one of the staff pressed it into his hand. Then he made a show of enjoying the scenery. He strolled through the garden, affecting what he thought might be an appropriate amount of appreciation for the arrangements, and made small talk with the people he passed close to in an effort to mingle. What the circuit told him was that Bek wasn't here, and that was good. Especially since he doubtless wouldn't be invited were it not for association with *her*.

Ferrash frowned into the stream, breathed clear of the thought, then turned his head to examine the dais.

The Magister – Fabien – leaned with a forearm resting against the railing, his face glowing with the breadth of his smile. He held hands with a red-haired woman a fraction taller than him. A safe bet to assume she was his new wife.

An informal queue led up to the dais, clusters of people chatting together as they waited to speak with the happy couple. No doubt they would make a fuss if he tried to skip ahead, even if only in tuts and whispers.

The hairs on the back of his neck prickled. He had a lot of eyes on him – no doubt some that he couldn't see, too. But try as he might, he couldn't move away from the spot. His feet were rooted to the floor, to the solid rock of Rythian architecture, his gaze locked on Fabien's face. As if that attention brushed his cheek, Fabien turned, smile dipping momentarily as he sought out the source of his discomfort. His gaze swept over Ferrash, found nothing, returned to the man he was talking to. With each second, his brows creased further. When the man gave his farewells and walked away, Fabien spared a moment to search the crowd again.

Their eyes met.

Fabien frowned at Ferrash, confused. Then he brought his wife's hands to his lips, said something to her, made his way through a door at the side of the dais.

Ferrash didn't take his eyes off him until he was out of view. He started to follow, but to his surprise, Fabien re-emerged at the edge of the garden, making straight towards him through the murmuring crowd. A large portion of the crowd didn't seem to mind this. Those in the queue were as content with wife as they were with husband.

'Have we met?' Fabien asked, his eyes narrowed.

Ferrash smiled. If they did this in public, it had to have every semblance of polite conversation. When he spoke, he pitched his voice low enough that only Fabien would hear him. 'We haven't, no, but I imagine you might have heard of me. My name is Vannis Proglimen. I apologise for the subterfuge, but this was the only way I could reach you. I am the chair of the Protectorate's Proctorate committee. I am the Proctor.'

Fabien stiffened. 'I see. I would say I'm pleased to make your acquaintance, but circumstances being as they are…'

Ferrash shivered, drew in a breath. 'I need your help.'

'I find that hard to believe.'

'The Protectorate is about to be pitched into revolution. Worse than Munab. It'll spread across the whole sector of space. But it's not going to plan. Could get messy. Could need outside help. I'd ask that that help be yours.'

Fabien laughed, and though he smiled, there was definite annoyance riding in his features – and a note of rising curiosity. 'Why?'

Realising he'd let his speech pattern slip, Ferrash took more care with his next words. 'For the same reason I'd guess you've sent people to Munab. You want to help. Supporting the people to change the Protectorate is a benefit to you as well as them. Imagine if in a decade's time they're a society not far off the Confederated Outer Reach. They wouldn't be perfect, but they'd be better than they are now. The Chair has consolidated too much power of his own.'

Fabien pursed his lips. 'You say "they", not "we". Why is that?' Contempt rode on his next words. 'Do you consider yourself above the rest of the Protectorate?'

Put on the spot, Ferrash folded his arms behind his back, beneath his cape. His next words were as true for him as they would have been for Proglimen. For any prog. 'I've never really been one of them. Not really. Not from the vats.'

'Then why try to change something that isn't yours?'

Ferrash narrowed his eyes at Fabien despite the need for politeness. 'Because it's broken, and it's hurting people. It'll keep hurting people until it's fixed.'

Again the pursed lips. Something else ate at Fabien's mind, something he was holding back from the conversation.

'There's more to it than just humanitarian aid,' said Ferrash. The

bigger the ask, the more likely he'd get given a small ask in com-
promise. 'There's another step before the revolution can happen. A
crucial one. I need to get onto the Prime Nexus – into one of its dead
tubes, probably – and stay there until it's done. I can't trust any of the
Protectorate's fleets with that, not with the Chair's influence. If I had
the protection of your fleet...'

Fabien's frown had morphed from restrained anger to curiosity.
'What are your intentions with it?'

'Sabotage.' A half-truth. 'It'll knock out the Keepers long enough
to get them out of the way.'

'Hmm'

Ferrash resisted the urge to look around him, or show any other
signs of impatience. Yet he was distinctly aware of eyes on him, of the
queue growing a little more discontent.

'How much of the operation on Munab are you aware of?' Fabien
said a moment later. 'The movement of free agents, perhaps? The
orders they have been given?'

'None,' he said, perhaps too quickly. 'That's not my purview.'

'Have you been there lately?'

'No.'

Fabien quirked an eyebrow and stared into the distance to his right.
'Palia was. She went to find you.'

The floor fell out from underneath Ferrash. One short conversation with Fabien and he already knew exactly who he was. Or maybe
Rythian security had whispered something in his ear. You could do a
job for years and still be *scatz* at it, apparently.

His throat suddenly tight, Ferrash asked, 'Is she here?' *Is she safe*?

'I haven't seen her yet, but she has been invited. She should be
arriving today. You recognised her name, which implies you remember her.' Of course, they wouldn't know if Ferrash remembered – he'd
vanished before they had chance to find out. 'You should stay. See
her.'

Ferrash started shaking his head before Fabien had finished his sentence, his body gripped with a sudden dread. His mouth was dry again, and he swallowed to try bringing moisture back to it.

'I can't,' Ferrash said. 'I...' How did he summarise the way he saw Palia? She was just a bunch of memories devoid of context – a bunch of memories he tried to put aside again and again but always came back to. He shook his head. Munab was a bloodbath. She had gone there for him. 'What about Bek?'

'Recovering. He was injured on Munab.'

Snapping his gaze up to meet Fabien's again, Ferrash asked, 'How badly?'

'I hear they had to amputate his arm. Palia says keepers attacked the mech they were fighting with, collapsing the compartment Bek was in.'

'They were in a mech? Why?'

With a pointed look, Fabien said, 'To follow the trail you left. The kill order for your father?'

Ferrash sighed, shifting on his feet, acutely aware of the noise around him, the press of other human bodies, the freedom and clamour of civilisation after so long spent on Hesperex. He opened his mouth, closed it again, tried to match words with emotions he wanted to shunt aside.

At last, he said, 'This is something I have to do alone,' but the words felt flat. 'And Palia...' Her name stuck in his throat. He stared at a point on Fabien's shoulder as he waited for it to come free, but it remained lodged there. He darted his gaze up to meet Fabien's, an unconscious cry for help, but he tore it away again just as fast.

Something in Fabien's stance softened, if only a fraction. 'We will help you with the Prime Nexus, when the time comes.' Ferrash gathered from its being mentioned first and the ease of the reply that this had been the easiest concession, which he hadn't been expecting. 'As for providing support after this... revolution, we will monitor the situation. If there indeed turns out to be a humanitarian crisis that we can help with that wouldn't be aiding a yet-established enemy, we will do so. Will you be able to contact me when that time comes?'

Ferrash nodded, but said nothing, his muscles straining to get him gone.

'And that's all you wanted to ask?'

That feeling again, rising, clutching. It was all Ferrash could do to force the words out. 'Please don't tell her. Don't tell her I was here. I... don't know I can deal with any of that yet. And I have work I need to do back on Hesperex.'

Ferrash could see the thought pained Fabien – it was etched upon every disapproving line of his face – but he inclined his head regardless. 'I understand. I'll leave that choice to you.'

'Thank you.' Ferrash turned on his heel to leave, his heart thumping.

Then he saw her, and he swore it stopped.

Palia stepped out from the colonnade, her attention fixed on the dais. Her white shock of hair framed a drawn face, and the lines of her body in her dress seemed gaunter than his memories had shown. That instant, before she noticed him, was the perfect time to slip away. But he hesitated, caught mid step. All the memories that had been plaguing him since the previous Magister's death jumped to the front of his mind. They clamoured for his attention. They wanted to be compared against the real thing, mapped to whatever feeling they might have lost.

Was he feeling that now? Had his whole stomach flipped upside-down when he had first known her? Had his chest burned and tightened? Had an ache nestled behind his eyes and threatened to bring tears to them? He didn't know. Couldn't know. Wouldn't. That was all lost to him, and whatever he felt now was his mind filling in the gaps. It wasn't real.

It wasn't real.

As she began to turn towards him, he jerked back into motion. He closed his eyes, breathed, opened them again with a smile on his face.

Palia approached two metres from him, smiling at someone over his shoulder, maybe Fabien. For a fraction of a second, her gaze flicked over to him, then away, registering nothing. She passed within a foot of his shoulder. He could have reached out and taken hold of her if he wanted, and he desperately wanted to, like some drowning man sighting a rope in the water. But he couldn't. He couldn't touch her. He couldn't pretend she meant anything to him when the Empyrean could take meaning from anything. Could and had.

He couldn't pretend he wanted to keep walking, either, even as his feet took him further from her. He wanted to rush back, apologise, introduce himself, find out how much she really remembered.

But he used so much concentration walking away that he didn't hear her come after him. A hand tightened on his wrist. He whirled, heart hammering, poised to fight.

Palia stood before him, her green eyes wide. Her throat worked silently, and they stared at each other for a moment before she breathed, 'Ash?'

CHAPTER THIRTY-THREE

PALIA HAD NEVER FELT more watched than she did walking through the palace complex. Every Rythian she passed looked at her with some combination of pity, contempt and mistrust, and she found herself walking faster just to outpace their stares. More alarming, they didn't seem to fear her. They *must* have seen her as empyrric. They must have seen the white hair and known that's what it was, but to know that and not be afraid... Maybe they thought she had just been scarred by one. Maybe it was all too distant when Rythe had no empyrrics of its own.

It had spies, though, and in abundance. Four of them moved in her awareness, shadowing her movements from other floors, probably following her via camera feeds. They wanted her to see them. Even Hesperex hadn't felt like this – though she supposed the trap of Hesperex was that the spies were the people who lived there.

As Palia grew closer to the music, she let the material of her one-piece reshape from trousers back into a skirt, then brushed the fabric smooth. They had told her she would travel beast-back, so she had dressed for beast-back, little knowing the transport carriers were more comfortable affairs. No matter. At least she had the choice again, after losing most of her clothes on Everatus IV.

Palia stopped by the entrance to a walled garden, drawing a deep breath of fresh air. Birds – no, flying reptiles – tipped their heads back to gulp water from the central stream, heedless of the chattering crowd.

If only Bek could have been here for this. It wasn't like him to miss a party – or not like she knew him – but he had insisted on staying up on the ship. The surgeon had pronounced him well recovered, physically, so that couldn't be the issue.

She scanned the crowd. Rythians mingled with those from the Hegemony, the two peoples surprisingly difficult to distinguish. The Rythians had dressed as they chose, and she supposed most of the Hegemites had been briefed to match them, out of diplomatic courtesy. Palia hadn't, but transitor families like hers were closer to Rythian fashion than the heredrae and the voidfarers anyway.

Spotting Fabien in conversation with another man, Palia smiled and moved out of the way of the door so she could wait for him to be finished.

Whatever they were talking about, it didn't sit well with either of them. Fabien had his lips pressed tight. He clasped his hands together so hard in front of him that his knuckles were white, then he inclined his head, once. Relief surged through the tangled mix of the other man's emotions, and he chose that moment to leave the conversation.

Palia set off to make sure she reached Fabien before anyone else, glancing to the dais as she did so. A lot of the crowd's attention seemed to be focused on that spot. At a guess, the red-haired woman towering over those around her was Fabien's new wife. Handsome, Palia thought, and not at all young.

Palia turned back to Fabien, her smile a little more heartfelt, and perhaps the man leaving the conversation thought that smile was meant for him, because he smiled back. The smile tangled a trail of dancing nerves straight into his core. She darted her gaze away, trying very hard not to blush. As he passed by her shoulder, the feeling grew. Butterflies became dragons, leaping in their haste to escape. She shuddered as something in her responded in kind: the untethered rope, looking for something to latch onto.

Not this. He's not him. Palia brought the picture up for a millisecond just to check, satisfied herself that he didn't have any of the scars Ferrash did, but still couldn't shake the feeling that something was wrong.

Fabien spotted her. For a moment, his smile faltered. It teetered between up and down, and she saw the flash of pity even though she didn't want to.

That was what told her she was right.

Palia spun on her heel, locked her gaze onto the man's retreating back and sprinted for him, every muscle in her body urging her on. His emotions flared like a star in its death throes, as painful to witness as she imagined they were to possess. When she caught up to him and grabbed his wrist, they stabbed through his body in an explosion of light.

He whirled to face her, jerking his wrist so hard he almost pulled her off her feet, all that whirling emotion etched across his face.

'Ash?' she breathed. This man looked nothing like the picture. His hair, while too short, was maybe the right colour, but he was paler, his eyes wide and bulbous, his facial structure all wrong.

Silence stretched between them. Had Palia been wrong? Had she interrupted some stranger's personal trauma?

The man breathed, sudden and sharp like he had only just remembered to do so.

'Palia.' His voice was little more than a hoarse whisper.

Delight danced through Palia's veins. She let out a relieved laugh, a grin spreading so wide across her face it pinched her eyes almost shut. In that moment, she sensed her thread that had been cut reaching still, closer and closer to a twin that coiled and lashed around Ferrash's psyche. She took a step towards him and went to place a hand on his chest, but he stopped her with a snatch of his hand.

It was like a door had slammed down across his face, all trace of emotion gone but for the storm she could see in the Empyrean. His gaze darted all around them.

'Not here,' Ferrash said. 'We can't be seen together like this.'

Her heart in her throat, Palia glanced around the room. They had it to themselves, though someone could come through from the courtyard or an adjoining room at any moment, and she caught a glimpse of Fabien still watching them.

Ferrash took a step back and let his hand drop, his grip shifting from her wrist to her hand. 'Come on, I've got a room booked. We can speak there.'

Something in Palia did a confused little flip at going from a surprised reunion to a clandestine talk. Her guts had tangled themselves up in knots. It was all she could do to keep the Empyrean in check as she walked hand-in-hand with Ferrash through corridors that she barely even noticed. A green pall followed on the wall alongside them – an Empyrean glow, courtesy of her own skin. There would be explaining to do if they bumped into any Rythians.

Ferrash seemed to realise this, as he squeezed her hand a little tighter, his footsteps becoming more urgent. He took corners more suddenly than had he been planning to go that way.

At length, they came to a door. Ferrash unlocked it and nudged her inside before turning to lock it behind them. Palia leaned against the wall, reassured by the solidity of the stone against her back.

Ferrash turned to face her, his brows drawn close, a lost expression in his eyes. Palia reached across the small gap between them and laid a hand on his waist, and she swore something in the core of his psyche shattered.

Chest heaving beneath his slit-collared shirt, Ferrash placed a hand on the small of Palia's back and cupped the side of her head with the other, his head so close their foreheads almost touched. Palia snaked her free hand over his chest, rested it on the hard angle of his jaw and leaned in. When their lips touched, Ferrash seemed to thaw. He pulled her against him, his fingers tightening in her hair, his breath warm against her face.

There was no thread anymore, or no telling where it might have been. Together they formed one blinding light, no beginning nor end to their emotions. Palia lost herself on the tide of it, grabbing at Ferrash's belt for purchase, letting her other hand roam from jaw to neck to collarbone, where she traced the shape of it and watched the electric thrill of Ferrash's emotions race away from her touch.

They broke apart for a moment, eyes locked, their breath coming hot and heavy. She didn't know this face. She didn't remember her time with Ferrash. She didn't need to.

She kissed him again, drew her hand down his chest, smiled at the way it made his breath hitch. Ferrash let out a strangled laugh and turned his face aside, planting a string of kisses from her ear to the base of her neck before pressing his lips against hers again. She ran her hand along his belt, found the buckle, and began fumbling for the clasp.

Ferrash pulled back. 'Wait,' he said. His emotions danced like static, blinking on and off in patches, fuzzy and vague where they had been vibrant before.

Palia blinked up at him as he staggered a couple of steps away from her. His face had gone even paler than before. She rushed in and caught hold of him just as one of his legs gave way, grunting under the weight, then pulled his arm around her shoulders and helped him onto the bed.

He sat there, eyes going in and out of focus, swaying on the brink of consciousness. Palia knelt on the floor in front of him, poised to catch him if he fell forwards.

'Are you okay?' she asked, squeezing his knee in case that brought him back to awareness.

Ferrash leaned onto his elbows with something between a sigh and a groan, wrapping his hands over the top of his head and screwing his eyes tight shut.

'Sorry,' he said.

'Don't be. I just... What was that? You looked like you were about to faint.'

He nodded and took hold of her hands. 'I think I did, for a moment. Inhibitors. I took too many, and then I took none, and... Turns out that's not such a good idea.'

Something about his words itched at the void in her memories. 'How long have you been taking them?'

Ferrash eyed her cautiously, then asked, 'How much do you remember?'

Sighing, Palia drew herself upright and sat down on the bed beside him, their shoulders touching. 'Wherever there was a memory with you in it...' Her breath caught in her throat. 'Now there's nothing. My brain just skips over it. I can't go looking no matter how hard I try.'

Ferrash nodded, unsurprised. 'Empyrean does that.' The thought wrapped a strand of bitterness around his core. 'But if you forgot me, how...?' He paused, throat working in silence, brows drawn low. 'How can you still love me?'

The words dropped into her psyche and burst like water hitting glass. 'I just... felt it. It was the only thing left. The only reason I recognised you.' That and the sight of his own emotions, spiralling out of control.

'*Scatz*.' Ferrash dragged a hand over his hair. 'And I left you to deal with it. I'm sorry. I thought... I thought I was nothing to you anymore.'

'But at least you remember me.' Relief spread through Palia at the thought. She hadn't torn his memories away as well. Just hers.

Ferrash chuckled, raising his eyes to the ceiling. 'I stopped loving you. Lasted all of a minute. Good thing about getting emotions stripped is they usually come back.'

'And memories?' she asked, trying to smother the desperate hope that Ferrash knew a way to get hers back.

He shook his head.

A sick feeling settled in her stomach. She closed her eyes. There was no hope, then. No hope but to make new memories, and as saccharin-sweet as that sounded, it would never make up for it.

Ferrash slipped an arm around her waist and drew her close. She nestled into the warmth of his shoulder.

'You did what you had to do,' he said, then shrugged. 'Just badly.'

Palia laughed, but his words made her think of the order he had been given on Munab. 'Ash, your father—'

'Is dead. I know.' A sliver of sadness wound around his psyche. 'I kept a watch on him when we all left Munab. I knew as soon as he died, but the Protectorate didn't. So I set the kill order on him and assigned it to myself to make them think I was out of the way, but...' He shook his head. 'I'm sorry you went after it. That's my fault. I heard what happened to Bek.'

Blanching at the memory, Palia shivered.

'How's he holding up?' Ferrash asked.

'Bek's fine, he just hasn't seen me the same way since what I did to you, which is fair enough.' She sighed. 'And he's hurt you've been hiding things from him.'

Ferrash exhaled and flopped back onto the bed, kneading the bridge of his nose between thumb and forefinger. '*Scatz*, I've been hiding things from everyone. Pretty sure that includes me.'

'Then stop hiding.'

He took hold of her hand again and turned to stare at her. 'Palia, there are things I need to do back on Hesperex that it's best everyone else stays out of. Could get violent. *Will* get violent, fast. There's a lot hanging on not being caught and you... you didn't exactly do a great job of that last time.'

'Then at least take Bek with you. There must be something we can do to help. Whatever it is you're up to, we can do it together.'

Ferrash stared up at the ceiling for several seconds, and the emotions flowing through him receded as he thought. Feelings were giving way to logic, and Palia had no idea if that was a good thing or a bad thing.

At last, though, he turned back to her and nodded. 'Okay. I think I have a job for you.'

CHAPTER THIRTY-FOUR

THEY SPENT ANOTHER HOUR or two together. For the first time in weeks, though Ferrash hadn't meant to drift away, he had a dreamless sleep. A part of him was glad his little fainting episode had stopped them going any further too fast. They had needed the time to talk.

As it was, he woke to Palia shaking his shoulder gently. He blinked up at her, bleary-eyed, and summoned as much of a smile as he could.

Palia smiled back. He could get used to seeing that when he woke.

'Hey,' she said. 'I didn't want to wake you, but Fabien keeps sending me messages. He wants to talk.'

That, he was less pleased to wake to. He rolled out of bed, accepting Palia's help to stand up, and tried to pat the worst of the creases out of his clothes. Palia stretched up on tiptoes and smoothed back a few rogue strands of hair. He kissed her when she dropped back down, past the point of caring what impression his appearance would give when he stepped out of the room. Everyone who mattered here had seen through the disguise, anyway. His pride still chafed at that.

They made their way back to the courtyard hand-in-hand, not quite sure if the party would have remained in the same place, but still able to hear the music. It had slipped a few notes quieter since their last visit. When they walked out into the sunlight, it was to see Fabien leaning against the dais accompanied only by his wife.

She noticed them arrive first, grinning at them and jostling Fabien with her shoulder to get his attention. Fabien looked their way. Relief washed over his face, then he came down the steps to greet them.

'You know,' Fabien said, 'I had this whole speech prepared for Palia about how I'd changed my mind and she could go to Hesperex to find you after all, if for nothing other than a little espionage, but to be wary that you might not want to be found.' He spread his arms wide in a gesture of defeat. 'I think if that were the case, you would have run a little faster when she recognised you.'

Ferrash laughed, but he didn't miss the accusatory glint in the Magister's eyes.

Fabien inclined his head. 'In any case, it's good to see the two of you together again, even if you *are* wearing the wrong face.'

'Speaking of being together,' Palia said before he could continue. 'Aren't you missing an introduction?'

'Oh, yes.' Fabien glanced to his wife on the dais. A little grin flashed across his face at the sight of her. 'Lady Charante.'

Lady Charante waved at them, told them not to mind her, then waggled her eyebrows at Fabien before retreating into a side room.

Fabien drew a deep breath, and Ferrash caught him examining him from the corner of his eye. He didn't trust him, and Ferrash couldn't blame him for that. It was Ferrash's job to do things that made him untrustworthy.

Fabien said, 'Something told me you weren't going to stick around Rythe much longer, so I thought I should catch you before you left.'

Ferrash nodded. This might have been a whistle-stop tour, but he had originally intended to stay the night and leave in the morning. Now that he didn't have to worry about seeming suspicious, the only thing that mattered was speed.

Beside him, Palia shrugged. 'Not meaning any offense to your wedding or anything, but I only came because you wouldn't let me go to Hesperex otherwise. And I didn't really need your permission, in any case.'

'Is Hesperex still the plan?'

Palia glanced to Ferrash, nodded. 'It is.' If she told Fabien the whole truth of what Ferrash had asked her to do, Fabien likely wouldn't let her go, permission needed or not.

Fabien sighed, then chuckled to himself, shaking his head. 'Okay then. But Ferrash? You make sure you both stay out of trouble over there, you hear me?'

Thinking of all the many dangers he would be bringing the others into on Hesperex, Ferrash nodded. 'Sure.'

Ferrash had to leave in the same ship he had arrived in to avoid suspicion from the Protectorate, so he wouldn't be flying with the others. They would arrive on Hesperex separately, with only Bek registered on the manifest, claiming that Ferrash had died in his mission on Munab.

On the subject of Bek, of course, he had a reunion and apologies to make.

Ferrash gripped the control column tighter than he needed to, making last-minute adjustments to dock with his old ship. He had caught sight of Bek in the cockpit as he made his approach, completely oblivious to who he was about to meet. The *Etheron*, like most ships, had a viewscreen instead of a traditional canopy. Bek wouldn't have been able to see in. And if he had, Ferrash reminded himself, he would have seen Proglimen's face, not his.

The presence of Palia's hand on his shoulder indicated just how much his nerves were showing. Ferrash took a few steadying breaths to melt them away, but flinched at the sound of the docking clamps.

'Come on,' Palia said. 'He's going to love this.'

Ferrash very much doubted that.

They climbed through the docking tube together, Palia at the front, taking it slow so the gravity flip didn't mess their heads up too much. Ferrash had left his half-cloak over the back of his seat in the cockpit and Palia had done something to her dress that turned the bottom half into a pair of trousers. He briefly pondered which looked best on her before bringing his mind back on track. No use trying to distract himself. They were here.

Ferrash heard Bek greet Palia in the lounge, asking something about the food, as he pulled himself clear of the tube. There was a definite strain to his voice, though he'd made some attempt at hiding it. Ferrash hesitated for a moment before walking towards them.

The moment Bek saw him, he leapt in front of Palia and drew his pistol, the stump of his other arm jutting out beside him. Ferrash stopped with his hands in the air, his heart aching at the damage.

'*Bile and blood*, Palia,' Bek spat. 'What're you doing bringing this *ostat* sannot on board the ship?'

Ferrash raised an eyebrow, glancing between Bek and Palia. 'Was kinda hoping the first thing you would have done is warn him about the disguise.'

Eyes wide, Bek lowered the pistol. He took a step forwards, squinting down the corridor, trying to see with his eyes what his ears had suggested. 'Ash?'

When he nodded, Bek holstered his pistol and strode towards Ferrash. Ferrash tried to speak, but Bek slammed him back against the bulkhead, his face screwed up, tears glistening in the corners of his eyes.

Ferrash didn't want it to be like this, but it was like it because of him. That truth wormed around his gut, gnawing at everything it could find.

'One message,' Bek said, pressing him against the wall again for emphasis. 'One message to let me know you were okay. Could you at least've given me that?' He turned his face towards the cockpit, away from Palia, and spoke his next words so quietly that even Ferrash struggled to hear them. 'I thought she'd killed you at first. I thought you were gone. It was only when she said there'd been someone else left alive that I realised she'd just forgotten you.'

'I'm sorry.'

When Bek turned back, he must have seen the truth of that in Ferrash's eyes, because his shoulders fell. He swiped his tears away with the back of his hand, then carefully put his remaining arm around Ferrash and pulled him into a light hug, like if he squeezed any harder, he might just disintegrate. Ferrash had never been this physical with Bek before, and for a moment he froze. In an instant, Bek had crossed a line Ferrash had taken great pains to draw. He had drawn it from fear of feeling, though, and while he couldn't say he was over the fear, he was certainly done avoiding it. He hugged Bek back, mumbling another apology into his ear as he did.

They parted a few seconds later.

'Come on,' Bek said, starting down the corridor. 'I'll get the drinks out. You can fill me in on what you've been up to.'

Ferrash grimaced. 'I can't stay.'

Bek raised his eyes to the ceiling. 'Can't you, now.'

Before Ferrash could reply, green light reflected off the walls to either side of him. He whirled to see a stern woman looming in the corridor. Empyrean flames bathed every inch of her body, reflecting as sparks in her eyes. *Scatz*, he *recognised* her.

'What is the meaning of this?' asked Archivist Lilesh. She peered around Ferrash, her eyes narrowed. 'Palia, do you have any idea just who you have brought aboard this ship?'

Further behind him, Palia replied, 'It's Ash!'

Lilesh rolled her eyes, lips caught in a sneer. 'Ancestors save me from memory-wiped...' Then she blinked and frowned at him. 'Oh. Oh no, quite right, it is you.'

Would it hurt for just *one* person not to see through his disguise today? This was the worst of them. He had bumped into Lilesh once about... what was it, six, seven years ago? He had been on a mission in Hegemony space and he hadn't *strictly* been following orders, which had seen him working in the Hegemony's interest for a spell. He'd done it before, and since, but always just as coincidence, not with any actual contact with their forces. Too risky that way. But apparently his meddling had annoyed Lilesh so much she'd made it her personal mission to find out who he was. The closest they had come was locking eyes across a server room before Ferrash had terminated the mission and bugged out.

She *still* recognised him after all this time. *Empyrrics*. At least she had only done so after Palia pointed it out.

Putting his annoyance aside, he said, 'That's right. You can put the flames away.'

'Oh, certainly I *could*, but I don't see why I should. I would have regarded the real Proctor as inconsequential in the grand scheme of things – another cog in your Protectorate machine, scrabbling for whatever power he could, making whatever deals he could to keep it. Making a deal with *him* would almost be predictable. But you? You haven't been the Proctor all this time, unless you can be in two places at once. I don't know what your agenda is. I just know you are up to something, and you are never who you say you are.' She turned to Palia again. 'Pestor, you cannot trust this man.'

With a start, Ferrash noticed Palia had appeared beside him. She held a fist out in front of her, sheathed in an emerald fire that lit her face and hair in monochrome. He resisted the urge to move aside. The threat of the Empyrean twisted in his gut.

Before she could do anything stupid, Ferrash rested his hand on Palia's shoulder and shook his head.

'Have you heard of the Reiart?' he asked Lilesh.

'You work for them,' Lilesh said, matter-of-fact, like it was the most obvious thing in the universe.

Ferrash bit his lip to hold back a string of profanities and shut his eyes. Bek moved closer, his footsteps quiet on the floor panels

'That's bile,' Bek said. 'You've always told me the Reiart is a myth. Ash, tell her.'

'I lied, Bek.' He didn't want to open his eyes, didn't want to look over and see betrayal on Bek's face all over again. 'They exist. I worked for them, for a while, and now I don't. Not exactly.' He squeezed Palia's shoulder without really meaning to, and she shifted in his grip. 'Now I run them.'

Bek drew in a sharp breath. 'But you... They... The things they've *done,* Ash. You told them to do all that?'

Ferrash shook his head and opened his eyes. Lilesh and Palia had withdrawn their flames, though he knew how fast they could summon them again. Light from the overhead panels glinted from the accusation in Bek's eyes.

'No,' Ferrash said. 'It doesn't work like that. It's... complicated.'

Lilesh's voice came again, cold and sharp. 'Give me one good reason why I shouldn't kill you for what you are.'

'I can give you three,' he said. None of those reasons would be the death of the Empyrean. Lilesh was too tightly coupled to that power to take its loss likely, he reckoned. 'One: Palia would try to kill you for it. Two: everything I have done as Reiart has been in pursuit of overthrowing the Keepers and establishing fair order in the Protectorate. And three: the Magister knows that, and is willing to help me. I'm guessing he didn't pass the message on?'

Lilesh just glowered at him, then her eyes unfocused, presumably as she messaged Fabien for confirmation.

Bek started to say something else, but Ferrash took hold of his arm to cut him off.

'Bek, you have every reason to shout at me for all the lies I've told you, but this isn't the time. I have to go back to Hesperex in my own ship. I'll meet you there.' Perhaps, anyway. There was a good chance he wouldn't see Bek for at least a few days once they landed, a good chance he wouldn't see Palia for a few weeks more, a good chance he would never see either of them again. 'Palia knows the plan. There are parts of Hesperex I don't have eyes on anymore. I need you two to cover those gaps and feed information back to me. I've asked Palia to infiltrate a group of the Kept down in the lower levels. She's a better chance blending in with them than Keepers. I'd like you'd to embed yourself within the Landers... if you want to go along with this, that is.'

Bek turned and walked away without saying anything, and that was worse than an argument. Ferrash stared at the docking hatch in the floor, relieved to have his family whole again and regretting meeting them at the same time, unsure if things could ever go back to the way they were before.

Palia stared down the corridor after Bek. 'I'm sure he'll help once I explain.'

'It should be me doing the explaining. I should have let him in on this years ago. He's...' He didn't have words for what Bek was to him. Closer to a brother than a son, but not quite either. 'I should have told him.'

Palia grabbed his hand and squeezed it. 'You can fix all of this, when we're through.'

'Sure,' he said. *If there's anything left to fix.*

CHAPTER THIRTY-FIVE

FERRASH WOKE TO THE sound of a proximity alarm. He jerked upright in his seat, confused for a moment at Bek not being in the cockpit beside him, then remembered he had switched back to the *Etheron*. He leaned forwards to examine the control panel.

A whole fleet of ships sat out there, just the other side of the canopy. Ferrash squinted through it, but couldn't make anything out. Another look at the panel told him the fleet was spread wide enough that he wouldn't spot them with the naked eye and they mostly lay behind him. One sat right on top of him.

'*Bile and blood*,' he swore when he scanned it – a Protectorate ship, from one of the void packs.

The void packs were the equivalent of free agents within the Protectorate's military: independent vessels with the freedom to follow their orders however they saw fit. Ferrash tried to remember where the packs were supposed to be stationed at the moment, but couldn't, not off the top of his head, and for the ship to be this close it must have spotted him. He'd almost completed the route he'd planned into the auto-pilot. The nexus just visible as a bright cross in the distance was Rembra's, the last stop in Hegemony space before the Protectorate and Hesperex.

He opened a channel to the ship. '*Hunter Tannis Four-Five-One*, this is the *CVL Etheron*. Is there a problem?'

Ten seconds passed, then another ten. If Palia and Bek had left soon after him, they might run into this lot as well. Ferrash scrubbed at the skin under his eyes with one thumb, trying to remove all trace of sleep, but his borrowed face always felt strange when he woke. He pinched the bridge of his nose tight to bring his thoughts together. When a whole minute had passed him by, Ferrash opened his mouth to speak again. The *Tannis* beat him to it.

'*CVL Etheron*, we see your code is an ESF signal. Are you with the ESF?'

Ferrash froze. That shouldn't have been a problem. They shouldn't be mentioning it. The External Security Force ran a changing set of transponder codes to identify free-agent ships to other Protectorate vessels. They didn't want their undercover agents getting swept out of the sky every time they tried to fly a non-Protectorate ship back home, and the rest of the fleets respected that arrangement. You see a ship flying ESF codes, you look the other way. You don't ask questions.

'*CVL Etheron*, do you read us?'

Ferrash cleared his throat, toggled the channel open again. 'Yes. Loud, clear. My code is as described in the registry. Is there a problem?'

Another delay. He brought up the rear cameras in the viewscreen and panned until he could see the *Tannis*, its drab metal bulk blocking out much of the void.

'*CVL Etheron*, we need you to dock with us.'

'Why?'

'Comply, or we will open fire.'

For a second, he just sat there. He checked the readouts in his implants to make sure he was awake and not dreaming this, then doubted reality when he saw he was awake. He stared at the ship. It showed signs of battle damage. A great gash had been torn in one side of the hull: a heavy collision with another ship, maybe, but far too much damage to have come from one missile. Their weapons were active, trained on him.

'Okay,' Ferrash said. 'Hold your fire. I'll turn and dock.'

He didn't have a choice. The ship had snuck up on him, unregistered as a threat due to their shared faction. In theory, the ship was on his side, but if that were the case, why would they disobey standing orders like this?

As Ferrash disengaged the auto-pilot, he pushed the questions aside and focused on escape strategies. Being disguised as the Proctor didn't mean much if they'd gone rogue. Worst-case scenario, they shoot him. Wasn't much he could do about that. But if they just captured him, he had a thousand ways to escape and get back to his ship. Flying away without getting blown to pieces was a different matter. He'd need to sabotage them, get their systems down as long as possible.

Above, the *Tannis'* hull blinked with docking lights, pointing the way to an external hatch – easier to blast away from than a conventional hangar.

Ferrash thought back to Palia at the party, to the feel of her lips on his skin. The last time he had been captured, the rescue mission she'd staged had culminated in a violent, catastrophic display of empyrric power. He consoled himself with the thought that at least she didn't know he'd been kidnapped this time as trouble rolled closer.

Ten gun muzzles welcomed Ferrash out of the docking hatch. He moved slow and held his hands up to indicate he wasn't armed, but the nearest man grabbed him and slammed him against the wall. Ferrash grunted, resisting the urge to fight back. Someone had a gun pressed against his temple. The man who had grabbed him pressed against his back so hard it felt like he was trying to force his ribs through the wall. They patted every inch of him twice, trying to find a weapon that wasn't there, until they eventually gave up searching.

The pressure lifted from his back. He drew in a deep breath, stumbling as someone spun him by the shoulder.

'Satisfied?' Ferrash asked.

The man who had grabbed him – and very much looked like he wanted to punch him – curled his upper lip. A thick moustache covered it, and the rest of his jaw had only been spared a similar coating by haphazard shearing. He was old. A prog, maybe in his seventies. The other nine were all vatborn, all towards the end of their lives, all bare-faced, neither male nor female. Void packs operated in deep space, isolated from the rest of the Protectorate for years on end. They liked to fill the crew with people they thought wouldn't pose a problem.

Apparently, that hadn't worked.

Ferrash licked his lips. 'What's this about, then?'

The bearded man answered. Ferrash would have to get closer, hand-to-hand, if he wanted to read his ID. 'Was goin' to say we can't have you runnin' back an' rattlin' to your overseers about us. Wouldn't do well. But I recognise you. Our own Proctor in the flesh, flyin' under a false flag.'

Ferrash glanced down the line of vatborn. Each of them had their eyes fixed on him, and he shivered at the hate behind them.

'My business here is legitimate. As is yours,' Ferrash said, hoping his nonchalance at their obvious treachery would ease their nerves a bit. 'You're on your way back to Hesperex, same as me. I don't have a problem with that.'

'Oh, if you've no problem with us, I've no blood in my veins. But you've skin in this game. Anythin' you know is somethin' you'll try to use at some point. Can't be havin' that.' The man spat on the floor, then turned to the vatborn. 'Throw him in the brig. Might be we can use him for some legitimate business of our own when all this is done.'

Ferrash tensed, instincts screaming to make a break for it, but every single gun twitched towards him in the same moment. They'd kill him if he so much as put a foot out of place.

'Captain.' One of the vatborn nodded and took Ferrash from the bearded man's grasp in a grip just as strong. Another took hold of his other arm and a third fell into place behind them. They jabbed their gun's muzzle between his shoulder blades.

'Move,' they said.

Ferrash stepped away, jostled between the two soldiers, trying to pick up on some clue in their behaviour that might tell him what was going on. They didn't want him passing their presence onto the Protectorate before they reached Hesperex. What were they planning? A fleet this big... he tried to remember how many he'd seen on the scans. All of them, he thought. Every ship in the void packs. A fleet this big could lay siege to Hesperex if it wanted to.

Biting the inside of his lip, he resisted the urge to swear or ask his escort for confirmation. Ida should have been keeping the void packs in line with his plan. It had been her job to hold them off until the time came. But Ida was dead. Unless she wasn't.

'Where have you come from?' Ferrash asked.

The vatborn didn't answer, though they jabbed him again with their gun for his trouble. Those they passed in the corridors frowned at Ferrash as he was marched by.

'Were you at Corumma?' A jump into free space was just the void packs' sort of thing. They were leaving Hegemony space, and leaving without the Hegemony's fleets on their heels. Retreating, perhaps? 'Do you know if Void Marshal Ida survived the jump?'

No reply again, but the vatborn to his left tensed for a moment.

'If Ida's alive, I need to speak to her.'

They ignored him. A couple of metres further and they bundled him into another room, tiny, with a small bench and a hygiene unit in one corner. Ferrash tripped over the rim of the bulkhead door and fell against the unit, jarring his elbow.

'Let the captain know I need to speak to Ida!' he called, but they slammed the door in his face.

CHAPTER THIRTY-SIX

ELECTRONIC SABOTAGE WAS HARD to achieve on any Protectorate vessel. Harder than Hegemony ships, in any case, where every surface was connected to something else and all you needed to do to find an entry point was touch it. Harder than Laresic ships, which could be accessed with similar ease despite well-maintained systems developed that side of the millennium. Ferrash knew this. The door to his cell had nothing electronic about it. If he wanted to escape, he would first have to escape this room.

The solutions: cast a wider net, see if he could latch onto a signal and interfere remotely; wait for someone to pay him a visit, jump them, and make his way from there; or just wait and see what happened next.

He preferred the second option, but it was too obvious. Sometimes obvious was the best trick you could play, but sometimes it got you killed. This was probably one of those times. So he waited. He took a seat on the cramped bench, leaned back against the metal wall, rested his hands on his knees and waited. Footsteps echoed in the spaces around him, a constant surround sound that had him mapping the layout of the ship from where the feet fell.

All the while, Ferrash cursed himself for avoiding it. Avoiding Palia. Avoiding Bek. His brain ticked over with trivial tasks and theoreticals, and all the while his heart ate away at itself in a way it couldn't have if he'd still been using inhibitors. When he finally gave up what felt like hours later, he let himself feel.

It hurt.

It hurt that he had been close enough to talk to her, to touch her, and he had done nothing. It hurt that she had been the one to fix things between them. Back after they had killed the Magister, Ferrash had been stripped, emotions devoured and destroyed. He had been surprised, and his emotions' sudden absence had shocked him, but that was all. Different now, with every emotion a splinter in his flesh that he couldn't pick out.

You always run. He closed his eyes. That was the truth. He always ran from pain. Not physical pain, so conditioned in him that he almost embraced it, but emotional pain. He suppressed it every moment he could, had been doing so for as long as he could remember. That, in itself, was painful to know. He had walked past Palia on Rythe, when he should have embraced her. He had run from her on the flagship, when he should have stayed to help her remember. He had let his father die fighting on Munab when he should have insisted he leave. He had chosen cynicism and subterfuge when his mentor was executed. He had run from Munab, and deadened the loss of the love he left there with inhibitors in every moment until he could put her out of mind.

Because before he loved Palia, he had loved her.

Her name had been Juuni, and his mother had killed her.

Ferrash had spent fourteen years of his life by that point in the caves on Munab, never once seeing the outside world except perhaps when he was very young, in the company of his mother. The fact he couldn't see the Empyrean had made him a prog, but his mother told him he didn't have to be. Hurl enough of the Empyrean at someone and the shock should let them see it. That was the concept. Survive that and come out the other side empyrric, and he would be a full-blooded Mannae.

That never happened. His entire life on Munab was a series of lessons and experiments: learn what it was to be empyrric, try to become one. After fourteen years, he had been ready to give up. Every day brought a new escape plan. He'd tame a beatwing and fly it out through the cave exit in the desert. He'd lure a lake demon to their shelter while his mother slept and hope it distracted her long enough for him to slip away. He'd take the boat across the water and beg one of the workers at the water treatment plant to get him out of there.

He opted for the lattermost option, but when he landed on the shore by the plant, *she* was there. Juuni, beautiful under the passing bioluminescence. All pleas for rescue tripped over his tongue before they could materialise. He was fourteen, awkward, and smitten.

Over the course of a year, they spent more time together. On the rare occasions his mother left the caves, that included the nights. In his naivety, he thought he could go on forever that way. But then Juuni became pregnant, and with even greater naivety he hatched a plan of escape so they could live together, far away from Munab.

That's why he did his best not to remember. It was the stupidity. The absolute stupidity of not realising it was too easy. His mother had been watching him the whole time. He had meant to meet Juuni on the orbital platform, but he had only found his mother. His mother, who told him Juuni was dead, along with the life she bore. She had killed them both. A final lesson, she meant, that even love was a weakness, and perhaps the greatest one of all.

So he had run from the memory, just as he had run from Palia's.

He let that sink in. He let the ache of sadness tighten across his chest and shiver in his bones. How long had he been without feeling things like this? Too long, though he couldn't remember the emotions of his time with Palia. He supposed that not remembering was the same as it being too long ago to count.

Footsteps sounded on the other side of the cell wall. Metal squealed. Ferrash pushed himself upright, wincing at the stiffness in his joints, and stood up to face whoever was opening the door.

The bearded man stepped in, unarmed. Ferrash wondered if he thought bringing a gun in was more dangerous, considering the consequences if Ferrash got hold of it first.

'I heard,' the man said, his eyes scanning Ferrash from head to toe, 'that you were wantin' to speak to Ida?'

'Yes.'

The man pursed his lips. 'Why for?'

'We had an arrangement. Me, her, your void packs. If she's still alive, if she didn't die on Corumma—'

'You had an *arrangement*? Thought you only arranged stuff with the committees an' stopped them all getting wrong ideas. You makin' arrangements of your own, that starts to sound a little like splittin' to me.'

Raising an eyebrow, Ferrash said, 'Constitutionally speaking, the Proctorate committee is the moral centre of the Protectorate. If we look like we're splitting, it's everyone else who's split.'

The man snorted. 'Come on. What're you up to, really?'

Ferrash narrowed his eyes. There might be no other way out of this situation, but still... He stuck his hand out in front of him, inclining his head to it to indicate the man take it. He did so after a moment's hesitation, giving Ferrash full access to his genetic identifier. Captain Scada Progvarrias.

Ferrash raised an eyebrow. 'So you're the one Ida slept with.'

Progvarrias pulled his hand away with a scowl. 'It was more than that.'

'I know. Is she...?'

The man's chest rose and fell. 'Went to the void with her ship.'

'I'm sorry.'

'How'd you know about Ida?'

Ferrash's genetic identifier would have shown him as Proglimen, and he didn't have any indication Progvarrias had delved further than that information – his cover should be safe. So he said, 'The Reiart knew.'

'You're with them?'

'I am.'

Progvarrias scraped a hand through his beard and paced the short distance between the cell walls. 'Bet if I ask you to prove it, you'll just claim you can't be givin' away too much. But you'll forgive me if I don't trust your committee sort so far as I can throw you. Don't matter which committee it happens to be, they're all leechrot, through and through.'

The void packs might work for the Protectorate, but that didn't mean they liked them.

'The Chair of the Primary Committee is on a road to destruction,' Ferrash said, trying a different tack. 'Kill me or keep me captive and he gets his way. The Protectorate burns. The void packs die in silence.'

That stopped Progvarrias in his tracks. The packs dying in silence had been a phrase Ferrash had agreed on with Ida, if he ever needed to meet with her or a subordinate and be trusted. The void packs would never die in silence. They would sooner roar their death into the void and take as many with them as they could.

'There is no silence where the packs fly.' Progvarrias breathed out heavily and clapped Ferrash on the shoulder. 'We had no need of detainin' you, it seems. But you can understand our caution.'

Ferrash peered past him at the corridor, but the man made no move to leave. 'I'm not entirely sure I do,' Ferrash said.

'This revolution the Reiart wants us to help with. Ida told me to be ready. After Corumma, it's all we want to do. Been wantin' to do somethin' similar for a long while. The Protectorate used us, got us killed. We're takin' the fight home like the Reiart asked.'

Mouth ajar, Ferrash tried to find a way to convey the intricacies of timing to Progvarrias, but he couldn't imagine him wilting at the fact that early moves could kill too many. It was in his eyes: hunger and pain. Pain at Ida's death and the death of so many of his comrades. Hunger to avenge them.

'Can you hold off?' Ferrash asked. 'It's not time yet. Outside the scope of the plan.'

'Too late for that. Haven't you heard the engines? We're through the nexus. Hesperex knows we're here.'

* * *

Ferrash had exhausted the Protectorate's vocabulary of curses by the time they reached the bridge, well on his way through Hegemony phrases in his head.

Each void-pack ship was an individual design, built upon by its crew over the course of many lifetimes. The shielded bridge of this one focused around a circular projection unit, with a tall dais standing at one end. Ferrash joined the captain on this, earning perplexed looks from the rest of the crew.

Hesperex may have known of the void packs' arrival, but it didn't know how to react. Around the projection of Hesperex, its fleets remained in their usual orbits. The radio blurted bursts of communication from planet-side control systems, both automated and manual. One of the crewmembers sat around the projection spoke into a headset. Ferrash didn't know if they were replying and couldn't hear what they said, but they flashed a glance to the captain as if searching for affirmation.

'What's your plan?' Ferrash asked.

The captain replied, 'Hit them where it hurts.'

Trying his best not to appear too condescending, Ferrash twisted to face the captain, eyes narrowed. 'Elaborate, please.' Where it hurt could be anywhere.

'We convince them we're home for new orders, since we've escaped Corumma. We get in orbit. We launch coordinated strikes at the important bits. It all crumbles.'

Ferrash bit his lip. 'Have you ever been to Hesperex?'

'Twenty-three times, for the breeding programme.'

'A while ago, I take it?'

He puffed out his chest, proud at reaching his years. 'Last one was forty years ago, give or take.'

'And can you remember where they are? The important bits?'

His chest deflated. 'Not exactly. You could point them out, though. You've targets in mind? From your plans?'

None of Ferrash's plans had involved orbital bombardment. The void packs were meant as a deterrent more than anything, a final nemesis appearing on the horizon to show what hadn't defected of the Protectorate's military that it was time to give up.

'There are no targets on Hesperex that you could strike without killing thousands of innocents, at the least. Public opinion matters here. If you start bombing them, the plan falls to cinders.' Were there any innocents? Were there any at fault? Or was it all just a blur of painful choices and haphazard morality?

'We're here now. They'll figure us out if we just sit in orbit.'

That was probably true. Even now, the Admiralty might be tracing the void packs' flight path back through the nexus. Protectorate forces getting so far through Hegemony space unscathed – bar damage from Corumma – would raise eyebrows. But it was too soon. Far too soon.

'If you get me back to my ship,' Ferrash said, 'I can spoof a command from the Admiralty to get you to Munab. They'll notice as soon as they ask the "sender" about it – I can't rely on Ida's station anymore – but it's long enough to get you there. If you want to hit them where it hurts, hit the fleets by Munab.'

Progvarrias scoffed, giving him a sidelong glance. 'You want the Hegemony to take Munab? That's what happens if we take out the fleet.'

'Hegemony, Munabis, Rythe...' Ferrash shrugged. 'Does it matter who takes it, as long as they're free?'

'I guess not.' The man stood for a while, examining him, his hands clasped behind his back. Then he nodded. 'Alright, we'll get you onto Hesperex. I'm trustin' you on this. Don't mess us around.'

'I won't.'

Despite the captain's claims of trust, they wouldn't let him out of their sight until they'd received the fake order. So Ferrash set to work, crafting an order in much the same way he had laid his false trail to Munab the first time round. Ducat would have done it faster, but Ferrash hit send ten minutes after getting on board.

Satisfied, they piled him into one of their own shuttles, making the fair point that he would be more likely to pass unnoticed this way than if he piloted the *Etheron* down himself. A minute later, the docking clamps released with dull thumps. The pilot nudged the shuttle towards automated Five-Fifty-Four descent and Ferrash watched the void packs turn back the way they had come, towards the nexus. He wished them luck. They'd annihilate the fleet at Munab, but they'd take a lot of casualties in the process. He thought about that great gash down the side of Progvarrias' ship. So much for structural integrity.

With Hesperex becoming bigger in the canopy, he tried to focus on next steps. But it was hard to do that without thinking about the role his mother played in all of it, and recalling all the reasons why he hated her.

CHAPTER THIRTY-SEVEN

'I wasn't expecting you to be up this late,' Palia said to Bek once Ferrash had left them.

Bek raised an eyebrow and walked to the raised projection table in the lounge, his face highlighted by the glow of whatever he had been looking at before they arrived.

'One trip to the surface and you're already out of Standard Chron,' he said. 'It's morning. Seven.'

'Ugh.' She had been awake for eighteen hours today. She couldn't stand the thought of staying awake another full day.

'Seriously though, when all this is over and everything's back to normal, I need to have words with you two about enjoying yourselves. Should've stayed longer at the party.'

With tired reluctance, Palia made her way out of the corridor to join Bek. 'I can enjoy myself. Just not when I'm worried about...' She waved a hand in the air, fell against the doorframe with a thud.

'Finding happiness in times of stress is the surest way to make hard times less stressful.'

'I'm not sure that's how it works, Bek.'

'Sure it is. Has to be. Ash taught me that.' When she raised an eyebrow, he shrugged. 'I was paraphrasing.'

The fact she knew to question Ferrash had spoken like that made her feel a little more confident, like she had retained more of her memory than originally thought, or picked some up just from seeing him again. She knew that wasn't the case, but it was good to pretend, just for a while.

'So,' she asked, 'why were you up this... early, anyway?'

Bek's face grew so serious that Palia almost regretted asking. He tapped the fingers of his remaining hand against the table, the stump of the other covered by a fold of fabric. His stance looked like it belonged to someone else – both too stiff and too casual at once. She wondered if he was copying it from Ferrash, whether intentionally or no. Filling in in his absence.

'I've done a little more digging,' Bek said. 'Into the systems. Into what Ash left behind.'

Nodding, Palia nudged herself off the doorframe and walked to the couch, where she lowered herself onto one of the seats. 'Well, we know he was up to stuff now. He must have to keep track of a lot, as the Reiart.'

At the table, Bek wavered. He dipped forwards, as if that one arm couldn't support his weight. His forehead creased into thick lines, and he chewed at the inside of his cheek, then checked down the length of the corridor before replying. 'I can't remember if either of us mentioned it before, but have you ever heard us speak about the Reiart?'

She examined her memories. She only recognised the word from Ferrash mentioning it earlier; trying to find it elsewhere had her skirting the voids in her mind. She shook her head. Then, because Bek hadn't seen, she said, 'Not that I recall.'

Bek let out a long breath, then came to join her on the opposite couch. 'The Reiart is another Protectorate intelligence agency, more enforcers than anything else, so secretive that they only really answer to themselves. If you're warning vatters not to step out of line, you tell 'em the Reiart'll get them. There's no proof to say they exist, just stories. Myth. Keep in line or they'll make you disappear. Enough people disappear all the time to make you believe it. You don't fear the ISL or the ESF – even they're scared of 'em.' He grimaced, tapped a finger to his brow. 'Case in point.'

He paused to stare out of the viewscreen above them. The distorted white star of the Rythian nexus sat reflected in both eyes. 'Ash always said they weren't real. Said they were just that: a story, nothing more, made to scare us. He was lying the whole time.'

Palia pulled a face at the floor. It had been too much to hope that Bek saw past this. Ferrash had been right to worry about the betrayal of trust. How long would this haunt Bek?

Bek drew a hand across his face. 'I can't believe he works for them. The whole thing with the ESF just made it easier to cover his tracks. Our whole *job* was a lie.'

'Maybe he was ESF first and then joined the Reiart?' Palia wished she'd asked for specifics.

Bek shrugged. 'He did all our missions together, but he always ended up doing his own things on the side, always knew more than he should. They call the committee that governs Protectorate intelligence the Board of a Thousand Ears, but I think all thousand of those must've belonged to Ash.'

Twisting in her seat, Palia followed Bek's gaze to the nexus. 'Do you believe in his plan? You think it'll work?'

'He's playing with chaos,' his reply came back, cold and hard. A lump formed in Palia's throat. 'But I'll always believe in him.' He chuckled, then, the noise sounding out of place. 'I knew he'd be on Hesperex. A bit of a shame you found him first.'

'You knew where he was?' Palia rocked forwards in her seat, eyes wide. 'How?' She guessed he'd only just found out, otherwise he would have told her.

'He's been getting sloppy. I got into the ISL database. They've a kill order out on him. Tracked him to Triff's underground, then lost him. Report says a Keeper helped him escape. His mother. Kill order on her head, too.'

That made no sense. Through all the gaps in her memory, she remembered the image of Ferrash's mother – a green-armoured figure riding in a palanquin atop a giant siggerith, her eyes boring straight into her. At the time, Palia had been relieved not to be discovered. That stare had filled her with fear. With all her emotions on view, she was sure she had been found out. But she had turned away. Had she seen Ferrash and trusted not to intervene? Were they working together even then? Why hadn't Ferrash mentioned her?

Palia sighed. 'I guess we have even more questions to ask Ash next time we see him. Can you plot the route?'

Bek nodded and unfolded himself from the couch, staggering a little as he started in the direction of the cockpit. Palia watched him go, her mind reeling. When the cockpit door membrane reformed behind him, she brought up the image he had given her in her implants, and there Ferrash was – not the man she had kissed on Rythe, but frustratingly familiar. She stared at it for an age, terrified that if she closed it again, she would just forget, as if the second he wasn't right in front of her the memory of his face would slip back into the void. Scars covered the left side of his face, the pain mesh buried underneath but still showing through. She traced them through the air with a finger in the space where her brain said the image should be.

She recalled how he had appeared on Rythe, the churning emotions, the untethered rope reaching out for an anchor, and cursed herself for never upgrading her implants to include a memory catcher. She may have reunited with him, they may have come *together* again, but would she ever be able to remember his face, once he lost the mask? And *what if...* what if all this was a cover? His love for her, his love for Bek. What if nothing else mattered but what he wanted to accomplish as the Reiart? Her heart beat so fast in her chest she was afraid it would make a break for freedom.

The thought burned through her mind, leaving fire in its wake. Her skin began to glow with the curse of the Empyrean and she shoved her hands under her armpits in case Lilesh or Tessa should walk in. She had seen his love. There must be something genuine there. Maybe Bek's stories about the Reiart were overblown. Maybe Ferrash had had nothing to do with the worst of it.

After a while, Palia dragged herself into the sleeping quarters. Tessa walked out as she came in, clothed only in a towel, the horns on her head shining after a fresh clean. The arsaeria inclined her head briefly, then went to join Lilesh in the dining room opposite. Here, of course, 'join' simply meant to share the room. They sat apart, facing away from each other, and Tessa resumed her art.

Palia didn't think she would be able to sleep. But once she had stripped naked and lain down under the blankets, she found herself drifting down through the layers of consciousness.

Where before she would have dreamed of the space between memories, the dead in the tides of Varna, she dreamed his face – the real one, the one she couldn't touch. She fell asleep to an enigma: an expression she couldn't read, a mind she couldn't truly know.

Of faces, Ferrash had two: the one she had just seen on Rythe, the one that claimed to love her; and the hidden one, the one that worked in shadows and played a game that may or may not have been a lie all along.

CHAPTER THIRTY-EIGHT

THE MOMENT THEY JETTED out of the end of the Prime Nexus, every alarm on the ship went off.

Palia jerked bolt upright in her bunk, cracking her head against the bunk above. She swore, cradling it in her hands, and tried to blink away the pain. The alarms sliced into it. Then, just as sudden as they had started, they cut off. With a groan, she swung her feet over the side of the bunk and stood swaying, her head fuzzed with static. Clutching the blanket tight around her like a cocoon too comfortable to shed, she walked to the cockpit.

Tessa and Lilesh already stood there, blocking Palia's view of whatever lay beyond. She could just make out the side of Bek's head through the gap between their elbows.

'What is it?' Palia asked. Lilesh stepped closer to Tessa, leaving room for Palia to stand alongside.

'See for yourself,' said Bek.

A long train of ships stretched across the canopy from the direction of Hesperex, passing straight by them to a different entrance in the Prime Nexus. They travelled in a cylinder ten abreast, and she could only just make out the end of the line.

Palia blinked at the sight in amazement. 'If they're not after us, why did the alarms go off?'

Bek said, 'One of them locked weapons just as we came out of the nexus, but they've dropped us now.'

'Suspicious?'

'Maybe just surprised to see us, until they saw the codes.'

The ships passed by so fast that they appeared as a continuous blur, like a rope tying the nexus to Hesperex. She could only make out individual ships when she blinked, but three blinks later the last of them vanished. Hesperex grew larger in the glass.

'Where are they heading?' Palia asked. If they could warn Fabien, it might help the war effort.

Bek's eyes became unfocused, his attention on his implants. With one hand occupied on the flight controls, he had rerouted many of the tasks he usually used control panels for so he didn't have to rely on his missing hand.

'Munab, apparently,' he said. 'Good thing we didn't stick around longer.'

Palia grimaced, picturing the besieged planet in her mind's eye, seeing all those ships appear in the fray. That many would plant advantage back with the Protectorate. Munab was edging closer to a lost cause.

'Do you mind if I send a message to Fabien? It shouldn't get picked up. It's encrypted.'

As Hesperex grew to the size of her head, Bek turned and raised an eyebrow. 'Encryption exists to be broken.'

'I sent one before, after you and Ash rescued me. He never noticed, that I remember.' Of course, she *wouldn't* remember.

'I don't remember him mentioning it,' Bek said, 'but it's just as likely he knew the second you sent it and just never said anything. Did you get a reply?'

Heart sinking, she said, 'No.'

'Might've blocked it.' He faced the canopy again, chewing at his lip. 'What'd Fabien do if you told him?'

'I don't know.' Fabien wouldn't just leave Munab, that was for sure. And with Rythe about to join the fight, maybe they would end up evenly matched.

'Best not, then.'

Lilesh had stayed remarkably quiet through the exchange. If she was a spy for Fabien, perhaps she had her own, secret ways to get a message back. Or maybe she had just followed the same line of reasoning as Palia. Tessa, meanwhile, had her eyes fixed on Hesperex, her hands clutching at the back of Bek's chair.

Concerned, Palia opened a private channel. <Are you okay? >

Tessa's shoulders twitched. She turned, startled. <I'm fine.>

But then she looked back over her shoulder as if she could see the departing fleet through the hull, and Palia saw how worried she really was, underneath it all. If Palia got uncomfortable knowing there was one empyrric aboard who could see her feelings, how did Tessa feel knowing there were two? Out of respect for that, Palia turned away.

Hesperex beckoned. Once that part of the journey was done, everything could go back to normal. Tessa could return to the arsaeria and never look on the person who had got Austela killed again. Lilesh could go back to doing whatever it was she really did as archivist. Palia and Bek and Ash... well, something would happen.

She took a seat in the chair that used to be Bek's and smiled across the panels at him.

He looked up from the controls, fixed his eyes on her. 'Time to see if Ash has made a mess.'

At the spaceport, once the automated systems had spindled them away inside the megastructure, Palia rose and made for the armoury to get some warm clothes. Lilesh shot an arm out to stop her.

'Your present course of action is unwise,' Lilesh said, her eyes narrowed to slits. 'The Magister tasked me with keeping you safe. You cannot be safe upon Hesperex.'

Palia raised her chin and pulled her arm away from the woman's grasp. 'Then tell on me, if you like, but Fabien already knows I'm going. You're staying here. You too, Tessa.' Palia nodded to her horns. 'Unless I missed something last time, they don't go in for gene mods on Hesperex.'

Tessa nodded, if anything relieved not to have to step outside, but Lilesh stood her ground. 'If the Keepers catch you, I'll never hear the end of it. The mother of the Magister's son, be he alive or no, is a bargaining chip. Walking straight into the heart of them is madness.'

'If the Keepers catch me,' Palia said, shrugging into a long, fleece-lined coat she had bought specifically for Hesperex, 'they'll kill me. The only reason blood matters to them at all is to breed more keepers. If they even know my relation to Fabien, which I doubt, they won't see anything meaningful in the connection.'

Palia hesitated before putting her gloves on. When she did, she kept her gaze fixed on her fingers as she pulled the fabric over them. After so long spent in the archivist's company, she had grown used to that snake, coiling around her psyche. She only remembered it now, in preparation for the sterile landscape beyond the spaceport walls.

'Can you sense any keepers?' Palia asked.

Lilesh cocked her head to one side, then shook it. 'No.'

'Good. That gives you time to calm down.'

'Excuse me?'

She looked up at Lilesh, unable to keep a sly grin from creeping over her face. 'You'll stick out a mile here. All that energy, burning away. You need to get rid of it. They'll see you, otherwise.'

From Lilesh's stance – feet planted at shoulder width, shoulders tense, head held high – Palia thought she was about to argue. But then she looked deeper, realised half of Lilesh's energies were fuelled by tension and desire. She didn't want to fight Palia, she wanted to fight *them*. A whole planet full of keepers and she wanted to meet them head on.

'I think it's for the best, don't you?'

Lilesh sucked in a lungful of air. 'You're quite right.' Her voice came out clipped, not far different to normal but laced with all the tension she held. That began to wane. Not the fastest way to bleed off excess empyrric energy, and they needed it gone fast, but it was something.

Palia turned to Bek. 'Are you ready?'

They left the spaceport the same way they had come last time, familiarity blurred by vanished memory. It wasn't snowing, but the air was ice. It cut into her even through all her layers. She balled her fists tight in her pockets to try keeping them warm, but her toes ached in her boots. She had hidden her tell-tale hair under a combination of headscarf, hat and hood. If the clouds ever disappeared overhead and let the sun shine through, would it melt away the gloom of Hesperex? Light made you notice things the darkness hid, provided your eyes were open.

'Where do you need to go to get your arm fixed?' she asked.

Bek pivoted on a heel as he walked, brows raised like he hadn't expected to see her there. 'Thought that comes later?'

She shook her head. Only a few others shared the street with them, making it quieter than last time, and they hurried on their way with eyes downcast. It made the orange-coated soldiers even more conspicuous. She saw more of these patrolling the city than she saw the city's residents.

'You get your arm first,' Palia said. 'If anything goes wrong, you'll need it – and I guess it would be harder to fit in with the landers without it. That's okay, right?'

Bek sighed, his breath misting in the air, and stared at the stump of his left arm. 'It feels cold. It's not there, and it's bloody freezing.' Swallowing, he looked away again. 'Come on, walk with me while we work it out. Can't stand talking in the street.'

She wanted to point out that they had seen four or five people talking in the street on their journey already, but she followed after him. The fact felt odd even to her. This wasn't quite the same Hesperex she had been to before. Something had changed, or was in the process of changing.

'I'll need to ask about the arm at headquarters,' Bek said. 'They'll recognise you, so you can't come with. I mean, Ash told them you'd defected, but... They weren't too keen to begin with. Was only him arguing it that saved you.'

More evidence to suggest Ferrash might not be far from who they thought he was. 'I've been there before? I don't remember. Maybe just talking to you, in a... waiting room?'

'Yeah. Doesn't surprise me you don't remember more. You wiped your memory of the escape back. That plus your other gaps, and... well, not much left to go on.'

Palia shook her head, though it was far too late to scold herself for her mistakes.

'Ash said there was someone I should meet, so at least I have somewhere to go.' A flurry of snow cascaded to the ground ahead, dislodged from one of the buildings lining the street. She wished they could go together. She felt like there was nothing she could do, alone, in the midst of the Protectorate, no matter what job Ferrash gave her. She had never lived here. She could blend in just as long as she was walking or mingling with a crowd, but how could she infiltrate the Kept when she didn't know how to speak with anyone without giving herself away?

'He tell you who?' Bek asked.

'A keeper, apparently. A friendly one.'

'No such thing.'

Palia shrugged.

Bek sighed and looked at her sidelong. 'You don't have to do this.'

'Ash needs our help. If I can't stop him doing what he's doing, I can at least get involved.'

'Fine.' He pulled a face. 'Just don't try too hard, alright? I'm not... I'm not sure how much I trust his judgement anymore.'

At the corner of a street, Bek stopped, looked both ways, then removed his glove with his teeth and held his hand out for her to take. He inclined his head to it, gesturing with his eyes. When she removed one of her gloves and placed her hand in his, he transferred a batch of files to her implants. He gave her hand a light squeeze, then withdrew and struggled back into his glove. Palia resisted offering to help once she had slid hers back on. He didn't seem in the mood for help.

<Open those files,> he sent.

Palia trusted him enough to ignore her virus scanner's warnings. Opening the files didn't do anything drastic, from a functionality perspective. It just added an extra layer around her existing systems.

<What's this?> she asked.

<Fake genetic identifier, fake database entries, a mask for your open networks. No public net on Hesperex, so if anyone scans you and sees you searching for one, they'll have you as a splitter. Remember you can't message anyone safely unless you're standing close, so you'll have no contact with me or Ash. We might be able to get messages to you, but you don't have the hardware.>

<This'll help me blend in?>

<It claims you're a free agent. Stay away from keepers – 'unfriendly' ones, anyway – and you'll be fine.>

Palia examined their surroundings: grey buildings, the same as all the other buildings in the city, stretching up until they were lost in the murk.

<I don't know where anything is,> she sent.

<Didn't Ash leave a map for you?>

Palia checked, and it turned out he had, complete with markers for where she had to meet the keeper. It was only five minutes from the spaceport. She wondered when he'd slipped that in.

Bek stopped again by the back entrance to a nondescript building, fiddling with the stump of his arm and eyeing the recessed door. 'I don't know how long this'll take,' he said. She wasn't sure if he meant his arm or Ferrash's revolution.

Palia examined the door, but found nothing of note beyond a slight twinge of recognition. 'I'll be heading back to the ship when night falls anyway, or earlier depending when I finish. If you can't make it, just send me an update, alright? And keep sending one every hour so I know you're okay.'

He laughed, too loud, and peered down at her. 'I'm not the one in danger here. You'd better be there when I'm back.'

Although Palia smiled, her chest tightened. She hoped arms grew back fast.

CHAPTER THIRTY-NINE

'You look awful, Honeras,' said Archivist Lilesh.

'Thanks.' Fabien dragged a hand across his face, trying to knead as much sense back into the flesh as he could, but there was no use. His skin weighed so much it might just slough off onto the floor. He could only make out the projection of Lilesh clearly if he squinted, and then he kept having to remind his foggy brain that she wasn't really there.

At length, when Lilesh ventured no more words and Fabien was convinced he wasn't about to fall asleep, he said, 'I haven't slept since Rythe.'

'Your relations with your new wife are not my concern.'

'*No*, that's not what I meant.' Glaring the best he could, he tried to pick out her surroundings, but the projection had clipped to her form well enough to exclude them. 'I've just been worried.'

'Given your role, Magister, might I suggest you work on managing your concerns, rather than let them consume you?'

Turning from the projection a moment, Fabien crossed to the lounger and folded onto it, knocking a glass from the side table as he did. He lunged for it, missed. It thudded against the carpet, unbroken. Everything was laid out different on this ship – one of the few in Rythe's fleet designed for people instead of machines – but hitching a ride with Rythe was the only way he could follow their eventual attack on Munab at their own pace. It would be a while until anything was familiar. *Wake up.*

'Can anyone else hear or see you?' Fabien asked.

'This link is neural only. As far as anyone who might be watching is concerned, I am asleep.'

That explained Lilesh's complete lack of movement, beyond her face. No shifting of weight, no involuntary movements. Her face only moved at all because such projections animated to match the words transmitted.

Fabien nodded, satisfied. 'How's Palia?'

Lilesh hesitated longer than was usual for her. 'Fine. Tense. Why?'

Was the archivist being evasive? He couldn't see any reason for her to lie. 'Back on Rythe, at my wedding... Ferrash visited me there, to ask for help, but disguised as the Protectorate's Proctor. He tried to leave just as Palia arrived. They saw each other. Palia recognised him.'

The guilt had been gnawing at him. Every time he shut his eyes, he saw the two of them passing in front of him, felt afresh that stab of indecision and sorrow. Sure, the two of them had ended up together again and it had worked out fine, but Fabien had been about to lie to Palia. Ferrash had been *right there*. But Fabien had promised.

'I learned as much myself,' Lilesh said, 'considering they both came aboard the ship and he outlined his plans.'

'Well, I'm glad he's at least starting to be more open. Is he still with you?'

'No. It would look too suspicious. And I wouldn't credit his openness a great deal. His outline was just that – the surface of his intentions. I imagine he left a great deal out. I remain suspicious of whatever he has omitted. I can't say I agree with your decision to help him.'

'I'm sure it'll be fine.' It probably wouldn't. 'We can talk more about this later.' He probably wouldn't get around to it. 'Look, I need to ask your opinion on something. Are you aware of the engineers I've set to work on the flagship?'

'Analysing the former Magister's modifications to it, yes.'

He hadn't told her that, and no one else should know, but it was her job to find things out, so he shouldn't be surprised. 'And do you know about the prototype technology Palia found on Munab?'

'Considering you sent us there to recover it, certainly.'

A fair point. Fabien flicked at a control on the side table and it poured a cup of chai. All the better to keep him awake. 'Through examining both the prototype and the nexite pathways within the flagship, the engineering team found similarities. At a likely guess, Magister Lavennon planned to unleash it on Hesperex, controlling the effect himself as implied by Palia's admittedly limited report from fighting him. They also got quite excited about more insight on nexite arrangements that we could use to arm our nexus against unwanted traffic, but that's a long-term project for them. It's nothing we can act on immediately.'

'So if it follows the effects of the prototype,' Lilesh said, and her fake projection crossed its arms somewhat stiffly, 'It stands to reason he was going to cut every keeper on Hesperex off from the Empyrean. How much energy did it require? Was he going to use all the energy gained from destroying Everatus Four in one attack, or would he have gone on to the other planets in the Protectorate to finish the job?'

'That's more than we can answer yet.'

Silence. Then came the important question. 'Do you intend to complete his objectives?'

It would feel dirty, using the still-stored energy that had killed his own son as a weapon of war. Less dirty if he reframed it, made it a weapon to *end* war. But reframing was the art of excuse and justification, and utilising it was as good as admitting guilt, no matter the extent. Not to mention, millions of people lived aboard the flagship. Manoeuvring it into a combat situation again would be rash, and certainly wouldn't sit well with the populace. Still, they could evacuate, and the Keepers *did* need to go...

'Once we have the Prime Nexus,' Fabien said, 'Hesperex will be cut off. We can travel in with the flagship and a skeleton crew, then have an empyrric trigger the weapon.'

'What if it uses more energy than you expect and you don't have enough to get back?'

Fabien picked the cup of chai from the side table and sipped at it, wincing. 'We have a contingency to deal with that.' The contingency was Rythe, and ships that could travel when and where they wanted, and an evacuation until they could drag the flagship back into recharge range of a nexus.

'Well then.' Lilesh couldn't look less impressed. 'Kindly let me know when you plan to carry this out – I would hate for Palia and I to still be on that accursed planet when it comes under fire.'

CHAPTER FORTY

THE SHUTTLE THE VOID packs used to send Ferrash down to Hesperex contained their wounded. In normal circumstances, they would have kept them aboard, but their ships had suffered too much damage in the assault on Corumma to be able to care for their own as they always did. As they approached the planet, vatters wrapped bandages around Ferrash's head, bloodied and soiled a little, so that Proglimen's face would be entirely covered.

With a little adjustment of rotas, the medical staff who came to collect him were members of the Reiart, embedded long ago.

As they hovered him on a gurney through the drab corridors of one of Five-Fifty-Four's hospitals, Ferrash took the time to go over his assets. Since he had taken control of the Reiart, he had added a second layer to its operations. The first layer, as ever, consisted of independent cells of agents. The majority of those weren't even cells, just individual agents. Their daily lives saw them embedded in some other role in the Protectorate. None of them reported directly to him. There were other ways to dispense orders . No one in the Reiart knew who he was.

The second layer, the new one, was even further removed. These didn't take orders. For the most part, they didn't even know they had been played. But they were splitters, all of them – people the ISL would have done away with if the Reiart hadn't shuffled them out of danger first. Sometimes they got a hint of the larger plan, told their time would come and they should wait for a signal, but mostly Ferrash just had the Reiart scare them enough that they stayed model citizens. A lot of them fed reports into Ferrash's web, whether they knew it or not.

Ferrash closed his eyes as a particularly glaring set of ceiling lights passed by overhead. Before the purge, that second layer had been massive. Around thirty percent of the Protectorate's total population – not just on Hesperex – had been a part of his web.

After the purge, there had only been five percent.

The full number had never really sunk in. He'd seen the reports live, but hadn't had time to mull them over until much later, when the events were further removed. His gut churned. How many billions had that been? Ferrash wondered what the committees had discussed that day, whether they had all shrugged and the food representative had felt a weight lift from their shoulders at another few years avoiding famine.

Aware that he hadn't been jostled in a while, Ferrash cracked open an eyelid and peered about him. Bare grey walls hemmed him in, disturbed dust thick in the air beneath a single light panel.

Alone, he levered himself upright, limbs creaking after so long lying down, and stripped the bandages off his head. He was ages from the nearest safe room, but they'd left a thick patchwork coat and hood in the corner for him. With another day until he was expected at the next committee meeting – he had been cutting it fine – he had time enough to sleep and shower.

Ferrash ran his fingers through the unfamiliar length of his short hair, trying to ignore the way Proglimen's face dragged on his own. He couldn't wait to get out of this thing. But it would be a long time before he could wear his real face again, at least within the Protectorate. He was the Proctor now, and would be until his plan either fell through or succeeded.

With a weary sigh, Ferrash headed for the shower. At least some of his plan's rested on surviving tomorrow's committee meeting. It wouldn't do to stink of Rythe and a void pack's jail cell.

No one paid Ferrash much attention when he arrived in the committee chambers, which was a good start. The first thing the committee chose to speak of, of course, was the void packs' appearance over Hesperex and their subsequent withdrawal.

'I thought I had made it clear, representative,' the Chair said to the spacer woman, his back perfectly straight as he sat at the head of the table, 'that the fleets were to remain in Corumma.'

The woman's face was a picture of serenity. If she hid anything, she hid it well. Ferrash wondered if his mother saw any different.

'Our fleets have remained in Corumma,' the spacer said. 'Only the void packs have returned.'

The Chair shook his head. 'Their actions are unacceptable. They knew where they were needed.'

Ferrash cleared his throat. 'By definition, the void packs' actions can never be unacceptable. They were created to be self-organising.' It was what made them one of Ferrash's best potential weapons. 'The most that can be done with them is point them at a target and let them loose. They were let loose on Corumma, they succeeded, and they returned.' Success, here, was a relative term.

The Chair narrowed his eyes at him down the length of the table, and Ferrash tried to suppress a smug smile. A part of him found playing nitpicker to the government too satisfying. He wondered if Proglimen had enjoyed his job, then shuddered when he remembered he was wearing the man's face.

'In any case,' the Chair said, 'they moved on to Munab. Why did they return here first? Why not travel straight to Munab? Their display here reeks of ostentation.'

Ostentation. It wasn't often the full word got rolled out over *ostat.*

'Is it possible their communications stopped working after Corumma?' Ferrash asked before anyone else could step in. 'If they could only receive in-system comms, perhaps they returned here for directions. I assume they *were* directed to Munab?'

The spacer stared at him for a second longer than he would have liked before nodding. 'We pointed them there, yes.'

Ferrash wasn't looking forwards to whichever meeting happened once the void packs turned on the Protectorate's fleets at Munab. It would be a few days before they arrived, at least. Then a thought occurred to him.

When a gap opened up between some tangential conversation, Ferrash said, 'I heard the Keepers have sustained heavy losses on Munab. Would it be wise to send reinforcements?' That would certainly kill two birds with one stone. The Keepers would arrive at Munab to a hostile void pack. No keeper had managed to attack far across the void yet – the best they could do would be to hold out a little while with shielding.

'Absolutely not.' The Chair's voice rang out across the room. 'Should the rot of Munab spread elsewhere, we need them ready to redeploy.'

Ferrash glanced to his left, to his mother, who had apparently retained her position, but Ayt also shook her head. 'Ignoring, for now, the fact that the Keepers take no orders from any of you, the problem of Munab lies with the Board of the Fist. It seems a wise move to have redirected the void packs there. I am sure they will turn the tide without our intervention.' She gave Ferrash a hard glance as she finished speaking, as if she had been able to glean his exact motives through the Empyrean. She might be supporting his disguise as per the plan, but she wouldn't go as far as sending her own people into the fire.

Throughout the meeting, the woman representing the vats had fidgeted in her seat, chewing at her lip every now and then. As a pause stretched following Ayt's statement, Vats took the opportunity to speak up.

'If we're done with Munab,' she said, her voice surprisingly soft, 'I have a matter to bring to the attention of this committee.'

The Chair leaned back in his seat, brow furrowed, and gestured for her to continue.

Vats tapped at the table in front of her, flicking a schematic across its surface so the table projected it as a holographic representation of a section of building. She left it hanging there, unexplained for now.

'About a week ago, one of our vat tenders was conducting a routine verification of our genetic stocks when they uncovered something that seemed out of place. They were only filling in for another worker that day, and they initially sought confirmation from fellow vat tenders as to whether they had seen a problem correctly.' Vats licked her lips, a nervous habit. 'Each of them dismissed the problem, but the way they did so made the vat tender suspicious, following which he brought his discovery directly to me.'

Ferrash eyed the hologram with a sinking feeling, half certain he knew where this was going, completely certain that it was not where he wanted it to go.

Sighing, the Chair asked, 'Do we have more gene-code corruption?'

'Worse,' Vats said, staring unblinking at the table. After a pause, she glanced at the faces around her and continued. 'There was a virus in the code banks. It had spread to sixty-three percent of our material. When we ran automated forensics programmes to identify whoever tampered with them, they wiped our records. The programmes had been tampered with as well. So we have no way of knowing how long this virus has been in effect, not without taking samples of varying ages of vatborn.

'With the help of the committee for digital infrastructure, we were at least able to conduct some manual forensics on the programme modifications. The suite of scripts used appears to be an adapted version of those created by either the ISL or ESF – we haven't been able to narrow down further than that. Whoever modified the programmes logged into the vat servers' – and here, the hologram lit up to highlight a workstation near the centre of the building – 'presumably using faked biometrics, considering the account owner was halfway across Five-Fifty-Four at the time.'

The ISL representative folded his arms across his chest and glanced sidelong at the ESF representative. 'There's security footage of this, surely?'

Vats nodded. 'They appeared identical to the account owner. When we followed their trail, they disappeared into a black spot and never re-emerged. We found what remained of a body at the location, but it was... unidentifiable. Its genetics weren't in the records.'

Ferrash clasped his hands over the table and rested his chin on them. 'Back to the most important question – what does the virus *do*?' He knew full well what it did, of course. He'd had the virus made well over three years ago. He'd ordered a Reiart cell to make sure it got applied two years later. They hadn't even been sloppy, just unlucky, and one of them had killed themselves to keep quiet. That hadn't been part of the orders. Perhaps they'd thought they were being followed. Ferrash had put the sabotage to the back of his mind, handled by his auxiliary AI, one sub-plan amongst a labyrinth. Now, it had come back to haunt him.

Vats looked surprised at his interruption. 'It, ah... It grants immunity.' She licked her lips again. 'To inhibitors.'

A deathly silence fell upon the table. With the Protectorate falling back on using inhibitors to suppress the more rebellious parts of its population in recent years, this situation was their worst nightmare. Each new generation of vatters made with that code would be a generation they couldn't control. And that was the point, of course, but they hadn't been meant to find out about it. This was all meant to happen behind the scenes, until one day everyone was immune and inhibitors wouldn't be a stumbling block anymore.

After what might have been a full minute, the Chair asked, 'You have *corrected* the fault, of course?'

'The backups were infected as well,' Vats said. 'We have gene coders working on it. Given they know the extent of the changes – unless there are any that aren't common to all infected codes – they expect to revert the immunity code within the week. We've suspended all new growths in the meantime.'

Ferrash leaned back in his chair as if satisfied at the announcement, but his mind whirled into gear. With population-wide immunity out of the question, he had to claw something back from this. If people couldn't feel, they wouldn't see a need to fight. There might be an inhibitor shortage, but there was still enough to keep Hesperex numb for a year, and he needed to move before then.

Once the other representatives finished questioning Vats – and after a particularly heated exchange of blame between the ESF and ISL – Ferrash said, 'If someone's trying to impede the effects of inhibitors, they won't stop here. They broke into the vat servers, and that building's arguably quite secure. Our current stocks are just scattered through warehouses and water treatment at the moment, aren't they?'

Both the water and physical infrastructure representatives nodded.

'Then we should move them somewhere with higher security.'

Vats nodded. 'I agree. Now we know about the virus, they're less likely to attack along the same route. We can't let them get to the inhibitors.'

The Chair peered at her, nodded once, and craned his neck over to Physical Infrastructure. 'Do you have a space?'

Ferrash slipped back into the flow of the conversation as they discussed where best to move the inhibitors, satisfied that his job was done. With the inhibitors in one location – one that he'd be able to find quite easily, even if no one revealed it in this discussion – all it would take was one well-placed explosion at the start of the revolution and they would be out of the picture for good.

He felt his mother's gaze on him, cold and calculating as it ever was. He stared back, wondering how long it would be until he felt a knife in his back. Or felt nothing at all.

CHAPTER FORTY-ONE

AN ALERT FROM HIS implants let Ferrash know Palia and Bek had arrived as he scaled the mountain to his hideout. The tracker on his ship – his old ship, not the one he'd borrowed for his trip to Rythe – had been picked up leaving the Prime Nexus. He squinted back along the cloud-capped ceiling of Five-Fifty-Four, knowing he'd have to stand here long enough to freeze to catch sight of their landing, then opened the hatch and dropped into the hideout. He tried not to think about the dangers of the tasks he had given them.

To warm his hands, he headed straight for the stove and a brew. Son and the Observers, he guessed, were still in the lower levels. He'd have time to check on them later.

'An eventful trip?' his mother asked.

His back tensed on hearing her voice. Juuni's death still weighted the edge of his memories, and Ayt's voice was just as harsh now as it had been then. She came into view at the edge of his vision, her hands folded across her chest in a gesture distinctly *his* that he didn't remember her using before. Dark bags nestled beneath her eyes. Instead of making him curious or sympathetic, the sight irritated him. It irritated him more that she had arrived here before him after the committee meeting.

'That hate is fresh,' she said.

Ferrash clunked a mug down on the worksurface and poured the brew in, spilling some thanks to his shaking hands. He raised it to his lips, blew. 'I was reminded of something.'

He could feel her eyes on him. A phantom pain bloomed where his pain mesh cupped his skull. He knew it wasn't her – the mesh hadn't activated – but his mind expected it.

'Ju—'

Rounding on her, Ferrash bared his teeth. 'Don't say it. You don't get to say her name.'

Ayt sighed, and her shoulders fell, almost as if he had disappointed her. The notion made hot fury bubble up inside him. He closed his eyes and leaned his arms against the worksurface, his fingers gripping the edge so hard it felt like his bones would press through the metal.

'I didn't kill her.'

Fury came to a screeching halt. In its place, an emptiness rang between his ears. 'Juuni's alive?'

'She died fighting the Kept five years ago.'

'What?' He pushed away from the worksurface, his brows pulled tight together. That was crazy. Juuni was a maintenance worker. 'Why was she fighting Kept?'

'She was a Keeper.'

'No.' Ferrash shook his head. Without meaning to, he stepped back. 'She was vatborn. Told me she was.'

'That's what we told her to say.'

Both hands balled into tight fists, he stayed in place, chest heaving, resisting the urge to fight or flee. 'You tell her to say she loved me, too?'

His mother opened her mouth, drew in a deep breath. 'Yes.'

Ferrash lashed out at the worksurface and sent the contents of the mug splashing against the wall. Didn't matter. His heart beat fast enough to warm him more than the brew could. For a moment, the first fuzz of the light-headedness that had come over him when he reunited with Palia rose up, but rage pushed that feeling aside. It had to be a lie. It had to. He had seen the love in her eyes and in her touch... when he was a teenager, and naïve and stupid. Keepers could stoop that low, but no, no, it couldn't...

'—lost cause.' His mother's words cut back over the ringing in his skull. 'They wanted you for the breeding programme instead. We compromised. I knew you'd run and get yourself killed if you went to Hesperex. They agreed to send their candidate to Munab.'

'We... we were together over a year. She was pregnant when you...!' He trailed off, panting, his entire body shaking. Without another word to his mother, he turned and left for the hatch. The thought of a child of his, born to the Keepers, when he had planned a normal life for them until he thought them dead... What had they been? Blood or prog? Keeper or fodder?

As he hauled himself back out of the hatch, his mother called, 'Ferrash, your daughter—!' but her next words were lost to the wind, and the snow, and the fires in his mind.

Ferrash made a beeline for Bek. It wasn't difficult to track him down. He knew where the ship had docked – right next to his own, by pure chance – and he'd had face-recognition algorithms sweep through the path of the nearest cameras to follow him. Ferrash was done keeping secrets from him. He'd go to Bek, tell him everything, finally have someone he trusted at his back instead of his mother. The lies surrounding Juuni screamed in the back of his mind, but he ignored them, as much as he could.

Sometimes, it was better to forget.

When he slid through the broken wall of a building on the outskirts of Five-Fifty-Four, he slowed to a halt, then removed his skis and hid them inside the exposed insulation layer. This he loosely covered with a curtain of broken wires tugged through from behind. Not the best hiding spot, but it would only be compromised if they knew exactly where to look or went over the place with a fine-toothed comb.

He braced himself for the cold, then whipped off his coat as fast as he could, turned it inside out and tugged it back on again. Plain, dark red fabric more suited to committee members and intelligence agents than the majority of workers gave way to a colourful patchwork.

He drew a hood out from inside the collar and pulled it over his hat, which he also reversed. There were enough people in similar clothes on Hesperex that he wouldn't draw much notice, and he had a scarf to keep Proglimen's face mostly hidden.

Satisfied, Ferrash left the building and immersed himself in the crowds. He'd accidentally timed it for one of the city's many shift changes, so even with lower traffic levels than usual, he had plenty of space to hide.

He checked the latest locations as he walked. Bek and Palia had split up. Bek sat in a waiting room at ESF headquarters. Palia waited in the safe house where his mother was supposed to meet her.

Slowing his breathing to maintain calm, Ferrash scratched a forefinger against his thumb and glanced between his options at the junction ahead. Right, and he could find somewhere to wait for Bek to come out of the headquarters. Left, and he could return to the spaceport, let himself on board the ship and wait for them there. His skin crawled at the thought of leaving Palia alone with his mother, of her wandering Five-Fifty-Four afterwards, after what had happened last time. So many ways she could get caught out just by existing on Hesperex. As if it wasn't hard enough for someone who had always lived there to survive.

He craned his neck up as if he could see the improbable curves of the Prime Nexus through every layer of cloud and smog. That was his objective up there. He couldn't forget that, but at the same time he realised he could no longer face the full scope of his plans alone.

The junction arrived. He turned right.

It felt strange, after so long working for them, to tread the road to the ESF headquarters and know that building was forbidden to him, now. Ferrash watched it grow closer, almost nostalgic at the loss, then turned into the building opposite. There he met with a patchwork sea of coated figures at pounding machines. Some nearer the front worked a conveyor belt, sweeping rains of bullets off the sides into crates before passing those onto another belt. There had been a time when all this was done by machines, but they had broken. The vatborn were replaceable, and just as mechanical in their motions.

Ferrash touched his hand against the signing plate on the dais above the workfloor, a fake identifier marking this as his place of work, and stepped down to join the others. He took up position at one of the presses and settled into the mechanical motion of working it. Electricity and automation were expensive. Muscles were cheap.

As he worked, he checked on Bek's position. Still in the waiting room. The Protectorate had no idea Bek had defected, but Ferrash would have been a little nervous at waltzing in and asking for a new arm, regardless.

He worked for another hour, watching, waiting. At last, they let Bek into the committee chamber. When they questioned him about his association with Ferrash, Bek gave the simplest lie he could: Ferrash had betrayed them, left them alone in Protectorate space. Left them for dead. Not all of that was a lie, and they believed it. In return for the regrowth of his arm, they asked one thing: that Bek pursue a kill order on Ferrash.

Bek was only too eager to accept.

Ferrash focused on the machine for the next few seconds in an attempt to make sure his distraction didn't show. Ignoring Bek's reaction – surely nothing more than a good act – the kill order was new. Had they traced the virus back to him? When he dared check in on Bek again, he was moving down, through the levels of the headquarters. He tried to extrapolate where they might take him. If you got injured as a free agent and it was something you couldn't fix on the job, you went to the medical bay on the lowest level before you got to the holding cells. Regrowth was different. Regrowth meant being resubmerged in what might well be the same vat you had been grown in, if you were vatborn. The nearest set of vats on the surface was the same set they had all spent the night next to when they brought Palia to Hesperex, but they were taking Bek down. Down meant the vats two levels below.

Ferrash had another five hours left in his fake shift, but he needed to go after Bek. Nerves stitched his chest tight: a growing sense that something wasn't quite right, that everything was about to fall sideways. First the attack on the underground, then the void packs returning too soon, now Bek and Palia in the heart of it all.

Ferrash made his exit when a conveyor belt caught for half a second. It scattered bullet casings into the air, showering the workers to his left, then resumed with a jagged grinding noise. As the others abandoned their stations to scoop up the mess, Ferrash slipped back out of the door. He scanned his hand on the way out, presenting a modified timestamp. Due diligence. If anyone checked, the fake persona he'd used would be shown as working a whole shift.

The streets were empty again. Grey clouds hung low between the buildings and mist coiled around his ankles. He kicked through it, headed down to the next level at the first set of stairs he could find.

Bek had stopped. Waiting again, or already in a vat? Hard to tell. He hadn't visited these vats in a long while, and the maps weren't always good at showing boundaries.

When he found himself free of onlookers, he broke into a sprint, charging down the steps three at a time, almost spraining his ankle as he hit the floor of the first level. His breath came in hard gasps as he ran between that and the second set of stairs. Map open in his implants, he didn't notice the ESF agents until he had already barrelled past them. They cried out in his wake. He heard a whine as one of them armed a gun, but he was already clattering down the next set of stairs. The dot representing Bek had moved on the overlay again, was still moving.

Ferrash spun at the bottom of the stairs, whipping his pistol from under his coat. He fired two shots at the agents chasing him, still moving backwards. The first shot hit an agent square in the throat as they braced to fire on him. Their chin snapped forwards to hit their chest and they staggered back before collapsing to the floor. The second shattered the other agent's shin as he started down the stairs.

It jerked out behind him and he fell, arms raised to break his fall. Ferrash put another shot through his spine and carried on.

Not long after, he arrived by the wall separating the main thorough-fare from the vats. Their chemical stench wafted through a vent high above him. It wasn't low enough to try looking through, and it was too exposed out here. He made his way further along the wall, aiming for a specific point on his map where chemical waste got funnelled away from the vats. When he arrived, he crouched, pulled a tool from his belt and unbolted the maintenance panel before dropping through.

Ferrash splashed knee-deep into assorted effluvia. If it smelled bad out there, it was worse here – offal and excrement hummed beneath eye-watering ammonia. Pressing a hand against his mouth and nose, he waded through slowly, so no one would hear him as he got further in.

After entering the building, the waste pipe split into smaller ones that ran the length of the vats. One of the ceiling valves along that route opened as he peered through, letting a stream of vat liquid slosh through the opening. The way was too small for him to go any further.

Ferrash searched for heat signatures immediately above him, found none. Then he loosened the bolts of an access panel and peered out from beneath it to see Bek, some hundred metres distant, being escorted down the row of vats.

One of those vats contained a man, and the man wore Bek's face.

CHAPTER FORTY-TWO

PALIA WANTED TO HAVE complete confidence in Ferrash's instructions, but she couldn't help worrying herself stupid on her way to meet his 'friendly' keeper. She pushed aside the anxiety, of course – she had to – but thoughts occupied her mind enough that she made it to the designated safe house without even noticing most of the journey. That, in itself, was also worrying. She needed to pay more attention. She began to wonder how Ferrash coped doing this his whole life, then she remembered the inhibitors.

The safe house Ferrash wanted her to go to was inside the Admiralty. Such an odd term, for a structure inside the Protectorate, where rank was supposed to be some strange horizontal thing muddled by the hands of a thousand committees. Almost like the people who served in their fleets were a society unto themselves, with their own rules and social strata. When she sighted the building, she breathed deep, the cold air stinging her nose. She tried to imagine she was Ferrash. She took all her nerves and shunted them aside, leaving only a cold core of calculation and observation. She needed to do it anyway, for the Empyrean, to stop it getting into one of those vicious little circles that spiralled outwards and ended in everyone dying.

She walked straight through the front door, then headed to a mirrored surface on the wall on the right-hand side of the foyer, which the map said was the building's reception.

'Excuse me,' she said when she was close to it.

The surface shimmered, then became translucent, revealing a woman in a deep red coat. 'What is your purpose here?' she asked.

'I need to speak to someone regarding ship requisitions. Can you point me to who?'

'Identity, please.' The woman stretched out her hand and it slid through the membrane between them, making the surface ripple slightly around her wrist.

Confidence. Palia took hold of her hand, meeting the woman's gaze until she let go.

'Do you need a ship, or are you reporting one destroyed or missing? Given the frequency of the latter recently, the former may be more difficult to guarantee.'

Palia shook her head. Two similarly uniformed people passed in the corner of her eye. 'Neither. I'm just chasing something up for our records.' She had no idea what the sequence of words meant, decoded, but she'd said them exactly as Ferrash had told her.

'Turn right from here, then go two levels up the first flight of stairs,' the woman said. 'Logs are administered in the third room on the left. I will warn them of your arrival.'

'Thank you.'

As she turned to leave, the woman blinked, leaning back a fraction in her seat. Palia searched the conversation for anything that might have given her away or sounded strange, but found nothing. Perhaps giving thanks was unusual? Not unusual enough to cause too much fuss, she thought as she ascended the stairs, or there would be someone after her already.

The room the receptionist had mentioned was smaller than expected. A man and two others of indeterminate gender sat around three back-to-back monitors, their hands immersed in the control interface of a particulate projection field. On seeing her enter, the person who had been facing the door stood up. They drew their hands out of the controls, letting the screen go blank, and stepped around their colleague to open a side door for her.

Palia nodded at them and continued through the door into a thin, ill-lit corridor. This eventually led her to another room, windowless and empty but for a narrow bench and hygiene unit. No one else was there.

She dropped down onto the bench, faced the doorway, and settled in to wait.

Ferrash stared at the copy of Bek from his hiding place. Regrowing body parts didn't mean regrowing them on a whole new person and harvesting the parts. The only reason to ever duplicate a person was to replace them entirely.

Bek hadn't seen his clone in the vat. His face was downcast, troubled in a way Ferrash had rarely seen him before, the stump of his arm moving as he walked. At last, as his escort slowed, he shifted his gaze upwards. His brows darted low, then rose again, eyes widening. Bek grabbed for the pistol at his belt, but the woman on his left took hold of his arm and drove a sharp hook into his abdomen. Bek doubled over, gasping. Before Ferrash could even think of intervening, the other escort, a man, jabbed him with a stunner. Bek's entire body spasmed, his face forced into a rictus grin, then went limp in the woman's arms.

Ferrash had both hands on the lip of the hatch now, breathing in lungfuls of foul air. The man gestured from Bek to the copy of him in the vat, and the woman nodded. She lowered Bek to the floor and the two of them started stripping him.

Legs bunched beneath him, Ferrash let a hand drift to the grip of his pistol. But the hatch was too small. His shoulders wouldn't fit through that gap. And if he fired from here, even if he killed the escorts, what then? He'd have to run all the way around the building to get to Bek, by which time the hundreds of people working here would have beaten him to it.

The woman wrapped Bek's unconscious form in a heavy robe, then hoisted him over her shoulder and began to carry him back the way they had come. She reached the end of the room. Instead of taking the stairs up, she went down. Ferrash tried to bring up Bek's position again when they vanished beneath the floor, but couldn't find his signal. Blocked. They weren't taking any chances.

He could follow. He could race back out of the building and pick up their trail again. It was the only way not to lose him. Draped over the woman's shoulder, Ferrash's face-recognition algorithms wouldn't be able to track him down. They'd take longer to find her, too, with her hood covering most of her face. And then there was the clone. The man left behind worked at the vat's control panel, priming the sequence for it to release its contents. Bek's clothes remained in a heap on the floor by his feet. Waiting for their new occupant.

<Son,> Ferrash sent, wanting with every fibre of his being to go after the real Bek but knowing he had to watch what happened here. <I need your help.>

Ferrash gripped the hatch tight as he waited for a reply. The vat's valve opened; its contents gushed into the pipes below. When the smell hit him, he gagged, and a moment later felt the liquid ooze around his calves, chased by a flush of icy water. The clone hung there, limbs dangling from the straps that held it. It would be waking now, opening its eyes, drawing in the first sights of the world around it. They would have preloaded it with a skillset, at a minimum, but if they wanted it to be a convincing replacement, they'd give him memories, too, from the real Bek. They'd jack into his implants, connect the two of them, let the real Bek's dreaming subconscious fuel the remembrances of his clone.

Ferrash couldn't let that happen. Not now Bek knew at least a part of his plan – even the fact that Ferrash was impersonating Proglimen. This had been exactly what he'd been trying to avoid by not telling anyone in the first place.

<Son!>

Son's reply came a moment later. <Here. What do you need?>

Ferrash stopped just short of sighing. <Do you still have anyone in the underground? Any Observers who weren't with us when the Keepers attacked?>

<Yes. I told them to leave the city. It wasn't safe. They should have all moved on.>

With a silent but heartfelt curse, Ferrash left the conversation unfinished and opened another with the one option left to him. In the vathouse, the side of the vat casing slid open.

<I've a job for you,> he sent to his mother.

<Ferrash?>

<Yes. Need you to track someone down for me.>

<And this is more important than my escorting Palia to the Kept?>

Ferrash narrowed his eyes at the clone as the man helped it stumble out of the vat. He used a towel to wipe it down with rough movements, almost knocking it off balance as he worked to dry off the vat's remnants. The clone blinked at the room it had been birthed in, saying nothing, unperturbed by the handling.

<Yes,> Ferrash sent. He could tell her to take Palia with her, but he genuinely did need someone within the Kept. <I've sent you image files and a vector at last known location. Find the man. Make sure he stays alive. Rescue him if you can.>

As soon as she had agreed, Ferrash focused all his attention on the clone, using his implants to better pick out any audio. The man was helping him get dressed now, using the pile of clothes they had stripped from the real Bek.

'—ails loaded in your implants. You will have a link established soon. Who are you?'

When the clone spoke, it did so with its eyes wide, as if surprised by the sound of its own voice. 'Saralbek.'

'No. Saralbek Julius Nossar.'

The clone frowned. 'That's not my name.'

Yanking a sleeve over the clone's shoulder, the man said, 'The name is on your file. You use it for operations outside the Protectorate. You prefer the extra names.'

'Why?'

'Split if I know. Hege names are *ostat*. The real you must have had illusions of grandeur. Are you ready?'

The clone stuck its arms out in front of it, examining them, then did a turn on the spot to take in the room. 'I'll be ready when I get that link. Don't know where to start until then.'

Lip curled in distaste, the man brushed vat fluid off his clothes. 'Start at the spaceport. That's where your ship is docked. Refrain from approaching until you have the link.'

Cloned Bek nodded, but Ferrash had tuned out of the conversation. He lowered the panel back over the access hatch, rebolted it, then followed the flow of waste back outside the building. He re-emerged when he was sure the street was clear, then headed directly for the spaceport. The agents' corpses still lay by the stairs, ignored and unclaimed except by the snowshrieks after a free meal. Ferrash took a different route anyway. If those stairs were part of a regular patrol route, an investigation was only a matter of time.

He couldn't keep his thoughts from Bek. Bek, who he had worked alongside for ten years, had taught how to be more than what the vats had made him, who had taught him much in return. And now he was replaced by a hollow shell from those same vats, his fate firmly in the hands of Ferrash's mother.

With every step Ferrash took away from the vats, pain lanced through his heart.

CHAPTER FORTY-THREE

SOME TEN MINUTES INTO Palia's wait, the door membrane disintegrated. She leapt off the bench, heart thundering in her chest, to see a spacer in a red coat and hood step in. No, not a spacer. Palia had no idea how she'd missed it, but the black hole lodged in the landscape of the Empyrean where the newcomer stood meant they were empyrric. This was Ferrash's keeper.

The woman stood regarding her for a moment, hood still shadowing her face.

At last, the woman said, 'I suppose it's a good thing Ferrash wants you to infiltrate the Kept and not the Keepers – you wouldn't last a second.'

Palia glared at her and pushed aside her moment of panic. 'That's what you're for, isn't it?'

The woman reached both hands up to her hood and pulled it back, revealing a scraggly patchwork of grey-streaked brown hair. Scars criss-crossed most of her face, and Palia could make out the tracery of a pain mesh like the one Ferrash wore underpinning them. The sight was familiar, and not because of Ferrash, but she couldn't place it. She got so carried away in the sensation that she forgot, for a moment, to feel afraid.

With a slight shake of her head, the keeper asked, 'Have you encountered the Kept before?'

'Yes.' Palia blinked back into focus. 'I – *we* – fought some on Munab.'

'Yes, they are quite endemic there. Did you have any meaningful interaction with them?'

'Unless you count slicing one of them in half, no.'

'Pity.' The woman rolled her eyes, which were the same piercing amber as Ferrash's. 'And no, that doesn't count.' She waved to the bench. 'Sit.'

Palia backed up against the bench and sat back down with a *whumph*, tensing as the keeper came to sit at the other end of the bench. Palia turned a fraction to face her and shuffled back slowly until her backside overhung the edge.

The keeper regarded her with something between contempt and weary resignation. 'Do you know who I am?'

Palia shook her head.

'I am Head Justicar Ayt Mannae, and I—'

'Wait, *you're* Ash's contact in the Keepers?' Palia couldn't help it. This was Ferrash's *mother*.

Ayt narrowed her eyes. 'If I were not, I wouldn't be here speaking with you. Why? Is there a problem?'

Palia tried her best to still the band of animalistic terror that tightened around her gut. Ferrash had... well, she couldn't remember if he had ever mentioned his mother, but her emotions apparently had the muscle memory to indicate he hadn't mentioned anything good.

'No,' Palia said, mouth dry. 'No problem.'

'Good.' Ayt turned away from her and stretched her legs out, massaging her knuckles over one knee. 'As I was saying, I am in charge of anti-Kept operations on Hesperex. As such, I know where the group's members are and how they operate. I can't give particular insight into how you should behave with them – for the most part, we killed them on sight. While we have infiltrated their ranks before, we only noticed that they did not possess as severe an emotional deviance as was theorised. In public, they will be trying to seem as much like keepers as possible. Most are never far enough removed from the public to do otherwise.'

'Most?' Palia asked.

'Recently, we have begun to consider that there may be a hidden conclave of Kept in a section of undercity separated from the rest of

Five-Fifty-Four. Having recently had the… opportunity… to explore a forgotten mountain base, I believe there are blocked-off tunnels leading down to it. The tunnels' trajectory matches our best estimates as to their location.'

'So I get to them by going through those tunnels?'

Ayt shook her head. 'Ferrash would want you to because it's known, and because it's safer. But if you enter via a blocked route, the Kept may grow suspicious. No, I believe there is another route. It—' She paused, staring off into space, eyes unfocused.

Palia said nothing, not willing to invoke the keeper's anger at being interrupted.

A moment later, Ayt blinked and rose from the bench in one fluid motion.

'I'm needed elsewhere,' she said. 'I've just sent both locations to you – the best route is approximate. I strongly recommend trying that one.'

Palia opened her mouth to speak, but Ayt had already raised her hood and disappeared down the corridor. That was it, then. Palia waited a few more minutes to avoid suspicion, checking the new markers on her map in the time that allowed her, then got up to leave.

There was a distinct criminality to walking out of the Admiralty building uncontested, but walk out she did. Sounds seemed louder now she wasn't clinging so hard to deception. Packed snow squeaked under her boots and the wind whistled around the edges of her hood. Her breaths seemed abnormally loud, but she convinced herself it was just because the hat pressing against her ears trapped any sound she produced in with her. None of the people walking by in patchwork gave her a second look, though they kept a wide berth.

Relieved to be free of a keeper's gaze, Palia picked out a path to the spaceport and followed it. She should probably run the route past Bek before trying anything. She had said she would be there that night, but the trip to the lower levels sounded like it would take longer. The Empyrean sat quiet, with only a muted hum of emotions coming through from Five-Fifty-Four's denizens. Soothing, in its own way. So much quieter than anywhere she could go back home. Quieter than Rythe, and a thousand times quieter than the flagship.

It was in this state of walking watchfulness that she noticed them: a keeper buckling the weft of emotions around them, sat somewhere in one of the buildings above. Ayt, perhaps? But no, she had gone the other way.

Palia stopped mid-stride, swore, then continued around the corner onto the main road, hoping the keeper hadn't noticed. They didn't shift. Nothing fluctuated in the energy surrounding them. Despite that, Palia couldn't shake the feeling they had seen her and taken a curious interest – like something feline watching a creature pass in the water below it. She shivered, and hurried the rest of the way to the spaceport.

Ferrash never should have left. He never should have lied. Bek should never have had to search for him on Munab. This was his fault.

The walk to the spaceport was the longest he had ever taken. He daren't take the train. Too public. Too empty at this time of day. Too easy for someone to recognise him as Proglimen. Whatever block they'd put on the real Bek, they'd put it on the cloned version, too. It was its own giveaway. If he'd been tracking Bek before and seen him vanish, he would have known to look. If they were being clever, they would have blocked the real one and let the clone be tracked. More believable that way. Easier to think, if he hadn't seen the exchange in person, that the Bek he found eventually was the real deal. As it was, it left him blind, with no idea if the clone had already gone on ahead.

Ferrash forced a stop near the admiralty building for a change of clothes. Patchwork didn't go in the spaceport. He found his hands shaking again as he hurried to change into a spacer uniform, swearing under his breath as he went, his heart thudding against his ribcage. The Keepers were blind today, or occupied elsewhere. He strapped a knife to his wrist, beneath the sleeve.

Suitably clothed, he strode along the bridge, the sea raging at the struts below, and into the hulking spaceport. With all but a basic defence fleet gone from orbit, it was quiet. Repair workers eyed him as he passed. They were taking advantage of this moment's calm to weld the superstructure back together where it had started to burst at the seams. Though the metal floor felt reassuringly solid beneath his feet, Ferrash wondered how extensive the damage of ages was, how many generations of vatborn would have to work on it before there was nothing more they could do.

He checked his map. Still no sign of Bek, cloned or otherwise. No sign of his mother, either, though no doubt she had hidden herself to avoid recognition from her former colleagues.

Taking the lift up, he tried to quiet the usual thoughts. Scenarios played out in a thousand iterations: what if the clone had beaten him there; what if he was on the ship, with command of the weapons systems; what if he had Palia? None of those scenarios were useful. Damn having a plan. He'd take this one as it came.

Ferrash exited the lift a level above where he should have got off, though not by accident. He had the map overlaid on his vision. To his right, floor panels gave way to a railing-lined drop where the mechanism that carried ships from the outside landing pads to their berths cut through this part of the building. Three hundred metres below and perhaps two hundred distant, his borrowed ship, the *CVL Etheron*, sat with its ramp open. A cluster of grey-clad figures busied themselves around it. ISL agents. It came as no surprise that they'd found his ship, but their curiosity couldn't have drawn them here at a worse time.

Contrary to the silence on lower levels, a constant stream of dock workers ferried equipment between a cargo bucket running on a separate rail beside the standard mechanism and a medium freighter parked next to his ship. His real ship, the one Bek would be heading back to, sat innocuously to one side, partially hidden by an intermediate wall.

Ferrash paced along the railing, then crouched low so he could see the whole ship. Palia wasn't there, or if she was, she hid inside. The clone wasn't, either, but his implants told him the lifts were moving again, on their way to the ship's level. Ferrash turned and took a different lift down one level. When he emerged, he headed straight for the crowd of dock workers. By the time the lift arrived, he had a crate of materials cradled in his arms – just another worker on their way to the cargo bucket. A few of the other workers shot questioning glances his way, but the ISL agents, preoccupied with his ship, didn't notice his arrival. They were the only ones he needed to fool. Dockers were always thankful for extra hands.

Halfway across the bridge, Palia heard feet on the metal behind her, jogging to catch up. She let panic spike and gathered it up, ready to hurl at her attacker, but then Bek called, 'Palia!'

She twisted on the spot, eyes wide, then fell into step beside him. Glancing at him sidelong, she saw he had his arm back – not a prosthetic, that was for sure. If she hadn't been the one to cut it off, she wouldn't have known they were different.

'That was quick,' Palia said, once she had checked no one was nearby to listen.

Bek grinned at her, his face seeming to shine from within, making him appear more youthful than she had ever seen him. 'Turns out they've improved the vats. Got it done faster than I expected.'

'I thought this city was falling apart?'

They passed under the spaceport entrance. Bek shrugged. 'Vats are our most important tech. If anything gets improved, it's that. Always other planets.'

'What about the committees? Don't they usually take ages to agree to anything? You said you'd have to argue your case, but it sounds like you haven't. What if they agreed too fast? What if there's a catch? What if they've—'

Bek waved her off, then placed a hand on her shoulder. She cast a nervous glance at some maintenance workers welding nearby, but they hadn't noticed.

'It's fine, Pal. Don't worry about it. Though,' he grimaced, drew his lips into a thin line, 'there was one condition.'

Dreading the answer already, she asked, 'What?'

'There's a kill order out on Ferrash. They must be onto him. They gave the order to me.'

Not caring who might see, she whirled around to stand in Bek's path. 'They *what*? And you took it?'

Bek glanced around them, then took her by the shoulder and guided her inside an empty lift. He waited for the doors to close before he said anything. Even when he did, it was in a whisper she struggled to hear over the lift mechanism.

'Didn't exactly have a choice. If I'd said no, they'd have wanted to know why.'

Palia stared at the bottom of the lift door, watching light flash through the thin slit remaining as they travelled up through the spaceport's levels.

After a few more seconds' silence, she said, 'Are you going to do it?'

'Do what?'

'Try to kill him?'

Their eyes met. The overhead lighting panel cast only a pale light over the lift's interior. It left a good part of Bek's face in shadow, and most of what she saw of his eyes was the dim reflection they cast, like mirror flashes set in the hollows of his sockets.

'Even if I wanted to, I don't think I could kill him. Don't think I'd ever have the upper hand.'

Bek kept staring at her as if that was the only answer that mattered. But given how long he had spent with Ferrash, how much he had pined for him in his absence... how was simple inferiority the only reason he could muster as to why he couldn't kill him? If anything, she would have expected that love would stop him. That the fact they were working together again would. She tried to voice it, but the words got caught in her throat, so she looked away.

'How'd the meeting go?' he asked.

Palia didn't feel like mentioning who the friendly keeper had been. 'I'm not dead, so—'

The lift ground to a halt, opening to reveal the level where their ship was berthed. More had landed since their arrival; a small crowd of dock workers blocked the walkway as they ferried cargo between a ship and some kind of container on the rails to their left.

They started walking towards the workers. Behind the body of the freighter sat the *CVL Etheron*, Ferrash's ship, with a horde of grey-clad workers bustling around it. What were they up to? Three of them talked, examining a datascreen and indicating the ship with gestures. Another two inspected the bottom of the hull. A few panels sat against the landing gear, exposing sections of hull to reveal the circuitry beneath. Another worker stood halfway up the ladder to the cockpit, rummaging through its contents.

In case they noticed her watching and thought her too curious, Palia fixed her attention on her boots.

<Is this a problem?> Palia sent to Bek before they got too close to any of the workers.

<Don't think so.>

Palia frowned at his vague answer and dodged around a dock worker with a crate. <What are they doing?>

Bek, a couple of paces in front of her now, glanced towards the ship. She hoped she looked as relaxed as he did, but tension rode in the air, something wholly outside the presence of the workers on Ferrash's ship.

<They're ISL,> he sent.

Bek's message continued, but it skipped over her attention. Mental hackles raised at the tension, Palia turned her awareness to the Empyrean to find out what it was.

Every single dock worker was terrified. The terror bunched in their chests, leaping whenever one of them happened to face the ISL agents.

All of them, that is, bar one. She felt the shadow of their presence behind her, too close, sending a thrill of adrenaline shooting up her spine. This one wasn't afraid. Beneath the bright steel framework of determination, an entire ocean boiled. No time to make sense of that – it might have taken her an hour to pick apart the patterns and work out their causes. She tensed, gathering the energy of that adrenaline, wondering if she could get away with just draining their emotions so they would be too calm to try anything, but then they passed by. In that instant, their resolve crumbled, replaced by a skin-gripping vice of guilt.

She breathed out. The sooner they got off this planet, the better.

Metal squealed, just audible above shuffling boots and the *thunk* of crates landing in the bucket. Ferrash dropped his in and glanced left on his way back to the freighter.

Palia and cloned Bek exited the lift together, deep in conversation. Both shut their mouths when they saw they were walking into company, and Palia's eyes lingered in one spot for a few seconds before she frowned down at the floor. In those moments, Ferrash had thought she was staring at him, but when her gaze hadn't followed him to the freighter, he realised she was staring at his borrowed ship. Did the ISL agents worry her?

Ferrash's hands sweated inside their gloves as a dock worker handed him another crate. Bek – cloned Bek – had to die. Ferrash had to stop him siphoning too much information from the real Bek before he could relay it to the Protectorate. He had to get rid of him before they decided Palia was less use as an informant and more use dead. Worse, he couldn't just tell Palia any of this because at this close range, anyone around him could intercept the message. The dockers wouldn't know how. False Bek would.

They were ten metres away now. They began to weave between the dock workers. Ferrash hurried to get his crate to the bucket, the edge of a concealed knife chilling the flesh of his wrist.

He turned back to the freighter, a hand up his sleeve, gripping the knife handle tight. Bek walked on the other side of Palia. If Ferrash wanted to take him down, he'd have to cross behind them, get a clean kill in that wouldn't have the clone cry out, get away before anyone could realise what had happened. His arms felt like they'd locked into position. Palia stepped across in front of him, her movements stiff, her shoulders tense.

One step, two, and Ferrash was behind Bek. His tongue was welded to the roof of his mouth. His hand still gripped the knife.

Then he passed behind them, and Bek and Palia continued on their way to the ship.

He couldn't do it. Not because it looked like Bek, not because he didn't have the guts, but because she would know. Palia would sense Bek's life leave him, would turn, would reduce this whole building to melted slag from the shock of it.

So he kept moving and let go the knife. Bek and Palia moved out of sight beyond the wall and he stayed there, shuttling cargo from freighter to bucket until the ISL agents had finished with his ship, all the crates were gone and the dock workers moved on to other tasks.

As he left the way he had come, he wondered which was worse: leaving Palia in the company of the enemy or killing the man she thought to be Bek right in front of her.

CHAPTER FORTY-FOUR

STILL NO WORD FROM his mother, and Bek's clone had tucked away aboard the ship with Palia. The plan, Ferrash thought, could have gone better. Not that he'd really had one.

He slumped into a chair at the nearest pastehouse and stared into a cup of brew. Tiredness, aching and bone-deep, had crept over him since leaving the spaceport. Adrenaline gone, all he had left was a problem bigger than the one he'd had this time yesterday and the knowledge that he hadn't slept since before being picked up by the void packs. He wondered if they'd reached Munab yet, instantly dismissed the question as a waste of time.

As much as he wanted to tell Palia what was going on, that ran three risks: First, that the clone would intercept the message. Second, that Palia would try to take matters into her own hands and either get killed or alert Hesperex to her presence, which would lead to the same conclusion. Third, that she wouldn't, but she wouldn't be able to hide her newfound knowledge from the clone. So Ferrash had to watch, and wait, and pick his moment to strike.

Taking a gulp of brew in the hope it would slap him back to sense, he turned his mind's eye to the camera feeds. No one had left the ship since he'd been there. The dock workers hadn't re-emerged, and the freighter must have left while he was on his way out. Somehow he hadn't heard it, or hadn't been in a state of mind to notice.

Ferrash halted with his mug to his lips. On the feed, the ship's ramp lowered and Bek's clone stepped out. He crossed the partition wall separating them from his borrowed ship, where the ISL agents had dwindled to two individuals. They turned to bar his way when they realised he was headed for the *Etheron*, then Bek said something – the feed didn't have audio and he couldn't make it out from squinting at his lips. Ferrash forced another sip from his mug. Getting frozen mid-action wouldn't look good to observers.

Bek put his hand out and one of the agents took it. Authorisation to search the ship, perhaps? A gift from the ESF to the clone. Did the clone remember that Ferrash was Proglimen yet, or was it just interested in the ship? In any case, it wouldn't get anything from the *Etheron*. He'd wiped it clean before leaving, with only a one-way back door in case he needed it again.

Ferrash accessed that back door now, hoping the relay delays wouldn't stop him making the changes before Bek got on board. This was the perfect opportunity.

On the feed, the agents nodded to Bek and let him pass. Ferrash took his time, building a believable set of loose ends and unscrubbed communications for Bek to find that would lead to the underground, but not seem too obvious. He didn't know how far the clone's believ-ability stretched – whether it fully accepted whatever blind faith the real Bek possessed or whether it kept its own veneer of incredulity over that perception. The proof would be in whether he followed, and perhaps the proof of his guilt would be in whether he took Palia with him.

Without waiting for Bek's search to begin, Ferrash drained the last of his brew, gathered his patchwork coat around him and set back out into the snow of Five-Fifty-Four.

Ferrash had chosen one of the lower levels, appropriate for someone the clone might imagine to be avoiding discovery. By happy coinci-dence – and maybe a little subconscious design – it was also one of the warmest spots on Hesperex. Where he lay in wait, his knees drawn up against his chest so he could fit inside the access layer, was so hot he'd had to strip down to his undershirt. His skin itched beneath Proglimen's face, but he resisted the urge to scratch. It made a pleasant change from the mountain.

Below him, around three dozen vatborn worked the forges. They, too, wore only one layer of clothes, and sweat slicked their faces. Their shifts were shorter than most, so it would be easier to blend in, but without his face covered there was no way to hide from Bek. He was fortunate most outside the committees wouldn't actually *recognise* the Proctor's face.

Eyes glued to the entrance down below, he saw Bek's clone arrive. It strolled along the centre of the room, head turning every which way, trying to spot a place Ferrash might hide. The workers took in his plain clothes, still with all their layers, and gave him a wide berth. Their obvious fear didn't faze the clone. The real Bek might have smiled at them, potentially making them fear him even more, but this one was a predator on the hunt, oblivious to anything else. He had one hand on the grip of his pistol, and all the manner of his walking suggested he was hungry to use it.

Ferrash waited until he turned along a side path. Soon, Bek would be directly beneath his hiding place. Ferrash readied his pistol, feeling a chill where it nestled in his palm. One shot. That's all it would take. One shot and the clone would be gone and Ferrash could focus on rescuing the real Bek.

But then, in the corner of his eye, Palia entered the room. She had her face hidden, just like last time he'd seen her, but he recognised the clothes she wore. He couldn't send a message without the clone intercepting it. His heartrate spiked. He couldn't get enough air in his lungs in the stuffy confines of the access layer. Pretending she wasn't there solved that. He focused on Bek again, saw him stop and examine a loose panel on the wall. Still not close enough to shoot. He could only see what he could from a combination of cameras and having his face pressed right up against the ceiling vent.

Come on.

Bek – the clone – frowned and left the panel alone. He turned to look back over his shoulder at the workers. Maybe he thought he'd have more luck questioning them.

When he hadn't moved a moment later, Ferrash gritted his teeth and flicked a loose bolt down through the open side of the vent. The machinery clanged, clattered and hissed. He didn't hear it land, but the clone did. It snapped its head around and brought its pistol out in front of it. It moved carefully, placing each foot so it made as little noise as possible. A few steps later and it would be in range.

Ferrash twisted so his knees straddled the open hatch, his back pressed up against the floor of the level above, one hand on the panel in front of him. He held his other hand as straight as he could, bracing it against the edge of the hatch, his implants connected to the sights. A pistol appeared, then a foot, then the blond hair combed back and tied behind the clone's head.

He took the shot.

The pistol bucked in his hand. Bek's head snapped sideways, a red spray exploding from the other side to splatter the floor around him. Ferrash almost dropped the pistol, but then he was scrambling away, dragging his clothes after him, tucking the pistol into his belt as he went, heading for the open hatch that led to the floor of the next level. He thought of Palia following, could feel the imagined tug of the Empyrean poised to drain him, the fires rushing up to devour him whole, or both at once, whichever way she chose to end him. He couldn't get the sight of Bek's corpse out of his mind. *Clone. The Clone's corpse.* Except it wasn't. That was the same blood as Bek's blood, the same brain as his, just deprived the same experiences. The sweat on Ferrash's hands might well have been blood. The clone had still been Bek. Given the same time together, the same chance to be more than a puppet for his handlers, this one could have been just as vital. Just as free.

<Palia,> he sent now the message wouldn't be intercepted, his eyes stinging. <That wasn't Bek. That was a clone. The real Bek's still alive.>

Palia didn't reply.

When Bek had left the spaceport, Palia hadn't hesitated to follow. She didn't know what he had been up to on the *Etheron*, but he had been acting weird about Ferrash, and he had accepted the kill order on him – obliged to or no. Maybe he was just going to warn Ferrash the Protectorate was onto him without sending a message. That was the last thing Bek said before he left – don't trust any messages. If they were trying to flush out Ferrash, they might try to get to his contacts first by pretending to be him. Bek insisted that, as he was familiar with the underground and she wasn't, he should go alone.

As if he hadn't told her about the kill order. As if she didn't believe, in some part of her gut, that was what he was going to do. After everything they had gone through to find Ferrash, Palia wasn't about to let Bek kill him just for some perceived betrayal that they had since resolved.

She used the Empyrean to follow him, her awareness always centred on the suspiciously blank slate of his emotions. She dared not draw her attention elsewhere as she went – its appearance matched many of the other citizens they passed, on their way down. That changed with each successive layer they visited. She found patches where emotion was freer, patches where all she could sense was fear, and they got more frequent the further down they went.

Bek abandoned the descent at least ten levels down, though by that point she had lost count. As she followed, she found herself dwarfed by giant forges. An orange glow radiated from every surface, wavering in the heat. Sweat swam beneath her clothes, but she had to keep her face hidden.

As she stepped into the next room behind Bek, she wondered if that was wise after all. Sweat-streaked people in thin shirts stared at her – only for a moment before continuing their work, but long enough to show how out of place she was. She blinked sweat out of her eyes.

Bek had disappeared around a corner, but she hoped he wouldn't stay here long, given he must be feeling the same as her. No discomfort showed in the Empyrean, but she struggled to see far past her own. The heat might be hazing her awareness as well as her vision.

Palia passed across the main work floor and turned where Bek had gone moments before, careful to keep out of his line of sight.

So intent on Bek's trail, Palia almost missed it. But then Bek paused, and in that moment of stillness she saw energy kept tense, vibrating like the skin of a speaker in the ceiling above Bek's head. Surprised, she stumbled, then sprinted for Bek as fast as she could, all pretence at hiding forgotten.

The ball of emotions flared into brilliant incandescence, a shock against the quiet of Hesperex. Palia gasped and screwed her eyes tight, rounding the corner to a sharp whip-crack and a thud.

When she opened her eyes, Bek lay on the floor before her.

Every nerve screaming, she skidded to his side. The Empyrean slithered along her forearms, its light offsetting the warm fireside glow with its own deathly pallor.

'Bek.' Palia grabbed his shoulder, shook it. 'Bek, ancestors damn it, talk to me. Bek!' Blood on her hand, on his shoulder, on the side of his head, on the floor, on the machine wall beside them. She couldn't see his eyes, couldn't see his face, could maybe see skull in all that blood but no, it couldn't be, he couldn't be. She got a message claiming to be from Ferrash and angrily dismissed it. Bek had told her Ferrash's messages would be faked. Whatever it was would be full of lies. If Bek had come down here to find Ferrash on the back of one of those messages, those same lies had led him to his death.

'Bek.' More of a whimper now. A desperate plea for the real to be unreal, for the bad to undo itself and just stop happening all around her. She rolled him over, saw those warm brown eyes staring, cold now, glassy like mirrors. His once-blond hair was streaked with red, lay glued to the sides of his face. A clean strand fell across the ridge of his nose, the tip of it riding a snake-shaped meniscus on the blood below.

Her head spun, tingling, numb. Her thoughts condensed to a high-pitched whine and the sensation of falling out of herself. Before she could faint, she brought up her other hand and slapped herself hard across her face, then again. She couldn't do that. Couldn't go under and wake up on a corpse and a pool of blood, couldn't go through that discovery a second time.

Bek was dead. Even if she refused to believe her eyes, she couldn't find the faintest spark of his life in the landscape of the Empyrean, and that was undeniable.

She raised her eyes to the ceiling, fixed them on the point where she had seen those emotions, rose to her feet. This was a trap. A pretence for murder. Whoever had done it thought they had got away with it, was making their escape right now.

They wouldn't escape her.

CHAPTER FORTY-FIVE

Palia ran, barely able to breathe in the stifling heat of the forges. She shed layers of clothes as she went, not caring who saw her, not caring if they saw the blood stuck to her hands, her face, her knees. Her hair hung heavy, slapping against her neck, drenched by sweat. Whenever a worker saw her, fear shot through them. Palia dragged it from them before it could fully form, coiled it into the ouroboros she had seen and lamented in Lilesh. And as she ran, she hunted.

Whoever had killed Bek had vanished. She couldn't find them in the Empyrean again. Their emotions, so bright only a few minutes before, were lost to her.

She expanded her awareness as far as it could go. Hyper alert and with adrenaline coursing through her, that covered thousands of people. She ran with the patterns of their emotions, no matter how frail. Where she found the faintest glimmer of surprise, she went. She dared any of them to stop her. Palia wasn't robed as a Keeper, but her hair marked her Empyrean-touched and really, who else would run in the open down here?

Away from the forges, the air grew colder. More reason not to stop moving. She raced past arrays of hydroponic tubes, past servers piled high and blinking, up stairs and through rooms whose purpose she couldn't guess at. Above her, a ripple of shock and uncertainty wove through the workers.

Following her map, Palia sprinted up another set of stairs. She couldn't feel her legs, and wasn't sure if that was due to the cold or the adrenaline that pushed her past it. She barged through a door membrane into a room filled with rows of hexagonal sleeping pods. A few people were climbing up these to reach higher bunks, prevented from kicking any feet in occupied bunks by a membrane coating the ends. Boxed in like bees in a hive. By entering in such a hurry, Palia destroyed all trace of the ripple she had seen. It flashed into sparks of alarm, settled into fear.

She drew to a halt, panting, pacing the floor, her eyes fixed on the ceiling. She still couldn't see them, whoever had killed Bek. All trace of them had gone.

Turning to one of the climbers, she asked, 'Has anyone come this way recently? In a hurry?'

Fear gripped the woman, who stopped mid-climb to stare at Palia. Her bone-thin limbs trembled. She shook her head, then pointed to the ceiling. 'A thumpin' moved in t'up.'

'What?' Palia looked where she pointed. Something thumped up there, moving. That must be the next level – or was there a crawlspace in between where a murderer could hide? She remembered the emotions flaring above Bek, wondered if that's where they had hidden there, almost got stuck wondering why they had felt anything at all.

'Please,' said the woman, 'dinnet bite t'Keepers. T'ey take all vatter jus' to look you.'

'Then don't tell them I was here,' Palia said, hoping she had understood them well enough, that they thought she was Kept. Then, without another word, she left – at a walk this time, annoyed there weren't any spare coats lying around for her to take. The vatters wore them to bed, given even these packed hives weren't heated.

When Palia had left the last of the hives behind – it took twenty minutes to clear them – and finally found herself alone, she dropped into the space underneath a set of stairs and curled into a foetal position to think. She couldn't keep striking upwards blindly in the hope she would notice something. She wouldn't. Hesperex was still an alien place to her. It didn't matter that she had a map – whoever had killed Bek knew their way around without one, could easily slip away no matter how fast she followed. And the further up she went, the more likely someone less fearful would find her. Keepers, or those ISL agents.

She shivered, teeth chattering. Bek's blood had frozen on the outside of her gloves. When she clenched them into fists, it crunched and cracked around her knuckles. If she wanted to find the murderer, she had to get help from someone better at tracking people down than she was. As a spy, Ferrash was that person. She would be coming to him with two pieces of unwelcome news: the fact that she hadn't even started infiltrating the Kept and the fact Bek had died. And, she supposed, the fact she hadn't been fast enough to save him. Whatever Bek had gone after down there, it had been planted as a trap.

The only means Ferrash had explained to contact him was to meet at his base on the mountain – the same place Palia would have needed to travel through for the 'easy' route to the Kept, anyway. But she should probably go via the ship, first, and let the others know what had happened.

Chilled to the bone, Palia searched the map for anywhere that made or laundered clothes, then picked herself up and jogged towards it, sticking to the shadows as much as she could. She slowed to a walk when she got within a few metres. No one stopped her taking a patchwork coat from a hanger as she passed, so she shrugged it over her shoulders, wishing she hadn't abandoned her other layers in the forges.

Now the adrenaline had worn off, her legs ached. Abandoning the prospect of the stairs, she found the nearest lift instead. The workers in there made room for her as she entered. Some even changed their minds about their routes and hurried out. She rubbed her hands together, trying to dislodge the blood. When she felt the pressure of eyes on her, she fumbled at the neck of her stolen coat and found the hood. She pulled it over her head and tugged the drawstring tight so it covered all but her nose and eyes. Her hair thus covered, she let herself relax a fraction. She let the energy she had been carrying dwindle into obscurity.

The lift rattled upwards, shuddering in the shaft. All she could smell past the stinging in her nose when she inhaled the freezing air was oil and grease.

Three or more layers passed in silence. The map didn't make it clear where some layers began, as there were layers within layers all the way to the surface. At times, the lift stopped to let more on and some off. New arrivals paid her no attention, but they picked up on the tension in the lift, gaining some measure of communal anxiety.

Surrounded by people, Palia's heart ached. It shouldn't be possible to feel so alone in a crowd. She kept her gaze fixed on the ground by her feet, counting the rivets in the panel beneath her and trying to ignore the blood on the toes of her boots. The lift stopped again. Its door slid open with a breathy whir. Palia counted four pairs of booted feet marching in, saw green robes flick past at the edge of her vision, heard the door slide shut again.

The air in the lift froze. Palia didn't dare look up from the floor. She could sense them now, and cursed herself for not maintaining her watch. Their fear – hers and the workers' – had become a vortex around the keepers. They stood in the centre, emotionally inert.

They could see her, surely? Palia clenched her fists in her pockets. If she reached for the Empyrean, tried to hone it into a weapon to use against them, she would be signalling for her own death. She waited for them to make their move, but nothing happened. The lift went on juddering. The shaft groaned.

At the next stop, Palia followed every other worker out of the lift. No one, it seemed, wanted to share a ride with keepers. But they hadn't tried to escape Palia – they knew she was different. She thought back to the woman asking her not to bring the Keepers down on them. The only other empyrrics on Hesperex were the Kept, terrorists intent on killing every other empyrric including, eventually, themselves. They must think Palia one of them.

Did the Keepers think the same?

She realised they were following her a few minutes after leaving the lift. Stood at the foot of some stairs with her attention on the map, a movement in the corner of her eye made her freeze. They appeared: four keepers, somehow at the top of the stairs rather than the bottom. They hung there like shadows.

Should she call out to them? They weren't moving. They just stood there. Surely if they wanted her dead – or suspected her enough that it would be worth the minimal effort – they would attack?

She couldn't contact Ferrash. Desperation crept through her.

'Can I help?' Palia asked. Her voice came out louder than she had intended, more aggressive. One of the keepers raised a flame-cloaked hand.

Palia ran.

As she ran, it felt more like they were herding her than trying to kill her. She tried and tried and tried again to find a route to the surface, but every stair or lift she came to gleamed with Empyrean flame. They forced her down, level by level, until she was convinced she would never see the sky again, no matter how dismal this city's was. Panic beat in her chest. They didn't try to snatch it from her.

Screw staying quiet. This was life or death now. She sent a message to Lilesh, knowing it might be intercepted, knowing Ferrash would be miles away and busy. Besides, even he would be hard pressed against this many keepers. <Lilesh, are you there?>

<Unless I dug these implants out of my skull, I could hardly be otherwise.>

Palia almost laughed. Almost. <I need help.>

<Where?>

No protests about her chance of discovery if she left the ship. No admonishments. Just a question: straight to the point. Palia sent her a live location feed. <There are four keepers chasing me. Not attacking. Don't know why.>

<I'll be with you as soon as I can. Do they know who you are?>

Palia ran down another set of stairs, so tired now that she felt she might throw up at any moment. When she next looked behind her, the keepers weren't there, but that didn't mean they had left her alone. <Don't know. If they don't, they'll think I'm Kept.>

< Describe how they're chasing you.>

<From a distance. They block any move I make to get to the surface.>

<They may hope to scare you into leading them to more Kept.>

That made sense. Ayt Mannae suspected the way to the Kept was in the lower levels. Was this her doing? Or were her former colleagues just chasing the lead she had left? < What if I don't find any?>

<I imagine they will grow bored and kill you.>

A tram was coming down the street towards her. It filled the boxed-in horizon on this level, getting closer, the track in the ceiling above it humming. Palia waited until it was almost on her, then hurled herself across in front of it. She felt it pass a millimetre from her toe. That might slow the keepers, if they weren't already ahead of her.

A message came in from Tessa. <Palia?>

Palia doubled over in an alcove just off the street with the tram, panting. Her mind fumbled over her implant before she could send a coherent message back.

<What is it?>

<Lilesh got bored while you were out, so we started monitoring communications. I've got something that could help.>

When Palia tried to breathe deep to calm down, the air hitched in her lungs and she ended up coughing it all back out. Her knees trembled, barely able to support her weight. Even if she found out where Ferrash was now, she wouldn't be able to get to him.

Tessa continued. <Lilesh tracked Ferrash's electronic signature through the city by cross-referencing with some traces he left on the flagship and in your implants. Don't tell him. Anyway, I've got a few locations that could be safe houses you can escape to.>

Palia glanced along the street in both directions. No sign of keepers yet. A note of muted triumph sounded in her mind: having access to communications without express permission meant her suspicions about the archivist hadn't been unfounded. It served in her favour, this time.

She wondered if the keepers had grown bored, or if somehow in their chase they really had lost sight of her. If Ferrash's safe houses were closer than Ferrash himself – and she didn't know where he was, so they might as well be – she would be better off going there first and trying to find him when she had recovered a little.

Palia stared down the length of the street. Overhead lights did little to diminish the gloom, and the panelling disappeared in a distant spot of darkness. Hesperex was a never-ending labyrinth of sight-swallowing grey. Somewhere in that labyrinth was Ferrash.

She straightened, rolling her shoulders to ease the tension in her back.

<Send me the locations,> she sent.

CHAPTER FORTY-SIX

WHEN PALIA STRUCK OUT for what felt like the thousandth time that day, it was with a destination in mind. One of Ferrash's safe houses lay all the way down in the lowest levels of Five-Fifty-Four. Down was good. If the keepers were still on her trail – and she was sure they must be – down was the only way they would let her go. And maybe she would find some sign of the Kept while she was down there, kill two birds with one stone.

Despite their visibility earlier, however, the keepers still didn't make themselves known, even when Palia plucked up the courage to board a lift that would take her all the way. She exited some thirty minutes later with her nerves in shreds, convinced that if the keepers wanted her gone, they could just knock the lift off its pulley and let her plunge to her death miles below.

She peered into the corridor ahead, viridian flames spilling from her hands to pool around her feet. The light it cast around her made it seem like the corridor was underwater. It soothed her, to watch it ripple across the ceiling. But then, lava would have the same effect and only feel more dangerous for the heat.

Then she received another message from Lilesh. <Pestor, I thought you said you had four keepers after you?>

Palia closed her eyes, nerves returning in force. <I saw four. I don't know where they are now.>

<There are a lot more than four.>

<On all of Hesperex, sure, but how many are close to me?>

<All of them.>

Green blended to turquoise, then a clean-water blue as Palia approached the first set of side chambers. All she could hear was her own footsteps, the irregular *plip plip* of water hitting metal. When she breathed in, it felt like she was eating the air rather than inhaling it.

<How many, exactly,> Palia sent, <and how close?>

<Of the seven thousand or so remaining on Hesperex, five hundred reside in this city. Two hundred maintain patrol routes throughout the city. Three hundred are on the level above you.>

Palia licked her lips, recoiled at the taste of blood. <So, not all of them, then.>

<Semantics. Unless you think you can take three hundred?>

At the moment, Palia didn't think she could take one. She carried on along the corridor, trying to work out how to get to the safe house. It should be below her, a few hundred metres in front and one or two hundred to the left. So she entered the first hydroponics chamber level with it, passing rows of rotating glass tubes, searching every part of the room for something out of place. Three hundred keepers were *there*, not here. If she couldn't beat them and couldn't escape, there was no point thinking about them.

When she got to the end of the chamber and met nothing but a blank wall, she sighed and turned back. What was it Tessa had said about the map markers? They *could* be safe houses. Tessa hadn't been sure. It looked like she had been wrong.

For the first time since leaving the hunt for the murderer, Palia opened herself to the Empyrean, letting the light ripples lull her back into its awareness.

<In case you were wondering, Pestor,> Lilesh sent, <I can also not take three hundred.>

<Just get close enough to help me out if I find a way past them.>

Palia's mind touched upon souls on the level above her, then life in the space below. Not human life, but something animal. Nothing like the siggerith she had discovered on Munab and had to leave behind – none of these animals noticed her attention – but moving in much the same manner. In all her scrambling between Hesperex's levels, it had been easy to forget this was an ocean world. But here she was, on a level beneath the waves, so far beneath them that there was life.

How she had missed the keepers, she did not know. They loomed by the lift on the level above, their presence overpowering the nearby workers, and yet Palia almost had to force herself to notice them. Maybe they knew some way to mask their presence in the Empyrean, remove the memories of their existence from someone's mind. Maybe that much power in proximity made her brain deny they were real.

Then came another sensation. Even further below, further than the location she had meant to head for, there was human life. Empyrric human life, but not keepers. Keepers were a deathly void to look upon, but these empyrrics had emotions flittering amongst them. The Kept. They must be.

A thought struck her. Ayt Mannae's directions could have been a trap. Maybe she had sent Palia after the Kept, then the Keepers after her, in an attempt to flush her out. That would explain why they had stopped the level above. They were waiting to see where she went. If she found the Kept, she would reveal their hiding place – but then again, the Keepers would just kill her if she tried to avoid doing so.

She couldn't tell how many Kept there were – the landscape of the Empyrean was always shifting, making it difficult to count individuals, especially moving ones. She trained all her senses on that distant point and her immediate surroundings. She took two paces, ten, twenty. Then she stepped onto a floor panel that felt different to all the others. Only a fraction, but enough to make her pause.

Palia knelt and felt around the edge for a way to lift it. It didn't sit flush against the wall, but she couldn't get her fingers into the gap. At last, she stepped back and concentrated. Tension sliced from her fingers and shone out as a condensed blade of empyrric energy. She stabbed the end of this into the gap by the wall and flicked her wrist. The panel popped out of its housing and clanged against the opposite wall, leaving a hole in the floor where it had been.

Palia peered into it. A ladder led down into the dark, its bottom lost to it. She lowered herself in and coiled another whip of energy to haul the panel shut behind her.

Her glowing skin illuminating bare metal struts and wires, she stepped down the ladder. One jet of flame would end all this. That was all the Keepers had to do. But all three hundred remained on the level above.

After a few metres, her feet hit floor. She let go of the ladder and turned to see a door set into the side of the shaft. She looked around for windows, but saw none. Anything could be on the other side.

She sent another message to Lilesh. <Question: Do Empyrean shields hold back water?>

<Why do you need to know?>

<It's more a 'just in case' question. A hunch.>

A pause. <It requires utmost concentration. Any shield you create must remain impermeable as long as it is in place. The most I managed was a minute, and that was not out of choice.>

Palia tried to gauge the distance between her and the empyrrics who might be Kept below, but without any landmarks, found she couldn't. The map didn't show the shaft she stood in, let alone what was on the other side of the door. It showed what should be there: ocean. Given how close those small flickers of life were, Palia believed it. She placed a gloved hand on the door, felt the chill even through the fabric. Keeping open water between them and the rest of the Protectorate certainly seemed like a good survival strategy for the Kept, though she did wonder how they travelled between their location and the city.

In any case, down was the only way left to her, and Ferrash wanted her to find the Kept. Keepers or Kept – with one, death was certain.

Palia closed her eyes and concentrated. She let herself panic at the thought of water rushing in, at biting cold dashing her against the ladder's rungs. Then she took that panic and stretched it around herself, forced it to circulate: an outwards ouroboros. Whenever she saw a thin patch, she shifted the flow until the surface evened out. As she did so, she panicked more: at the number of patches, at whether she would be able to concentrate, at the disastrous consequences of putting even one foot wrong. She remembered a time in a luminescent cave, falling, green lights swirling, the water below caved by the edges of her shield. She had done it before, sort of, though the details were fogged by misremembrance.

Palia spun the door wheel then, when water didn't shove it back at her, she pulled it open and stepped through the hatch. Another door sat in front of her, with the same wheel-lock design. Recognising an airlock when she stood in one, she closed the first behind her and set to work opening the second. Her shield buckled where her hands touched the surface so it formed a second pair of gloves around her hands. It thinned where she almost touched it, but she didn't dare strengthen it in case she melted the wheel.

Vents opened in the door as she turned and water began to pour in. The temperature in the airlock dropped a few degrees. Goosebumps prickled her flesh. Her feet didn't feel wet, but she didn't look down to check the shield was working.

The door *had* to lead somewhere. They wouldn't just build an airlock for no good reason – unless it was just for maintenance crews to get back in, or undersea vehicles to dock, or another habitable module that had since been removed.

After a few more turns, the wheel *thunked* and refused to turn further. The water lapped around her waist now, rising fast. She drew the aching pain of the cold into her shield and hoped she wouldn't end up blissfully unaware of a bad case of hypothermia or frostbite.

Drawing her hands back to her sides, she strengthened the shield where it had thinned and waited. Sparkling under the light of the shield, the water level rose, like a storm-tossed ocean in miniature. When it passed her mouth and nose, she couldn't help but hold her breath. She let it out a moment later when she realised the water hadn't made its way in. Holding her breath would only make her gasp when she ran out of air. She needed to take slow breaths. Unless she had accidentally made a shield that filtered air from the surrounding water – which she doubted, and doubted was possible – she had a limited supply.

Unrestricted by pressure, the door swung open. Palia pushed off from the floor and drifted into a pitch-black void. For the little she could feel against her skin, it might well have been space. Her breath seemed too loud in her ears. She tried to juggle her semi-artificial panic with the need not to hyperventilate, but she was too focused on maintaining the shield, keeping it spinning. She thought she saw a cluster of lights in the depths below, near where the empyrrics lay in her awareness.

She thrust her arms out in front of her and clawed back, the shield extending around her. It stretched into two ghost-like wings, caught against the water, propelled her forwards. It worked, sending her faster than her arms ever could have done, but it sent shockwaves rippling through the shield. She gasped on feeling ice water splash her back. She closed the hole as fast as she could, but she could feel it all unravelling, her panic too chaotic to be confined to a shape for so long.

The lights grew closer. They nestled atop a metal cuboid, most of which was still lost to darkness. As she rocketed towards it, she caught light spilling from its lower edge. Where there was light, there might be an entrance.

Palia dived the last hundred metres with water chasing the toes of her boots and splashing through gaps in her shield. At the last moment, she flipped and came straight up at the bottom of the building, where the surface of a pool glimmered. She burst through it so fast that she cleared the water's surface and crashed against the ceiling with her arms up to protect her face. Then she fell, flailing, for the water.

A vivid green membrane pulled taut and caught her before she could reach it. Another shield, not hers, but she was too busy gasping for breath to identify an origin.

The shield tilted, rolling her off to one side, and Palia landed face-first on a damp metal floor. She pushed herself up on shaking arms, still struggling to draw air into her lungs, then a hand clamped around her elbow and hauled her upright.

Palia staggered, boots squelching, and blinked water from her eyes. Her shield had vanished. In the wake of the panic it had eaten, she felt calm and alert.

'Don't be trying anything.' The voice, harsh and gritty, came from the woman who held her arm. Thick patchwork swathed her figure. Three others stood around the room, all in patchwork.

Palia tried to pull her arm away, but the woman's grip was iron.

'I'm not a keeper,' Palia said.

'No,' said the woman, 'and not Kept neither. But you've gone led them to us. And now none of us can leave.'

CHAPTER FORTY-SEVEN

FERRASH HADN'T MEANT FOR Palia to see it. When he'd seen Bek alone, the plan had been to kill him, then go back and tell Palia what had happened before she found out herself. But she had been there, following, and he had no doubt she'd seen Bek's corpse lying there on the forge's floor. If Ferrash hadn't run, she might have killed him. It might have served him right.

Now he sat in one of his safe rooms, nursing sore shoulders from his scramble through the access layers to hide his trail. Palia had just abandoned the chase. He finally had chance to breathe.

He tried another message to his mother. <Have you found him?>

No response. He swore, then stood and passed through the disguised door membrane separating the safe room from the warehouse beyond. He knew the messages were getting through – to her and to Palia – but apparently no one was in the mood to reply.

If his mother couldn't be relied on to find Bek, Ferrash would have to do so himself, picking up the weak trail where he had left off. It wasn't as hopeless a situation as it could be, but it would be time-consuming.

Ferrash walked through the shadowed corridors of the fourth level until he was beneath ESF headquarters, ready to resume the search.

He brought up the camera feed, rewound it to the point where the woman had carried the real Bek downstairs. Then he accessed the next camera on their trail. Where she exited the building, Ferrash began to follow on foot, repeating the same process every time she vanished from sight. With the feeds overlaid on his vision, it was a bit like chasing ghosts. At a junction between a tram terminus and a collection of habitation blocks, he lost her. The feeds had the woman crossing the tracks just before a tram came through. By the time it had passed, she was gone.

Ferrash paused by the tram stop with a bunch of workers, trying to process more angles from cameras further along the street. As he did, a rippling murmur passed through the crowd. He looked up, caught sight of a dozen keepers heading down the stairs across from him. He thought of Palia and the unmistakable trail she had blazed through the belly of Five-Fifty-Four to hunt him down.

He sent another message to his mother. <Please answer your messages. Could really use your help.>

Begging his mother left a sour taste in his mouth, but he swallowed and pushed pride aside. He couldn't push his other feelings aside, though. Not this time. Doubt gnawed at the back of his mind. Palia had at least been conscious the last time he'd seen her. Bek didn't have that luxury. He was unconscious, replaced and, now his clone was dead, extraneous. If his former colleagues realised that and reached him before Ferrash could...

There, on one of the adjoining streets: a woman wheeled a large crate before her. Same clothes, same stature. The box was large enough for a man crammed tight inside, and it looked insulated. A little heat bled out on infrared.

Ferrash checked the way was clear of keepers and, as the next tram rolled into the stop, crossed the road in front of it. Back on the trail again, he resisted the urge to run. He followed the woman and her box across mesh bridges where the ocean glinted underneath, then down onto lower levels beneath the waves, where water sometimes dripped onto the heads of those below.

The further down he went, the more keepers he saw. He counted forty-seven just on one level, sixteen of those moving as one unit towards the stairs. In all his time on Hesperex, he'd never seen this many out in force. You sometimes got twelve in one group to track down Kept and sometimes two groups of twelve happened to come together, but never this, never so many all heading the same way. The only time he knew of where similar numbers of keepers had mobilised was during the purge, when they had let themselves loose on the population to exterminate any splitters. Whatever this was, it was the same; it wasn't just for Palia.

The trail led him, at length, to a barracks block squatting low in the company of warehouses and habitation. There, the feeds died. The building had no cameras inside – not that he could access, at any rate – but he could tell the woman hadn't left. Or rather, she hadn't left with the box, but she could have made another change of container.

Dark even in the dim-lit street, the barracks stood out from the buildings surrounding it. Others contributed to the general illumination by the strip lights over their doors, but the barracks had no such light and Ferrash struggled to make out the door itself until he got closer. He skirted it twice, but found only one entrance. The maps marked it as one big square of barracks. Its interior had never been recorded, not even in the landers' archives.

He sighed and left the door to pursue another route. Since so many keepers had passed by recently, all the workers had fled. Ferrash had the streets to himself, along with the surety that he likely wouldn't bump into any keepers. It had been a while since he had seen any – they must all be in the lower levels. So he turned down a dark alley between two warehouses and climbed, using ductwork as handholds.

When he reached the top, he kept low and double-checked that no one was watching. Then he sprinted for the edge, his footfalls ringing out in the emptiness, and leapt for the roof of the barracks. He rolled on landing, then lay still in case anyone in the barracks had heard and decided to investigate.

It would have been much easier if his mother could have just done as he asked. As a keeper, even one wanted by her colleagues, she would have been able to walk through the front door without risking confrontation. If Ferrash tried the same, he'd be shot. Sure, he had contacts in the landers, but none in here and, he was sure, none with the authority to get him in.

Convinced no one had seen his climb, Ferrash got to his feet and began to pace. He cast about for entrances, vents, anything as he went, but found nothing. He pinged Bek's implants again in the hope he'd at least get a location to aim for, but it was still blocked.

If Palia hadn't followed the clone, Ferrash would have been able to backtrace its connection to wherever they were keeping him.

After a half-hour search turned up nothing, he returned to floor level and lifted a panel to clamber down into the access layer. He'd spent more time in these cramped spaces in the course of... however many hours this had been... than he had in all his previous time on Hesperex. This time, he came up empty handed. He crawled all around the perimeter of the building. The wall extended through the access layer, so he couldn't get underneath. All the access panels were alarmed and he couldn't risk deactivating them in case they were connected to a larger monitoring network. All he found was an inlet/outlet system for vat liquids, much the same as he had waded through in the other vat building. Except this one had a metal grille preventing him doing the same.

Ferrash reached inside his coat and pulled out a hover disc. They might detect it flying through their boundary, but it was the only chance he had to find Bek.

Connected to his implants with the disc's feed showing in his vision, he sent it through the grille, whirring quietly. The waste pipe went straight for several metres, then split into an irrigation grid. He chose the nearest and sent it along, hugging the side in case any of the vats emptied right above it. But the waste pipe seemed dry through the disc's cameras – it hadn't been used in a long while.

When he saw light shining from one of the vat openings, he sent the disc up and hovered it inside the base of the vat. He kept it low at first, but when an infrared scan showed no one outside, he flew it higher to get a good view.

Around half of the vats were occupied, with six rows of eight vats. Small, for a vat chamber, but given its position in the heart of a well-secured barracks, this didn't exactly pass for normal.

Spinning the disc, Ferrash searched for Bek amongst all the naked bodies, half expecting to see his own face among them. But the clone had been birthed in another chamber. Unless they'd moved it from here to headquarters to make the transfer easier, he couldn't have expected to find others here. Having the mock barracks as a secure location for living transmitters made sense. Easily disturbed originals were easily foiled infiltrations.

He found Bek three quarters of the way round the turn. Half-hidden behind three other vats, Ferrash almost missed him, but caught sight of blond hair floating free in the liquid and knew, even before he zoomed closer to check.

Relief flooded through him. Ferrash leaned a shoulder against the side of the building and closed his eyes. Every hour he'd spent on the run weighed down on him then, like it had just been waiting for permission. It was all he could do to stay awake.

<I've found him,> he sent to his mother. <Get in touch if you can.> The message was futile, but he hated leaving loose ends.

He considered scenarios. One: his mother had been discovered and killed by other keepers. That would be an underestimation of her abilities, and the keepers had started moving en masse too late for them all to be going after her. Two: his mother had been playing a longer game and had returned to work for the Keepers with all her new understanding of his plans. Doubtful. She would have just killed him. Three: his mother had been distracted by something more important than a search for someone she didn't know and was too busy with that to reply to him. Plain rude, but true to form.

Whatever the truth, the best place to find her was back on the mountain. There was nothing more he could do here. He hated to admit it, but he didn't have the skills or equipment to break into the barracks and rescue Bek. So he left, even though it felt like he left his heart behind him. All he did leave was the hover disc, hidden on the floor of the vat he had flown it into. He knew exactly where Bek was, which is where he would send help during the coming revolution, and he'd be alerted the moment anything changed. The disc could release a knockout gas, if needed, to give him time to rush back.

On his return to the surface, Ferrash didn't encounter a single keeper, but orange-coated landers huddled on every corner and patrolled the streets. A few of them nodded his way as he passed – an unfamiliar gesture for Hesperex. Too personable. Too feeling. He wondered if they would retreat again the moment the keepers returned, or whether this was their first coordinated move in the revolution he had set in motion. Too soon, if that were the case. Everything too soon and out of control.

He searched for his mother when he reached the mountain hideout, not expecting to find anything. He didn't. He couldn't find Son, either, or his Observers, but the hideout extended a long way into the heart of the mountain and Ferrash was tired. By the time he reached the same level as the bunks, his knees were buckling beneath his weight at every step. He staggered back onto a bed to rest them, just for a moment. Then, without meaning to, he slept.

CHAPTER FORTY-EIGHT

'So you're Kept, then?' Palia asked.

They had taken Palia through to another room, away from the lapping ocean pool. While she sat shivering on a low metal stool, her new guards watched her, forming an empyrric ring that tugged at the edge of her senses.

One of the others pushed through them with a pile of dry clothes and motioned for Palia to change. Given how soaked her coat was, she was grateful it hadn't gone through too many layers. She might not balk at nudity, but shared shower rooms were one thing and an audience was quite another.

'We *all* be Kept,' said the woman who had pulled her from the floor.

By placing emphasis on 'all', Palia guessed she meant to encompass everyone in the Protectorate rather than just their congregation of empyrrics. The natural consequence of having keepers, she supposed, but hardly helpful as an identifier.

'Yeah, but' – Palia peeled off her socks and patted at her feet with a towel – 'are you the...' Her tongue tripped over the word 'terrorists'. 'Are you the ones who fight the Keepers? Not just like everyone else, I mean. The ones who want all empyrrics dead.'

The woman had her arms folded over her chest, as did most of the people encircling her. 'We want the Empyrean gone. Empyrrics bein' dead is no but a sad side effect.'

'Including yourselves?'

She shook her head. 'Us Kept began with a man who chose on sterilisin' himself when he got called up for the breedin' programme.

We all be makin' that same choice when we join. Can't birth people, can't carry on the blood. Same choice keepers get given provided they be sensible and not fightin' back.'

As Palia shrugged into the new coat, she wondered why that option hadn't occurred to her before. It made sense. Blood was the only way for the Empyrean to travel from one generation to the next, and the bloodlines were already on their way out, almost entirely devoid of the Empyrean in the Hegemony. You couldn't grow empyrrics in vats. You couldn't easily shock them into existence. She wondered how long it would be before empyrrics died out without the Kept's interference. Maybe they would be better just waiting.

'Anyhow, if you ain't one o' them and you ain't one of us, who *do* you be with? An' why come to us?'

'They chased me down here. I was trying to head for the surface, but they wouldn't let me reach it. I didn't mean to bring them to you, but I sensed you, and I thought I'd be safer where you were than with them.'

'What led you here? There be no way of sensin' us from anywhere but right above. You with the Observers?'

'I don't know who they are.'

The circle of Kept exchanged glances. A man with a full-length beard poking from underneath his hood narrowed his eyes. 'She's a Hege.'

Palia didn't deny it. There wasn't much point.

The woman examined her for a few moments, then waved the others away and pulled another stool out from under a bench to sit in front of Palia. Another woman lingered behind her, a steaming mug cupped in her dark hands. Palia caught a flash of amber before the woman turned her eyes away.

'What did the Hege send you here to find?' the seated woman asked.

Palia glanced back over her shoulder at the pool, its surface lit by the lights around the opening. If the Kept were interested in empyrrics, chances were they wouldn't be interested in Ferrash. Just her, potentially.

'In the level above this, where I came from,' Palia said, 'I thought there might be somewhere I could hide from the Keepers. They were chasing me because I... someone killed my friend, and I got carried away trying to hunt them down' She shivered, picturing again the side of Bek's head coated in blood, thankful to be rid of the clothes that bore it. 'I didn't find a way to reach it before I found all of you. I don't even know if it really existed.'

The woman tilted her head, eyes tracing paths in the air. 'Must be thinkin' about our recent neighbours. Though you said you no know about Observers? Was them were up there, and more besides. Would have been safe to hide, once.'

'I didn't realise. The location was all I had. What happened to them?'

'Keepers found 'em. Was interestin' to sense, I hear, while I weren't bein' around to see it.'

Palia gripped her knees hard. 'They're all dead?'

'No. Escaped. Had a keeper fightin' their side for 'em. Strange, that. Day later, we hearin' the fighter be Ayt Mannae. Head Justicar goin' rogue ain't something ever been seen. Shame she not one of ours.'

At the mention of 'Mannae', Palia sat bolt upright. So Ferrash's mother really was on their side – unless the fight was a lie. 'Who else was there?' she asked.

The woman shrugged. 'Vatter called Son woulda been there. Observers are his. Think they been livin' with Technocracy vatters, since most of 'em escaped in a submarine. We heard it pass above.'

'Where did it go?'

'No clue. We thinkin' it unimportant. They got away and they didn't get us found. Not like you. Mannae, we followed her. Went with others hikin' up the mountain. Kept built those tunnels they usin', long ago. Better access, better escape, but you no able to get to it from below no more. They be goin' overland, up the slopes.'

Breathing out a relieved sigh, Palia relaxed back into her seat, only just managing to correct herself on remembering the stool had no back. Tiredness hung on every bone and limb, trying to drag her mind down under its weight. She rubbed at her eyes.

'Is there somewhere I can sleep?' she asked. Behind that question, another: would they let her live?

'Sleep?' The woman raised an eyebrow. 'Depends on if the Keepers come. But you can try. Dakaga? Since you be standin' there, you show this Hege to the bunks.'

The woman with the mug turned her head, then gestured for Palia to follow her. While she had seemed outwardly surprised, Palia couldn't sense any of that reflected in the Empyrean as she stood up. She couldn't detect much, in fact. If all of the Kept used to be keepers, perhaps this Dakaga was a recent addition.

Dakaga finished her drink and dropped the mug on a counter. Then she led Palia through the room – a communal dining area, it looked like – and into a long corridor. When they reached the bunks, she indicated an unmade bed far from the door. Palia thanked her, but the woman made no move to leave.

After a moment in which Palia considered the least awkward way to ask her to go, Dakaga said, 'When Hetan mentioned the head justicar, you recognised the name. Why?'

'She's a well-known Keeper.'

Dakaga's eyes, caught by the light of a wall lamp, reflected gold. 'That is not your real reason. There was more to it. What do the Mannae mean to you?'

Palia sat on the edge of the bed and slid her boots off. 'Nothing.

'Then why did the Hege send you?'

'They didn't. I chose to come here. It's... personal.'

Even when she swung her legs onto the bed, Dakaga had her eyes on her. Palia shifted, too uncomfortable to lie down.

'Ayt Mannae is my father's mother,' Dakaga said. 'I have no intention to harm her, if that is what you worry about.'

'I don't care what happens to that woman.' Palia shook her head, half to support her statement, half to dispel the sudden rise of distaste.

All she had against Ferrash's mother, unless there was something else hidden in memory, was that she was a keeper. And even that may not be true anymore.

Then Palia frowned. Was Ferrash Ayt's *only* son? She peered at Dakaga, noting her amber eyes, the scarred and puckered brown skin only a fraction cooler and darker than Palia's. The scars made her seem older than her years, she thought. At first glance, she would have guessed late teens or early twenties. Looking closer, she wasn't sure. 'You're a Mannae?'

'No. A Lay. My mother was a keeper. I get my blood from her.'

From both, of course, but the names didn't work that way. That implied her father hadn't been empyrric, but had been related to the Mannae – only possible if he was a prog.

Palia brought up Ferrash's image in her implants, compared it to the woman in front of her. Dakaga had his eyes. Not the shape – hers weren't as hooded and they sat too shallow in her face – but the colour was that same amber. Palia couldn't imagine Ferrash having a daughter. But when she imagined children, she pictured families, pictured her and Derren living together above Everatus IV before the disaster. A very Hegemony mindset. Children on Hesperex would only ever be keepers, progs, or unsanctioned. Did Ferrash even know she existed?

Palia realised she was staring. Clearing her throat, she broke her gaze.

'You know him, don't you? Ferrash Progmannae.' Dakaga furrowed her brow and knelt by the side of the bed. Her hands rested in her lap. Palia couldn't sense much in her, but some kind of sadness rippled below her breast.

Palia said nothing.

'I have never met him. We do not get to meet our parents, unless they are keepers, and then that is only for training.'

'So you trained under your mother?'

'Until she died, yes. Juuni, her name was. Juuni Lay.'

'I'm sorry.'

Dakaga tilted her head back, raised a thick eyebrow. 'Why? Training to be a keeper does not induce good feelings between blood relations.'

Not knowing what to say to that, Palia opted for silence again. Tiredness kept her from controlling her emotions as well as she could. Dakaga could probably tell she had thoughts whirling around in her mind, and that she was battling herself on whether to trust her. Dakaga might know where Ferrash was. Maybe that's why she was talking about him. What other reason could she have? Dakaga didn't strike her as the sort of person who took pleasure in idle chatter. None in the Protectorate did, excepting Bek. Palia's throat closed up at the thought of him.

After a moment, Dakaga continued. 'That is why I want to meet him. He... The vatborn do not claim to be family, but they treat each other as such. Having seen them, and having heard of other worlds beyond the Protectorate, I felt I lacked something. Ferrash Progmannae is all that I might count as family. Your reaction to hearing Mannae's name... you believe if she has gone against the Keepers, she must be helping him?'

'I can't claim to know her motivations.' Palia wished there were others in the room with them, yet every bunk but hers lay empty.

'If they are working together, it is only logical that they escaped to the same location. The mountain. We could go and find him together.'

Palia's heart raced at her conclusions being voiced aloud, but she shook her head. 'They said they had to go overland because the other way was blocked. Even if he is there, I can't reach him without being spotted. Or freezing trying to find it.'

'I know the way they say is blocked. Anything blocked can be unblocked. If you like, I will clear the way for us while you sleep, and we can go together to see him when you wake. But please' – Dakaga reached a hand out and laid it on Palia's knee – 'tell me, is he a good man? He will not give me up to the Keepers?'

Palia gave her a small smile. 'I think so.'

CHAPTER FORTY-NINE

FERRASH CHECKED HIS HANDS for blood when he woke. His memory rang with the sound of the shot that had killed Bek. The scene had played over and over all night, keeping him too restless for it to fade as dreams should.

He pulled his knees up in front of him, his palms pressed together and holding the weight of his forehead. He needed to get another message to Palia, needed to tell her what had happened, but she hadn't replied the first time. He wouldn't be able to explain what had happened without seeing her in person.

Ferrash found a message when he went to make a cup of brew, etched into the worksurface by something fine and hot enough to melt it. His mother's work.

No communications. Your signature has been identified. They know who you are. They know who you pretend to be. Have taken your friends elsewhere, somewhere safe. Will contact you as chance permits.

A cold fear lodged in Ferrash's chest. That explained her failure to find Bek. It also meant he couldn't contact Palia even if he pulled together the words for it.

Worse, it meant his plans were undone.

Ferrash stared at the message for a minute or more. Only the sound of boiling water broke him free, and even then he almost spilled it over his hands as he poured.

His plans had been falling apart with every passing day. He had never truly been on top of this situation. He'd been a fool to believe otherwise. His impersonation of the Proctor had been a laughable last grasp for leverage. If it weren't for him, Bek wouldn't be in danger and Palia... was she in danger too? Of course she was. He stared into his brew, willing the depths to give him solutions, but all they did was warm the air.

His mother had been hasty. Having his signature didn't mean the Protectorate could find him – he'd made sure it couldn't be traced. But it did mean everyone he'd been in contact with could be traced. That meant her, Son and a few others who he wouldn't have usually contact if it wasn't for the hole the purge had left in his usual contacts.

He'd last contacted Ducat through the long-distance array, which was all but untraceable. Son had been in the hideout when Ferrash had last messaged him, but that was recent. Ferrash changed his signature at random intervals. Any messages sent to the hideout had been sent after a change.

So it hinged on which signature they had. He massaged the bridge of his nose between thumb and forefinger. Too early for this. He wished he knew when in the past few days he'd stopped being a morning person.

Ferrash found a chair and sat down, knowing he should just leave on the off-chance they knew where he was. Then, taking a sip of the brew, he forced his brain into gear.

When he'd seen the keepers, they'd been heading down. If they wanted to get to him, they'd carry on straight until they reached the mountain, unless they planned to come from below and unblock the passages. He doubted they even knew they were there. He'd only found them from this side of the blockage after exploring the hideout. Leftovers from the civil war, by the age of them. Maybe they'd belonged to the faction that had been wiped out, leaving no one left to reclaim them until now.

Over the next few seconds, Ferrash ran tracking algorithms on all the camera feeds from the keepers' movements earlier. He only ran them on the first few levels – any more might take too long – before getting them to extrapolate the overall picture. Soon enough he had a mile-square estimate for where they'd been heading. Not anywhere near where the mountain tunnels should connect. No, all it contained was the spot Son had chosen to hide out with his Observers. Not a current signature. He was safe here.

Any feeling of safety vanished the moment the news alert arrived.

The Chair, his image usually absent from Hesperex's propaganda, today sat tall and staring harsh-eyed into the camera. Ferrash's heart started to beat faster. He knew what was coming.

'Citizens of Hesperex,' the Chair began. 'Brothers, sisters, all. I come to you with grievous news.' He licked his lips, and the sight made Ferrash bare his teeth in anger. 'For some time now, there has been a sinister faction within our committees, manipulating events, stripping rightful authority from the hands of you the people into their own arsenal. They have abused an historically trusted position to steer the Protectorate towards their own ends. They have desecrated the consensus enshrined in law. They have erred... and they have been discovered.

'It is with shock and dismay that I must reveal the treachery of the Proctorate committee, whole and entire. The Proctor has led it, and us, astray. He will be found and brought to justice. His committee is rotten, and that rot has leeched to other committees, to other worlds. Our only recourse is to dismantle all committees bar the Primary with immediate effect. The Protectorate, from this moment, is under temporary martial rule until such time as we may re-establish committees that we know to be untainted.'

The *sannot*. The Chair knew full well that Proglimen was dead and his identity stolen – Ferrash's mother had just said as much – but he hadn't mentioned that. He'd kept up the charade, used it as an excuse to take complete power for himself.

Ferrash tore the reconstruction mesh from his face and hissed at the pain. He lurched upright, making brew slosh over the sides of his mug, then drained the rest of it despite the heat. Just as he set it on the side, a noise sounded from deeper in the hideout. He froze, face stinging. The noise came again: a sharp, metallic squeak, muffled by distance.

All senses on alert, Ferrash clipped a utility belt on, shouldered his rifle and took hold of his pistol, then started towards the source of the noise. He walked slow, placing each step in case whoever was there heard him. Too late to run back to the hatch and get his skis on, if they were keepers. He'd had a choice of two directions and hadn't even thought of fleeing. Stupid.

Above him, one of the lighting panels flickered. He passed the rooms where Son's people had been, saw their food abandoned mid-meal. Ayt had got them out of there fast. The leak had spooked her – rightly so.

Metal squealed again, louder now. Ferrash tightened his grip on the pistol, staring down the length of the corridor at the dark rectangle that was the membrane at the end. Farming space lay on the other side. The growing lights were so powerful he'd kept them turned off, otherwise they'd drain more power than the hideout's generator could supply and switch to the planet-wide grid, which would eventually reveal his presence.

On reaching the membrane, Ferrash paused, listening. Could be a hundred keepers on the other side. Could be right in front of him, about to open the membrane and surprise them both. But he couldn't hear anything.

Ferrash touched the membrane and commanded it to become translucent one way. He couldn't make out much on the other side, other than to say no one stood right against it. So he opened it and stepped through with it disintegrating around him. His feet crunched on old, coarse soil. When the membrane reformed, he stopped and listened. His breath misted in front of his face and the seconds ticked by with only his breathing audible. It was like all sounds had been confined to the millimetres around his skull. Just when he was about to keep moving to investigate further, the noise came again, screeching through the silence.

Green light splashed against the wall at the back, where the stairs down opened up onto the fields.

Ferrash sidestepped until he could hide behind some abandoned equipment, then peered through a gap with his pistol aimed through another. Footsteps sounded at the edge of hearing, light but unmistakable. They came up the stairs, taking their time. A figure emerged from the top.

He closed his eyes and switched the lights on. Hundreds of individual lights flared into brilliance like a lightning strike – Ferrash winced even through his eyelids and heat touched his shoulders almost immediately. He aimed his pistol at the intruder via his implants.

His finger froze on the trigger, and his heart froze in his chest. He couldn't shoot a ghost. Juuni stood side-on from him across the field, solid as life, the dark tones of her skin flattened by the bright light. But this wasn't Juuni as he had known her. Not quite. Here she wore patchwork and a faint veil of Empyrean fire. Just as his mother had said.

Ferrash bit hard into his lower lip to check he hadn't dreamed up some vision of his mother's assertion that Juuni was empyrric, but he was truly awake. Then she turned fully to face him and he understood what his mother had been trying to say when he'd stormed out.

Your daughter.

Ferrash couldn't move. She started walking up the field towards him, fully aware of his presence.

When she was halfway across the field, Ferrash found his voice. 'Don't come any closer.'

She stopped, hands held out to either side. He couldn't stop staring at her, couldn't get away from the grip of his memories. She looked so much like her, so little like him, but those eyes...

'Ferrash Progmannae?' she asked.

Though suspicion crawled over his skin, he stepped out from behind the machinery. He still held the pistol out in front of him, trained on her heart. Not as confrontational as sighting to her face. Before he spoke, he sent a crawler into the Keepers' database. He'd avoided this, before. Now he needed to know.

'Name?' Ferrash asked. It came out as more of a croak. He cleared his throat. 'What's your name?'

'Dakaga Lay.'

It meant nothing to him. To him, Junni had been vatborn. A second name would have shown that cover, if cover it had been, as a lie. Ferrash planted his feet more firmly, adjusting his grip on the pistol. 'Lineage?'

'My blood stems from Juuni Lay.'

'And?'

Dakaga tilted her head, considering him. It was such an animal gesture that he shuddered.

'And you,' she said.

The shuddering gripped him, making his hands shake and his breaths come faster. He tightened his hold on the pistol to counteract it. That the truth hurts was common knowledge, but he hadn't imagined it could hurt like someone driving a drill through your skull. He inhaled sharply through his nose, the cold air searing through his sinuses. When he swallowed, it was like forcing a rock down his throat.

'How do I know you're telling the truth?' he asked.

Dakaga held a hand out to him, inclined her head to it. 'It will be in my identifier.'

Ferrash stayed put, and eventually she returned the hand to its previous position. Her lips twisted down as if he'd disappointed her, but he couldn't help seeing it as a veneer over something dangerous – a taught expression rather than anything genuine. She wore patchwork, and she had come through tunnels that only the Kept should have known, but that didn't prove anything. The Protectorate knew who he was. They knew he had betrayed them. Logically, they would send someone after him. Who better to catch him with his guard down than his own daughter?

'Are you with the Kept?' he asked.

'I am.'

The crawler was taking too long. He needed those answers now. 'Why'd you choose to join them?'

'The Empyrean is a curse which needs to end.'

A rote answer. The Kept's standard line. And she said it without a hint of emotion. Ferrash took half a step forwards and shrugged his shoulders. 'Nothing personal? You just decided that one day and jumped ships?'

Dakaga hesitated, lips downturned again, maybe something a little more genuine in the expression this time.

Empyrrics can't be trusted.

Her eyes locked his soul, caught it in a web of wonder and angst and despair, but behind that lock his mind whirled, playing out scenarios, working out how likely it was that he'd be able to walk away. He didn't like the odds.

Time stretched around them. Further back in the mountain, the generator coughed and died. The overhead lights dimmed, then rose back to full strength, working off the grid.

Then Dakaga said, 'My mother told me how they treated you,' and that's when he knew it was all a lie. The crawler came back on the tail of her words. Dakaga Lay was still recorded as a keeper. An attendant in the Keepers' Inspectorate, to be specific – part of his mother's old task force against the Kept. Dakaga may be in the Kept now, but only as a spy. This was all a lie. It looked like she took after him after all.

Ferrash relaxed and holstered his pistol, leaving his hand close to his belt. He grinned, imagining it toothy, as animalistic as her earlier gesture had been. Violent tension shivered in the air between them.

'Your mother didn't even tell me what she was,' he said.

They both moved in the same second. Ferrash flicked a disc grenade from a belt pouch and hurled himself to one side. Dakaga burst into radiance. Her entire body glowed green. Flames billowed around her arms. She threw that flame towards the space he had just vacated, then slashed sideways. Coruscating light rushed at him, but in that instant the grenade went off. Her empyrric blade faltered, cut off from its energy source by the cloud of nexite particles he'd released.

Whipping his pistol out, Ferrash fired two shots at her, but she'd shielded most of the grenade blast and his bullets disintegrated as they passed into the remaining energy. He lurched to his feet with another two disc grenades wedged between the fingers of his left hand.

As he stood, her fingers twitched; something tugged at his soul. For a moment, he was outside his body, his breath stolen from him. But then he let loose the two grenades and snapped back into himself, panting. He blinked. His thoughts jumbled in his mind. When he moved, the sensations didn't line up right. Stepping with his right foot made his right palm ache with no sensation in the foot. It twisted underneath him and sent him sprawling on his face.

Either the fall knocked it out of him or the effect just faded. The cause didn't matter. He rolled to his feet as a coiling tendril stabbed the ground beside him.

Dakaga's face contorted with pain, glowing along the lines of her pain mesh. Forced to rely on that, she couldn't tear him apart outright, but she was still more than strong enough to kill him.

Strength was her crutch, though. As he dodged another two lashing attacks, Ferrash realised she had no finesse. In her eyes, if she threw enough at him, she'd win. He had one more grenade. If they were still fighting once he'd used that and the nexite clouds wore off, she'd be right.

Dakaga rushed for him. The Empyrean scythed in front of her, washed out under the sun strips.

Only one way to do it. Ferrash sprinted across the field towards her, jumped the leading edge of the scythe and flung the last grenade straight at her. It exploded against an impromptu shield, but she staggered back, and the flames faded into the light. Then Ferrash landed. In the moments before she could regain her abilities, he barrelled into her. They both tumbled to the ground, but he kept his grip, his arm curled tight around her neck. She drove her elbows back into him as he fumbled in his belt pouches. He twisted to deflect the worst of them, then came up with a syringe clutched in his free hand. He stabbed it into her neck and depressed the plunger before she could react, though she clawed it away and threw it across the room a second later.

She threw all her weight sideways, arms reaching for the pistol he'd dropped trying to reach her. He wrapped his other arm around her waist before she could get to it. Any second now. Any second now, and the drugs would knock her out and he could put her in the box where she couldn't hurt him. Any second now.

Too late, he caught green on the edge of his vision. Eyes widening, acting on instinct, he reached into the sleeve of his coat and pulled out his knife. He plunged the blade into his daughter's heart, and then the Empyrean hit.

CHAPTER FIFTY

PALIA DIDN'T REMEMBER FALLING asleep. There had been Dakaga's hand on her knee, her questions, and then... nothing. She didn't remember being asleep. She woke like coming round from unconsciousness, head swimming with confusion, alarmed, temporarily misplaced from the circuit of time. She fell out of the bunk and crawled along the floor. She couldn't get her eyes to focus on anything. The universe tilted on its axis. Distantly, she could hear people moving, metal screaming, someone closer trying to say something.

'Hege!' The sound resolved itself. Strong arms hoisted Palia from the floor until she stood, wobbling, on two feet. The woman from earlier – Palia couldn't remember the name Dakaga had used – stood before her. The universe seemed to flip again. The woman took hold of her shoulder before she could fall.

'It's keepers,' she said. 'We bein' attacked. That's flux you can feel, the pull 'tween then and us.'

Sense slammed back into Palia. She gasped, then focused on the woman's face, the scars crossing her skin. 'How are they attacking?' she asked. 'There's a hundred metres of water between us and them. You'd fight them off fine if they came one at a time through that hatch.'

The woman's eyes flicked to the roof above their heads. Tension rode in her shoulders. 'They tryin' crumple the hull. We be fightin' back to that.'

Palia tried not to think about them all being crushed inside a metal box. Instead, she cast about for Dakaga, but this woman was the only other person in the room.

'Where's Dakaga?'

Creasing her brow, the woman shrugged. 'I haven't seen.'

'*Fires.*' Palia rubbed a hand across her chin. 'The tunnels. The ones you said were blocked on the way to the mountain. Can you get to them from here?'

The woman blinked. 'If they can be unblocked, we be able to flee one by one, 'til Keepers crush us... We can get there, yes.'

'Show me.'

Palia's heartrate accelerated as the woman led her to the tunnels. It wasn't the threat of the Keepers that did it, but a burning shock and suspicion that grew with each step, like she had made some catastrophic mistake and was just about to see the consequences. When they came upon the tunnel entrance and she saw the blocking metal melted away to a human-sized opening, bile rose to her throat. Dakaga had gone that way, and Palia didn't trust her intentions anymore.

Palia didn't stop to thank the woman. She vaulted through the hole and ran, and she never looked back.

Palia found Ferrash kneeling in the middle of an indoor field with his back to her, rocking back and forth on his heels, Dakaga's body held tight to his chest. The sight rooted her to the spot. So focused on getting there as fast as she could, she had managed to ignore everything she could sense in the Empyrean, but now it hit her like a landslide. All that grief, confused and tangled, blazing like a star about to turn supernova. Tears sprang to her eyes. She staggered forwards. Blood pooled on the ground around Ferrash's knees, soaking into the tail of his patchwork coat.

'Ash.' It came out as a whisper. Something in the air confused her senses, making the edges of the supernova dance in her vision. 'Ash.' She knelt on the ground beside him, just behind Dakaga's feet. His face looked red and raw, completely changed since last Palia had seen him, but his hair and presence were the same. She matched the face to the photo Bek had given her, then remembered the last time she had seen Bek, resting in a pool of his own blood. She had to tell Ferrash about that, but not now. Not while he was dealing with this.

Palia hunched her shoulders over the ache in her chest and placed a quivering hand on Ferrash's shoulder. 'I'm sorry.'

As she waited for him to respond, her eyes traced down to a singed tear in his coat. On seeing it, her grip on his shoulder tightened. There was a hole in his flesh three inches deep, V-shaped, like something with a long jaw had taken a bite out of it, but the edges were perfectly smooth: cauterised.

Something clamped over her hand and she jolted, surprised. Ferrash had taken one hand from Dakaga's body and covered hers with it. He squeezed, hard. Blood welled out from the fabric of his gloves.

He hadn't turned to look at her, but with his other hand cradling his daughter's head, he laid her down on the soil before him. Then he doubled over, his forehead almost touching hers. Palia's hand slipped off his shoulder, but he kept hold of it, squeezing it so hard she had to bite her lip to keep from crying out.

'I'm sorry, Ash,' Palia said, her voice cracking. 'She heard me talking to the Kept about your mother, and where she'd gone, a-and she figured out the same as I did that you'd come up here as well. She said she'd clear the way, but I didn't know to trust her and... I think she knocked me out? I'm sorry.' She drew in a deep breath that turned into a sob. 'I-I should have stopped her. Should have got here first. Should have warned you. This didn't—' Again, she bit her lip – this time to stop herself saying it didn't have to happen. That would make it worse. Retrospective what-ifs always did. It would cause the same guilt she'd shackled herself with after Derren's death.

Was it worse to lose a child you had never wanted or a child you had never known?

Ferrash straightened. Pain flashed through him, spiking from the injury, and his face – his real face, the one her mind had erased – was contorted when he turned towards her. Blood streaked its left side. It ran over his pain mesh and into his hair, spiking strands of it into ragged paintbrushes. A depth of pain lodged in the gold discs of his eyes, stung them with tears.

When Ferrash opened his mouth to say something, no sound came out. He let go her hand and threw his arms around her, pulling her so tight against him she could barely breathe. Palia hugged him back, arms rising and falling as his chest heaved. His crying was too quiet – not sobs or wails but sharp gasps, breathy laughter turned too far to abject sorrow. She didn't know what to do, so she clung on, hoping that just by being there she could give him the support he needed.

Then she remembered the keepers below. Had they torn the Kept off their perch yet? Had they left it to sink to the bottom of the ocean and gone on their way? Or had they launched a full invasion, crossed the water, killed the Kept and found the tunnel entrance?

'We need to go,' Palia whispered, even though it was the last thing she wanted to say to him. 'It's not safe.'

Ferrash took a few moments to regain enough composure to talk. He made a strangled noise in the back of his throat, then said, 'I know.' He stood, his arms falling from around her, his teeth bared and stark white against the surrounding blood.

Palia rose with him. He turned to look at his daughter's body again. But for the blood, Dakaga looked as if she might still get up and walk away. Her eyes betrayed her death. They stared sightless at the sun lamps, capturing their reflection for eternity. Palia felt like she should close them, throw a shroud over the mirrors, but that was Ferrash's decision.

'Do you want to bury her?' she asked.

He shook his head, eyes closed. 'No time.'

Palia pulled some of her grief out of her hand and into the semblance of a flame, then regretted it when Ferrash flinched away from her. But he nodded. As she turned to scoop a hollow in the soil, he moved in her peripheral. When she turned back, Dakaga's eyes were closed. Ferrash scooped her into his arms, a sob catching in his throat as he looked upon her one last time, and lowered her into the grave. He stepped back, brows low over his eyes, and gave a slight nod. On that signal, Palia lifted the soil again and poured it into the grave, leaving a disturbed mound under the blazing lights.

Ferrash picked his pistol from the floor. Every movement pained him, sent spikes of agony screaming through his psyche.

<Pestor, are you well?> Lilesh sent.

Blinking, Palia double-checked the time stamp on the message. It had arrived some time after she had entered the tunnels, along with a dozen other messages, but had been sent several hours before.

<Only just got your message,> Palia replied, not sure how to explain how far from 'well' things were.

Ferrash took a step towards the far exit, then beckoned for her to follow. 'This way.'

Palia followed, stepping around the unmarked grave. She imagined she could smell the blood on the air, and her senses still tingled with afterimages from whatever clouded the atmosphere. As she followed Ferrash, the near-silence weighed on her, a pressure she couldn't yet see to lift. There was nothing she could say to make this better. The only news she had was news of Bek, and her heart broke just to think of telling it.

Lilesh sent another message. <I had just about given you up for dead. You realise there is a war on, do you not?>

<Of course I know about the *zashen* war.>

<Not *the* war. A new one. I can feel it several levels down and rising. Are you near it?>

Remembering the mind-lurch of her waking, Palia grimaced. <I was. I felt it. But I'm away, now. Hopefully the Kept will escape the same way I left.>

<Good. Do you still need me here or do you have a clear path back to the ship?>

They passed through a door membrane and into the corridor beyond. Palia stepped out to walk by Ferrash's side, sticking close, hoping her presence might reassure him.

'Is there space for the ship to land where this comes out?' she asked.

Ferrash swiped at the blood on his face with a sleeve, mixing it with the tear tracks. His voice was heavy when he replied. 'It's a mountainside. Room to hover, but you'd get shot out of the sky before you made it a mile from the spaceport.'

'So we go on foot?'

He shook his head. 'There's skis. Just one set, so either I'll have to carry you or you can make yourself some green ones.'

Without meaning to, Palia glanced at the wound in his side. He stiffened at the observation. He probably could carry her, but it wouldn't do him any good.

They emerged into a medium-sized room with a stove and seating. A shiny metallic box rested to one side, occupying a null zone in her awareness, and a mug lay on the floor with its contents still drying in a trail around it. Ferrash kept going, but she paused. Wind whistled, muffled, down the corridor to their left.

Sensing that she had stopped, Ferrash turned and followed her gaze. 'There's something I need to do first. Won't be long.'

Ferrash made his way to the comms array. As the air temperature dropped, Dakaga's blood began to freeze on his face. He pawed at it again, then realised with the state of his gloves that he was probably just making it worse. He pulled his hood up instead and tightened it, sick to his stomach. His mind kept dipping towards that first fuzzy stage of unconsciousness. Dragging himself back from the brink again, he sent Palia a message asking her to run some hot water from the stove so he could wash the blood off. Bad idea leaving there if it'd just crack his skin the moment he stepped into the snow. Maybe he deserved that. He hadn't *meant* to...

Ferrash screwed his eyes shut and jammed his fist into the power switch on the comms array, grinding his knuckles against the surface. Anything to keep the thoughts at bay.

Once the generator had brought the array to life, he patched his implants through to it, prepared the automated set of messages he'd had ready for years and hovered over the command to set it all in motion. It might already be too late. If he'd done it right, if he'd kept everyone quiet and safe until the time was right, it might have happened in one moment. One button to flip the order of things in an instant, without bloodshed, without question. A theoretical button. It never would have happened like that. But it was still a threshold. One word from him and a fight between thousands here would become a fight between billions, all across the Protectorate. One word from him and the Keepers would be truly challenged, but still in possession of all their powers. The blood on his hands...

But he already had blood on his hands. They all did.

He pressed the button. Messages streamed from the comms array to bounce themselves around Hesperex, through the relays in the orbiting fleet, through the Prime Nexus, to every planet the Protectorate claimed to own. Not messages, as such. Each was a virus, each unique, each designed to evolve and multiply in as many ways as possible. The Protectorate didn't have a societal network. All it had was the central news system, so that's where the bulk of the messages travelled.

When the last message sent and the first hit Five-Fifty-Four, he turned the machine off and limped to join Palia. Pain seared across his left side, but it had begun to grow numb.

'Are you ready?' Palia paused in her pacing of the stove room.

It hurt to meet her eyes, but it hurt less than the real pain. His chest tightened. Feelings he didn't have strength to process gripped him. Every bone ached.

Ferrash started towards the hatch and the snows outside. Somewhere out there, a million riots were starting, and a million riots would roll into a hundred battles and one great war. It should have been as simple as roles switching. Should have been as simple as most of the people in power saying things would be different now.

Things *would* be different.

He breathed in as deep as he could before the pain became too much, then he turned to Palia. 'Let's go.'

CHAPTER FIFTY-ONE

THE COMMAND DECK HUMMED with energy. Fabien could feel it in the air, tingling at his skin, standing the hairs on his arms on end. The Rythian navy embodied a precise, military efficiency that even the greatest ships of the Hegemony fleet couldn't quite match. Military and civilian overlapped and merged too much in Hegemony life. This, perhaps, was different. Perhaps it had to do with the AI they used, even aboard this ship with its rare human crew. He could only see the surface of their navy, after all – most of it was machines.

Fabien glanced to his right, where the high marshal stood leaning over the rail to the projection oval. Set into the floor, it acted like a window onto the battlefield of Munab. Hegemony ships displayed their projections at eye level. This made you feel more like a god, surveying all beneath you.

What there was to see wasn't good.

The rebels had had a hard time of it. The precision strike on the Munabi cave system, while presumably effective at its intended purpose, had left a gaping hole in the cavern roof. Suddenly they had three entrances to protect, rather than two, and the effort stretched them across miles of unfortified desert. In this hazy orange landscape, the vast swathe of the Protectorate's armies oozed like a great grey fungus. Mobile barricades as tall as mechs stood rooted at the edge of their encampments. Their tanks belched so much smoke into the air that in places, poisonous green fog had been superseded entirely. Their mortars pounded at Hegemony shields, blossoming against them in bright, fiery silence.

Of the mechanised division, only one unit remained. If Fabien squinted, he could just see it standing guard beside the main cave entrance.

The high marshal lifted his gaze from the projection. 'Looks like a stalemate down there.'

Fabien inclined his head. 'We've suffered losses, but not as many as the Protectorate has. Then again, they outnumber us by a considerable margin.'

Nodding, the high marshal leaned back and tapped at a screen embedded in the rail. 'I'll bring us in opposite the Protectorate fleet in orbit. We can drop assets, then retreat to engage the fleet. What matters is that we get more units on the ground.'

'Agreed.'

As Fabien bent to examine the scenes below in more detail, a message from the commander of the Hegemony fleets in-system popped up in his implants.

<Watch your backs. We've registered a new fleet travelling through the nexus.>

Fabien relayed the message to the high marshal, who frowned and gestured at the ceiling to bring another projection down from it. This one showed the nexus, tube ends beginning to glow for arriving ships.

'That changes things.' He turned to address an officer at a side terminal. 'Bring our rear around. Spherical. Outwards. Be prepared to fire on my instruction.' To Fabien, he asked, 'Are you expecting anyone else?'

'No.' Not unless Palia and Ferrash had needed to come back here, in which case Lilesh would have told him.

A moment later, a stream of ships burst out of the Munabi nexus, like a string pulled suddenly from a reel.

Fabien ground his teeth. 'They're Protectorate ships.'

The revelation didn't seem to concern the high marshal, who had his arms folded across his chest, staring up at the projection with a look of quiet curiosity.

'Orders, sir?' the officer asked.

'Hold fire.' The high marshal drew closer to Fabien and pointed to the projection. 'See their flight path? What do you make of that?'

The Rythian fleet, thanks to its blink ships, had appeared ninety degrees away from the nexus on the plane of Munab's orbit. If this new fleet wanted to attack them, they would have to come a good deal closer. Yet as Fabien watched the projection, they kept their existing trajectory, decelerating towards Munabi orbit.

Fabien shrugged. 'They intend to usurp orbital superiority. Burning for the planet makes sense.'

'At the angle we're approaching Munab, they can't tell if we're aiming for orbit or slingshotting to hit the nexus. If we were already in orbit, we would be committed. If they see us out here, they see us as little enough a threat to ignore us. You said there was trouble within the Protectorate. I don't think they've come for us. Besides which, I'm not entirely sure anyone has spotted us yet. The Protectorate's sensors aren't particularly effective. If they're still having to rely on a lot of manual monitoring, they might not notice anything that hasn't come through the nexus.'

Fabien opened his mouth to protest – a little unrest was one thing, but rogue fleets were quite another – when the projection lit up with overlaid trajectories.

The officer didn't even look away from her terminal. 'Missile launch,' she said.

The high marshal gave a small, smug smile. 'Projected path?'

'Incident on the Hegemony fleet in orbit, sir.'

Teeth clenched, Fabien tried to put his thoughts in order, but even as he considered reprimanding the high marshal for his nonchalant attitude, he found himself infected by some of the man's curiosity. This *was* odd. Fabien didn't need to warn the fleet – missiles fired from such a distance were simple enough to avoid or destroy. Half of them might well miss without anyone trying to move out of the way. If the newcomers were serious about causing damage, they would get closer before firing. So this made no sense.

Fabien ran a thumb along his jaw. 'You think they're powered missiles?' If they were, they could adjust their aim later in their journey. The Hegemony fleet was prepared for incoming fire, so an adjusted aim wouldn't do much good, but if the newcomers were to aim at the Protectorate fleet instead, they might not have time to react before the missiles hit.

'That's my theory,' the high marshal said.

'Sir,' the officer had a hand covering one ear, 'intercepted comms chatter between the two Protectorate fleets. Orbital fleet is praising incoming fleet for their arrival. Minimal response from incoming fleet.'

The high marshal nodded. Terse responses weren't confirmation of rebellion by any stretch, but it seemed to satisfy him.

'There's more, sir.'

At the tone of her voice, Fabien stood up straighter and frowned, one hand gripping tight to the rail.

'The nexus is moving. Relay telemetry indicates connection to neighbouring nexus.'

A cold fear clamped about Fabien's heart. He let out a long breath. 'They're pulling it out.' Of course the Protectorate was willing to cut off their own system to starve their enemies out.

The high marshal eyed him, calm, crimson irises glinting ill in the light. 'I wonder if they'll put it right back when they realise how we got here.' Rythe's ships could, of course, go wherever they pleased, nexus or no.

'It still leaves my fleet stranded,' Fabien said. 'If we need to withdraw...'

'We won't. We came to help you win this war, and we will. You don't need to worry about our new arrivals, either. Look.'

Back on the projection, the missiles had penetrated within the moons' orbits. Fabien's heart leapt into his throat at the sight of them so near his fleet. But even as he watched, the missiles changed course. Their indicators pulsed to show engine burns, then faded with their path set around the planet's circumference – a slingshot straight towards the Protectorate fleet.

Fabien leaned closer to the projection, hands gripped tight to the rail. At the last moment, the Protectorate ships in orbit burned to escape. Their fleet slid into disarray. Blocky hulks sideslipped and brought flak screens into life, but not fast enough. The incoming missiles tore into the fleet, spraying shrapnel across whichever ships didn't fall to the first hits, detonating in bright flares where they met flak. In mere moments, a quarter of the Protectorate fleet was gone.

Whatever had come through the nexus, it truly was a rogue fleet. Protectorate against Protectorate.

Fabien weighed new odds in his mind, wondered just how many of those rogue fleets there were.

'Sir,' the officer looked to the high marshal for guidance, 'the accent is a little hard to understand, but I believe our new allies just identified themselves as void packs, and offered their assistance.'

CHAPTER FIFTY-TWO

Palia skated down the mountainside on a raft of empyrric energy. It made no wake around it.

She kept Ferrash firmly ahead of her, her eyes and awareness both glued to him in case his pain made him fall. His skis kicked ice into her face every time he twisted to avoid a rock, blinding her with snow.

She wondered how he stood it. So many times, she had hesitated on the brink of taking the pain from him, but she knew he would refuse if she asked, somehow, and would notice if she didn't.

Lilesh awaited them somewhere in the city below. All Palia could see of it, when she didn't have snow in her face, was a single spire poking through the clouds. Those clouds churned just beneath her, grey and angry. Another layer of clouds above her made the sky finite, enclosed and inescapable. Lightning flashed from the top layer to the first. It washed each impact site with light, delineating sweeping bulges and troughs of clouds, picking out the edge of the spire in bright white. Another struck the rod atop the tower, and the crash that followed shuddered through her sternum.

Passing into the clouds, she lost sight of Ferrash. Palia's heart quickened, yet he still shone bright with pain in her awareness, so she could keep track of him. She hadn't lost control of the raft yet; there seemed no end to her supply of power. Everything had hurt for so long now that she had been forced to coil it into itself like Lilesh did. If she didn't, it would become too much and escape her. Better to feel and be deadly than to be dead to emotion.

They emerged from the clouds soaking wet and chilled to the bone a few seconds later. Ferrash turned by the side of the first building they came to, then toppled onto his hands and knees when he tried to halt. Palia let her raft hiss away into the air and took his arm to help him up.

'I'm fine,' Ferrash said, but he leaned into her as he staggered to his feet.

Palia helped him upright by holding her arm against the small of his back. The simple touch made her insides churn, more intimate than it should have been. Everything that had come untethered since losing her memory had latched onto him, bright and so strong that she worried she would never be able to walk away from him again. So she stuck close, following him inside the empty building.

'Can you walk to the ship?' she asked. 'Or do you need to take the tram?'

Jaw clenched, Ferrash shook his head. 'Trams won't be running.'

'Why?'

'You hear that?'

Palia paused. The wind howled. Thunder shook the ground beneath them. The sides of the building they stood in rattled as hail struck it.

She shook her head. 'Just the weather.'

Ferrash grimaced. 'Not weather. War.'

He limped across the room without further explanation and peered into the street from a side door. When Palia drew close, distant conversation washed through the blizzard outside. No, not conversation. She wouldn't hear that over the wind. Shouting. It took a while for the fact of that to sink in, but when it did, a weight sank in her gut. In all the time she had spent on Hesperex, she had never seen a crowd – not a coherent one, with everyone there for the same purpose. She had never heard anyone raise their voice and rarely seen anyone talking at all. But now there was shouting.

A gunshot cracked across the city.

Ferrash glared at the ground by his feet, the muscles of his face taut. 'Can't go overland unless we want to get caught up. Might still get caught up, but could be safer a couple levels down.'

'What are they fighting for?'

'Freedom.' Ferrash sighed and propped himself against the wall. 'Bloody freedom. My fault, too. Chair's disbanded the Proctorate committee because he found me out, but that was enough to make the people rebel. Doesn't take much, when they're already on the brink.'

Palia nodded, trying to hide her dismay at the guilt grasping Ferrash's psyche, trapped in the depths of his eyes.

'We can only go down a couple of levels to avoid it.,' she said. 'When I was looking for you, I... it was a lower level somewhere. Near some hydroponics – apparently one of your safe rooms should have been there. Anyway, the Kept were hiding down there, too, and now the Keepers are attacking. They might all be dead by now' – she hoped they had managed to escape to the mountain – 'but that just means the Keepers will be coming back to the surface.'

Ferrash's face went through varying degrees of surprise and anger, then settled with an eyebrow raised and his lips twisted into a half smile. 'You're assuming the Keepers'll be the ones to survive it.'

Palia remembered what Lilesh had told her: three hundred keepers on the level above her. How many Kept? Palia had only seen those in the room when she came out of the water, but there had been at least thirty of those, and she had walked past plenty more rooms on her way to the tunnels.

'Should I let Lilesh know where we are?' she asked.

More gunshots split the air. A barrage, this time. The noise of the crowd rose.

'Not safe for her. Or us. Come on,' said Ferrash. He ducked out of the building and walked a hundred metres down the street until he reached some stairs.

Palia kept pace behind him as he took the rest of the stairs three at a time, then the next set. After so long with her memory sliding off his image, she couldn't take her eyes off him. Since parting with him around Rythe, she had been worried she would forget again, that without him standing right in front of her, she wouldn't know who he was to her. She was glad to see that hadn't happened, but where her eyes fell, her awareness followed. Guilt and grief clawed their way up to Ferrash's brain.

They reached the bottom of the stairs and a loud *boom* thundered above them. It left Palia's ears ringing. Ferrash widened his stance and a moment later, the ground lurched beneath her feet. She stumbled forwards, only her grip on Ferrash's arm and his other shooting out to catch her stopping her from falling. The explosion continued, rumbling, a throaty roar without an origin.

'*Bile and*—' Ferrash's teeth flashed as he grimaced. 'They've blown the munitions factory. Idiots.'

He pulled her away, hand tight around hers, pushing even further through his pain. Every few seconds, something else cooked off in the explosion and the shockwave shuddered through the floor. A ceiling panel slipped free and landed half a metre behind them. It bounced loudly across the floor before crashing down onto its side.

Ferrash didn't lead them straight. He jinked and weaved into any side passage they came across, seemingly at random. He couldn't have looked more conspicuous if he had tried. He looked more like he was escaping.

With some reluctance, Palia dragged her awareness away from Ferrash and concentrated on the space surrounding them. Far in the distance, two empyrrics fought. The levels here were almost empty, like everyone on Hesperex had decided to make for the surface at once.

Ferrash's hand gripped tight. She followed his movements on instinct now, freeing up all her attention to find any pursuers. Then she spotted them, closer than the keepers, their emotions so dull or, she thought, non-existent, that they only showed up through the flicker of their lives' energy. They kept pace to either side, heedless of the walls that separated them.

'Who's following us?' she asked.

'Reiart.' Letting go of her hand, Ferrash drew his rifle from over his shoulder and plugged the wires into the flesh of his arm. The motion was familiar, if sickening.

Palia frowned and followed him through the door of a tall building. 'I thought they work for you?'

Ferrash gave a harsh chuckle. 'Looks like they want a change of management.'

The building they had entered was dark, with empty, dust-covered vat tubes stacked on their sides near the back. With the curved sides facing them, it looked like a sinuous glass wave coming out of the darkness. Ferrash jogged to a staircase, which led to a mezzanine floor overhanging the tubes. Palia cast about for another door, but she had only seen the one they came through, and that was too small for the tubes. She looked up. The shadowed ceiling had a small crane folded away underneath it. If it had been brighter, she imagined she might have seen a way for the roof to open.

'We're holding this place?' She joined Ferrash by the railings and crouched next to him.

With the barrel of his rifle resting on one of the bars, he pulled a pistol out from under his coat and handed it to her, grip first. He nodded. 'Don't tell your archivist we're here. They'll intercept any messages, send someone to find her.'

Palia took it from him, surprised to find it lighter than expected. 'Lilesh can deal with them.'

'They've more or less the same training as me. Don't count on it.' His voice hushed now, he touched her shoulder, then pointed to the ceiling. 'Shoot anything comes through that.'

'I can shield—'

He shook his head. 'Only when I tell you. Or a last resort. They see that first and they'll know to counteract it. It's how I...' The last word choked in his throat, his emotions flaring brighter. In the darkness, his face seemed ghostly, all too real and yet transient, like she might reach out to touch him any second only to find him gone. She found herself transfixed by the creases around his eyes, deepening as he moved and the pain from his wound bit deeper.

Then she did as he had asked and watched the ceiling. So no one could sneak around behind her, she dropped back into a shadowed corner. There, she had a good field of fire over anyone dropping down. In her awareness, she sensed the Reiart gathered outside, still silent.

Why do we call them mirror eyes? Palia looked into these souls and saw nothing, not her own emotions reflected back at her. More like being in a void, she thought, with the only sensations the ones confined to your self.

Ferrash lay prone in the centre of the railings now. His rifle muzzle drifted with his breath. Outside, two of the Reiart approached the door.

'Brace yourself,' said Ferrash.

Sat so far back from the edge and with her attention trained on the ceiling, Palia couldn't see the door. There was a crack and an electric hiss. The rifle muzzle flashed in the corner of her eye. Metal clinked, then light flashed and noise exploded into the room.

Palia cursed, ears pounding, wishing she had thought to cover them. The floor trembled underneath her. Vat tubes bounced against each other with dull clangs and she heard one roll away from her along the floor. Above, the stowed crane shuddered and groaned. Pain bloomed where once there had been silence by the door. She glanced back down, found the panels around the entrance buckled and torn, a bright splash of red picked out by the illumination outside.

Something metal glinted, rolling through the doorway. Palia cupped a hand over her left ear in preparation for another blast, glancing between the door and the roof. Nothing happened. The next time she looked to the door, smoke hung barely visible, blocking out most of the light from beyond it.

Then Ferrash started shooting, and that sound she did hear.

Back in the landscape of the Empyrean, life glimmered on the rooftop. Palia guessed at four or five people. A pale slit appeared in the ceiling, and the building juddered a fraction as a hatch began to creak open, though she couldn't hear it. Quieter sounds started to make their way back through the ringing in her ears. Ferrash was trying to say something, but she couldn't make out the words.

<I can't hear you,> she sent.

She pulled her knees up to her chest so she could rest her elbows on them and keep the pistol aimed at the widening gap.

<Pistol has link-in optics,> Ferrash sent back. <You found them?>

Palia checked the connection where her skin met the grip, but couldn't find anything to indicate she could link with it. <No. How do I do it?>

Ferrash fired three more shots in quick succession. Each shot brought with it a new spike of pain from the area of his scars, but nothing compared with the pain from his existing wound.

<Hold on,> he sent. <I'll set it up.>

Before she could ask how, her vision crashed into itself. Spots danced around behind her eyelids. She recoiled, but a moment later they were gone and so was the gloom. She could see the crane fully, perched in the centre of the ceiling. Light blazed from the gap beyond it. Her aiming point wavered to either side of it, and the optics picked up infrared from the people beyond. Six, now. They stood at the far edge of the roof, directly above the door, with the gap by their feet.

Palia took aim through the gap. It was too bright to see them, but she could make out what looked like the heat of a head, so she drew that level in her sights and pulled the trigger. The pistol bucked in her hands. The heat signature jerked, wavered, then fell into the street below.

<Can't you jam the hatch or something?> she asked.

<Nothing they couldn't get past.>

Palia risked a glance back at Ferrash and the door. The smoke had cleared, for the most part, with the Reiart covering behind the buckled doorframe. With Ferrash shooting at them whenever they broke cover, they couldn't get back into the room.

Something thudded above her. Palia looked up to see the crane nodding. One of the Reiart had jumped down onto it through the gap, cradling a carbine in their arms. Palia flicked the pistol towards them and fired. The shot hit their groin and sprayed blood over the girders behind them. They fell back, screaming, thumping up against the supports, then slipped sideways and fell over the edge. Palia sensed the wash of their pain pass her by, resisted the temptation to take it as a weapon. With a groan, the hatch halted, a metre's gap in its centre.

The remaining five Reiart jumped atop the crane at once. Palia gave up any attempt at aiming carefully and squeezed off a burst of rapid fire. The optics must have compensated for it, as she caught one of them in the arm, dropping his weapon, and made the others dance away from flashes on the struts beneath their feet.

As she lined up the next burst, the one who had dropped his weapon reached into a pocket and withdrew a grenade. Palia shot him in the chest just as he threw the disc out towards her. She watched it sail through the air for a moment too long before she came to her senses. She grabbed for the falling man in the Empyrean, dragging his pain from him, and then his life. With his energy coiling around her, she shot out both hands and met the grenade two metres from her chest with a wall of actinic green.

It exploded. It happened too close, the other side of her wall, its shrapnel disintegrating as she forced the wall outwards. Three of the Reiart jumped back through the ceiling, but one was too slow. The woman's alarmed cry cut to silence when the wave swept past her. The energy petered out just short of the ceiling, leaving the crane squealing in half-melted supports.

Gathering herself, Palia scanned around for more attackers. The four on the roof remained there for now. Three more were climbing up the wall to join them. Four stood ready by the door, still locked in a fire fight with Ferrash, and one more…

'Ash, look out!' Palia bolted from the floor towards the spark of life she had seen climbing the stairs. Green fire danced through the air beside her, coiled into an arcing tendril. She hurled it forwards when she reached the top of the stairs. It stabbed clean through the person's head. She whipped her hand sideways to cut across and it seared into the metal of the wall. The person hung in place, momentarily held up by their own body, then tumbled forwards onto their face.

Shredding the corpse to draw the rest of their energy, Palia lashed out at the door. A chevron of flame darted into the frame at waist height, sliced straight through, took the heads clean off the two who had been crouched nearest the door.

Ferrash shouted again, but her head was spinning now. The Empyrean danced everywhere she looked. Life flashed where it wasn't. Interlacing waves that seemed like joy spread themselves in empty space with no one there to feel them. Blinking, she tried to find something to orientate herself, tried to find Ferrash's pain as an anchor, but everywhere she looked was something new and brighter. She turned, stuck in her awareness, then bumped her hips against something and fell, her hands grasping at thin air just as her mind grasped for something comprehensible.

CHAPTER FIFTY-THREE

THE MOMENT HE SAW the nexite grenade, Ferrash knew there would be no stopping it. He tried to shout a warning to Palia, but it was too late. The grenade exploded, setting the air shimmering for a moment with that characteristic green haze. Palia flailed, her back turned to the door.

Ferrash grabbed the handrail and launched himself onto his feet. The wires in his arm tugged as his rifle barrel caught in the railings. Pain shot across his waist and lanced all up his left side. He let out an involuntary cry, staggering towards Palia. His back tensed as he ran. Enemies lay above him. Any second could see a shot between his shoulders.

Palia stepped back, her heels hovering over the edge of a step. She backed into the sloping railing and slipped, tipping backwards, with a fraction of an inch between falling to the side and falling over it completely.

Ferrash lunged for her, caught a fistful of her coat fabric and heaved. It looked like she might fight him, but then her eyes snapped into focus, and recognition came with it. All resistance gone, he pulled harder than he meant to. She crashed into him and sent them both slamming down onto the staircase. He would have cried out if the impact hadn't jarred his teeth together so hard. He wheezed, tasted blood.

Palia rolled away from him, crushing his arm against the hard steps as she did. When he tried to follow, static crowded his head. He gasped and lay back, everything reduced to the confines of his own skull, the separation sneaking through his limbs. It was that sensation that brought him snapping back to the moment. Too similar to the Empyrean. Too similar to the numbness that must come before death.

He made to get up, but Palia held him down by his shoulders. She put a finger to her lips, then jerked her head towards the door. Frowning, he let her help him sit.

Gunfire sounded from the street outside. Close. Much closer than before.

Ferrash searched about in his implants for a camera nearby, found one on a building opposite. The Reiart by the door were all dead. Three remained on the roof, but fire flashed from all around. Ferrash couldn't see where from, but the Reiart were outnumbered. Not long ago, he might have felt something at that. Nothing emotional, so much – more an urge to see them out of danger. But the Reiart had never really been his. He'd just been pulling the strings, and now they knew, they weren't happy about it. He might have felt guilty. Maybe he did, but he felt so much else that it was hard to tell.

Patchwork moved by the door. Ferrash began to lift his rifle, but Palia shook her head, then called out, 'Tessa?'

The figure bounded up the stairs towards them, lowering her hood to reveal dark hair crowned with horns. She slid into place in to Ferrash's memories: the surviving arsaeria from the flagship. If she'd been on the ship with Palia, he must have missed her in his brief stop after Rythe.

'Is he hurt?' Tessa nodded to Ferrash, to his bandaged side still showing through the hole in his coat in particular.

'Not enough,' Ferrash said.

Palia shot him a hard glance. Ferrash hadn't meant it to sound like he deserved more pain. He'd just meant he wasn't too hurt to move. Maybe later, he'd have to think about if he really had meant anything else by it, but now wasn't the time.

'Lilesh sent me here,' said Tessa. 'Couldn't come herself. She has gone back to protect the ship.'

Ferrash shortened his rifle's barrel and removed the wires from his flesh, wincing at the suction. 'Who'd you come here with?'

Tessa shrugged. 'People. They heard the sound of fighting and rushed to join in. It appears they will fight anyone not dressed the same as them, with exceptions. There are some others in uniforms but with patches sewn onto their sleeves.'

'That'll work just as long as it takes someone to realise they can fake it.'

Palia had her head cocked to one side. Listening or sensing, he couldn't tell. Then she said, 'We should head to the ship. Straight line. Keepers are coming. Fast.'

Tessa shook her head. 'You go. I'm staying.'

'What?' They both said it at the same time. Palia seemed horrified.

'This is history in the making, Pestor Tennic. If I am to record anything in my life, it should be this.'

'If you even survive it.'

Tessa gave a small smile. 'There are many of them, and I believe few of the attackers. Or defenders, whichever way around this is. I will be safe enough. Safer than on the flagship.'

Mentioning the flagship made Palia's jaw tighten. She drew a deep breath that he felt more than heard where their bodies pressed together.

'Go then,' said Palia. 'And good luck.'

Tessa made her way back down the stairs, leaving the two of them alone.

More of Ferrash's weight rested on Palia than he would have liked, but he couldn't find the strength to move. Cold clung to his skin, even through the coat.

'Can you make it?' Palia asked. She was afraid for him, her brows downturned, her hand covering his.

Ferrash met her eyes, found Empyrean green staring back at him. He tried to speak, but his mouth opened and closed without sound coming out.

'Do you need me to take some of the pain?'

Shaking his head, he tried to stand, but the pain threatened to rip him in two. He collapsed against the wall, panting. The spaceport was ages away. He'd never make it like this. So he locked eyes with her, trying to say without words how much he didn't want to have to say yes, then nodded. The pain released a second later, sliding away to leave only a dull throb.

It was bliss.

Palia helped him to his feet, squeezing his hand through their paired layers of gloves. When Ferrash started down the stairs, she followed a fraction behind. Ready to catch him, he guessed, if he fell. He should have been looking through his implants and the camera feeds to find a clear path back, but he couldn't muster the energy to send a coherent command, not anymore.

Stepping out into the enclosed street, it was like his world had shrunk. His view limited itself to the two or three buildings in front of them and the road in between. He could feel the ceiling pressing down above, but wasn't aware of it, and couldn't bring himself to focus on any details in their surroundings. Even sound came muted. Gunfire might as well have been crickets. Explosions sounded distant and muffled, like he was hearing them underwater.

Vatborn streamed past, a sea of patchwork. For once, the colours stretched to their faces. Grime covered, blood streaked, they let their faces feel. So many crowded the streets that they jostled him from side to side. Palia took hold of his elbow – he guessed so she didn't lose him in the crowd – and it didn't even seem out of place.

The sight gnawed at him.

Ferrash asked, <How far did you say the keepers were?>

<Next level down. They're running. They must have finished off the Kept and realised they needed to come to the surface.>

They didn't have to be running *towards* something, but Ferrash didn't say that. Instead, he pushed his mind into his implants, found the nearest stairs, started heading that way. They battled their way up against the flow. Palia pushed past to walk in front of him, driving a wedge that he lacked the strength to make himself.

All those people heading down, straight into the hands of the Keepers – how many could they kill? There wasn't a limit, not really. An empyrric could reduce a thousand to nothing but energy and release it again to kill a thousand more. Chances were they couldn't handle that much and they'd explode, but how many would be dead by the time that happened?

When they reached the surface, Ferrash stared up at the dark underside of the clouds. The sooner they got to the Prime Nexus, the fewer people had to die. If he focused, really focused, he could make out the spaceport in the distance, looming in its haphazard monstrosity over the streets below.

'Come on.' He began walking faster with that goal fixed in his sights, but Palia stiffened. Her grip on his elbow spun him. When he followed her gaze, he saw them: keepers, dozens of them, swarming out of one of the lifts. They kept running even when they were free of the stairs, just barging through the crowd at first. But as the crowd started to resist, Empyrean flames flickered into life.

Ferrash pushed Palia in front of him, towards the spaceport. 'Run!'

She took hold of his hand and he sprinted after her, panting hard, struggling to keep up. Green flames danced beneath the sleeves of her coat. If anyone else saw, they might think she was Kept. He didn't know if that was a good thing anymore, but even if the vatborn didn't attack, the keepers would.

From the screams behind them, the keepers weren't discriminate in their attacks.

<They're fighting each other,> Palia sent.

<What?> Ferrash grappled with his implants. Palia's grip, bone-crushingly tight, gave him the focus he needed.

<The Keepers. They're under attack on the lower levels. That's why they're running up here. I think the Kept must have survived and chased them all the way up from the ocean base, somehow.>

Ferrash glanced back at the green-robed swarm cutting their way through whatever remnants of the crowd stayed in their way. The keepers had formed a perimeter around the stairs entrance, preventing any retreat below. Ferrash would have watched longer, but Palia stopped, jarring his shoulder as he kept forwards.

'What...?' he began, but trailed off as green robes approached through the wall of patchwork hoods in front of them.

One of the keepers pointed their way, shouted something, commanded the vatborn before them to move.

Palia shoved Ferrash towards the edge of the street. He put a hand on his pistol as he staggered sideways, ready to shoot if he had to. Lightning flashed through the belly of the clouds above. A crash and rumble shook the street a moment later, sending snow flurrying from nearby rooftops. Where the keepers moved, the vatborn stepped aside – not as keen to fight as their siblings further up the street, or not as stupid.

Palia had drawn her flames back, but the keepers were still heading for her. Ten of them. Twenty. More came up the stairs behind.

One step further and Ferrash had his back pressed up against the buildings lining the street. Palia bumped into his chest, then stepped forwards and pulled her hand away. His fingers trailed after her touch.

<Is there a way past them?> she asked.

He couldn't answer her. There wasn't. Not that they could get to in time. But he wanted to say they could. He wanted to say everything would be alright for once, that things weren't as messed up as they appeared, but they were. Ferrash reached for a grenade, but he had spent all his. He'd used them all to kill his daughter and now he had none left to save Palia. Or himself. Or anyone.

When the first keeper appeared at the front of the crowd, Palia speared him through the chest with a jet of energy so intense that Ferrash flinched away from it. He edged right and fired a couple of shots, but they disintegrated on meeting the other keepers' shield. It rose into the sky above their heads, tall and growing taller. Palia sent more jets at it, but while it buckled, it never broke.

Ferrash tried to move away from the wall and skirt around to get a clear shot, but Palia grabbed him and held him back. She had her own shield up, thin and shimmering. Glass under the iron of the keepers' wave.

As the shield tilted over their heads, a shape flitted over the top of the keepers. Another keeper dropped to the ground behind the others, swung their arm out and slashed a line of fire through their midst. Taken by surprise, they didn't even put up a defence. Each stumbled as one, cut in two. The wave faltered, faded. Palia kept her shield up, but took half a step back until she was pressed against his chest again. Ferrash thought he could feel her heart beating against his chest, rapid as bulletfire, but it could have been his own, echoing from her back.

The new keeper stepped over the bodies of their fallen comrades, their arms outstretched. It might have been a gesture of good intent, if their hands hadn't been weapons in themselves. On their shoulder, a white patch had been sewn against the green.

His mother removed her hood. Ferrash grabbed at Palia's arm before she could try anything stupid, just in case she didn't recognise her.

'It's okay,' he said.

His mother shook her head. 'It's not.'

Palia dropped her shield, but he could tell by the way her shoulders tensed that she didn't trust Ayt. Understandable. She relaxed a fraction when his mother flicked her wrist to send two approaching keepers crashing into the opposite building. The underside of the clouds above them glowed green, reflecting the fighting further down the street. His mother kept glancing that way, wary.

Taking a step towards her, Ferrash lowered his voice so Palia couldn't hear and said, 'I'm going to get out of here and head straight for the nexus. Can't do this if I don't know how. If you found anything about how we can kill the Empyrean without the technology—'

'I found a lot, but there's no time. You don't have the capacity to understand it, anyway. Her.' She stepped around Ferrash, clipping him with her patched shoulder, and stared at Palia. 'Are you sure you trust her?'

'Wouldn't be alive if I didn't.' His chest tightened as he voiced it.

Satisfied, Ayt stuck her hand out in front of her. She inclined her head for Palia to take it. Palia hesitated.

Ferrash craned his head over both of them to see the fighting. More keepers had joined from Five-Fifty-Four's surface. They held position around the stairs, the air between them and it torn with a chaos that hurt to look at. Green met green in wave after wave of coalescing force. The nearest vatborn, too slow to move or too engaged with the fight, were on their knees screaming, buckled in pain. Sannots, sworn to serve the Keepers as punishment for their unsanctioned births, stabbed at the wounded, twisting knives and inflicting pain any way they could to fuel their masters. One held a vatborn's hand in his, lips trembling. Then he turned and plunged the knife up into the back of the keeper nearest him. The keeper turned, and green lightning whickered across the crowd.

'Palia, just take her hand,' Ferrash said. His mother had said he didn't have the capacity to understand her discoveries, which meant it was empyrric business. Her outstretched hand, he guessed, was meant for knowledge transfer – whether by implants or the Empyrean, he had no idea. 'Whatever she wants, do it. We need to go.'

He had his pistol aimed at the keepers, but if they came further this way, he wouldn't stand a chance. He could only grit his teeth as Palia clasped hands with his mother. Palia recoiled at the touch, staggering back, but Ayt held her fast. Half a second later it was done, whatever 'it' was – it couldn't just be a simple transfer of knowledge via implants, or she would have sent it to him, wouldn't she? Or had she meant only an empyrric would understand the data? His mother stepped away, and he didn't have time to ask her.

Unsupported, Palia fell. Ferrash shot out an arm to catch her, hissing between his teeth as her weight pulled at his side.

'You okay?' he asked.

She nodded. In the corner of his eye, his mother's robes flicked.

'Wait!' Ferrash let go of Palia and threw himself across the gap to grab his mother's sleeve. 'Where are you going?'

Ayt faced him, expression unreadable, her eyes flickering with the reflections of distant lightning. 'To create a diversion.'

Ferrash stared into her eyes, trying to see what lay behind them, but that was something he'd never been able to do. Then he leaned in closer and spoke quickly so that no one would overhear. 'The man I told you to follow, the kidnapped one? I know where they're keeping him. Find him for me, please.' Without thinking, he moved his hand to her arm, squeezed tight. 'If you do one thing for me, make it this. Save him.' He sent the location marker across to her implants a moment later, after she dipped her head a fraction to acknowledge she would do it. Then she strode away from both of them, her fingers curled, ready to strike.

'Come on,' he said to Palia, taking hold of her hand. 'We've got to go.'

They wove through the crowds together, the press of people so thick that anything faster than a brisk walk was at times impossible. Gunshots were rare. Where the vatborn met resistance, fights broke out. An elbow struck the side of Ferrash's head. Pain shot through his skull. He keeled over sideways, held upright by Palia's grip, almost slipping into blackness as he fell. She said something to him. A lot of things. A constant chatter of panic-edged noise muffled by the blunted edge of his subconscious.

He came to when she shoved him in the small of his back. He lunged forwards, knees buckling, then broke into an unsteady sprint. Blinking his vision clear, he saw the way ahead: the ice-coated bridge stretching away across the ocean, empty for now, and the spaceport rising as a shadow high above.

CHAPTER FIFTY-FOUR

THE RYTHIAN FLEET DROPPED their payload of unmanned attack vehicles like a black rain upon the surface of Munab. Fabien watched them descend on the projection, from the belly of the fleet in orbit by the ceiling and down, down past his eye level, flaming with the fury of re-entry like reactive metal shavings scattered across water. Black trails followed in their wake. They plunged through choking gas clouds and still down, until they punched through the roiling flame smoke from the battle on the floor and were lost from sight. Once grounded, they could be given their target.

In a disorienting lurch of graphics, the projection's view shifted to a slightly different section of desert, beneath the clouds. Fabien leaned over the railing to get a clearer view. Pitch smoke trails stretched across the surface of Munab, almost obscuring all of the dismal sands. A series of high plateaus jutted out of the smoke near the bottom right. One of those had an outpost held by the Hegemony. A lot of blood had been spilled to keep it that way. Hegemony forces sat almost entirely atop one mesa, pushed back and pushed back until the high ground was the only ground they could manage.

Because there, taking up most of the view, was the Protectorate – so many of them, their tanks and people seethed like a grey ocean.

Fabien had read the reports. He had seen images from the ground, from the air, from orbit. He had seen this view projected, the same as he was seeing it now, a hundred times or more. But there was something about seeing it and knowing he was there, something about the tantalising proximity, that made his skin crawl.

He scanned the ground for any sight of the Rythian vehicles, but couldn't spot them. A larger view on his datascreen told him they should have landed due north of the plateaus, beyond the Protectorate position, off the projection.

Then they appeared at the side of the projection oval, still glowing with the heat of re-entry. Bright orange dots, they crept down from the north, cooling to dim-glinting black. The Protectorate forces buckled, a sudden hive of activity as they tried to react to the new threat and wrap their lines around two fronts. They weren't fast enough. A new cloud formed above Rythe's forces, thick, shifting. It rocketed across the ground like a shadow cast by something high above, only as it went, it sowed destruction. Protectorate aircraft diverted course to meet it, but their shots met thin air. The cloud reformed around them, then swept back at their attackers. Fireballs bloomed above the armies.

Under the protection of that ever-changing cloud, the ground attack vehicles rolled onwards. Orange flashed again as the Protectorate's artillery began to pick them off, piece by piece, but half of those explosions were diverted misses or mid-air interceptions. A few broke through and perhaps fifty dots vanished, but there were more. There were enough.

Fabien wondered how it looked from the mesa. An unknown threat from orbit, chewing through enemy ranks towards their position. The Hegemony soldiers might have been briefed, but they wouldn't know what to expect. Fabien was the only person in the Hegemony who knew about Rythe's best-kept secrets.

'So that's all AI down there?' Fabien asked the high marshal.

The first Rythian vehicles smashed into the Protectorate's rear lines. A few of them had used the cover of a crashed Protectorate ship, shot down by the void packs, to flank further.

The high marshal turned from his conversation with an officer, then made his excuses and walked over. 'Yes,' he said. 'We don't put people on the ground unless it's a last resort. We retain them for the defence of Rythe.'

'Don't you find AI... quirksome?' Fabien asked.

'How so?'

Fabien crossed his arms, trying his best to put the thoughts together. In all his studies, he had to admit he hadn't paid much attention to software. It just wasn't interesting. It was there, and it worked, and that was that. But he remembered... 'We stopped using AI because they couldn't keep up with augmented humans. They were too unpredictable – no, too predictable. And that made them unreliable. Humans were always better at improvising.'

'"Were" being the key word. Who knows where your AI would have been by now?' The high marshal shrugged. 'In any case, we would rather some unreliability than lives lost, wouldn't you?'

Unreliability leading to a lost battle could mean an enemy advance, could mean besieged worlds, could mean dead civilians. Then again, if you picked as few fights as Rythe, perhaps that didn't matter. Fabien wondered when their two civilisations had diverged. Probably when Hegemony citizens started augmenting their minds and Rythians didn't.

'Sir.' The female officer again, taking quick strides towards the central viewing rail. 'Movement from the Protectorate fleet.'

The high marshal raised an eyebrow. 'They're withdrawing?'

'Not exactly.'

Waving a hand at the projection, she brought a view of the fleets back at eye level, leaving the ground view laid out below. Each ship in view was a Protectorate vessel. After their first missile strike, the void packs had closed to engage and chased the main Protectorate fleet in orbit ever since. The Hegemony fleet had done likewise, though from a greater distance, unnerved by the void packs' close-range ferocity. Where they had fought, ship splinters and broken spines littered space. Some had decayed in their orbits and burnt up in Munab's atmosphere. Others still raced through the void, death traps to any ship caught without adequate shielding.

In the midst of all that mess, it took a while for Fabien to pick it out. But then he saw it: the Protectorate fleets peeling off from combat, all burning for escape velocity bar one.

That one ship dipped its nose below the lowest plane of combat and plunged. It slipped free of the void packs, its hide shimmering with the flak of countless detonations, and dropped like a great, ponderous arrow for the planet's surface. Seeing what it was doing, the void packs abandoned their chase of the escapees and wheeled after it.

'What are they aiming for?' Fabien asked. The question came out louder than he had intended. Harsher.

The officer started to shake her head with a gesture half a shrug. She couldn't read their minds.

'Can they hit the main battle site from their position?'

She nodded.

Fabien swore. That ship was massive, a bulky monolith as long as a mountain was tall. The void packs were gnats against its sides, biting and biting but never able to pierce flesh. Something that size crashing into a planet...

He brought the *Gigamet Carvan's* prestain up as a projection from his datascreen.

'I've seen it,' the prestain said once she recovered from the surprise of the call. 'We're sending ships.'

'You won't reach it in time.' This from the high marshal, whose face bore its first traces of true concern. He leaned over the rail, staring at the swarming troops below.

Fabien curled the fingers of his left hand where they wouldn't see, clenched his fist tight. 'Can you hit it with the lance?' he asked the prestain.

'Yes,' she said, 'but the debris...'

'Unless the void packs can attach grapples and haul it out of there, we have the option of one big, steerable chunk of debris or lots of smaller bits that could land anywhere. Neither is good, but the latter is the lesser ill. Do it.'

The prestain nodded, her face pale, and disintegrated in the projection.

Fabien watched the ship falling, burning, on the main display. Its rear engines had gone, spewing smoke instead of their normal exhaust. Ice glittered amongst it and in a fanning spray to either side where they had jettisoned their fuel to avoid explosion. Then everything became polarised: ships white on one side, black on the other. A fraction of a second later, the *Carvan's* empyrric lance burst into the projection, straight into the side of the falling ship and out the other. When it vanished, Fabien blinked his eyes back into focus and saw ten void-pack ships spiralling away from the wreckage of their prey where the lance had punched through before attenuating.

With a hole bored through its side, the ship fractured under gravity's influence. First into two parts, then three, then suddenly a disintegrating jumble, its injuries piled up to the point of no return. It fell, flaming, towards the planet below.

Being bombarded by the death dive of their own ship was the last straw for the Protectorate's army on Munab. By the time the smoke cleared – as much as it could in such an atmosphere – a half of them had already surrendered. On seeing that fact, the remainder followed suit. Some, mostly amongst the Keepers, had objected and been overthrown – but keepers did number amongst the surrendered.

Fabien stepped out of the lander that had brought him to the surface, sweating beneath the transparent faceplate of his helmet. The outpost at the top of the mesa sat before him, a smoking ruin. Debris had hit the right-hand side, caving in the domed roof and taking out what remained of the turrets on that side. The air passing through his filters smelled hot, filled with the tang of smoke and metal. As he watched, Hegemony troops walked out of the other side of the complex carrying laden stretchers between them.

He walked to the edge of the mesa.

It was a bloodbath. Munab's desert had been churned and pitted and scarred, its cliffs pocked and crumbled, its people stamped out. One mech stood far in the distance, but that was all the evidence he saw of the rebels. He wondered how many were left. How many people had made their lives here only to lose them in rebellion? Was it worth it? The land before him was a sea of charred wreckage and bodies, with Rythe's swarm thick in the air, maintaining control. Their vehicles had withdrawn in the past hour. He could just make them out in the far distance, deactivated and waiting for pickup.

'Magister,' a man said behind him.

Startled, Fabien took a half step back and wheeled to face the new arrival. The adjutant officer's eyes widened, flitting between Fabien and the edge. A streak of blood smeared the side of his helmet and one shoulder, and a woman stood just behind him. Watchful eyes stared hard as steel from her scarred and pitted face. She was Protectorate, in their orange army uniform, though she had ragged white patches sewn onto each sleeve.

'Adjutant. I apologise, I was lost in thought.' Fabien glanced at the woman, making the movement obvious.

Taking his hint, the adjutant recovered, cleared his throat. 'This is Division Commander Adrati Progeura, commander of the surrendered Protectorate forces. She wishes to formally offer her surrender to you.'

'Is that true?'

Progeura inclined her head, a sharp motion, like she was trying to shake off something balanced there. 'This fight was senseless, no matter what our orders were. But I followed, and it led me to killing my own people. The broadcasts would have us believe they were traitors, but...' She shook her head – that same sharp motion, made horizontal. 'After the ship fell out the sky, when command fell to me, I knew we had to stop. And we have orders from the Reiart, now. We should have listened to those sooner.'

Fabien frowned. 'What orders came from the Reiart?'

'Rebel. They told us to rebel.'

Fabien looked away, then, up towards the sky and where the nexus should be. What was happening out there, in the rest of the galaxy? Without the nexus to relay messages, they couldn't tell, not unless Rythe sent a ship out and back, not until they nudged the nexus back into position. He wondered at the secret police Lilesh had mentioned, her implication that Ferrash was somehow involved, Ferrash's own warnings about revolution and his goal to sabotage the Prime Nexus. This was his doing, he was sure.

What else had that man planned?

CHAPTER FIFTY-FIVE

WHEN PALIA SAW THE ship, she cried. The tears stung her cheeks in the cold, but they were the most comprehensibly real sensations she had felt that day. She had to support a good portion of Ferrash's weight as he limped with his arm around her shoulders. He was flagging – she could sense it. His emotions had come untethered. They floated around the confines of his psyche like loose threads, each barbed and painful, writhing to the surface one after the other. Of all of them, the only one that didn't seem to cause him pain was the one tethered to her. Her rope, his... she couldn't tell. There was something reassuringly familiar about that ambiguity.

It was what lay beneath his emotions that concerned her: the weak ebb of his life, retreating further and further into his core.

He was dying.

<Lilesh,> she sent. <The door.>

The ramp swung open when they were ten paces from it, and Palia began hauling Ferrash up the slope the moment it touched the ground. His arm slipped from around her shoulder, but she grabbed his hand and hauled back, then the archivist appeared by his other side and took the rest of his weight.

Between them, and with Ferrash dragging his feet as best he could, they rushed him into the corridor and sat him with his back propped up in the corner. Palia took his face in her hand, tried to make eye contact, but he kept drifting in and out of focus.

She swiped at the tears on her face, sniffed, and pushed her rising panic aside.

'Can you get us out of here?' she asked Lilesh.

'I should be able to. Where—?'

'Anywhere.' They had no time for specifics.

Palia fumbled with the zip on Ferrash's coat, willing him to stay alive, willing herself to find a way to keep him so. She tugged a patchwork coat flap aside to reveal another layer, diagonally fastened. The hole in his side stood out worse here. It had been hidden amongst all the colours of the patchwork, but now it stood red against black, livid. She unzipped the second layer and peeled it aside, hoping it wouldn't take any flesh with it, then swore when she got to a layer of undershirt.

One of Ferrash's hands pawed at her wrist. She looked up to see his face tense with pain, eyes closed. He pawed again, pushed her hand closer to the wrist of his other arm, which he held up, shaking.

Confused, she rolled the sleeve back to check for injuries and saw the straps of a knife sheath wrapped around his arm. Understanding hit her. She twisted his arm and unsheathed the knife, then used it to cut the bottom half of his undershirt away from him. A dark bruise spread from the hole and across his chest. It faded just to the right of his belly button. Every time he breathed, it moved, and his pain spiked. Her hands hovered near the wound, fingers twitching. Her mind had frozen. She reached into it, trying to find some action, any action to take, but everything had fogged.

'Third...' Ferrash rasped, then screwed his face up. 'Third shelf. Top. Near... door.'

Palia nodded and dashed for the armoury, one hand on the door-frame so her momentum swung her to face the nearest shelves.

'Other side!'

Turning, she picked out the third shelf from the top. She lifted out the entire box marked 'Medical' and carried it back out, almost crashing into Lilesh in the corridor. The engine noise came into focus then, the fact that it was idling and they weren't moving at all.

Teeth gritted, Palia stepped around the archivist. 'What are you doing? We need to leave.'

Lilesh stayed behind her as she knelt, her presence tingling along her spine.

'Where is Tessa?' Lilesh asked.

'She wanted to stay behind. Her choice.'

'And Bek?'

Palia froze with the box's lid half open, seeing Bek's blood on her hands even though she had washed it off and changed her clothes. Tears prickled at her eyes again. 'I... He...' She drew a deep breath and began to rummage in the box, but she couldn't stop her hands shaking. Blood stung her mouth where she bit her lip.

'Bek's... alive,' said Ferrash.

He didn't know. He hadn't seen what she had. He hadn't had Bek's blood on his hands.

Palia found what she was looking for – a black membrane sitting folded and obvious on top of the other supplies – and started to wrap it around Ferrash's abdomen. The material clung to his skin, stuck to itself where it overlapped. When she let go, the circuitry embedded in it activated and a readout appeared on its surface. Where the wound lay underneath, the material rippled. Beneath, it should have expanded to fill the gap.

Ferrash found her hand where it still rested on his waist, placed his over it, gave it a weak squeeze. She couldn't meet his eyes. She couldn't contradict him. She couldn't—

'One you saw shot... was cloned. I killed it.'

Palia stared, her throat tight, into the space beyond the floor. Then she let her gaze drift up, over their hands, over his chest, to the blood he hadn't managed to clean from under his chin, to his eyes, bright and shining, so deep she might see clear to his centre.

'Real Bek's alive,' he said.

'And you don't wish to save him?' Lilesh asked.

'Got people... on it. Can't go back. Have to...' He cried out and rocked forwards before he could continue, crushing Palia's hand in his and clutching at his waist.

'Get us out of here, Lilesh.' Palia turned to her, pleading, wishing she had the strength and respect to make it an order. 'Please. We need to go.'

Something crashed outside the ship, loud enough for them to hear it. It might have been lightning striking the spaceport or something altogether less natural, but Lilesh heard it and made her decision. She strode to the cockpit. A moment later, the engine pitched up and they rocked off the ground.

Ferrash leaned towards the box, dipped a hand in and came up holding a clear, partitioned pouch of cartridges and a syringe unit.

'Hey. Hey.' Palia put her palm flat against the hand that held the bag, preventing him moving it any further. 'What are you doing?'

He frowned, peering out at her from under sweat-coated brows. 'Seriously?'

She looked at the bag again, saw labels for painkillers and anti-inflammatories.

'Sorry, I thought...' Confused, she drew her hand away and watched him slot a few of the cartridges into the unit before pressing it against his neck. She didn't know what she had thought. The syringe had come out, and she had assumed... something that she couldn't remember.

'So... it was you,' she asked, 'near the furnaces?'

He nodded, his head back against the wall, and let the syringe tumble out of his hand.

She let out a breath, unsure how long she had been holding it back. 'I could have killed you.'

'Wouldn't be the first time.'

Her heart skipped in her chest. 'What?'

Ferrash grunted. She thought he might have meant it as a laugh, but she couldn't be sure. ''Course you don't remember.'

Thunder rocked the ship and the floor bucked under them. Palia steadied herself with one hand and stuck the other out to stop Ferrash falling on his face, leaving the box to crash against the wall. Medical supplies spilled across the deck.

Putting aside whatever she might have forgotten, Palia said, 'Let's get you somewhere you won't roll around,' and dragged Ferrash to his feet. When he was up and she had his arm around her shoulder, she shuffled him through to the sleeping quarters and helped him onto his bunk. Every time he drew a sharp breath, she saw the pain and winced. For his sake, she hoped the painkillers kicked in soon.

She set about taking off his boots, which were dripping ice water all over the sheets. 'We'll take you to the flagship,' she said. 'They can fix you up there. You'll be fine. You'll pull through.'

'No.' She felt the pressure of his hand on her shoulder, the weight of his gaze on her back. His words came out slurred. 'Need to head... to Prime Nexus.'

'Yes, then the flagship.'

'No.'

He squeezed harder. Palia dragged the last boot over his heel and dropped it on the floor with a thud before turning to face him. He had levered himself half off the bed. It looked for all his stupor like he already wanted to get up and go, straining towards the cockpit. Palia put herself between him and the door and grabbed his shoulders to keep him on the bed.

His gaze locked onto her again. He took hold of her elbow. It sent a shiver through her, despite the heat of all the layers she hadn't had chance to remove.

'What... did you get from my mother?'

Palia drew in a deep breath. The moment Ayt had passed her information to her – in a combination of electronic data and some kind of shared understanding through the Empyrean that she didn't realise was possible – it had been like having her brain crushed by a rockslide. She had pushed the moment of contact to the back of her mind but now, with Ferrash's eyes boring into hers and the question of what it contained buzzing around her mind, she was forced to look.

It crouched in the deep parts of her mind: an aching weight of information, boulder-like, poised to roll and gain momentum. Taking the reassurance of Ferrash's grip as an anchor, she approached it, the edge of her awareness raised to press against it. It unfurled, flower-like, the many threads it contained unspooling around her to settle where they belonged. In the space of a heartbeat, she had memories that weren't hers, knowledge she had never gained, plans she had never drawn up. Her breathing hitched. They could never be the memories she wanted.

'Palia?'

She opened her eyes to see Ferrash's face drawn tight with concern. 'She gave me... understanding. But I don't know how much – I mean, it's just *there*. What was she meant to give me?'

'The... Prime Nexus. What do you understand about that?'

The plans came to her mind unbidden, but alien. They were on the tip of her tongue before she recognised they had never been hers to begin with. She hesitated, then forced herself to pick through the information slower so she could process it at the speed she spoke it. 'We need to go to the Prime Nexus because... we need to destroy the Empyrean? Ash, that's exactly what the Magister was trying to do. Why he burned Everatus Four. Is that... Is that what you've been planning all this time?' As her thoughts edged towards panic, she shook his shoulder and regretted it instantly. Ferrash sank back down into the mattress with a grimace. He waved off her apology, but she hadn't meant to hurt him.

Once he had taken a few deep breaths, he wrapped his hand around hers on his chest and looked her in the eyes. He could barely keep his open. 'I... can't. There's too much.'

Letting out a breath of her own, Palia closed her eyes. Ferrash pressed his lips to her knuckles, so soft that she only felt it as a light touch and a breath of air across the back of her hand. When she opened her eyes, their hands rested together on his shoulder. His eyes had closed. His breathing was shallow, but he was asleep. She lingered on his face, the way it looked so peaceful now he wasn't awake. Not emotionless, like in the picture Bek had given her, where he was cold and blank, but just blissful, and warm, and vulnerable.

She settled down with her back to the wall, her head against the mattress and his hand still in hers.

<Lilesh,> she sent. <How long will it take us to reach the nexus?>

<Eleven hours, twelve minutes.>

<When we get there, don't send us through. There's something we need to do first.>

CHAPTER FIFTY-SIX

IT WAS THE FIRST long, undisturbed sleep Ferrash had had in weeks. Instead of waking with a start or watching each hour slide past as his mind raced away, he drifted into awareness. His limbs felt heavy. That and the small warmth of Palia's hand held in his caught him there, wrapped in the still unfamiliar embrace of comfort. For the first time in a long while, he felt safe.

As his mind cleared, he tuned into the engine's drone. The thrusters weren't firing, so it was just background noise: a steady whir he'd miss if he hadn't been listening for it. He had missed it. He'd missed having somewhere that felt like home. He'd missed the little safety net that was the ship's slight separation from Protectorate scrutiny. He'd missed Bek. Their reunion had been too brief.

Opening his eyes, Ferrash turned his head sideways on the pillow and found Palia, leaning against the side of his bed with her arm trailing onto his chest. Pressure built in his stomach, fluttering like a second pulse and working its way up to his breast. Their roles had been reversed, once. She had been the one on the bed, her skull almost split, her hand in his as he rested on the floor beside her. The two images superimposed themselves in his mind. He had saved her. She had saved him.

Now all they had to do was save everyone else.

'Palia.' He squeezed her hand then, when she didn't move, tried to roll so he could nudge her shoulder. Pain slashed across his abdomen. He cried out and curled in on himself, crushing Palia's hand without meaning to.

Jolted awake, Palia clutched his hand tight to her breast. Her face appeared in front of him, eyes shocked wide. She reached out and touched the side of his face with her free hand. He smiled, but when her frown deepened he guessed it must have come out more a grimace than anything else.

'You're alive,' she said.

He laughed, the smile growing to tug at his cheeks. 'Looks like.'

Palia's shoulders relaxed, losing all their tense angles. Her coat was bunched up around the wrist where they held hands – she'd been too warm to sleep, but hadn't wanted to disturb him. He resisted a sudden urge to let go and run his hand along the curve of her neck.

She shook her head, eyes downcast, and breathed out a shaky breath. 'I didn't think I'd sleep. I was so scared I'd wake up and you'd be...' When she couldn't finish, she met his gaze, eyes crinkled almost in apology.

Ferrash squeezed her hand again, but when he tried to think of words, he couldn't find any. The second he ran at them, they scattered. So he closed his eyes and breathed deep, brought his thoughts back under control. Difficult – her hand still rested on his face, her thumb tracing gentle lines along the skin of his forehead. He forced himself to concentrate.

'I tried to tell you about Bek,' he said. 'I'm sorry how that played out. It all happened so fast.'

'I got your message. Bek told me I shouldn't trust any new ones, since you'd been found out... but I guess that must have been the clone trying to put me off contacting you.' Palia sighed. 'Do you think he'll be okay?'

'My mother will find him.' It made his head spin to be putting his trust in her, but he believed it. 'As to whether he'll be fine after that... Well, he's the same odds as anyone on Hesperex now.'

'I should have realised something was off.' Palia drew her hand away. 'I thought he was just mad at you, but...'

Ferrash winced at the hurt in Palia's voice and opened his eyes to see her face twisted in on itself. Her knuckles whitened at the edge of the bed.

He rolled, anticipating the pain this time so it didn't cripple him. Then he reached out, cupped her face in his hand. The touch made her stop her search for words with her lips just parted, her forehead still creased but smoothing now. He leaned across to kiss her, but before he could she rocked forwards to meet him halfway. Their lips met, scratching where the cold had chapped them, but hers were warm, and she pressed them against his like she'd been meaning to do it again every moment since Rythe. His skin felt alive where her hand lay against his chest.

He pulled back, smiling, light headed. Excitement clashed against the pain in his side until he almost felt sick with it, like his guts had all twisted after touching her.

'I hope everything turns out okay for once.' Her breath brushed against his lips as she spoke. She still smiled, but her eyes had grown sadder.

He wanted to draw in for another kiss, but stroked his thumb along her cheekbone instead. 'It will.'

Palia's forehead creased again, and her gaze drifted down as she got lost in thought.

'What is it?' he asked.

'I just...' Palia drew her hand off his chest, the fingers curled, uncertain. 'It'll sound stupid, but *this* feels like I don't deserve it. I took all your emotions from you, Ash. And you say I killed you once, too. I'm not exactly sure how that worked, but... After all that, you can still bear to look at me. Still bear to be with me. How...?' A blush crept up her face. 'I mean, I don't know if you ever said as much, or if I did, but how can you still love me? I-If you do, anyway.'

He'd never said it, but he was pretty sure he had loved her. Thinking back, Ferrash wasn't sure he'd ever stopped. Sure, he hadn't felt it right after the fact. He'd known he'd lost something and felt that loss, but embraced the emotionless state he'd spent most of his life in, pushed the matter aside, focused on more important things. But the memories hadn't been content to lie idle. They'd replayed over and over and as they did, he'd felt for them. Maybe there was no way to know if his responses to the memories were the same as they had been when they happened for real. Maybe he couldn't guarantee he'd loved her in the first place. Maybe it had only been a liking, and now he'd blown it into something bigger.

Did it matter?

Aware that Palia was still staring at him, he took hold of her hand and said, 'Feelings can come back. Memories don't.'

If anything, the words made her more miserable. Her shoulders slumped. He wanted to throw both arms around her, but moving that much might well make him pass out. All he could do was squeeze her hand and curse silently. Her memories would never come back. She'd have to live with that. He wondered how complete the destruction was, how big a hole she had, how much of their time together she remembered. But she had felt enough to recognise him on Rythe...

'Palia,' he said, 'you can see what I feel, can't you?'

She grimaced, but nodded. 'I don't mean to.'

'It's okay. I know you don't. But...' Ferrash shifted back onto the bed with a groan. Staying on his side so long had hurt, and gone too long unnoticed. He stared up at the ceiling, trying to figure out how to phrase the question that had been bothering him since... well, since before he'd lost his feelings. He'd never mentioned it then. Never had time.

Next to him, Palia shifted, impatient. He spoke his next words with care. 'Do you think, after we first met, when you realised you were empyrric... Do you think you saw what I felt first, and that affected what you felt? You saw I cared and you found yourself caring back? Do you think... the act of observing an emotion changes its path, somehow?' *Do you think we would have come together anyway, or is all this just a consequence of bouncing off each other's observations?*

In the corner of his eye, the crease in her forehead deepened. 'I... maybe. But that would have happened anyway, wouldn't it? That's how it works. You find someone and something in the way they talk or act hints they like you, and you respond to that the way you like. Maybe you both talk and act and go on not noticing forever. Seeing it in the Empyrean just makes it easier to spot and harder to second guess the truth. But I don't know if that's how it *did* work. It just... is what it is, now. And I *like* what it is.'

'So do I.' His chest tightened. Ferrash wasn't really sure what answer he'd wanted, but Palia was right. It was what it was. He took a deep breath. 'How close are we to the nexus?'

Palia glanced towards the cockpit, head inclined. The ship's systems registered transmissions between her implants and another's. He hadn't been paying much attention when she'd brought him on board. He didn't know who else was tagging along for the ride.

'Lilesh says three hours, near enough,' Palia said.

That didn't leave long. Ferrash massaged his temples, trying as best he could to rub clarity back into his mind. His thoughts were all scattered, in part by the pain, in part by whatever drugs remained in his system and in part by the rush of endorphins Palia had brought to him.

'I need to send a message to the Magister,' he said.

'Fabien?'

'Well the other one's dead, so I don't know who else I'd be talking about. Yeah, I need to talk to Fabien. Help me up?'

Palia stood, after some hesitation, and held her hands out for him to grab onto. He took hold with one hand and shuffled so his legs hung over the edge, then tried to haul upright with as little movement from his torso as possible. Even so, weak legs sent him staggering sideways. Palia caught him, but the flash of pain in his side was so intense that it felt like everything from his ribs down on the left-hand side had been clamped in a vice. Static fuzzed his mind. When it cleared a moment later, his forehead was pressed against Palia's shoulder and she was struggling to keep him upright.

'I'm okay.' He swayed, clutched at her other arm with his free hand to steady himself. 'I'm okay.'

Palia twisted around him so she had an arm around his waist and had hold of his hand over her shoulder. He leaned into the comfort of the embrace. A part of him insisted it was just for stability, but he knew the truth. Denial wasn't a good look. He'd needed this.

Palia propped him up all the way to the lounge. When he raised the hover table, she suggested raising one of the chairs with it, but he shook his head. If he sat down now, he might never get up again. Instead, he leaned on the table, then rested a hand on the surface to interface. It pushed against his mind like an old friend welcoming him home.

'It didn't surprise me when I didn't have permission to retrieve data from the table,' said Palia, standing at the edge of the display table with her arms folded across her chest, 'but I was surprised even Bek couldn't get into it.'

Grimacing, he pulled up a system map on one half of the table and found Fabien's contact details. 'Bek should've had access to most of it, just not my activity with the Reiart.'

'Considering how much he couldn't get to, sounds like that was most of it.'

He sighed, supporting his weight through his hands. 'I'm sorry. I didn't want you following me at first. Either of you.'

'Why?'

'Didn't think Bek would understand. Didn't want to get either of you in trouble if it all split up. Didn't know how I'd act if you came into the picture.'

'We would have helped.'

'Yeah.' He laughed, and his lip curled. 'Probably would've meant fewer people dying in the process if I'd taken help from the start.'

He hadn't seen her move, but her hand closed over his on the table and he turned to face her as she put the other on his hip, just below the wound.

'You've got help now,' she said.

Only if she agreed to the next step. Only if she helped him wipe out all traces of the Empyrean. They hadn't had that discussion before he'd slept, or on Rythe. His flesh burned under her touch, hand and hip, and he felt himself leaning just to get closer to her.

They'd need to talk about it, and soon, but first they had to get all of the Hegemony behind them.

He called the magister's ID and watched the projection unit for a response. To the side, the image of their ship blinked ever closer to the Prime Nexus, and perhaps the end of it all.

CHAPTER FIFTY-SEVEN

WHY DID HOLDING HER hand over Ferrash's feel so utterly alien and yet so inarguably right? Palia's whole hand tingled, like she held it near static electricity. When the particles of the projection unit jumped to life, Ferrash's knuckles twitched under her palm.

Palia straightened. Ferrash couldn't do as much. He leaned over the table, his hair dangling, lank, over the other side of his scalp. The light of the projection unit made shadows of his scars.

'Palia?' Fabien said. His projection stood on the table, two feet tall, his hands clasped behind his back. His gaze shifted to Ferrash. 'Progmannae? It's good to see you both safe.'

Palia spoke without answering. 'There's a problem on Hesperex. There—'

'I know. Archivist Lilesh sent me her report on the rebellion ten hours ago, I'm guessing before you were back on board. Provided your plan works, we have ships ready to send through with aid and' – he grimaced and flashed a glance to Ferrash – 'whatever enforcement may be required. Are you still planning to sabotage the Prime Nexus?'

'We are,' said Ferrash.

'How close are you?'

'About three hours.'

Fabien nodded. 'We've had some of the fleet on standby waiting, so we can get to you in an hour. We might need that long to break through the defences. What are we dealing with?'

Ferrash slid around the edge of the table, leaving Palia's hand behind, and selected the system projection. The scale shifted, bringing

Hesperex and the Prime Nexus up together so they were identical in size. She tried to remember how big they really were in comparison to each other. The Prime Nexus was big enough to have its own gravity, so maybe they weren't too far off. The flagship was smaller, but still moon-sized.

'You've got two groups you need to worry about,' Ferrash said, then pointed to Hesperex. 'The Hesperex fleet is four-hundred and three ships strong at the moment. Range of sizes, most middling. Weapons fire indicates they're not seeing eye to eye, but fighting's sporadic. Some ships might be in the middle of mutinies. Volatile situation, no telling how it'll turn out. My worry is that Hege showing up in-system will give them a common enemy to fight against.'

'Do you have any influence over the fleet?' Fabien asked.

Ferrash shook his head. Anxiety thrummed through him. 'I played all my cards starting this. I've got nothing left.'

'So we should plan for all of them. What about the other group?'

Ferrash tilted his head to one side. 'Not as bad. Prime Nexus has a ninety-ship escort. Usually more, but they got spooked a while back by some ships passing through. Void packs. Should have been on their way to Munab. Did you see them there?'

On the projection, Fabien raised an eyebrow. 'That was your doing?'

When Ferrash nodded without elaborating, Palia asked, 'What happened? Is Munab okay?'

Fabien nodded his chin, once. 'Those ships... void packs. When they shot out of the nexus we thought we'd have to bring in reinforcements or risk losing the system. But they flew straight by us and hit their own fleets instead. There isn't a single Protectorate ship in the sky anymore, not unless it belongs to them or chose to switch sides. Thanks to that and Rythe's help on the ground, the war's almost done.'

A smile flickered across Ferrash's face. 'Glad to hear it.'

'The void packs left the system not long ago, shortly after we moved the Munabi nexus back into position. They didn't tell us where to, or announce they were leaving, for that matter. Is that your doing as well?'

'I called them back. Part of the bulk orders I sent out. If they're on their way, that's good. Means you'll have backup. Means the Hesperex ships won't know which side to be on. Any confusion might be the window we need.'

Fabien turned on the spot and gesticulated at someone behind him, on mute so all she could see were the gestures and his lips moving. He nodded, then turned back.

'I'm on my way to you now with the Hegemony fleet. Rythe is staying with Munab. With any luck, we'll arrive after your void packs and be able to join the fight from there. How long will this sabotage of yours take?'

Palia felt Ferrash's eyes on her. That information was in the memories his mother had given her, and she hadn't had chance to go through them yet. She dangled the question in front of her mind in case the answer was just sat there waiting, but got nothing other than a vague sense of uncertainty. Maybe even Ayt hadn't known.

Sabotage. Did Fabien know the full extent of what Ferrash had planned? She wondered if he would approve. In a straight battle between the Keepers and any Hegemony empyrrics, the Keepers would win outright. There were thousands of them and only a handful in the Hegemony. Reducing all of them to the same footing as anyone else by destroying the Empyrean would place superiority firmly back in the Hegemony's grasp. Fabien couldn't complain at that. Palia guessed she couldn't, either. Not just from that perspective, but from all she felt for the Empyrean, all it had done to her, all she had done with it. There was no room for something like that in existence. And yet... She thought of Derren, thought of Austela, thought of all the dead and their ancestors sitting in the empyrric haze of Varna. If it existed, which she had never made up her mind on, and if it worked the way they said – the place from which all life came and all life returned – what would wiping it out do? What would it do to life?

'We're not exactly sure,' Ferrash said.

Palia jumped at the sound of his voice. Her thoughts had run rampant and she had drifted out of the conversation. Back in reality, the scientific part of her brain stepped in and mentioned that the only species ever found to need the Empyrean to live was the kariassid. And they were extinct now, anyway. It would be fine. Of course it would.

Fabien had leaned in closer, eyes narrowed as he flicked his gaze between the two of them. He chewed at his lower lip, then said, 'Then I should let you know to expect movement as soon as you're attached to the nexus, assuming you will be attached. We have plans in place to transport the nexus from Hesperex to Origin. We'll finally have it back where it belongs.'

Beside her, Ferrash straightened. 'Moving it won't matter once we're done with it. Can't you wait to steal the Prime Nexus until you have control of the system? You'd be moving your fleet's only escape route.'

'Rythe can send help if we need them to, trust me. In any case, you can't guarantee how long it takes and I can't rely on you getting the job done in time. I'm sorry. But look at it from this angle: if your sabotage takes a lot longer than expected, moving you away faster than the Protectorate ships can follow keeps you safe until you can get it done. And if you reach us first, well, you won't even need to see it through. We can undo whatever you've already done and get you out of there.'

Through Fabien's speech, Ferrash had grown more and more stiff, his psyche underpinned by something halfway between anger and caution.

'You move the nexus,' he said, 'and you'll be leaving everyone on Hesperex stranded. You promised you'd help them. This isn't it.'

'We'll move one of our own into place when the Prime Nexus is clear.'

'And how long'll that take?'

'Our technicians give a conservative estimate of a month, but they really have no idea. The theory is that the nexus will keep accelerating as it gets closer to ours, but the rate of that acceleration will decide when it arrives. Deceleration should be a fraction faster.'

'Better hope it is. Overshoot and you'll swing it into a planet.'

Palia was speaking before she even realised it. 'If it takes us longer than a day to do this, we're doing it wrong. Move the nexus if you like. We'll either get it done or we won't, and either way it doesn't matter where we end up.' The fact had come to her mind unbidden, or been sat there all along. One of Ferrash's mother's gifts.

Fabien caught her gaze, nodded. She didn't want to squint at the projection, but she was fairly sure she would make out bags under his eyes if she did. Tiredness barely showed on his face, but she knew him well enough to see past any façade he could throw up.

'Is there anything else I can do to help?' he asked.

She shook her head. 'There are still a few things we need to talk through on our end. We'll let you know if we need anything. Unless there's anything else, Ash?'

'Apart from that I'd appreciate a hospital visit after this' – Ferrash raised an eyebrow – 'no, I'm good.'

'Okay,' said Fabien. 'I'll start coordinating the attack. You two make sure you stay clear of the fighting before *and* after we arrive, is that clear?'

When they both said it was, Fabien's projection spiralled back into its constituent particles and the surface of the table. Ferrash sagged lower, no longer trying to keep up any appearance of good health, though she was sure the ruse would have been obvious enough to Fabien.

Palia turned to him, resisting the urge to fold her arms across her chest. 'You haven't told him the full plan, have you?'

'No.' Manoeuvring himself around the edge of the table with both hands, Ferrash broke free at the edge and staggered to the lounge set. Palia followed, wincing as he collapsed into one of the seats.

'So you went all the way to Rythe to lie to him.'

'Needed help.'

'People are inclined to help more if you're honest. We should tell him. You should, I should. One of us, at least.'

Ferrash closed his eyes, rested his head on the back of the seat and pinched the bridge of his nose. A spasm passed through the skin beneath his implants. 'No point telling him if we're not doing it. And I can't do it without you.' He opened one eye. 'I've hidden things from you, but I haven't lied to you. Will you help?'

Palia traced the hard lines of his face, the weeks' growth of hair on his jaw, the bags around his eyes. That one open eye remained fixed on her – golden, earnest. She imagined she saw the white shock of her hair reflected back at her in his pupil.

She sat down.

'Ash, I can't remember our time together but I remember enough times when I've wished I'd never touched the Empyrean. If it didn't exist, I wouldn't have lost Derren and I wouldn't have killed all the people I did. The Protectorate wouldn't be what it is today. You wouldn't be who you are. But' – and this was the scientific part of her brain talking, the part that had never really turned away from rigour and research – 'you don't know what pulling the plug on it will do. You've done this all at the last possible moment with hardly any time to prepare. If your mother had known all the consequences, she would have passed that knowledge on to me and I wouldn't be raising this point. But I am.'

'What's the worst that can happen?' Ferrash turned to stare at the viewscreen and she realised it had overlaid a forwards view: the Prime Nexus sprawled in the dark of the void. 'You lose your afterlife? Varna? Even if it's more than a myth, is keeping it worth the cost?'

Palia didn't answer. Stars hung steady in their places, unmarred by atmosphere, shining their existence through the black. The Empyrean underpinned so much in the galaxy, yet they knew so little about it. Had they known more, once, before the records ended? Would they have been able to say yes or no to the question of whether it should be destroyed?

'What about the Kept?' she asked. 'Their plan would work, in the long term. With outside help—'

'How many would die before they succeeded? Even without rebellion across the Protectorate?'

Too many. If all destroying the Empyrean did was take out an afterlife no one was sure of, at least she could be satisfied that they would never know the consequences. As afterlifes went, it wasn't even a knowing one. You didn't go somewhere to live again. You just got reused. So if they went ahead with this, either it never existed and no one would know the difference, or it had existed all along and they still wouldn't. Until all the energy got used up, perhaps, and then what would happen?

'Energy can't be created or destroyed,' she said, more to herself than anyone.

Ferrash answered anyway. 'The Empyrean isn't energy. It's just how it travels. A transportation system.'

'And that's exactly why we can do this.' Standing up, she held her hand out to Ferrash. 'We're not killing anything, we're just making it inert. Come on. I'll help, but we'll need Lilesh for this.'

CHAPTER FIFTY-EIGHT

No one could fail to notice the void packs arrive in-system. The first Ferrash knew of it was when they sent a message to warn him of their arrival. Before he could say anything to the others, the nexus began to glow with incoming transport. He snapped his head to the cockpit canopy, where the Prime Nexus occupied half the view, and watched his unruly allies arrive.

They streamed out of one of the tubes, visible only by their sheer number and density as a silver thread against the void. At first, that was all they were. They threaded themselves through the eye of the nexus and out, past the docked patrol ships and nexus defences. Ferrash caught their chatter through his implants, a back-and-forth between them, the patrols and the fleets around Hesperex. The exchanges were too rapid for him to keep up with, let alone anyone else. It seemed like every ship in the pack was sending its own messages. Void pack ships were their own leaders, united under a theoretical banner, but this? This wasn't them jostling for position. This was intentional.

White flashed in his peripheral and Palia joined him beneath the canopy. Archivist Lilesh sat in the pilot's seat, her shoulder resting not far from where he gripped the seat for support. Ferrash hadn't spoken to her much, and they'd both stayed clear of the topic that they'd been enemies until not so long ago. So had Palia, in theory, but Lilesh played the game. Had done for a long while. He didn't like that she'd known him already.

'Those are the void packs?' Palia asked.

'Yeah,' he said.

'What makes you think they'll help us?'

The void packs hadn't captured and released him that long ago, though it sure felt like longer. Ferrash remembered the anger he'd seen on their faces when they thought he was one of *them*, and Captain Progvarrias' need to follow Ida's last orders. To avenge his comrades lost to the collision at Corumma.

'They're pissed,' was his answer.

As his words died away, an explosion bloomed by the lengthening thread. All at once, the void packs split off in every direction, disintegrating into a swarm of angry insects. They hazed against the Prime Nexus' superstructure. More explosions followed, a rough sphere of fire marking the boundary between their flak and the defence systems' missiles. Ferrash leaned forwards, breath caught in his throat. Stripped of sound, it was just a light show. Distant. Non-lethal. Like watching a clip of fireworks with the sound turned off.

The archivist half-turned her head to address him. 'Progmannae, you have contact with these ships, yes?'

'Can have.'

'Will they follow your orders?'

'To some extent.'

The lines of her jaw hardened. 'Will they follow them to the extent that they refrain from firing at both us and any of our fleet travelling through the nexus?'

'Should do.'

She grunted. 'Hardly the confirmation I was hoping for, but it will do. Where do you need me to fly us for this sabotage of yours?'

Ferrash glanced to Palia, then nudged her when she wouldn't draw her eyes from the view ahead. She jumped a little, startled, then chewed at her lower lip.

After a moment, Palia said, 'Anywhere deep inside the nexus should do.'

Lilesh raised an eyebrow. 'Deep inside? You can't get inside a nexus. If you go inside, you travel through it. That is the only option the systems provide. There are no maintenance shafts or access tubes – the nexuses maintain themselves. How do you propose getting into the centre of this one in particular?'

From where Ferrash stood, the Prime Nexus' tube openings just made its surface seem faintly porous, like an undulating, misshapen piece of pumice viewed from a distance too faint to resolve most of the openings. Hundreds of openings. Thousands, maybe. Very few of those saw active use.

He scratched at the coarse hair on his chin. 'Don't think all the tubes work. If we fly into one of those, we could work our way further in without issue.'

'Do you have idea any which tubes those might be, or do you plan to fly blindly at each one until we find one without a pull?'

Not quite prepared to admit that was better than anything he'd thought up yet, Ferrash drew in a breath, then took in Palia and the archivist with a glance. 'What do you two feel when you travel through a nexus? Anything?'

Palia shook her head, but Lilesh nodded. 'The effect is subtle, but there is... a warping of the usual fabric. I find it more noticeable on larger ships when there are more people to contribute to the picture, so it doesn't surprise me that you haven't chanced across it, Pestor. It was many years before I did. And I believe this is the only ship you have travelled through a nexus on, since your awareness came to you. We won't count the flagship's arrival in Hesperex under the old Magister, given you were somewhat preoccupied at the time.'

Ferrash tapped his little finger against the back of the chair as he waited for her to finish. When she did, he asked, 'That mean you can tell which tubes are trying to pull us before we're too far in?'

Lilesh inclined her head. 'Not much sooner than the additional acceleration would tell you, but I can try that, for want of a better plan.'

A chain of explosions ripped across the face of the nexus, one after the other. Turrets getting hit, he hoped, and not the nexus' structure. Then again, the Prime Nexus had been around for at least twenty-four thousand years, give or take, and at some point the Protectorate had stolen it halfway across this part of the galaxy. Must have been a fight for it then, and it was still sitting here in one piece. Nexite was brittle, but the Prime Nexus was coated in stronger stuff. Couldn't scratch it. Couldn't manufacture it, either.

Palia cleared her throat. He could read the tension in her shoulders, the way she drew herself a little away from Lilesh before she spoke. A knot of nerves tightened in his chest. If Lilesh didn't like the plan, she could put a stop to it as soon as thinking.

'When we get deep enough,' said Palia, 'which should be about a thousand kilometres, we should clamp to the side of the tube, or whatever space we end up in. Hopefully no one follows us, because we all need to do the next bit.'

'Are we leaving the ship?' Lilesh asked.

'No.' Her shoulders rose. Fell. 'Ferrash and I will use the same method we used to kill the Magister. Or what Bek told me we used, anyway – I can't remember it well. If Fabien didn't fill you in on that, it's a feedback loop. The point is to... *heighten* emotions through experiencing them. There's probably a better way of explaining that, but' – she shrugged – 'it just matters that it works.'

'And what do you intend to do with that energy? Compared to the energy travelling through the nexus hourly, it's nothing. You won't make a dent.'

'That's where you come in.'

As intrigued as he was by this new part of the plan, Ferrash's head was starting to blur, and it felt like his left hip had been clamped in a vice. He pushed away from the pilot's seat, passed behind Palia with an encouragement to keep talking, and staggered into the navigator's seat. A groan slipped out between his teeth and Palia hesitated, but he motioned for her to continue.

'The idea is, I direct that energy to you and you feed it into the nexus. Amplify it if you can, but keep it going. Once energy levels pass a certain threshold, you should see a response from the nexus. The

Keepers apparently tested its limits once. When they threw enough empyrric energy into its structure, the nexus returned it to sender.'

Those must be memories gleaned from his mother. Palia hadn't known this. She'd known some of it, before, when she'd taken a prototype of the Magister's weapon and used Ferrash as a power source to test its effects, but she'd forgotten that.

Lilesh pressed her lips into a thin line. 'You want me to invite the nexus to annihilate us as a threat?'

'No, because it won't be able to. When it strikes, you need to send its energy back at it, and keep doing that for as long as it takes. You should start to notice blank spots appearing in its output. Keep going even then, no matter what happens. You'll know when it's done. We both will.'

'Pestor, that is far easier said than done. How much energy can the Prime Nexus output compared to the two of us?'

'The Keepers didn't record that, or they lost the records.'

'My estimation is that it will be significantly greater. A small beam, even with great energy, can be diverted a small amount to avoid a target, but a complete reversal would take an impossible effort.'

'You don't need to reverse it. We'll be in the middle of the nexus. You just have to make sure it goes into the side of a tube, somewhere, and doesn't hit us.'

'Fine.' Lilesh huffed and narrowed her eyes at the canopy, where the fluctuating glare of battle was beginning to resolve into individual ships and missiles. Ten minutes away, Ferrash guessed. 'And what does this achieve? Is the goal simply to do enough damage to make the nexus inoperable?'

'No, the nexus shouldn't be affected. The goal is...' He felt the hesitation in Palia's voice more than saw it, the slight tremor as she gathered strength for the admission. 'The blank spots eventually increase in frequency and become all of the output of the target. When that happens, the target is no longer empyrric. That's what happens on a person, anyway. On the Prime Nexus, as the hub of all empyrric activity in the galaxy, maybe the universe... well, the theory is that we'll exhaust all of the Empyrean, or all the Prime Nexus can get hold of, and it'll be gone. Permanently.'

Neither of them moved when Palia finished talking. Nor did Lilesh. Her eyes reflected blankly from the surface of the canopy. On the nexus, two tube openings glowed, ready to spit out arriving ships. The entrances stood just to one edge of the expanding battle, though a line of defence turrets were ablaze nearby, neatly taken out in a strafing run from the void packs.

Ferrash's muscles tensed. His skin pulled taut, tugging at his injury, sending pain spiking through his side. He tried to spin it into adrenaline, but all that did was make his head spin. Lilesh's eyes flicked to watch him in the reflection. He hated that. Being seen. *Agree, damn you*. With Lilesh's help and a little time, he'd never have to worry about being seen again.

Eventually, Lilesh's voice came again, too loud after so long a silence. 'The Magister has agreed to this?'

As the answer was his fault, Ferrash cleared his throat and said, 'He agreed to sabotage. Doesn't know the details.'

'Tell him. Now.'

Suspecting the answer, Ferrash queried Fabien's details in his implants. 'Can't. He's in transit.'

'Then the moment his ship is contactable, you tell him. I am happy to follow your plan until we are in position within the nexus, but I refuse to participate in such abject destruction unless the Magister makes it an order. If it were my judgement call, I...'

The archivist blinked, her face awash with surprise. It was the first expression he'd seen her wear that wasn't haughty arrogance. Her brows creased.

Ferrash leaned forwards to rest one arm against the dashboard, making it look casual as he faced her. With his other hand, he brushed against one of the control screens and handed control of their flight path to his implants. Better safe than sorry. He could override her input if needed. Just had to hope she didn't take too much offence if she found out.

When she still hadn't spoken a second later, Ferrash waved a hand. 'Hard concept, huh. What's your gut say?'

The glare she shot him could have cut glass. 'My gut is hardly the appropriate mechanism by which to make a decision that affects the continuing fate of the peoples of this universe.'

'You think it'll affect them that much? Tell me, if the Empyrean disappeared right now, who'd notice? All the empyrrics, sure, but who else? Would they miss anything?'

'Unlikely in the Hegemony. Likely with your people.'

'And my people would be safer for it. So would yours. No Keepers is good for everyone. So's no empyrrics. There's no harm in helping us.' In fact, if she didn't, there'd be a whole load of people on Hesperex doomed to die, and a whole load of people further afield when the Keepers worked their way through them.

As he waited for her answer, a proximity alert popped up in his implants, and one of the consoles lit up red. He spun back round to face the canopy with Palia leaning over his shoulder.

Adrenaline spiked into his heart through the pain. A cluster of lights tracked across the canopy. Behind them, he made out the outlines of ships, and behind them were yet more lights. He flicked at a panel, made the image zoom in. Hard to tell which ships were which, given all Protectorate ships followed much the same pattern. Cubes were cubes, or cubish, no matter how many of them you stuck together. But the group at the rear were definitely in pursuit. The group in front shot down approaching missiles where they could, but they were fighting a losing game. One ship took a direct hit to its engines and went dead, knocked off course by the explosion so its neighbours had to steer away from it.

And behind even those, by the glowing nexus tubes, a fleet of daggers shot out into the dark. The Hegemony had arrived.

CHAPTER FIFTY-NINE

'PRIORITY CALL FROM ARCHIVIST Lilesh,' the communications officer said.

Fabien wheeled from his pacing to face the officer, then craned to examine the projection of the sky ahead. Coloured light faded to pitch void and the scattered bursts of ongoing combat. His shoulders tensed. Whatever situation they had flown into, they needed to get on top of it, and get on top if it now. So many ships travelling through the nexus lanes in such a short space of time had slowed their approach. The pilots hadn't even considered it could happen. The Prime Nexus was massive. Everyone assumed it could handle whatever came at it. Apparently not.

But Archivist Lilesh's news could be important. Perhaps they were in trouble.

He gritted his teeth and turned back to the communications officer. 'Project her on the secondary display. Consul Esselia, you have command.'

Fabien walked the five metres to the secondary display unit at the back of the command section. By the time he got there, it had manifested an image of Archivist Lilesh, Ferrash Progmannae and Palia, though Palia's distance from focus rendered her features indistinct. Fabien took up position beside a balding engineer, who caught his expression and trailed his datascreens along to the far end of the unit. Fabien could have taken the call in private, but he didn't see the need here – he didn't like being seen to hold secrets.

'It's good to see you all well,' he said. 'Report, Archivist.'

Lilesh turned her head a fraction towards the others, then back. The grim set of her lips tied a knot in his gut. *Please don't be bad news. Please let this just be your resting disapproving face.* He risked a glance back over his shoulder as the deck rocked beneath his feet. Esselia stood with her back to him, her hands clasped behind her. Harsh lights painted the faces of everyone around the main display unit.

'I have been made aware,' said Lilesh, 'that Progmannae did not furnish you with the full details of his plan before securing your involvement.'

Fabien nodded. 'I saw no need to press for details. Our existing plans had us defending the Prime Nexus during removal anyway. A little extra sabotage is good insurance, and on the chance Progmannae had been reporting back to the Protectorate for whatever reason, the opportunity to make our presence seem their idea was too good to miss. No offence, Progmannae. I had hoped you had good intentions, but it pays to be cautious. The Magister taught me as much.'

Ferrash inclined his head, but the movement was stiff. Fabien narrowed his eyes. The projection made it hard to tell with any certainty, but this man looked a world different to the one he had met on Rythe. It wasn't just that his disguise had gone and his implants were visible again – he looked to have aged years since their last meeting. His face was gaunt, and heavy bags lay under his eyes. He tilted to one side, off balance, and Palia's eyes darting to check on him was the only movement he could pick out in her face.

'Perhaps you should be more concerned, Magister,' Lilesh said.

'Why?' That couldn't bode well. Hackles rising, Fabien resisted the urge to check around him for anyone listening in. The audio streamed straight to his implants. No one else could hear their side of the conversation, unless they chose to lip read.

'Progmannae, tell him.'

Ferrash cleared his throat, then spoke in a voice almost as worn out as his appearance. 'The sabotage leans a little towards the... *permanent* side of things.'

'...Destructively permanent?'

'Nexus'll still be there afterwards, don't worry about that. Empyrean won't, though.'

'You...' The words hadn't even processed. Fabien stood there, a response stalling on his tongue, trying to force it to sink in. '*What?*'

'Well, think about it. It fixes everything. No Keepers, no real opposition for you, no more empyrrics losing control and disintegrating everything around them, no more Magisters bleeding planets dry for fuel. Not that *you'd* do that, of course, but you get the picture.'

'Isn't that precisely what the former Magister was trying to achieve on Hesperex? We've had teams of engineers working on the flagship. The whole ship would have acted like a focus similar to the Munabi prototype. Are you telling me you've asked my help in finishing what he started?'

Palia stepped forwards between the others, her face resolving more clearly now. Fabien drew in a sharp breath. While she looked nowhere near as bad as Ferrash, she was still haggard.

'Fabien,' she said, 'we don't have time for this. The Magister's methods may have been questionable, but they were reasoned. He didn't know Derren and I were on Everatus Four when he destroyed it. All he wanted to kill were the kariassid, to make sure the Empyrean couldn't come back once he'd cast it down. I don't know if I could have had a whole planet on my conscience, empty or no, but I don't think many would have complained at his results, do you? We don't even need the flagship for this. Not if we use the Prime Nexus. I'm just asking your permission. Let us do this.' She locked eyes with him across the projection. 'Nothing like anything I have seen this past year should ever have to happen again. Let us make that certain. Please.'

With a sigh, Fabien rubbed his knuckles across his forehead. This was... he couldn't think of a good term for it. Unprecedented. Galaxy-breaking. In his short reign as magister, he had already brought his people to war. Now he could see his future, and all of theirs, resting on the pivot point of history. It could go either way. He could be the Magister who righted the balance of things, or he could be the

Magister who set it all crumbling. Whatever choice he made now would decide that, he was sure.

And yet, they had a point. The Empyrean was and always had been a weapon. It always would be. It had no place in the galaxy beyond it.

He swiped at the display. A projection of the landscape outside showed itself in miniature. Their ships had speared straight into the heart of an ongoing battle, though it looked as though most of those ships were fleeing for Hesperex. The source of the call was just passing his position high above, heading for one of the tubes.

'Fabien,' said Palia, 'we need an answer. We'll have to cut off comms in a second or someone could follow us in here and hit while we're occupied.'

Squeezing his eyes tight, Fabien asked, 'How long until you get to where you need to be?'

A pause, then Ferrash answered, 'Depends how winding the route is. Half an hour minimum, if we don't mind scraping the sides on tight turns, maybe two hours max.'

Fabien paused for several heartbeats, weighing the threat of unknown consequences, then said, 'Okay. You have my permission to go ahead. Will you still be able to receive messages?'

'Yes, but don't send any our way. They could give away our position.'

He nodded and took a moment to take in all three faces before him, lingering on Palia's a moment longer than the rest. 'I won't. But I have to run this by my engineers in case there's something you haven't thought of. If anything important comes out of that, I'm sending it to you. We'll worry about anyone trying to find you if it comes to that.'

'Thank you.'

'Don't thank me. Just get this right. It's... I trust that this is a good thing you're trying to do, and for all our sakes, I wish you the best of luck with it.'

Palia opened her mouth to reply, but the projection fell back into the table before any sound made it through. That left Fabien staring into empty space, the sounds of the command room muted in his ears. That moment of separation was short-lived. The engineer had returned to stand uncomfortably close to his shoulder. Fabien turned, one eyebrow raised, but the man remained firmly within his personal space.

Then he said, 'Magister, don't be takin' this the wrong way, but... are ye friends *zashen* mad?'

Chills crawled over Palia's skin as the shadow of the tube opening fell upon them. The cockpit was still lit up from the overheads and the control panels, but the nexus' presence weighed over it all, bearing down on them though it must have been a kilometre away. Hard to tell in space, with no good references to compare against and no atmospheric haze to get a guess at distance.

They had permission. The second Fabien had given it, her nerves had started dancing all through her. It earned her a hard look from Lilesh, but Lilesh would have to put up with seeing a lot more of her emotions over the next few hours if all this went to plan. Ferrash refused to let Lilesh fly them in until she pointed out he could barely sit straight, let alone fly straight. After that, Palia led him through to the lounge and sat across from him, holding his hands in hers under the mirror surface of the blank viewscreen.

She stared at his hands, watching his thumbs trace along the sides of hers, barely feeling the touch but feeling it all too well at the same time. Chewing at her lower lip, she looked up to meet his eyes. The gaze she found was intense, and a little forlorn.

'Do you have any questions?' she asked.

The corner of his lips twitched up a fraction. 'Don't know what to ask.'

'Ash, we...' She sighed. All of this rested on them. Maybe she should have asked Lilesh to take on this part on her own and Palia could take the job of focusing their energy, but she knew she couldn't hope to control it as well as Lilesh could. That ouroboros Lilesh could bring into being would have been useful. Whether she could have kept it going long enough and strong enough to get the job done, Palia didn't know, but she didn't know if she and Ferrash could do it either.

It felt reasonable to doubt another person. Painful to doubt herself. To doubt what she felt.

Ferrash shifted in his seat and clasped her hands between his. She could read the concern beneath his furrowed brows and see it in his psyche, frayed from the end of the rope that connected the two of them.

At last, in a quiet voice, she said, 'I wish I remembered.'

'When all this is over, you and me can sit down and talk it through. I can fill in the gaps for you.'

Palia shook her head. 'That would be nice, but it's not the same. I wish I remembered what I... *thought* and *felt*. I mean, I can't remember anything from our fight with the Magister, other than a few big-picture snatches, and I'm about to do the same thing all over again, just bigger and more important. And I don't remember how I did it last time. You can't tell me that. You can't tell me what the Empyrean looked like just before the end. You can't tell me what I did wrong, when I started digging too deep and messed everything up. I don't want to mess up again, Ash. I feel like I only just found you.'

She had closed her eyes as she spoke, so the touch of his hand on the side of her face made her start. She opened them again to find the image of his face blurred.

'If you lose your memories and knock me back to a clean slate again' – Ferrash grinned – 'I promise I'll stick around this time. Long as we're both still around afterwards, it doesn't matter how we got there. We can pick up the pieces. And if it works, there'll never have to be a third time.'

Palia smiled, leaned into his hand and let her gaze drift to the viewscreen. All she saw was their own reflections, painted in the glass. Faint signs of movement rushed along in the depths behind it, but it was so dark that she couldn't make anything out. This was what a nexus looked like from the inside, when it wasn't transporting. Dark, inhospitable, uninviting. Much like the spaces between souls when you stared into the landscape of the Empyrean. With a pang of sadness, she realised she would miss that a little – those stars of souls, blazing for her eyes alone.

Lifting Ferrash's hand from her face, she stood and touched his shoulder. 'Get some rest while you can. I'm going to go over some last details with Lilesh.'

CHAPTER SIXTY

GET SOME REST. THAT had to be a joke. Even if he hadn't been in pain, Ferrash didn't think he'd be able to relax. He couldn't take his mind off the camera feeds he'd seen before leaving Hesperex – the munitions factory exploding, scattering debris across adjacent streets. It had flattened ESF headquarters. A great burning crater lay where the factory had been, slicing through the upper levels. He'd put his better judgement aside to try watching those feeds again, but their entry into one of the Prime Nexus's dormant tubes had screwed communications. Easy to get a signal lost. He wondered if the Magister would be able to reach them, even if he wanted to.

He picked at the edge of the membrane wrapped around his abdomen. It burned inside the wound, hard and blunt, like there was a hot metal bearing pressed up against it. Chances were he was still dying, just slower than before. Might be missing some organs without realising it. He didn't want to stare long enough to check. He couldn't have painkillers, or he'd be too zoned out to be useful to Palia and their plan would flop before it could even start.

So he sat, eyes screwed tight shut, trying to stop the contents of his stomach jumping up his throat.

'Ash.'

When he opened his eyes, something had changed. Darker, maybe. He squinted until he realised the ship had entered the first stages of its night cycle. Then he followed Palia's hand from his shoulder to her face.

'Are we there?' he asked.

422

'Near enough. Lilesh is flying us into the next junction between tubes. We'll set down there.'

Ferrash nodded. A normal nexus would only have one junction where the tubes met, and with each tube active, you'd be gone long before you could see it. The Prime Nexus had more tubes and junctions than you could count. 'Has anyone followed us?'

She shrugged. 'The nexite's getting in the way of scans. If anyone else followed, we won't be able to tell until they're almost on us.'

'Great.' He grunted and levered himself upright, wincing as his side ground against the membrane.

Palia blinked and shot to her feet, ready to catch him if he fell. She held her hands out in front of her and stepped between him and the door. 'You don't need to get up, Ash. We can do our part from in here. Lilesh can do hers from the cockpit. I, uh...' Her face flushed. 'We might be glad of the privacy.'

He raised an eyebrow, but remained standing. Seeing her this flustered had him grinning so wide his cheeks ached. 'There a part of the plan you've been holding back on? Can't think we'll be getting up to anything the archivist would object to seeing.'

'No, I... We're not...' Palia put her hands on her hips and stared down at the floor for a few seconds before continuing. When she looked up, it was with a grimace plastered across her face. 'What did we do last time?'

Ferrash attempted to turn his laugh into a cough. Probably failed. 'You pretty much had me in a death grip at first, though that's more because you'd just knocked me out of the way of something. I don't remember it too clear. Magister had just... tried something on me. Everything felt kind of out-of-body, then when it snapped back it was like recoil. But that was all it was.' It wasn't quite all. Right at the height of it, he remembered a kind of juxtaposition. Her hands were his hands, and they were not. The view from her eyes had been his, but he knew it couldn't have been. The memory wormed around in his skull, shifting, so he didn't quite know if it was real or he had imagined it.

The engine changed pitch just then, and he cocked his head as the muted sound of thrusters firing made its way through the ship's structure. Looking out of the viewscreen, the dark tube wall pivoted away from them. Soon, he could see where it curved over into the next turn, then they rotated further to reveal where the ceiling had given way to darkness. The Prime Nexus' disconcerting internal architecture stared back at them, all holes and shadows and impossible curves. Palia's face had gone pale. Goose bumps prickled her arms.

<We're here,> Lilesh sent. <Begin when you like, and I will be ready to focus.>

True to her word, Lilesh set them down on the tube wall. It bobbed in the viewscreen as the landing clamps latched onto it.

Palia wove her fingers through his. 'There's no going back after this.'

Smiling, he leaned in close and planted a kiss on her lips, then drew back to hover an inch from her face, with the smell of her sweat lingering in his nose.

'That's the point,' he said.

They settled down facing each other, their foreheads pressed together, on one of the couches. With the weight of what they were about to do heavy on her shoulders, Palia felt every detail. The padded couch cover pressed against her knees where she knelt and her heels dug into the back of her thighs. Ferrash's forehead was hot against her skin. Too hot. Feverish. His hair tickled the side of her face. In her awareness, his pain had condensed into the area by his wound, stronger but localised. She could take that from him, gladly, but that wouldn't last forever. What she was really interested in was the light skipping across his ribs, happy arcs of lightning weaving a bright cocoon. It was beautiful to watch. The energy inside him danced like filigree in motion, infinite patterns forming and coming undone, too delicate to trace any individual line, but strong and blazing as a whole.

'Are you ready?' she asked.

Ferrash's voice came closer than she expected, and low. It sent a shiver through her. 'Thought you'd already started.'

She laughed and opened her eyes a fraction. His were too close to focus on. 'I'll get on with it, then.'

Closing her eyes again, she took a few deep breaths and let her body grow heavy. Then she turned her attention to that shiver, which was still dancing around inside her, and focused all her will on making it grow. She was subtle about it. She couldn't just command it to be more and watch it become so, but by holding it in focus she made herself aware of it. When she turned back to Ferrash again, the sight of his emotions laid bare sent the shiver twirling. It wrapped around the bones of her arms, around her torso, around her heart. And as it flared, the first dregs of it began to bleed away.

She panicked, adding another flare to the brightness, and for a moment she wrestled with whether to let that panic fester. A shimmering trail of leeched energy led from the two of them to Lilesh. The archivist had seen it and begun her task. For now, all that meant was gathering it. The ouroboros formed again, writhing around her body.

What if Lilesh took all there was and they couldn't keep up? What if she stripped them bare, as Palia had done to Ferrash? What if they just couldn't feel fast enough the supply the energy needed? Panic might help. Or it might distract her from other emotions.

In the next moment, she realised the pressure of Ferrash's head had disappeared from her forehead. Then his lips were on hers, warm and insistent. Her heart skipped in her chest. There was so much light, so much going on. She could barely think. All she could do was ride the tide of feelings washing over them both, let its warmth encompass her even as it dwindled at the edges. As she leaned into the kiss, she placed a hand on his chest, felt his heart beating beneath his ribs, had a moment of doubt at whether it was his heart or hers. This close together, their emotions seemed to merge. She couldn't pick out the differences between them anymore, not unless she took a wider view, and she couldn't do that for long without losing focus. There was a zone that was distinctly her and one that was distinctly him, but where they met, it was all a shining confusion.

Vertigo gripped her. This had happened before. This same feeling. She remembered it, like muscle memory without any knowledge of how it came to be there. A dizzying gulf yawned in her mind where the void lay, and she felt herself falling into it, tugged by that sense of déjà-vu, driven by a burning desire to know whatever it was she had lost.

Ferrash's grip on her shoulder brought her back to herself. She gasped at the sudden pain, and at the feeling that it was her hand doing the grabbing. She ran her hand through long hair. Her hand or his? Whose hair? Her psyche tingled, bridging two bodies, like phantom limbs ghosting around her but all the limbs were phantom and none of them were quite hers. She saw nothing of the Empyrean past the inferno they had become. She didn't know how long it had been.

Something brushed against the edges of her mind, recoiled, then turned back.

Two messages blinked in her implants. No, one message, on two sets of implants. Palia read the information twice, digested it twice, lost track of her thoughts in a whirlwind of untethered confusion.

<URGENT,> the wide broadcast from Fabien's ship, the *Gigamet Horasin*, read. <Turn gravity field off. Turn engines off. Turn generator off. Turn all Empyrean-powered devices off.>

And a second, targeted message read, <URGENT: Do not proceed with sabotage.>

Moments, minutes, maybe hours later the significance of having Empyrean-powered devices when they were about to destroy the Empyrean sank in. They couldn't have stopped if they wanted to. A message came in from Lilesh, but by the time they read it, they had already floated free of the couch. Despite weightlessness, the message had settled as a sinking feeling in their guts. They held each other tight, no longer sure enough of which body was which to trust to any other motion, desperately trying to maintain some sense of identity in the face of their joining. Pain racked both of them, blazing alongside the love that kept them together.

Who were they anymore? Had one been wiped out in favour of the other? Or was there no 'one' anymore?

They put a hand out to brace against the ceiling before they hit it, with no idea whose hand it was, and bounced back the other way. Ferrash's breath brushed against her neck. A moment later, Palia realised she had been able to make that distinction. The thread connecting them to Lilesh had drawn more away. Their excitement floundered, fading without due cause. Palia let herself panic again, to give Lilesh something else to latch onto so she had time to catch up. Ferrash's senses still hazed over hers, but there was a definite separation now.

Palia could only afford to focus on the two of them. But out there, beyond the scope of her immediate awareness, something shifted. Fear jolted through her, more urgent than anything she had felt that day. It was the sight of a void opening behind her, ready to engulf them all.

Ferrash said something, but she couldn't focus on the words. Instead, she tried to lose herself in him, in the light of his soul, burying her face in his neck like it would block out the darkness. He had his hand on the small of her back, beneath her shirt, and then it was *their* hand, but not quite. Palia opened her eyes and drew back to see the light fading, Ferrash's eyes wide and staring back, her grasp on her awareness slipping between her fingers. The thread connecting them to Lilesh flickered and died, and a harsh note of fear flashed where the archivist should be in the cockpit.

Then the fear faded from Palia's vision, and she saw nothing.

CHAPTER SIXTY-ONE

'REPORT!' FABIEN GRIPPED THE edges of his command lectern so hard his knuckles turned white. His heart thundered in his chest, and his guts had tied themselves in so many knots that the only thing keeping him from throwing up was the act of saving face.

The engineer looked just a sick as Fabien felt, with his face illuminated by the projection unit and its display of the battlefield. The Protectorate had recalled some of its fleets from nearby systems. Fabien's plan was working – they were moving the Prime Nexus away fast enough that the Hesperex fleets couldn't catch up – but that didn't prevent other Protectorate ships travelling out through it.

Consul Esselia answered from somewhere behind him. 'No indication whether they've received our signal, Magister, but they are slowing.'

The engineer staggered across to the lectern and grabbed Fabien's wrist. It hadn't been long since his outburst that Fabien's friends were mad – just long enough for the engineer to outline how lots of things relied on the Empyrean to work. One of those things was the inertial dampers that stopped them all flying through the hull during manoeuvres.

They couldn't get hold of Palia's ship to stop her.

The engineer's eyes were wide, frightened. 'Ye've got to do it now, Magister. Kill all the ship's systems. Kill 'em dead. Or we'll be, sure as fire.'

Fabien locked eyes with him, willing him to be wrong but knowing he wouldn't be. On the projection, their battle lines traded fire with incoming Protectorate vessels. They could hold them off just fine as it was, but the second they shut down their engines, they would be dead in the water. All the ships in the fleet had received the same urgent broadcast, supplemented with an additional command: 'comply when ready'. Now Palia's ship was stopping and they still weren't ready.

He turned back to the engineer. 'If the Empyrean disappears and the only thing we've turned off is gravity, what will happen?'

'I can't answer that question without a full understandin' o' facts.' When Fabien kept staring, the engineer sighed, gritted his teeth at the projection and added, 'It might just be enough. No way o' tellin' until it happens. Could be generators'll explode, could be nothin' happens. If ye think the risk's better than bein' sittin' targets...'

Fabien nodded and issued the order to disengage gravity generation with a one-minute countdown. He broadcast the same order to the other ships in the fleet and made sure they sent a reminder across the rest of the galaxy, too. If the order to turn off all systems hadn't reached Palia yet, it meant the order to leave the Empyrean alone hadn't, either. And that potentially meant death to anyone who didn't read the message.

Sometimes, a system could become so embedded in the fabric of a society that people took it for granted. The Empyrean was one of those systems. It had two faces: the obvious one, where empyrrics could mine emotions for power, but no one had to worry because they were so rare; and the taken-for-granted one. Fabien had taken it for granted. It had taken the engineer and the work of a second's thought to see right through it to the catastrophe underneath. The Empyrean was more than a resource empyrrics could tap into. The nexuses used it to transport ships across the space between stars. The energy nexuses drew from the Empyrean was stored in nexite batteries for ships to run gravity generators from, and shields, and weapons. They relied upon it so heavily and thought of it so little.

What would happen when it was gone?

Fabien hoped Palia got the second message. He hoped they would stop in time, before it was too late. He imagined all those systems cut off from one another with no idea what had happened. All those systems that still weren't self-reliant.

Then he thought of Rythe, and their ships that didn't need the Empyrean to skip across the void.

As he ran to strap himself into an emergency harness against the wall, he called to the communications officer, 'Can you get a message to Rythe?' Gravity slipped away as he fastened the last clip.

'Want me to tell your wife you love her?'

'No!' Fabien cried. 'Tell them to come—'

The power died. Lingering momentum jerked Fabien against his harness and cries of alarm rang out across the ship. He breathed a sigh of relief when his harness became slack again, and opened his mouth to ask for a status report.

In the space between one blink and the next, the wall of the bridge burst inwards. Something flashed, impossibly fast, and slammed into his legs. The last Fabien saw before he passed out was streams of blood racing to escape through the holes in the hull.

CHAPTER SIXTY-TWO

THE EMPYREAN'S DEATH TORE *the galaxy's heart out in one shredding impact. Deprived of an energy source, nexite – and all it powered – became useless. Shields blinked out. Ships designed for style instead of atmosphere broke apart attempting to de-orbit. Gravity generators ceased to generate. Inertial dampers could no longer counteract the staggering forces of acceleration and deceleration. For those who hadn't heeded the warning, those who hadn't heard it, it was death. Families dining in artificial sunlight on ships they had called home for generations became missiles. They accelerated unhindered through bulkhead and hull, a spray of bile and blood and bone, lethal in sheer velocity.*

Ships gutted themselves. The water in their hulls became wrecking balls of solid force, punching through everything in their path to form icy gasps in the void.

Every nexus ever created became useless slabs of exotic metal. Ships transiting through their tubes exited before their journeys' completion, smashing themselves into stars and asteroids or waking to the yawning call of exile far from rescue.

Those few empyrrics whose watered-down blood had clung to its powers long enough over the millennia now stood mute. Some wept. Others couldn't comprehend the loss. Keepers, indoctrinated for so long to feel nothing other than pain, reeled to a fear more primal than any they had experienced, the loss of something so fundamental to everything they had ever been, to everything they had ever thought to be.

The Kept rejoiced, even as debris painted the skies above them.

The Empyrean died, and with its last breath, it brought death.

CHAPTER SIXTY-THREE

'PALIA. PALIA, WAKE UP. Bile and blood, please, Palia, please.' Ferrash pinched her earlobe, hoping to see some sign of consciousness return, but her head continued to loll in the absence of gravity. Her hair formed a white halo around her head, starkly beautiful. It was the clearest sight he could make out – the ship had gone dark. Shining half-moons marked where her eyes glistened beneath her near-closed lids.

She was breathing. He couldn't hear over his own ragged breath, but he felt it through his palm on the small of her back. Her skin was warm, and he'd found a pulse when he'd checked for one.

'Progmannae,' Archivist Lilesh called from nearby.

Tearing his gaze from Palia, Ferrash found Lilesh floating towards them down the corridor. It took him a moment to realise, once he had blinked his eyes clear, that she was upside-down with respect to him. Dim-glowing panels illuminated her just well enough to see her features outlined in blue. The same panels had begun to glow in the lounge, too, and they sparkled off his teardrops as they scattered.

'I can't wake her up,' Ferrash said, the words catching in his throat.

Lilesh took hold of the doorframe with one hand and swung in place, graceless. Shivers wracked her body. 'Does your ship have a backup generator? One that doesn't rely upon the Empyrean?'

He drew Palia a fraction closer. 'I can't wake her.'

As if noticing Palia for the first time, Lilesh's gaze tracked down to her limp form, squinting, eyes unfocused. 'Is she alive?'

'Yes.'

'Then it should pass. Do you have a backup generator?'

'I...' Ferrash screwed his eyes tight and drew in a sharp breath. This wouldn't help Palia. 'There's a small backup under the floor panels in hydroponics. Should have kicked in by now, though.'

'I shut everything down the second we received orders, including redundancies, I'm afraid, as I wasn't prepared to take chances. How long will it last?'

Lilesh was already making her way back down the corridor, so Ferrash tapped a toe against the ceiling and started drifting that way with Palia in his arms. Thinking he saw a flicker of movement on her face, he paused to examine it, but her eyes remained closed.

'Backups are designed to operate for a month on essential systems only,' he said. 'Theoretically long enough to get us rescued or planet-side, or fix whatever problem caused the outage.' When he reached the doorframe, he pulled himself further along, heading straight on into the main corridor. All the spaces around him seemed wrong, and it took all his concentration to push off at the right angles whenever he hit something. His mind still reeled from being not just *his* mind, from having to grasp two simultaneous streams of sensation. Beneath that ache, his thoughts slowly slotted into place.

At length, as the door to hydroponics drifted closer, he said, 'It's gone, isn't it? Completely gone, that is. We did more than take the Empyrean from empyrrics, we took it from...We killed it.' Palia had told them that would happen, but that was knowledge his mother had given her, and clearly even she hadn't considered the wider implications. They'd been in such a rush to get it done. If only they'd turned their brains on and thought, *really* thought, for just one moment...

Lilesh's voice came from inside hydroponics. 'Your ship's systems will not reconnect to the nexus. It is not the case that there is nothing to connect to, as such. The problem I can see is more localised, in that your systems don't appear to be systems anymore. No logic lay behind my attempts to restart them. Your nexite is nothing more than a useless mineral. It stands to reason that this might be the same for others.'

How had they been so blind?

Ferrash drifted past hydroponics, where Lilesh knelt next to the open floor panel, and into the cockpit. The moment the door membrane disintegrated, light burned into his eyes. He screwed them tight shut and grunted. Palia stirred in his arms – or perhaps she'd just bumped up against something. He peeled one eye open to check.

Harsh white light filled the cockpit, painting everything as bright as the inside of a medical bay. It hurt just to look at the glare. Having rotated to face the floor, he couldn't see where the light came from. When his back bounced off the canopy, he used the momentum to get in front of the seats, then wedged his toes underneath them so he could bundle Palia into the navigator's chair. Her eyes moved from side to side behind her lids, like she was stuck in REM sleep. Every now and then her lids opened halfway, then closed again. She batted at his hands as he strapped her in.

Floating in front of her, Ferrash craned his neck around to look outside. Still the nexus tubes. Still where they had been before. Except now, instead of dull metal lining the tubes, every surface shone with light. Nothing like any nexus lights he'd seen before. This was artificial, electric.

A hum started up in the belly of the ship. A few of the control panels flickered to life, washed out by the lights above them. Gradually, the canopy adjusted to the light and dimmed until it didn't feel like it was burning his retinas. Huh. He'd figured something that essential would have been made to work without power.

'Ash?'

Palia's voice startled him so much he almost slipped from the floor and started free floating. She had her head tilted to one side, and when their eyes met, she smiled. Lopsided, but so wide that her eyes smiled with it. He bit his lip, but he felt his own smile crinkle the skin around his eyes.

'It worked,' she said. 'I can't see any of it anymore. I can't... I can't see *you*.' Her last word choked into a sob. Still smiling, but bittersweet now. He wondered what she could possibly have seen in him to regret losing sight of it so much.

'Palia...' Ferrash folded his knees, bringing himself level with her, and took hold of her hand. 'There were more consequences than we expected.'

She pursed her lips. 'That transmission at the last second. I guess no one's getting home any time soon, huh?'

'Doesn't look like.'

Palia closed her eyes and nodded, then stared over his shoulder at the lights. Reluctant to leave her but eager to be tethered to something more than his toes, Ferrash pivoted over the partition and strapped himself into the pilot's seat. A *clunk* behind him indicated the side seat had been released. Half turning, he saw Lilesh climbing into it. Her hands shook at the buckles.

'We're moving,' Palia said. 'Or... *it* is.'

Sure enough, when he looked past the tube they were in, he could see the nexus' porous substructure shifting. Openings rendered strangely flat by the harsh light shifted at the edge of vision. At first, there appeared to be no pattern to it. Holes shifted and merged. Proportion stretched and compressed and remoulded into a thousand different shapes that hurt his eyes to follow. But the holes were getting bigger. With every new shift, he saw less material and more empty space. Like a chain reaction, it spread, irising, distant walls opening one after the other, drawing them in and casting them aside so the space that remained was cylindrical. A million tiny tubes merging into one.

It crept closer, too. Alterations juddered and rushed towards their section of tube. Ferrash braced himself a moment before it ground into motion. Metallic groans shuddered through the ship and through his bones, echoing between his ears. His stomach flew up into his throat. Acceleration pressed him down into his seat. The view beyond the canopy had become a light-washed blur of motion. No sense to be made in it. No sense in what was happening now.

Palia took hold of his hand. He rolled his eyes to catch her expression, found hers wide and frightened. Then he jerked sideways. His harness straps tensed and cut into his shoulders.

For the next few seconds, their grip on the side of the tube twisted them every which way. Heartbeats separated the moments between free fall, between shaking, between being pressed so hard in one direction that it was all he could do not to black out. Through it all, the darkness expanded. He squinted, muscles tensed against the turmoil, biting back a nausea that pressed insistently against the back of his throat. Faded grey turned to black. White specks and splashes of fire blurred past.

Stars? Ferrash reached for a control panel, but every time he got close, the ship moved again and knocked him off course.

By the time the movements became slower and more drawn out, he didn't need to check. They were stars alright. The nexus had opened itself up – or closed, perhaps, given all the space it had contained before. Craning his neck, he found the rest of its structure stretched out in a wide band, forming a ring the other side of which hung thin in the distance above them. He couldn't guess at a diameter, but given how big the nexus had been, how much material it had contained... it must be massive. You might just fit a planet through it.

Palia squeezed his hand, breaking his stare. 'Ash, we need to move. Look.'

Even as he turned to look, he booted the engines up. They sounded different, without the Empyrean, but he couldn't place the change.

Their ship sat on a section of the ring's inner surface far out from the middle, facing diagonally outwards towards the edge. Looking the other way, he saw the source of Palia's concern, and his heart beat faster. A thick lip had formed at the other edge of the ring. As he watched, another section of ring concertinaed up and crashed into place against the side of the lip, almost like a spring returning to form. It tugged their section along behind it, pressing him against his harness straps. If it was doing this to all sections and they were still attached by the time they reached the main ring...

Ferrash disengaged the docking clamps and gave the thrusters a burst to get clear of the surface, then turned to face the middle of the ring and edged back, slowly. Hovering further upwards meant the view ahead became more space and less ring, and that's when he saw them.

Ships. Or what once were ships. Cold gripped his shoulders and he tightened his hands around the control column. Palia leaned closer to the canopy beside him.

When they had entered the nexus, both the void packs and the Hegemony fleets had been chasing Protectorate vessels back to Hesperex. He shouldn't have been able to see any of them from here, not with the naked eye, but on the other side of the ring there was a new field of stars, moving fast, expanding out in all directions. Without a word to the others, he keyed into communications channels, but the system wouldn't connect. *No nexite buoys.*

Ferrash let out a breath. 'No instant comms. How far—?'

The backup channel sprang to life and he snapped his mouth closed. Panicked voices burst into the cockpit. One at first, which cut off abruptly, then a rush all at once, overlapping one another, no heed for etiquette. Tearing metal sliced through the transmissions, and screams, and the sucking rush of vacuum.

He couldn't turn to face Palia. He didn't want to see her expression. He wasn't sure he wanted her to see his. Instead he found a control panel and cut off the feed, setting it to record in the unlikely chance they'd want to listen to it later.

Before he could zoom in on the debris – he was pretty sure that's what it was – the last folds of the ring snapped into place and its inner circumference lit up, just as bright as when they had been inside it.

'Do you think it's repairing itself?' Palia asked, but the quaver in her voice betrayed how little she believed that possibility.

Other lights came on to either side of the wider ring, then began to rotate. Slow at first, then faster and faster into they were just two pulsating rings of light sandwiching the first. Just when it was becoming impossible to guess the direction of rotation, all three rings flared brighter. With a flash, the centre of the ring filled in with a membrane that rippled at the shock of its creation. When it became still a few seconds later, it hung like a glass pane, a light purple haze obscuring the stars behind it.

Silence reigned in the cockpit, so complete he could hear Palia's clothes rustling against her harness.

Then she said, 'Ash, turn comms back on. We need to know if anyone's survived.'

Ferrash swallowed before complying, expecting another wave of panicked messages, but all he got was more silence.

He licked his lips, toggled transmission on and said, '*Memnet Horasin*, this is the *CVL Barute*. What's your status? Over.' When he toggled off, he tried to steer his brain away from expecting an immediate reply, but found himself floating near the edge of his seat, teeth clenched.

'We should fly around and try to find them,' Palia said. 'They might have a communications malfunction, or they might not have turned power back on yet, or they might be damaged.'

Ferrash tried to work out the distances in his head, figured it would take around two minutes for their message to be heard and another two for a reply to come back, if they replied straight away. No way they could fly there in that time, but it wouldn't hurt to get a head start.

Peering over the side of the canopy to see how far they were from the edge of the ring, he started nudging them down and said, 'Do you think the *Horasin* would have turned off its dampers in time?'

'They sent the message, so if anyone would have, it's them.'

When you turned inertial dampers off, or if you had a power failure, they were designed to spool down slowly. You'd float fast, but not fast enough for anything but your last meal to cause issues. But that still relied on the Empyrean, on all the components working as intended. If your ship got unlucky and took a direct hit, the process would be sudden, and deadly. Except by that point, you were probably already dead. Ferrash tried to imagine a ship the size of the *Horasin* having its dampers cut off abruptly. Even if they got everyone harnessed, anything not bolted down would inherit a velocity it had been denied before. Bodies, cutlery, weapons, furniture all taking flight, punching through hulls and keeping moving. And all that water, suddenly turned into a fluid missile mass...

Something shook him. Light-headed, head buzzing with static, he blinked at Palia.

'Ash, take us around the ring,' she said.

'I am.' Frowning, he looked at the control panels. They were moving, but not the way he wanted. He tightened his grip on the control column and gave the thrusters more power, but nothing happened. Then he realised he could feel it: the slight downwards pressure as they rose up towards the centre of the ring. 'Hold on; I'm going to try the main engine.'

Spinning the ship on its axis – slowly, so he didn't turn them all to paste with too high a G – he pointed them straight down and slightly away from the ring, then punched the main engine straight up to full power. It roared through the ship's structure. Back down the corridor, the dining-room fittings rattled in their rail bolts. They slowed a fraction, but besides that, they were still being pulled towards the ring and its new membrane. He shot a panicked glance to Palia and Lilesh, then shook his head and cut the engine off.

'It's drawing us in. Can't outrun it. Might as well save power. Hold on...' One of the consoles was shining a light he hadn't noticed before. 'It's linked with our ship. Same signal as you get when locked into a nexus lane, but there's no coordinates for this one.'

Lilesh spoke up from behind them, her voice slow and quiet. 'A membrane is made for passing through. Perhaps we should see where it takes us. Granted, we have little choice.'

Ferrash shrugged, then winced when his wound flared up. 'Could fire at the ring.' But even as he said it, he knew damaging it wouldn't be possible. He activated a drone in one of their launch tubes and shot it towards the membrane, then rotated the ship back around to watch its progress.

Palia had her hands bunched in her lap. Her eyes kept drifting to the edge of the ring.

'Even if we could get to them,' Ferrash said, 'there's only so much we could do to help.' It wasn't exactly reassuring, but it was the truth, and it was all he had. The only reaction he got was a grimace.

Twenty seconds later, the drone reached the membrane. As the leading edge rippled around it, he could see its shape suspended in the membrane's fabric like a shadow on the surface of reality, and then it was gone. He waited long enough to be certain he still had its signal. Ten seconds later, more than long enough, it was still transmitting. Stars dotted the black on its camera feed. Stars other than these, he noted when cross-referencing with what that view should have been. When the feed stabilised, the shadows of unfamiliar ships resolved in the dark.

He couldn't take his eyes off the membrane, but he reached across the partition and took hold of Palia's hand. Under the gaze of that shining sea, the touch gave him comfort, the semblance of humanity within arm's reach.

'Drone got through safe,' he said. 'But whatever's on the other side, it isn't here, and we'll have company.'

Palia laced her fingers with his, her grip tightening as the membrane drew closer. With the canopy mounted so far forwards, their transition would be almost instantaneous. If it took offence to their ship in particular, they wouldn't have long to see any damage ripple across the ship's hull. Maybe that was for the best. They couldn't escape. Better to die in an instant than see your death coming and have time to consider it.

The light touched their nose, then slid around them like the line of a laser scan. Every muscle tensed, breath held, Ferrash scanned the view outside. Not too far off travelling through a nexus, except the light was static and blue, not the multi-coloured display that soared past in-tube. There seemed no end to it. Everywhere he looked was a fluctuating blue sea. He couldn't even see the ring anymore – though he thought the light was a fraction brighter where it should be.

In an instant, the light cut out. Blue flashed into solid black and he blinked, adjusting to the void again. Here were those unfamiliar stars, and there ahead of them, the drone he'd sent through first. Ahead, and around to either side, were the ships he'd seen on the camera. Great behemoths of them, turned broadside to face them.

Lilesh spoke first. 'I don't recognise their design. Whose are they?'

'Not ours,' said Ferrash. 'Not anyone's I've seen.'

Then the radio blared into life, and a clipped voice sounded through the cockpit in a language his implants' translators recognised, even if he didn't, each word as hard as gunshots. 'Unregistered vessel, this is Allied Reach ship *Ammit*. Disable your weapons, shields and propulsion and prepare to be taken aboard. In light of the breach of the terms of your banishment, you are hereby under arrest until such time as a trial can be arranged. Out.'

Mouth open, Ferrash looked to Palia and Lilesh for answers with more questions than he knew how to voice on his lips. But in the end, there was only one thing he could do. He complied, and they sat vulnerable and waiting for fate to reach them.

CHAPTER SIXTY-FOUR

BEK HAD LONG SINCE stopped trying to scream. A part of that was thanks to the way they'd wired him up. He had no control over his muscles and an oxygen mask rested over his mouth and nose, so even if he could have moved his throat to make a noise, it would have come out as a muffled groan. When he'd opened his eyes the first time after waking up, slime had rushed in to touch them. Closing them had just trapped the ooze behind his lids. He'd wanted to throw up, but hadn't been able to. He railed against his own body, mind a constant roar of animal noise, trying to move something, anything... and lapsed into calm a few minutes or hours later, exhausted in his soul. He felt crushed by the weightlessness of the fluid he hung in. Being born to a vat, you kept the sense memory with you. Being back in that same memory brought forth an almost primordial fear.

Then had come the neural link. He felt its movement in the vat, moving the sludge before it, and made it one of the few times he willingly opened his eyes. Nothing. Just a faint, green-tinged light shining through the sludge. He couldn't crane his neck to look up, but he felt something approach, like the movement of sludge over his naked body had become another sense. Then came a sharp pressure at the base of his skull. His heart thundered in his chest. As the pressure increased, he was sure he was going to pass out, and maybe he did, because soon the pressure stopped increasing and stuck at one, intolerable level.

It felt cold. Like he imagined death felt like. Like it had felt to be stabbed, the first time they had taken Palia to Hesperex.

The thought brought Ferrash's face to him, clear as if he floated in the vat before him. A fog clouded his mind. *Getting stabbed in the brain might have something to do with that.* But this was different. He felt... like his muscles were moving, even though they weren't. And at the same time, he floated from one memory to the other against a sluggish current. He couldn't tell if that current was him trying to exert control or something else.

Think, Bek, think. He had a needle in his skull. Neurigers, they called them. Stab them into the base of someone's – or something's – skull and you got some modicum of control over it. An animal with only basic intelligence and you could steer it. A human, and you had it open to suggestion. The problem with trying it was that being open to suggestion tended to be outweighed by having just been stabbed in the head. This was more than that.

As much as he wanted to avoid thinking about it, Bek examined the sensations in his head. Beyond the obvious throb of the needle, something hard was clamped around his skull's circumference. External readings as well as internal, then.

For some indeterminate amount of time, he juggled the two systems in his head. Every time he thought he was close to figuring out what they might be doing, his mind slipped off it and back onto a more familiar memory. They were all of Palia now. Irritation flashed into his mind, followed by guilt. Her fault he was in this situation, in a way, but he'd have come after Ferrash anyway.

Bek tried to think of Ferrash, but couldn't. His thoughts were firmly fixed on Palia. The memories weren't full experiences, just fragments out of context.

No, not out of context. With memories still flicking past at the forefront of his mind, he brought his attention back to the sensation of movement. Then sight, and the sight of Palia, and the sound of her voice, and none of it was a memory and none of it was him.

A mind link. They'd cloned him. They'd cloned him and hooked his mind up like a splitting database so the clone wouldn't have to worry about any missing experiences.

Bek felt like he might throw up again, wished he could move so he could jerk his head back and stab the needle just a little bit too far. The curse of knowing was the curse of seeing. So he saw it all, right up until the moment someone shot him. After that, he floated in the vat, blind and alone but thankful to that hidden figure with a bullet set for his clone. He pictured Ferrash, and now he knew the clone wasn't sifting his memories, he let the image hang there. Ferrash would come for him. Wouldn't he?

Pressure again at the base of his skull. Worse this time, even though he could feel the needle pulling out. When it was gone, the entire area burned, ice cold, and his teeth ached with the pain.

Then something loosened around his face. He opened his eyes again. The black tube of his breathing mask slipped away, taking the mask with it. Vat fluid oozed to fill the space it left behind. It slithered over his lips, then up into his nose. That was the point he instinctively tried to breathe. Sludge moved deeper up his nose, and when he opened his mouth, it rushed in. Gagging, he tried to kick to the surface, but his muscles still wouldn't move.

No, that wasn't true. He tried it again, felt his toes respond to his command. Heart pumping, he tried again, and again, moving more of his limbs each time. When his lungs began to burn, he breathed out, expelling all the carbon dioxide building up there. He sank a fraction as he lost some of his buoyancy, but then he was moving up, his legs flailing behind him. He moved about an inch through the sludge. He kicked again, got another two inches. He could see the retracted tube dimly through the sludge now. The sludge shuddered around him.

With one final kick, he burst to the top of the vat and hit his head on the lid, but he still hadn't hit air. *Bile and blood.* It was full to the brim.

He hung there for half a second with his hands pressed to the lid of the vat, screaming at himself to move, to think of something, to get himself out of there. He could feel vibrations through the lid. Not important. Bigger things to worry about. *Look for a valve, Bek.*

One shove with both arms pushed him back down the length of the vat. His heels knocked against the cold bottom surface. Whoever had captured him definitely didn't want him alive – the vat had been heated earlier, but they'd turned that off and it was cooling, fast.

Suppressing shivers, Bek curled up at the bottom of the vat. His lungs were cramping. He had to bite his lip to make sure he didn't try to breathe the sludge. He patted at the floor with both hands, searching, then found a circular opening in the centre. Half a foot further down, it was closed off by another slab of metal. He drew his arm back as far as he could and punched it, but the sludge's viscosity slowed it so he barely had an effect. He punched again. This was his only option. Punch it, and keep punching until something broke. That something would either be him or the valve.

Blood curled in the sludge. His blood, from his hand. The pain didn't even register. Then his lungs took control and he hauled in a breath. Sludge rushed down his throat and into his lungs. He knelt with his hand on the valve, coughing, gasping, making the problem worse. He scrabbled around the edges of the valve with both hands, but he couldn't find anything to get purchase on.

He was still scrabbling with bloodied fingers when the valve opened. The sludge dropped away, and the pressure of it carried him down. He slammed into the bottom of the vat, his arms stuck inside the opening. While he was bodily blocking the drain, the sludge couldn't go anywhere. So with the last of his strength, he dragged first one arm out, then the other. Then he lay on his back, watching the view above him grow brighter and less green.

By the time the meniscus broke over his face, he had drifted. Sight didn't mean anything anymore. His lungs felt frozen. He couldn't think to open his mouth to breathe. The sides of the vat hummed, retreating into the floor. It didn't seem important.

Something shoved him, hard. He rolled off the side of the vat, landing on his right arm on the freezing floor. He went to cry out, but opening his mouth made him try to breathe, and trying to breathe made him cough. He vomited a thick glob of vat sludge onto the floor in front of him and kept coughing the stuff up until he was pretty sure the sludge was more pink than green and the chunkier bits might have been his actual lungs. It felt like his bones and muscles were made of the same sludge. When he tried to roll over, he just flopped.

He stared at his slime-coated arms, willing them to do more than just twitch. Then he followed the line of one arm to the tips of his fingers, to the spreading pool of sludge, to the hem of a green robe.

With one kick from his legs, he rocketed back and slammed into the side of another vat. He fumbled for a gun, slapping wetly at his waist, but of course there was nothing there. So he held his hands out in front of him instead, as if that – or anything – would be enough to ward off the approaching keeper.

'Are you Saralbek, friend to Ferrash Progmannae?'

Bek gritted his teeth, arms trembling in front of him, his breath misting in the air. 'Y-y-yes.'

The keeper thrust something towards him and he pressed himself as close to the vat as he could. Then he blinked. It was a towel. He remembered the first time he'd slipped out of a vat, the people who'd been standing there with towels and clothes ready to help them out.

'Take it,' she said, her eyes averted, 'and hurry. The situation outside is spiralling. If we are to reach the spaceport alive, we need to leave as soon as possible.'

For a moment, Bek just sat there staring at her. She was a keeper. This wasn't how things worked. But she hadn't killed him yet, and she'd saved him from the vat, so... He snatched the towel out of her hands and threw it around himself, then used the side of the vat to support him standing upright. As he scrubbed the sludge off his skin, he examined her. Something about her was familiar, but it was only when he'd stopped scrubbing and she turned to face him that he saw her face under her hood.

'You're Head Justicar Mannae?' He hadn't meant to make it a question, but he just couldn't believe she'd ever help him.

Ayt Mannae nudged a pile of dry clothes across the floor to him. 'I am.'

When she turned her back, Bek hurried into the clothes, fumbling the fabric between numb fingers. The clothes were no warmer than ambient temperature, but they'd heat up fast. He wouldn't die of cold, at least.

'Why'd you save me?' he asked. 'You here because of Ash?'

Ayt turned to leave. As he made to follow, he noticed a man with close-cropped hair stood to one side, pistol in hand, wearing a patchwork coat. Bek hadn't noticed him earlier, but he fell into step beside them. Footsteps behind him indicated there were more.

Ayt cocked her head at the sound of an explosion outside, but kept moving. 'Ferrash has left for the Prime Nexus to complete his mission, along with the Hegemony empyrric. He gave me your coordinates and asked me to get you out.'

'You're... working with Ash?' *But he hates you.*

'I agreed with his goals, and he needed my help.'

Bek turned the fact over as they led him out onto the street. No amount of imagination could let him picture Ferrash going to her for help. But then he'd never imagined him leaving, either. Never imagined him keeping so many secrets from him. Never imagined him being the Reiart. Never really believed it even after he admitted the truth.

Through the deserted street, they took him to the lifts. What had been silence grew from the shadows. Distant voices became a murmur, became a roar, became a riotous tumult that drowned out the lift mechanism. Bek found his eyes stinging, tears freezing on his cheeks. He brushed them away before the others could notice them. Didn't suppose it mattered anymore, but crying in front of a keeper – or anywhere near one – should have been a one-way ticket to annihilation.

A massive bang and the floor lurched underneath him. He staggered sideways along with the others, ears ringing. When they all righted themselves, he noticed in the dim light that they all had a patch of fabric sewn to each sleeve, except for two who wore patchwork coats. A mark of allegiance. Must be. But... to the vatborn?

Before he had time to get more confused, the lift shuddered and stopped. The doors squealed open, letting a gust of snow-laced air sweep in. Bek braced for the cold, but the gust was mild, and it bore the stench of smoke upon it. As they stepped out, firelight gleamed in the distance. When he craned his neck right back, he saw black smoke fading into the night sky.

The *night* sky. Smoke-hazed but clearly visible through gaps in the cloud layer. When had there ever been gaps in Hesperex's clouds? In theory, there must have been some, but he'd never seen them. He'd never seen war on Hesperex, either. In that little patch of sky, lights flickered, fires winked as orange specks and explosions dashed them all across the night. Whose ships attacking whose, he didn't know. He just hoped Ferrash had got clear of them. He tried to send a message, but had no signal.

'Saralbek, focus!'

He jumped at Ayt Mannae's voice and hurried after her. He had to elbow his way past two landers to get there. There were people every-where now, not paying them much attention, though a few raised their weapons at Ayt before presumably noticing the patches and turning away. He flinched away from the sound of breaking glass. A couple more landers were leaning into a warehouse through a smashed window. Before he brought his gaze back to the front, they'd started passing weapons out to others in the crowd.

'How bad's fighting?' Bek asked.

A dark-skinned man in patchwork took up position beside him. 'Planet-side?' he said. 'The fighting is global, though centred on admin-istrative centres, and the threads of fate have not tilted the balance of either side. Five-Fifty-Four is meeting with more success – we are close to an assault on the Tower of Voices – but the fighting is fiercest here. We have lost many siblings today.'

'"Bad" would've summed that up nice enough.' Bek scanned the rest of their small cohort as he walked. 'Anyone got a gun I can borrow? Guessing I might need it.'

Ayt Mannae didn't look back as she replied, 'I will clear us a path. You shouldn't need to worry. We just need to reach the spaceport, and soon.'

Bek snorted. 'A keeper protecting us and we might as well stay in one place. Nothing'd touch us.'

To that, she had no reply, but the way her shoulders tensed sent a shiver through him. The head justicar was scared. Terrified, maybe. And even if she'd had every confidence in herself just then, he wasn't about to put all his trust in the hands of a recent enemy, even if she had saved his life.

As if sensing his dilemma, the man he'd spotted first down in the vat chamber stepped in close and offered him a pistol, grip turned towards him. 'T'ere be no harm in defendin' yoself, brutta. Fight be changin' each time we look.'

Bek took the pistol from him, nodded his thanks. 'Brother.'

In the moment between turning away and setting his next step down, the road ahead burst into emerald light. Ayt Mannae walked forwards at its centre, her arms raised. Gunshots rang out all around. Bek flinched at the noise, but nothing made it through the keeper's shield. Behind the faintly pulsing hemisphere, shapes huddled in side streets. Shapes with patches on their arms and guns raised to face them.

'Hey!' The man stepped out from behind him to walk by the side of the shield. 'Hey, vatter! We fight on same side. Save yo weapon fo t'real enemy.'

Intent on his companion, Bek walked straight into Ayt's back. He jumped back, but she didn't seem to notice. A crowd had barred the way in front of her, all in patchwork, all armed with guns and knives and metal bars and welding torches. Behind them, the spaceport rose into the sky. So close, and they had an empyrric, so surely she could just move them all aside. But he'd seen enough thrown rocks hit the shield in the past few seconds to know it might not be that simple.

'She be our enemy!' came a voice from the crowd. An approving roar followed it. 'She a keeper! She ne'er fight fo us. Yo tink a patch on an arm be foolin' anyone? We fight to free ot'er vatter from t'green.'

In another time, Bek might have agreed with them, but instead he stepped up beside Ayt Mannae and spoke in her ear. 'Can't you just move them? I've seen keepers throw people before.'

That look again. Tense, expecting an asteroid to appear in the sky above her head any moment. Her eyes flicked back to meet his. 'I would prefer to avoid aggravating them.'

'Nothing you do's gonna make them like you.'

She stared straight ahead for a moment, then nodded. 'Stick close to me. All of you!'

Ayt stretched both her arms out in front of her and slightly to one side, then swept them across to the right. The front of the shield whipped out and scooped the crowd aside. Angry shouts and gunshots filled the air, but then they were running, passing the heap of sprawled bodies, their feet pounding on the packed snow. Bek's heel skidded on his next step. He tried to correct his fall, but he hadn't had time to adjust from the vat yet. The dark-skinned man shot a hand out to catch him, then shoved him forwards.

Bek fixed his eyes on the spaceport. Reach it, and he'd be out of this fight. He'd see Ferrash again. He had to reach it. He fixated on it. So he didn't notice the attack until green flared sun-bright in front of him. Four or five people flew back into an alley, screaming. More adrenaline spiked through him, and he whipped his head around the rest of the street to check for pursuers.

'Behind you!' he said, and aimed his pistol through widening gaps in the shield.

Ayt Mannae spun on one heel, wobbling, off balance. Her eyes were wide, and the shield was almost gone. Bek fired three shots into the crowd while she prepared her attack, but there were too many heading for them. All it would take was one with a gun and they were sitting ducks. Ayt needed to get the shield back up, and soon. But when she shot her arms forwards, all that came out was a thin viridian stream that faded into nothing a metre from her fingertips. She drew both hands back and stared at them, mouth agape.

In the second it took the crowd to jump on her, she brought her chin up and let her gaze rest on the night sky, with the last emerald reflections dying in her eyes and a smile on her lips. Then they were on her, stabbing and punching, a blur of limbs and crimson splashing on the snow. And Bek just stood there, shocked, with his eyes fixed on that same sky.

Where there had been pinprick ships before, now there were a quarter that number. In the air around them hung a haze, shimmering, becoming more diffuse the longer he looked.

'You. You wit' or against vatter?'

A knife blade rested against his chest, point digging into the fabric, stained red with blood. He followed the hand that held it over patch-work to an unfamiliar face.

'With,' Bek said. 'I've never been anything but.' And he thought of Ayt Mannae, torn between the claws of his siblings even though she'd saved him. He wondered where the balance of her life stood – if her past crimes were outweighed by recent events – and whether anyone deserved that sort of death.

Far away, carried by that too-warm wind, a hum came. Off-beat and discordant but, when he bent his ear to it, distinctly musical. Receding gunfire formed its percussion, bolstered by the bass booms of contin-uing explosions from elsewhere in the city. Still the hum grew louder.

As the knife retreated, Bek caught the man who'd given him his pistol cocking his ear to it as well, a smile plastered over his face.

Bek asked, 'What is it?'

The man turned, raised an eyebrow. 'We been singin' it in quiet for long years wantin' no one to hear, but now we sing free again. You been too long away fro ot'er vatter. Learn t'is, Saralbek. T'is t'song o' we bein' finally in control o' our own destiny. T'is t'song t'at we are free. T'is t'song o' t'vats.'

TO BE CONTINUED

ENJOYED THIS BOOK?

It would mean so much to me if you could leave a review for *Bile and Blood* in the store where you bought it, or on Goodreads or The Story-Graph. As a new author, it's so incredibly difficult to get my books in front of readers. The more reviews a book has, the more likely those big algorithms in the sky will help me do just that.

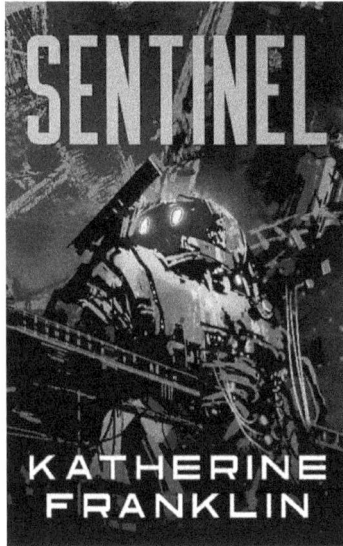

Subscribe to my newsletter for a copy of *Sentinel*.

If you're looking for more from this universe and want to find out exactly what happened to Ferrash's father on Munab, you can find out in a free short story by subscribing to my newsletter (FranklyWrites.com/newsletter). I send out updates once a month, and it's the best place to hear about new releases.

I also maintain a wiki with more information about the *Galaxy of Exiles* series. If you're interested, go ahead and check it out at WorldAnvil.com/w/Galaxy-of-Exiles-FranklyWrites.

ACKNOWLEDGEMENTS

It's weird to look back and think that I started writing *The Empyrean* back in 2018, little knowing that a pandemic was about to trot along and buck half the publishing industry off its back just when I would be ready to query it. When I, depressed, frustrated, and thoroughly miffed at my near-empty inbox, decided to sort the damned thing out myself, things happened fast. I paid for what I needed. I ran the Kickstarter. I published the book.

And everything since then has felt like full gallop.

Doing all this wouldn't be so manageable if it weren't for the supportive people around me. I would first like to thank my granddad – who regardless won't be able to read these thanks on account of being dead – for always being interested and being one of the first to support the Kickstarter. That meant a lot to me, and I'm glad I was able to share it with him while he was alive. My husband, of course, remained as supportive as ever, even as I increased the frequency of my panicked screeching to encompass the new and rather weighty concerns of social media and marketing. Find me someone who doesn't screech at those two and I will be scared.

Regarding the dedication at the front of the book: I had been outlining my plot to him on a long drive, somewhat excited, having brought things together in my head quite recently. He then asked that wouldn't that destroy the universe? I paused. I asked 'What?'. He then proceeded to explain the physics of my own setting to me, which I had until that moment completely forgotten about, much like the unfortunate characters of this book. And so The Blend was born.

Thanks, husband.

Thanks also to the rest of my family, who all ask after my books and conspire to make me blush with praise (which doesn't take much, to be fair). Mum, I'm glad you enjoyed *The Empyrean* much more than I imagined you would!

The various writing groups and communities I'm involved in are a constant source of motivation and inspiration, and I'm not sure where I'd be on the publishing side of things if not for everyone's dedication to helping each other. Having recently discovered I'm just a socially anxious extrovert as opposed to an introvert like I always believed, it has been good to socialise a bit more as well. To this end, I went to my first ever sci-fi convention. I'd like to thank everyone there for being so lovely and welcoming, especially the group who first noticed me sat on my own and drew me into the conversation. I'll definitely try to make my way to more conventions as and when finances and circumstances allow.

My thanks must also go to James Alper, who performed such an excellent narration of *The Empyrean* and was a joy to work with. I'm also grateful for the feedback from my beta readers and Kate at Nerd Girl Edits, whose analysis was just as thorough and helpful as always. Design for Writers, I haven't seen the cover for this book at the time of writing the acknowledgements, but I always get complemented on the cover for *The Empyrean*. You did such a great job with it, and I'm so excited to see what you come up with for this one!

ABOUT THE AUTHOR

KATHERINE FRANKLIN SPENDS FAR more of her days than is healthy glued to a screen, writing stories when she's not writing code, but she manages to venture outside once in a while as well. She loves science, but didn't love her physics degree enough to do anything about it. Fiction was always her first love.

Katherine lives in Yorkshire with her husband and a horse-sized dog, where she practices martial arts, miniature painting and far too many little hobbies to count in her spare time.

You can find her on Twitter and Instagram (@FranklyWrites), Mastodon (@FranklyWrites@wandering.shop), Facebook (@KatherineFranklinAuthor) or through her personal website (www.FranklyWrites.com).

Ingram Content Group UK Ltd.
Milton Keynes UK
UKHW012012100423
419951UK00003B/55

9 781915 007063